# THE REDEEMER

## ❅ IT IS WRITTEN ❅

A NOVEL BY

# MARK MORAN

# DISCLAIMER

The characters, institutions, entities and events in this story and novel, <u>The Redeemer: It Is Written</u>, are fictitious. Any similarity to real persons, characters, institutions, entities or events, which are existing, pre-existing, living or dead, is coincidental and not intended by the author. Furthermore, there is no true-life association with <u>The Redeemer: It Is Written</u> story to any of the excerpts from a literary work of non-fiction, <u>America's Lawyer Mafia: Railgate</u>, that are exhibited following <u>The Redeemer: It Is Written</u> story novel. They are included solely for purposes of marketing literary work(s) and merely as a marketing convenience to the author and publisher.

The Redeemer: It Is Written story written by Mark Moran Copyright © 2009 by Wild Horse Literary Works, LP, WGA-West Registration Number 1347722, 2nd Ed.

Cover design by Mark Moran Copyright © 2009 by Wild Horse Literary Works, LP

Public domain electronic copy of portrait of The Prodigal Son, painted by artist Pompeo Batoni, 1773, formatting by Mark Moran Copyright © 2009 by Wild Horse Literary Works, LP

Cover illustration by Mark Moran Copyright © 2009 by Wild Horse Literary Works, LP

Lettering by Mark Moran Copyright © 2009 by Wild Horse Literary Works, LP

Published and Printed by Wild Horse Literary Works, LP

Copyright © 2009 by Wild Horse Literary Works, LP for individual and collective works

Excerpt from America's Lawyer Mafia: Railgate written by Mark Moran Copyright © 2009 by Wild Horse Literary Works, LP

ISBN: 1-4392-5233-5

ISBN-13: 9781439252338

Visit www.booksurge.com to order additional copies.

# DEDICATION

This novel, <u>The Redeemer: It Is Written</u>, is dedicated to the memories of two fine and courageous men. The late United States Navy Reserve Commander, Michael T. Shelby, who served his country two-fold: as a US Navy SEAL Intelligence Officer, during Operation Desert Storm, and as a law-and-order US Attorney for the Southern District of Texas. He created the Anti-Terrorism Advisory Council, which was used as the model for other US attorneys nationwide, and more pointedly, he vigorously investigated and prosecuted white-collar crime (union lawyers involved in organized crime, Enron, etc). And my father, the late US Air Force Brigadier General Glennon T. Moran, Sr., who also served his country in two high-level capacities: as a fighter pilot and a commander of fighter pilots, in times of armed conflict, during World War II, Korea, Berlin Crisis, Cuban Missile Crisis and Vietnam; and in his capacity as a lawyer who, as the Missouri State Liquor Control Supervisor, successfully fought for first-ever legislation, against stiff nation-wide opposition from the brewing and distilling industry, to require photo ID's to purchase liquor, in order to reduce under-aged drinking and traffic deaths due to drunken driving. The fruits of his selfless labors were eventually adopted nationwide and ultimately served as one of the forces that helped grow the life saving organization, MADD.

Both men were lawyers.

Both men were highly decorated military men.

Both men were respected as giants in their fields.

Both men stuck out their necks in order to do the right things for the American people.

Neither man knew each other, but both knew the same dark secret. In the course of their careers, both of these good and honorable men learned of the startling depth and breadth of organized crime, albeit a *mafia*, operating for decades, for generations, within our American judicial system.

Both men were silenced.

Gentlemen, this one's for both of you.

*Semper Fi*, gentlemen, *Semper Fi*.

# ACKNOWLEDGEMENTS

Given the controversial nature of this novel, I am severely restricting my acknowledgements to persons who were most important to the creation of this book, in order to ensure the anonymity of those kind, hard-working and generous souls who might not have known the full scope of <u>The Redeemer</u>, when they were so gracious to lend me assistance. Your help was critical. I could not have done it without any of you. And I thank you sincerely for your help. My entire family was extremely supportive – thank you for believing in me. However, there are some specific people whom I can recognize.

My dear sister, Jeanne, to whom I owe the gift of seeing what it is like to struggle through profound, lifelong, physical and mental challenges, including a wheelchair and Autism – Asperger's Syndrome. She productively offers many prayers every day for persons of all faiths and colors, and she proceeds through life with a level of courage to which I can only aspire. She is one of my heroes.

Mary Russell is a hard working, kind person who has helped me immeasurably with this story, in the rigors of typing and organization, to her kind advice and her never-ending support. She deserves sainthood in triplicate.

My old friend Solomon Parker, with whom I discussed the story during its infancy, and upon a common interest in the military, lent me some audio tapes of Army and Marine Special Forces double-timing to their cadences. From the mental toughness Solomon honed as a Special Forces instructor, he was able to do the impossible – become the first documented person to overcome quadriplegia. He now walks. His will is legendary. He too is one of my heroes.

U.S. Senator John Danforth. He granted me a nomination to the United States Air Force Academy. And for that I am eternally grateful. Although I did not complete my studies there, I left with the honor of being at the top of my class (and the holder of the push-up record). I draw on the training I received at the Academy each and every day of my life. The lessons I learned, as a cadet, about honor, persistence and determination, and how to exceed oneself, in all things intellectual and physical, even when all looks lost, served me well, in life, in the writing of <u>The Redeemer</u>, and throughout the thousands of hours I spent representing an innocent man through the United States Supreme Court and beyond. I received the best education imaginable at USAFA. *Never give up.*

Double huge thanks to my editor and attorney, Ms. Debbie Austrin. She was masterful in her ability to place my work onto her editor's anvil, hammer out its wrinkles, sharpen the plot's edge and make the double-bladed story shine; all while preserving the unique ring to its steel—its voice. She is the best.

Thanks to all you proofreaders. <u>The Redeemer</u> is a much better literary work due to your input. I owe you all some beer and a barbeque.

But most of all, loving thanks to my tremendous and extremely patient wife, Kim, and our wonderful children. I love all of you beyond measure. Hey now we can play outside! Who calls dibs on first at-bat? Dad pitches.

# FOREWORD

This novel is based, in part, on a true story. If you are bored with the concept of social justice, please skip this foreword. Reader enjoyment is paramount.

~~~~~~~~~~~~~~~~~~~~~~~~~~~~~~~~~~~~~~~~~~~~~~~~~~~~~~~~

For thousands of years, novels, plays, fireside tales, and other works of fiction have been offered to the world in an attempt to bring about social justice by raising the audience's awareness of how things really are. The parable is powerful. The fact that stories educate so well is a testament to our ability to place ourselves in another person's shoes and gain a perspective that we never could have imagined simply hearing the cold, hard facts. There is one novel about the American experience and social justice that stands out, deserving to be mentioned here: Upton Sinclair's novel, The Jungle.

In 1905, Mr. Sinclair wrote the original version of The Jungle to bring transparency to the Chicago, Illinois, meatpacking industry, to raise awareness of the terrible working conditions of the people caught in that corrupt and greedy system. At the beginning of the twentieth century, mass-production meat processing was an upstart, thriving industry. It regularly consumed lives: some, quickly and violently, and some, slowly and with terrible heartache.

It is our firm belief that had Mr. Sinclair possessed the ability to self-publish, as we do today, he would have done so with no hesitation because he was required to cut almost one-third of The Jungle's stunning scenes from the 1905 version to allow him to be published with his 1906 sanitized version. (In 2003, See Sharp Press published the uncensored original, 1905, edition).

Reading the censored, 1906, version of The Jungle, America learned some of the revolting truth about meat processing before effective food and labor legislation was passed. Sinclair wanted readers to react to the way the meat-packing workers were abused. But much to Sinclair's surprise, it was the unsanitary, food-production practices to which Americans most reacted and focused upon. In response, Congress was forced to pass legislation that soon created the 1906 Pure Food and Drug Act, as well as many other regulations designed to improve the quality of our foods.

To attempt to promote social justice, we offer <u>The Redeemer: It Is Written</u>, as a latter day version of <u>The Jungle</u>. But with a focus on a different industry infected with corruption; railroad worker personal-injury claims, as personal injury lawyers pursue them. Perhaps it does not spew as much blood as the meat packing industry, but it does produce horrors, in railroad workers' lives, for consumers and taxpayers, and in our United States system of justice. In some legal circles, Lady Justice is no lady.

The genesis for <u>The Redeemer</u>, which in part is based, plainly and unapologetically, on a true story, was a story my dying father told me as we returned home from the hospital at Scott Air Force Base, Illinois, on a warm day in the summer of 1986.

My father's life had followed a unique path. He had been decorated as one of America's "Ace" P-51, fighter pilots in World War II; he became a record-setting trial lawyer; and he rose to the rank of Brigadier General in the United States Air Force National Guard (131st TFW). His picture hangs on the Fighter Ace Wall of Fame at the United States Air Force Academy. He was a loving, Catholic husband and a father of seven.

I was his sixth child and, that summer of 1986, a new graduate from law school. My future in the law looked grim to me because I had wagered quite a lot in my expectation that I would practice law with Dad. In fact, the goal of practicing law with my father was the primary reason I chose to leave the United States Air Force Academy when I was ranked at the top of my cadet class.

On that memorable day in 1986, I was driving Dad back home to St. Louis after he had received medical care for an advanced cancer in his stomach and lungs. We silently admitted that his end was near and I would never get to practice law with him. Our conversation somehow turned to the possibility of my practicing railroad work-injury law, and Dad immediately grew angry. With a sharp twist of his emaciated wrist, he snapped off the radio, which had been playing Elton John's song, "Rocket Man." My father clearly stated, "It's a fucking mafia!" (Although Dad had been a wing commander during the Cold War and a fighter pilot known to use salty language, he rarely used the "F" word.)

A long and startling question-and-answer session followed that day between father and son. Dad taught me lessons about the law that no one learns in law school. The most disturbing lesson was that there was a secret side to America's court system that allowed organized crime to be committed in the name of Lady Justice. Dad told me, in certain and sorrowful terms, how he had been denied a promotion and his second general's star, due to his innocently meeting with railroad-union officials in the course of his civilian job as a trial attorney. My head was swimming.

After I heard how the legal system really worked, I was angry with myself for leaving the Air Force Academy. When I had decided to leave USAFA, I thought I was stepping up from a career of flying jets to practicing law—up to what many have labeled "the most honorable profession." I was terribly hurt by my father's solemn instructions. But I did not let it show because I did not want Dad to feel badly for telling me the truth.

To understand the depth of my folly at leaving the Academy and a career as an Air Force officer, I asked Dad more questions about this mafia of lawyers about which he had warned me. He was forthcoming with all the information I requested; most all of it was heartrending to a believer in our United States Constitution.

Yes, he dropped some names.

Triple-ace, Brigadier General Glennon T. Moran, Sr., passed away that summer of '86, and I passed into the practice of law. The lessons I learned from Dad about a lawyer mafia that ran portions of the railroad-injury industry were stored away, in a dark closet in my mind, one that I believed I would never open.

I was wrong.

A number of years into my law practice, I was involved with defending a railroad-union official, a law school friend of mine, in the United States Supreme Court. The honorable man I defended had run for International President of a railroad union, on a platform that included cleaning up the dishonest practices of some of the railroad union's "designated" lawyers. For his attempt to clean up a sewer of corruption in the legal field, he was railroaded through our court system and sent to prison. His crime? Allegedly lying to a grand jury that was examining the railroad-injury industry. Through thousands of hours of unpaid, *pro bono*, legal work, my law partner and I gained a reversal of the perjury conviction our client had suffered. The poor man had been sent to prison merely because he told *the truth* about the railroad-injury "designated" attorney system.*

Railgate.

During those thousands of hours I spent representing an innocent man, I learned quite a lot about the shady sides and angles of the railroad-injury legal business. Talk about a system built with smoke and mirrors, lashed together with the thin rope of bipartisan support from our elected officials! It seemed that each injured railroad-union man had his own unique story about how the ethics laws had been shredded and discarded by some of the railroad-injury lawyers. Those stories of corruption made me remember the story my dying father had told years earlier and recall some of Dad's other characterizations for the railroad-injury system: "It's a barrel of Goddamned snakes" and, perhaps my favorite, "They're a pretty rough bunch," which Dad claimed in reference to their penchant for violence, doing whatever it took to keep other lawyers from getting railroad-injury clients.

<u>Please note: not all railroad-injury attorneys are dishonest</u>.

But a troubling number of them are. It should come as no surprise that a good number of railroad-injury lawyers have employed racketeering and organized crime to obtain personal-injury cases. And it makes some sense once you consider that, despite the staunch dissent of its own members, the United States Supreme Court, unintentionally, has sanctioned the chasing of personal injury cases. Forty-five years ago, that dissent pointed out that allowing lawyers to chase cases would lead the practice of law in America down a dishonorable path.**

Railgate.

At the back of this book are some excerpts from a future non-fiction book, <u>America's Lawyer Mafia: Railgate</u>. One of the excerpts is a copy of an official, federal court order, dated September 13, 2005, and written by a Texas federal district court judge. On page two of that order is <u>underscored</u>, for your convenience, where the judge officially finds that dozens of railroad work-injury lawyers admitted in his courthouse, under sworn oath, that they had participated in RICO, organized crime, racketeering activities in order to receive railroad-injury cases. That secret testimony, offered by some members of the lawyer mafia, in a very high-level deal struck with the government, led to the felony convictions and to the imprisonment of two International Presidents, as well as other railroad-union officials, for participating in organized crime in connection with railroad-injury lawyers obtaining cases in exchange for bribes of many sorts.

An excerpt of a sentencing transcript, for the imprisonment of one of the rail union officers, who was suckered into doing business with the lawyer mafia, is also provided.

Railgate.

In a scary commentary on the power of the lawyer mafia, every single one of the attorneys, who testified regarding using racketeering to obtain personal injury cases, dodged civil or criminal discipline. They were not even reprimanded by their bar associations. (And people wonder why America has lost much of its competitive edge.) It also appears that the U.S. Attorney who tried to turn over to their respective bar associations their names and sworn testimony resigned after a closed-door meeting with the newly appointed Attorney General Alberto Gonzales—before the judge changed his initial ruling, and ruled in favor of the admitted ring of racketeering lawyers. That US Attorney never testified before Congress regarding the allegation that Alberto Gonzales had fired US Attorneys on political grounds. That brave ex-U.S. Attorney, and ex-Navy SEAL, died of a gunshot wound; ruled a suicide.

The above referenced court order is offered as an excerpt from the previously mentioned nonfiction book <u>America's Lawyer Mafia: Railgate</u>, which we intend to publish some time in the future. That book would reveal, among many other things, that what would be illegal for most Americans appears to be legal for a select few of the railroad-injury bar.

The Railgate system of corruption has, by some estimates, cost the American public and taxpayers much more than the fifty billion dollar ($50,000,000,000) Ponzi scheme revealed in a recent, Wall Street fiasco. By one news report, Bernie Madoff raked in fifty billion dollars and never once invested any of it in stocks or other legitimate investments. Absurd. But could some of our public officials be just as greedy? Just as sloppy? As ruthless? To make matters worse, the Madoff, and other huge thefts, were all pulled off in the face of honest persons continually begging investigators to do the right thing — investigate. But whistle blowers are not treated well in America.

The result of top financial officers warning of a major financial disaster ended with Freddie Mac and Fannie Mae firing the honest people, the whistle blowers, who warned of a devastating financial collapse, world-wide recession, if the systems were not investigated and corrected. They were lone voices, sometimes accused of being crazy, warning that our society was being duped. But nobody listened, until it was too late.

Unthinkable. But it happened. And it is sinking our financial markets, our children's futures. But at least we can still leave them the power of prayer!

Enron is another example of amazing, massive theft, where regulators looked the other way in plain sight of powerful people intoxicating themselves on reservoirs brimming with money poured in by innocent people. Life savings, 401(k)'s, stock holdings of honest, hardworking Americans went "poof." And the monies were lost into another financial dimension that only the crooks, and perhaps some politicians, know how to access. Railgate is much the same.

In Railgate, sources indicate that the federal investigators and prosecutors stopped after they hit the wall of racketeering lawyers, who, by some sources are contributors to, or are related to, powerful politicians, in positions of legislative influence over our chief federal policing agency, the Department of Justice and its FBI.

These "mega-thefts" seem to happen due to similar causes: a lack of effective regulation and a fear of making powerful people accountable to the law. Uncorrected, the system of how railroad-injury cases find their way into lawyers' offices and through our judicial system, robs us Americans of billions and billions of dollars, collectively.

The Railgate expenses of bribery and corruption are unseen, but they are surely a waste, causing dogged inefficiencies in our struggling economy and in higher costs for everything: from each time we use electricity to the expenses of our shoes, our food, and our medical care. Make no mistake, we, the American people, are being robbed by an outdated judicial system that has been exploited by unscrupulous lawyers who want little but to gorge on the mountains of money to be made in the railroad-injury system; all to our loss.

This crooked system, driven by ruthless lawyers, that Dad explained to me, in 1986, has been ongoing, operating under unwritten rules of organized crime. It is now 2009, and the syndicate racketeering for injury cases has been gaming us all nationwide, at least since the mid-1950s—over fifty years. When will we find the courage to step on the toes of both political parties and stop these sanctioned crimes? Political pundits choose sides but we choose the truth!

For context, please note that my family and I have a long and, in some points, famous history representing injured workers and personal-injury claimants, one all the way through the United States Supreme Court.*** We are not anti-plaintiff or anti-defense, anti-corporate; we are pro-truth.

The fact that one federal judge had the courage to leave written proof, an official order, that some railroad-injury lawyers paid bribes and conducted other organized-crime activities *redeems* our American system of justice and our right to free speech. For that matter, revealing to the American citizens the crimes perpetrated in our judicial system *redeems* the entire United States Constitution. Almost as important, that courageous federal judge validates squarely—in the written opinion that he laid open to the public in a case involving hundreds of sealed documents that the public was forbidden to see— the scandalous story Dad told me that warm summer day. *Beware, my son.*

"It's a f_ _king mafia!"

~~~~~~~~~~~~~~~~~~~~~~~~~~~~~~~~~~~~~~~~~~~~~~~~~~~~~~~~~~~

We hope you find <u>The Redeemer</u> a novel with a great storyline and timeless plot. It is offered not just as entertainment, or only as a call to social justice, but also as a spiritual message about the power of prayer and meditation. We hope that, through prayer and meditation, we, as a people, find the courage to demand that our elected representatives pass legislation that will increase the transparency and accountability of our institutions. As a start, we believe it would improve our great country if the "Office of Public Integrity" Senate ethics bill legislation were passed. Our elected officials should admit that they cannot adequately police themselves. The age-old maxim still rings true: "Unchecked power corrupts." Letting politicians police themselves is like letting foxes watch the henhouse.

Do we, the people, deserve anything less from our publicly elected and publicly paid officials? That Texas federal judge had the courage to print the truth, unless you think he made it all up; that he was lying about a ring of dozens of personal injury lawyers swearing the truth, in hundreds of pages of testimony, that they knowingly participated in an on-going criminal enterprise to illegally funnel lucrative railroad injury cases to themselves. Was the judge lying? You be the judge of the truth. Truth has always produced the strongest fabric of government, especially in the hands of the American people.

This foreword is being typed in the State of Illinois, on the 200th anniversary of the birth of President Abraham Lincoln. And that begs the question: "What would 'Honest Abe' do?" We doubt he would turn his head to allow a lawyer mafia to pick the pockets of honest Americans and to have their way with Lady Justice. We believe Mr. Lincoln would have agreed with

Dr. Martin Luther King, Jr., who encouraged the world to act when he stated, "It is always the right time to do the right thing."

No matter how you, our dear reader, are moved or not moved by social justice, we hope you enjoy the story. It comes from the heart.

May God bless you and your families, and God bless America,

## *Jeanne and Mark Moran*\*\*\*\*

\* For you legal beagles, see <u>Waldemer v United States</u>, 98 F 3d. 306 (7th Cir. 1997).
\*\* See <u>Brotherhood of Railroad Trainmen vs. Virginia State Bar</u>, 377 U.S. 1 (1964), for its full opinion, including its clairvoyant dissent.
\*\*\* <u>Senko v. LaCrosse Dredging Corp.</u>, 352 U.S. 370 (1957).
\*\*\*\* A Catholic, sister-brother team; Jeanne does most of the praying and Mark, a lawyer, does most of the writing. Seeking social justice is an integral part of our Catholic religion.

## *It Is Written*

# THE REDEEMER

❧ IT IS WRITTEN ❧

# CHAPTER I

*"A Dream Is The Beginning For All Great Achievements.*
*It Is The Common Seed Among The Mighty."*
—Michael McRain

IT IS WRITTEN that to every thing there is a season and a time to every purpose under the Heaven: a time to be born and a time to die, a time to kill and a time to heal, but I knew, sure as Hell, there was no right time for a trained killer to baby-sit his henpecking, big sister.

I was the last child born into a large, Catholic family, and I was named after Saint Michael, the warrior angel. Eventually, the United States Marine Corps beckoned me, and the C.I.A. ordained me into its secret order of assassins. I became a killer angel. After a number of years moving unsuspecting souls into the afterlife, I wanted a change from spilling blood, to a career I believed would be a bit more honorable—practicing law.

Study at Harvard Law School refined my thinking and made me pause and reflect on my actions. It was in such a pause, at my father's deathbed, that I reluctantly accepted the duty of caring for my physically and mentally challenged sister. Be warned. Brothers and sisters are like fire and ice; one should not be nanny and chauffeur to the other, else he suffers a major meltdown of spirit. World War III. It was not long before I found myself trapped. I could not escape the blood oath I had sworn to my dying father: to be the lifelong protector of my domineering sister, Bridget Mary Bernadette McRain, Irish and hyper-Catholic. Better known as Hell on earth. I loved and I hated my sister Bridget. But through an unexpected quest, full of miracles, Bridget became my redeemer.

My sweet redeemer.

It started on the dark side of dawn, July 27, 1995. I was the epitome of sweet slumber, stretched out on my four-poster bed at the McRain estate in St. Martinsville County. Once my bedroom had been an island of comfortable refuge; back when I believed the law could make a difference. But the more I practiced divorce law and the more I cared for my sister, the more jaundiced I became, jaded at my stalled life. My room in my sister's home then pressed upon me, transformed into a dark cell of incarceration.

My bedroom was long and narrow. Crammed with heirloom antiques. Ageless scents of ancient dust and lemon-oiled hardwood floors wafted through the rambling Victorian mansion I called home. The house had been built in the nineteenth century by a sea captain, high on a white stone bluff overlooking the mighty Mississippi River. The chandeliers were tarnished and the oak floors creaked, but it was the place where I grew up with my five older brothers and a sister, Bridget. My blind and autistic older sister was now my landlady, but I babysat her on a promise to our dying Father.

Before I awoke that day, I dreamt deeply. The dream felt real:

*I was brought to a beautiful beach. Warm trade winds blew serenely through my hair. Soft ocean waves lapped white foam over my polished, Marine Corps boots, splashing onto my dress-blue pants. No worries. No problems. White, pulled-cotton clouds appeared pasted on a cobalt sky above shimmering, clear waters. I looked down at my feet as a gentle wave receded, leaving sparkling white sand over my uniform, my earthly image. When I looked up, I saw a great and majestic ship, its full sails billowing halfway to the horizon. A mighty three-master frigate on a tack to my quiet, little island and me. A thick fog overtook the ocean, then the beach. And me.*

I woke up.

Even in my dream, I should have spied on the horizon the hurricane of evil about to blast into my life. It would bring a storm of greed and deception and blood, the likes of which I had never seen. It was to be a reckoning I could not avoid.

# CHAPTER 2

# MAFIA MUSCLE

In a dark woods three hours away, the mafia flexed its muscle.

"Do it or you're gonna be coyote meat," said Knuckles.

Knuckles was in the parts business. Body parts. Pain and suffering. He jack hammered his brass knuckles into Billy's face. Again. No emotion. Just business. He snugged down his fedora and glared at his target through his one good eye.

Knuckles looked like a Grizzly bear on the scent of wounded game as he followed Billy, who was trying to sneak away, scooting backwards on his butt. Futile. Billy smelled the diesel fumes from the locomotive. The horrid breath from his assailant. Knuckles was playing with his prey. Billy knew what was expected from him. Knuckles had told him twice, between Billy begging for mercy and Knuckles pulverizing his face. Through the puffy slits his eyes had become, Billy could see he had bought himself scant time.

Billy McAvoy had heard the rumors. The horror-story talk from his union brethren, the railroaders. In the roundhouses and the rail yards, at hotels on layovers, elbow to elbow in beer-soaked, smoky juke joints. "Some day you might be chosen." A black duty. There was no good and no escape. This was bigger than the both of them.

"I told ya I'd pay ya anything."

"Sure, you'll pay him. I'm just picking up the collateral for the loan. This ain't nothing personal. Dutch just picked you."

"*Lucky me,*" thought Billy.

Again the union man looked around for escape. At Billy's back, a slow freight train crept out of the Ozark oak forest, as a hungry snake might. It slithered along winding, mountain rail tracks. Inch by inch through the cool night. The enormity of its cars made the train appear hungry to the injured man, as though it was sidling up next to him, sensing his body heat. Ready to devour him. Billy felt cornered by beasts who could not reason—could only lust for their food. Knuckles flattened Billy's nose with his shiny left fist, crushing Billy's face down onto the chalky rocks. Billy crawled on his belly towards the train. A loose sill step rattled like a sidewinder's warning before it strikes.

Knuckles' head jerked towards the sound of the train horn—three long, lonely wails from the moonlit distance. Time to act. Time to part. A nearby pack of coyotes began to dance, and yap and yipe, amongst their howls to the moon and the night train's offering. The train. They had lived off of its kill, its carrion, for one hundred years. A never-ending feast on the steel of man. They were shameless, for they too were beasts.

Billy looked up at Knuckles, standing astraddle him. Knuckles' long, black trench coat and plastic poncho swept over him. *"A blanket of death,"* Billy thought. He could smell Knuckles' foul breath even through the thick night air and the blood caked in his nostrils. It sickened him, all the way to his testicles. He felt like vomiting, but he could not. Billy stopped. Nowhere to go. Nowhere to hide.

Billy was sure as Hell this wasn't in the Continental American Railway employee handbook when he signed on. He wondered why he even paid union dues, if this is what paying dues got him. But he knew these were special dues he was paying. Secret dues.

He was afraid to turn to look back at Knuckles because he kept losing his teeth. Billy thought of his wife and children at home. Maybe for the last time. Knuckles interrupted this warm, fuzzy time with a brogan to the back of Billy's head and the unmistakable click of a switchblade opening. He yanked Billy's shirttail from his pants and sliced it off.

"Just in case you make it, kid," said Knuckles. "Don't wantcha endin' up like your dumb-fuck union brother last month; big pile of freakin' hamburger."

Billy shook. His lips quivered as he summoned courage to do something no man should have to do. Knuckles held onto the back of Billy's belt and stayed clear of the iron handgrips protruding from the passing railcars. Billy looked back one last time at Knuckles, his speechless nod a direct order: do it. Now.

Billy's head was below the undercarriage of the cars going by, just inches outside the nearest rail. He turned his head to watch the enormous freight-car wheels creep down the endless, twin serpents of steel. He mumbled a "Hail Mary" through blood-swollen lips.

William Andrew McAvoy blinked his eyes in deliberation. It was a momentary, desperate meditation—hoping for some type of salvation that he knew would not come. His entire life plunged past him in a blur of thought without time: *his mother's apron, first communion, his little brother drowning, Daddy dying, his wife's touch, their first-born child, a family picnic, last Christmas.* Billy's eyes shot open.

He screamed to his creator, "God!"

A minute later, the train's brakes screeched. Fingers as big as cucumbers pulled butcher's wrap from inside Knuckles' now blood-drenched poncho. Ghoulishly disregarding the nature of what he held in his hands, the huge man deliberately wrapped his prize, constricting the waxen paper with rubber bands. He branded the gory package "Ex. A" with a red marker.

Neither man, sorry souls, knew the why. The real why. The why involving time and money—and the power. The secret power that sprang neither from Heaven nor Hell. The unholy why.

A dark laugh escaped Knuckles as he smiled at his work. He was sure proud of it. He looked up the tracks in the direction of Billy. Blackness had swallowed the young brakeman. Whole.

"Dumb fuckin' Mick."

Knuckles tucked the package under his arm like a football. He stiff-armed the tall, Buffalo grass growing along the railroad right-of-way and disappeared.

*Pay day.*

# CHAPTER 3

# THE PROTECTOR

The blare sounded just like the morning bugler at Camp Pendleton. My hand smashed down on my alarm clock, stopping its familiar electronic revelry. I woke with a start that brought my dog, Gunny, to attention with a snort and a slobber. Gunny was a fine British bulldog; he slept on a USMC throw rug at my bedside.

For a moment, cool cotton sheets held me like a magnet before my taskmaster barked at me. My feet hit the floor. My six-foot, two-inch frame poised upright and ready for another day of splitting marriages and divvying up property—once earnestly hoped and prayed for—between man and wife.

I moved to the light switch on the wall and flipped it on. Stabbed into the wall just above the switch by a combat knife was a Polaroid photo of a tombstone. I had impaled it there the night before to be sure I saw it when I woke. I had to be doubly sure I would see it to inflict upon myself the first of many daily, internal floggings of guilt.

Gunny snorted impatience.

"Okay, okay, I know, it's PT time."

I assumed the position and started doing push-ups on clenched fists. When Gunny heard me say, "Fifty," he barked. I flipped over and started ripping out sit-ups. Sometimes Gunny would bark after I did ten, sometimes he would wait and make me do two hundred. This time, he barked when I said "Thirteen". I figured he had to go pee.

Some Special Forces guys swear by their guns. Not me. I am a knife guy. As I sprang to my feet, I grabbed the K-Bar knife I keep under the mattress at night. I threw it underhanded into the crotch of a silhouette target hanging on the wall between framed pictures of Jesus Christ and legendary Marine Corps General Chesty Puller. The two men around whom my life orbited.

"Let's hit the head."

Gunny wagged his nub of a tail all the way to his hips.

We crept out my bedroom door and tiptoed past Bridget's room to avoid her endless spiritual shrapnel. We sneaked downstairs, as quietly as the squeaky steps would allow. I opened the wooden screen door and walked out of the kitchen onto the large wrap-around porch, where I laced up my boots. It was a place of tranquility.

As I sat in an Adirondack chair, I listened to the resident whippoorwill sing in steady cadence. Smells of early lilac and morning-glory took me back to a childhood of comfort and security. The morning was serene. It gave no warning that my life would soon take an abrupt turn where I would face opponents as elusive as ghosts, but as real as death. Gunny and I left tracks in the dewed grass from the flagstone sidewalk to our favorite tree, a massive burr oak, where we stood to relieve ourselves. It was a ritual started by Father, the General, who had been Gunny's original master. When Father died about a year ago, I felt compelled to continue his practice of marking the trees as a territorial, male-bonding sort of thing. Gunny and I were a team stuck on tradition. We were proud to mark our turf.

That particular burr oak was the largest of the small forest of hardwoods at Twenty-Three Oaks. Looking at it, you could see it had been used through the generations for a lot more than nature's call. The oak's history was scarred with initials, messages, and symbols carved into its trunk by McRains back to the 1800's. The initials of my brothers, my sister, and I appeared there, in vertical order by age. The oak was a living totem pole spelling out the pecking order of our house. My initials were at the bottom. "M.O.M."–Michael O'Brien McRain. My five brothers were now scattered to the four winds: a surgeon; a computer engineer; a physicist; a Yale college history professor, no less; and an investigator for the I.R.S.

In the faint glow cast by the yellow porch light, I looked up and down the trunk of the tree. The initials J.C.C. were quite faint, but could still be seen in the aged bark, as a testament to the sea captain who built Twenty-Three Oaks. I wondered whose initials might have been grown over by the bark of a hundred years. More, I questioned why I was the only man on the list left residing at our childhood home.

CHAPTER 3

I knew the answer. I was the obedient son. The only one hyper-dutiful enough to be there tending to my autistic and blind sister. I was the black sheep. Literally. The only one of the six boys with dark, Irish features like my Father— Brigadier General Frank McRain. The General was a titanic, military legend in his own time, the highest decorated fighter pilot in American history. And I realized that was why my brothers had left, to return only for Father's funeral. None of them could ever find enough sunlight to grow, to become their own man in our Father's huge oaken shadow.

Under my breath, I cursed my blessed plight, that I was the son of a national hero. Gunny shook his leg and trotted over to his doghouse, following our routine. I knelt down, picked up the chain, and clipped it to his spiked collar. His doghouse had "Gunny" blazed over the door, and a small brass placard attached to its side read: "Break Chain in Case of War." He whined. He wanted to run with me. We had tried it before, but his short legs failed him halfway to the stone. I stood up and gave him a funny sort of salute as he sat looking up at me worshipfully.

"Stand guard for the crazy lady," I directed as I jogged off into the early-morning blackness.

When I got to the end of the hundred-yard gravel driveway, I turned up the street and looked over my shoulder towards the house. In Bridget's bedroom window, I saw the soft glow of the holy-devotion candles she burned in her perpetual rituals of prayer. I cursed to myself. Again. It was a good, Marine-Corps cursing.

I bowed my head and lengthened my stride into the chilly, dark night.

# CHAPTER 4

# THE REDEEMER

God blessed her and cursed her. Bridget Mary McRain had a photographic memory, but not much way to share what she knew with other people. Her talks with God stretched like a warm blanket across her every day. She had not asked to be born that way. Blind. Autistic. Catholic. God decided the first two, and my parents christened her a Catholic. Bridget had no weak will. Not in any sense of the term. She accepted all three: the blindness, the autistic Asperger Syndrome, and the structured spirituality of Catholicism. She gleefully reveled, shining like a beacon in her unbridled Catholic penchants, that never seemed a duty to her, but to others appeared as unceasing burdens she carried each and every moment of her life.

Bridget was a force that could only be explained by observing her behavior and experiencing her presence, which evoked a special peace. Her serenity seemed to spin turban-like, a celestial aura surrounding her. Her sense of smell was very strong. Her only vanity lay there. She wore sweet-spiced holy water, her own version of perfume.

She and God were as one. She never stopped, and she never gave up. Bridget was a human, praying machine—a conduit to Heaven. She prayed twenty-four, seven. I believe she even prayed in her sleep.

Bridget charged through her life, carrying what seemed to others as a puzzle in her gut, an enigma in her mind, and a physical suffering unique to the blind. Her sightlessness was a mystery only revealed to her as far as she could reach with the primary tool of the blind—a white cane. Bridget's cane was plainly Irish. It was a magnificent white shillelagh with a beautiful Celtic cross carved atop the hilt and a bright-red tip with which she would tap-tap-tap wherever she went. To those who did not know and understand Bridget, her life appeared an intellectually dim and physically lightless prison. But I knew that wasn't the truth. I knew Bridget had it all figured out—about life and love. And she lived her life accordingly.

They call that "centered" nowadays.

Her prayers were not just light, airy petitions tossed up to heaven. Bridget Mary packed some serious spiritual heat. A natural consequence of standing up for herself, the only girl in a home full of rambunctious brothers, Bridget developed a personality Dirty Harry might have had if he were a nun. Tough love. She had a heart the size of Texas, but God forbid if you messed with her praying or her rosaries. That would bring you a swift swing from Bridget Mary's shillelagh.

She employed an array of Catholic paraphernalia that would impress the Pope. And she called on a circle of holy heavies with whom Bridget spoke and to whom she prayed daily, both out loud and in her mind, a cocoon full of spirits and Jesus Christ. She knew of every saint who ever lived, and she treated each as her dear friend and protector, waiting to help her at a moment's notice. This was her faith, lived every day and every moment of her life.

She felt her way everywhere outside her home with the assistance of her long-staffed shillelagh and her seeing-eye dog, Ace. Bridget Mary Bernadette McRain tended to be a night owl. She could afford to, having only a simple job stringing rosaries together, bead by bead, at St. Cecilia's Workshop for the Blind three days a week. The rest of her time was spent in fervent prayer, "working the beads," as I called it, in a series of never-ending requests to a thousand different saints, to Jesus, and to God, and to the Virgin Mother herself. I suppose, because she was blind, autistic, and a Catholic, there was nothing else worthy of her thoughts.

In my prior career, before I became a divorce lawyer, I was a member of America's elite Special Forces, a member of the United States Marine Corps Force Recon. I admired Bridget—in a way, because I knew every Special Forces operative could only aspire to the unwavering focus Bridget employed. Her mind had a singular purpose: her own private little war to achieve good in the name of God.

CHAPTER 4

My older sister woke each morning in her second-story bedroom, in her featherbed, in a brief state of wonderment. She lay in bed and thought about lofty and high-brow subjects, like quantum physics, and friendship, and relativity. She even pondered the existence of God. But she always arrived at the same answer, facing east when she opened her eyes each morning. She realized she was a child of God in a world much in need of prayer.

It was a cool, summer morning when Ace lightly bumped his cold, wet nose against her hand, draped over the edge of the bed: the blind, lead dog's way of letting Bridget know he needed to go outside.

She gathered back her bushel-ful of long, red hair and wriggled her toes into her slippers. Grabbing her shillelagh, she shuffled out of her bedroom into the upper hall of the great home she inherited from our late Father. Typical of a large Victorian-style home, it was constructed around a beautiful, wide, long staircase. She navigated down, past the large portrait of "Daddy" the General, in his pilot's jacket, looking like an eagle standing sentry over the staircase.

There were nineteen steps from top to bottom, and she knew each one well. To Bridget, each stair step had a unique feel under her feet. The seventeenth and the fifth each creaked quite loudly. But it was the eleventh she enjoyed the most. Its light, long squeak sounded like a beginner's bow drawn across a cello in "D."

The home smelled of cinnamon and nutmeg, along with the scents of the different incense and candles Bridget burned in a devotion of prayer.

Like most of the blind, Bridget's hearing was keen. Paradoxically, she preferred her television loud and her music louder, to accommodate her autistic brain, that multi-tasked like a super-computer. She thought of the louder sounds of the world as an audio blanket, under which she murmured her prayers.

Earnest prayers offered: Prayers for the poor. Prayers for the trees. Prayers for the President. Prayers for the crops. Prayers for Ace. Prayers for me. Prayers for world peace. Prayers for the souls of the dead. Prayers for the Pope. And prayers for every other matter that might exist, on this world or in the universe. There was no end to the list of subjects worthy of her prayers.

I usually called her "Bridge" or "Bridgy" or "Bridget," but sometimes I jokingly called her "Bridgetiletto" to get a rise out of her. It was simply my attempt to break through her stone-faced, autistic veneer, so I could see her white, porcelain face contort, out of prayer mode, with a stern issue of the only name she ever called me: "Michael."

When she and Ace got to the fifteenth step, she was praying to Saint Jerome Emiliani to help the orphaned children in Africa, switching to Saint Ivo of Kermartin to help me in my law practice by the time she descended to the seventh step. When Bridget reached the bottom of the stairs, she felt the strong, hardwood floor, covered by a Persian rug. By then, her earnest fingers had progressed along her rosary to focus a machine-gun volley of "Hail Mary"s to ensure the Pope a safe voyage to Asia. As she prayed all these devotions, her left hand repeatedly pinched each station of a mahogany—beaded, Franciscan rosary.

With her right hand, Bridget prayed for God to cease all wars. These were her petitions for universal understanding and for human relief from Greed—the underlying reason for wars. For these prayers, she used a special, glass-beaded rosary, a gift from our late Aunt Virginia. When I listened to Bridget pray, I wondered if she was an innocent lamb or the end product of our evolution. Every time, my musings ended with confidence that the Marine Corps would still be guarding the gates of whatever Heaven or Hell we made for ourselves.

Bridget was the most genuine and sincere person anyone could meet. This was just great, unless you were her brother. Then it was a living Hell, an onslaught of never-ending prayer-speak. The only times she spoke clear English were when she was her angriest. It was then the knot in her tongue would loosen and she would speak. Such was the confounding world of Asperger Syndrome in which Bridgy lived.

Bridget opened the front door, and Ace led her out, onto the large, wrap-a-round porch. Ace trotted off the porch for his call to nature while Bridget smelled the air, sweetened by summer lilies. Bridget had called our

Father "Daddy." He left her the house, and, as a tribute to Daddy, she set her mind to keep the lilies every year. They were Daddy's favorite, and they gave Bridget a bouquet of memories of swinging on the porch swing with Daddy, for hours on end in quiet, contemplative bliss. This was her ageless image of her forever-loving Daddy. Her protector left her the whole estate in a trust administered by a crusty, old lawyer from a blue-blooded law firm in Chicago. He was someone the General could count on. An old wing man from Daddy's World War II, fighter-pilot days.

Bridget walked along the large porch, her shillelagh bumping into one of the three-foot-high chess pieces standing on the huge chessboard painted onto the floorboards. When we were growing up, everyone—the whole McRain family, and especially Bridget—took turns, moving one piece at a time in the family chess game. We were required to justify each move to our Father, who used the game to teach life's strategies. Thinking. Forethought. Strategy. Anticipation. Planning. Execution. They were all required in all of life's pursuits.

Bridget took my knight with her bishop and put the black horse and rider to the side, where she kept her captured pieces.

It had become just Bridget and me at home. With Father's passing, it fell on me to protect her. I had made a promise from son to father. *A deathbed promise.*

At the time of my promise to Father, I did not know that I was merely a dutiful soldier in a war I did not yet know existed. I learned that there come times when we escape the world and become as gods to the helpless.

But I was no god. I was just a pawn in Bridget's chess game. A game that would soon turn bloody.

# CHAPTER 5

# THE RAINMAKER

Delilah "DeeDee" DeVillay stroked her slender fingers through her jet-black hair. She wondered why she had needed to graduate from Yale Law School in order to become the Madame of a whorehouse. A brothel on wheels. Mobile sex for the union men—her firm's bread and butter. She chewed on her thumbnail. Natural, not fake. And she recalled all the hard work she had put into becoming a human machine, studying for eighteen hours a day and editing the *Yale Law Review*, to graduate at the top of her class. Nonetheless, she was proud of being the highest-paid call-girl in the American Bar Association.

DeeDee daydreamed between johns and sometimes when they were mounting her. It took her mind off how bad their beer-belching breath smelled. Plus, it helped the time pass more quickly. They were railroad union men. They didn't know how to treat a lady. Her expensive French perfumes were wasted on them.

For DeeDee, it was a simple trade-off.

DeeDee was one sharp chick. She was a student of history. She knew she could make a lot of money relying on the history of the railroad business. It was a history full of brutality: from the brute force used by the Pinkertons, who ran early American settlers off their land to make way for the railroad; to the harsh practice of treating foreign laborers like disposable mules, working them to death to build railroad tracks across the continent; to running a mammoth, black-cloud-belching locomotive that pulled people and promise across a wild country; or to the deadly Pullman strike, in which the Pinkertons killed striking rail-union men. Call it what you want: imperialism, greed, Manifest Destiny. They all fit because they all require brutality.

Delilah DeVillay knew that the history of the railroad was a brutal history that paralleled America's rise to dominate the world. You simply could not separate one from the other.

DeeDee was greedy. She felt a natural kinship with the railroad barons. She admired all the stories of their taking and creating wealth.

She realized these simple history lessons, and she accepted the railroad industry on its own bestial terms. DeeDee provided brute sex for the union men who, in return, sent her law firm very lucrative railroad-injury cases. It was that simple. And it wasn't a new marketing angle. Her law firm had practiced it for decades with regular whores. Not with a licensed attorney doing the scandalous work between the sheets.

As RVs go, this was the largest the law firm could rent. It was equipped with two bedrooms that they filled with DeeDee and some non-lawyer, working girls to service the line of railroad workers stretching deep beyond the door.

DeeDee looked out the window of the RV, into the inky blackness of the Louisiana night, while the beast on top of her grunted and shoved. The aroma of cigar smoke reeked from his flannel shirt and made DeeDee try to hold her breath for a while. He was an officer of the railroad-union local there in Baton Rouge, so she accorded him special treatment—a whisper in the ear and two or three "Oh God." That was the extent of whatever religion she practiced.

J.J. kept thrusting, and he was not getting anywhere. She coaxed him like a horse, holding onto his flannel shirt with both hands, like a bridle.

"Come on, J.J. Come on, Sugar. There ya go."

DeeDee called the men by their initials and not their names because that is how railroaders refer to each other. They use their first two initials because their railroad-union rank-and-file seniority lists are typed in that manner. As an unintended result, it dehumanizes the men, assigning their existence in life a number alongside some initials. It serves to foster their hollow lifestyles. Ghosts in their own homes. No longer real people, they are only machines operating for the railroad. They carry serial numbers and initials. And each man is issued a head, two arms, and two legs. That's the way the railroad likes it because it doesn't have time to molly-coddle its men. Not with schedules to meet and profits to make.

Damn it.

CHAPTER 5

DeeDee figured J.J. was some time from finishing, so she let her mind wander from her flat-back duties. *"If my Yale classmates could see me now."*

She recalled how she had been recruited and chased by all of the biggest, most prestigious law firms in New York, San Francisco, Washington, D.C., and even London. They enticed her with outrageous offers because God not only graced her with brains, but also with wicked, movie-star, good looks set high on a thirty-eight-inch inseam. Male heads of all ages turned to follow her when she walked by. Beauty and brains, loaded with panache and chutzpah. Throw in that she was ruthless, and you were looking at the perfect law-firm rainmaker. But there really never had been any other place for DeeDee to work, but her old man's firm.

DeeDee defied the logic that a person of her intelligence and professional polish could not be so stupid as to have sex with so many relative strangers. She knew all about STDs, and she reasoned around them. She placed herself in a category all her own, and that gave her a distinct advantage over her male competition.

DeeDee made sure each and every one of her johns wore protection. And she usually only serviced the union leaders. They were older and not as high risk as the young bucks. But it was the money that separated Miss DeVillay from all the other call girls in the whole, wide world. The girl was shrewd and had business smarts like a Harvard M.B.A.

She started her lawyering career as a junior partner at her step-father's law firm, right out of Yale Law, with the understanding that she had to prove herself by getting the R.I.O. personal-injury business. The more railroad-worker injury business she brought in, the more money she made.

DeeDee did the math and shattered the record books after the first three months. In her first year alone, she made millions of dollars in legal fees from the cases she brought into Falic, Moore & DeVillay. Not counting the little folding money the men would stuff in her bra when they were done. She sat down once and figured it all out. She divided her income by the number of men she sexed. On average, she was making over twenty-three thousand dollars each time she laid a railroad-union man. She was by far the highest paid call girl in the world.

Why? Because she held a law license and used it, like nobody else, on the most lucrative clientele in all of tort law. DeeDee was shrewd at marketing. She recognized an exclusive market flush with cash, and she met the clients' needs. Bingo. DeeDee fashioned her version of the magical golden goose. This one kept laying golden eggs, as fast as DeeDee could lay the union leaders.

The RV smelled like stale cigarette smoke and latex. And the place was a-rockin'. DeeDee was detached from her act of sexing J.J., but she still acted like she was enjoying it. She had it on autopilot. After a while, J.J. got up a head of steam and poured on the coal until they'd enjoyed another couple of gyrations. J.J. completed his taking with his own form of prayer, "Oh God. Mercy! Oh God." He finished strong and satisfied and gathered his breath.

J.J. was a tall, bearded man. A lot of railroad workers wore beards because of the wicked winds out on the rail. The beards protected their faces. He hitched up his pants in front of DeeDee and released a heavy sigh.

"Mercy, Miss DeeDee, you are the best. I'll say that. I see why they call you the Kegel Queen."

J.J. slipped his belt through a large, rodeo buckle and stood up straight. He had a heavy, muscled physique, accustomed to carrying one-hundred-pound railroad-car coupling knuckles a mile or more on uneven, rough-rock ballast. DeeDee liked railroaders. They felt like real men because they were real men—capable of handling themselves with thugs and hooligans and drifters who might ambush them at night, out in the middle of nowhere, to rob them of their money. But these men were lonely. Most of them spent fewer nights per year in their beds at home than navy seamen on nine-month voyages. Railroad life is extremely hard on families and marriages. The men's isolation showed as emotion in their voices. She could tell how long ago it was that a man had been home just by listening to him talk.

DeeDee hugged J.J. tight. As a marketing ploy, she liked to personalize things to give the men a false impression that they somehow touched her heart. She did that to make the union leader feel guilty if he referred an injured railroad worker's R.I.O. case to a rival, Designated, R.I.O. law firm. She practiced a type of psychological warfare on the poor souls who weren't smart enough to understand what was happening. But if they were smart enough to figure out that they were being used, they didn't care because DeeDee was the best at making men feel special. Ultimately, none of her marketing shtick would have worked if she had not been so damned good looking.

"We appreciate your business, J.J. And don't forget it. One of your boys gets hurt, here's my card."

DeeDee slipped J.J. her card and a baseball hat with the seal of J.J.'s railroad union, the Hog Heads, on the front and the law firm's phone number, 800-I-AM-HURT, on the underside of the bill. J.J. pulled a twenty-dollar bill out of his pocket and pushed it into her lithe hand.

"Here's a little somethin' for wigglin' and gigglin' like you mean it." DeeDee stuffed it in her brassiere.

When DeeDee let J.J. out of the RV, she looked at the train of men leading up to the RV's door.

Railroaders are a different breed of men who, like the nomad cowboys of the Wild West, enjoy a brotherhood glued with bestial manners. When the train of men saw a beautiful woman in a short dress duck her head out the door of the RV, they acted like a pack of wolves, howling together, hungry for flesh. They clapped and chanted in unison, "Kegel Queen! Kegel Queen!"

One man named R.J. tried to jump ahead in line. He got into a fight with T.B., waiting ahead of him. R.J. said, "T.B., you got a wife to screw. Now get back to the end o' the line." T.B. went chest to chest with R.J. and established he was alpha male. He said, "Yeah, I gotsta wife, but I been on the rail so long, I ain't been home for a month of Sundays. B'sides, I gots union seniority here. I'z Chairman." R.J. slid off and dropped back to his rightful spot in line. DeeDee led T.B. inside and shut the door before she went into her well-rehearsed spiel of appreciation.

"T.B.!" She shrieked with well-acted excitement. "T.B., I thought you'd never get up here. That line must be pretty long." T.B. nodded and grinned in anxious anticipation of receiving his very own slice of-her unique lawyer's bribe—flesh a la carte. "You're a local chairman. You got rank. You should'a said something and I woulda moved you up in line. You send us more cases than anybody else." T.B. stared at DeeDee and her amazing, long legs below slender hips, and he started to lick his lips. "I was going to have Charlene say 'Hello' to the next Hog Head. But no way, Jose. You're a leader and you're mine, buster."

THE REDEEMER: IT IS WRITTEN

DeeDee grabbed T.B. by his string tie and led him into her lair for a proper "Thank you for referring me a hundred-man carpal-tunnel, R.I.O. class-action case." The firm paid her an eight-hundred-thousand-dollar bonus legal fee on that case alone. And DeeDee showed T.B. how much she appreciated it.

It appeared to DeeDee that T.B. was part Clydesdale. But after she got a saddle on him and coaxed him to a canter, DeeDee let her mind slip back to her worry over why she held a law license while she was still living the life of a mobile Madame. She came back with the same three reasons she always arrived at. The pay was unbelievable, and she got her name on the door the day she walked into Falic, Moore & DeVillay. The biggest railroad-injury law firm in the whole United States. And then there was the third reason.

Incest.

The primary force pushing her to provide sex for injury cases was her stepfather, Felix Falic. He not only allowed her to use her body to snare R.I.O. cases, he encouraged it. It was a scandal of the worst kind. He was her pimp.

Felix strategized that to have a lawyer dish up the sexual favors gave his R.I.O. law firm a competitive advantage in the cutthroat world of railroad-injury law, where only the most unsavory, the law firm that gets the business, survives. He studied the situation and came up with the plan to consolidate the prostitution with the law practice while he was putting DeeDee through law school. Felix figured that, since lawyers were professional whores to begin with, why not take it literally. It worked great and without a hitch. Nobody else had a system like it because no other firm had the Kegel Queen. They were receiving R.I.O. cases from coast to coast because of DeeDee's shimmy in the sheets. But, ruthless as DeeDee was, Felix was many times more so.

He and DeeDee were quite comfortable with the whole idea of sex for pecuniary gain because Felix started training DeeDee at an early age. Father and stepdaughter worked out a little earn-your-allowance deal starting the week after DeeDee's sixteenth birthday. DeeDee's whoring was begun at a convenient time, when DeeDee's Mother was away in Montreal, shopping for furs. The whole family was a perverse study in ancient sins. Lust and incest. But mainly greed. DeeDee lived her life for Mammon.

"There ya go. Oh, sweetie. Uh-huh. Go, sugar. Come on."

CHAPTER 5

# CHAPTER 6

# A WARNING

The autistic seem to have a channel straight to God. I don't know if it's because they are more pure or they are terrible liars or because they are smarter and can see into a dimension we cannot. When it came to chess, Bridget played like a wily cat. She liked to allow me to hang on, so she could torture me by defeating me slowly, like a feline plays with a captured mouse before she kills it. She chuckled inwardly that my bishop would soon be hers and the match would develop and end as she ordained. I almost always lost, and not because I wasn't trying. Bridge was good. She was smart, and she used chess as a way to communicate with the world that we, the non-autistic, live in. The material, pretentious world that the autistic seem to have little use for.

Bridget could hear Ace's collar tinkle in the cool, pre-dawn air as he trotted from bush to bush, hesitating at Gunny's doghouse long enough to exchange dogs' customary, greeting sniffs. A nice breeze lifted her long, wavy, red hair. Bridget knew all about sniffing the air as a way of seeing. Blind from birth, she battled her black environment and slowly worked her way through it with her cane, her hearing, her keen sense of smell, and a profound gut instinct.

"Good morning, Gunny."

She spoke to animals as though they were human because she had such a close relationship with her seeing-eye dog, Ace. Her fingers were wrapped around a long, Franciscan rosary and the staff of her shillelagh as she stood, her feet still. She swayed back and forth on the porch, listening to the air, smelling of it. Bridget would say the rosary at least forty to fifty times by the end of the day. She worked through the beads one-handed, and many times two-handed since she had the multitasking, split-brain ability of autism. She would push a bead through her fingers like she was loading the firing chamber in a machine gun all the while, her rosebud lips would be pursing, whispering her prayers so quickly that she would be onto the next bead, and the next, and the next, until she got to the crucifix, where she would pause. She seemed only to come up for air and to reload.

She deliberately smelled the air, searching the source of a scent, not knowing if it was a harbinger of things to come at change of season or more by man's design. It was not the sweet lilac and morning-glory she smelled, for their aromas left her olfactory and were replaced by the distinct scent of fear.

Some claim dogs can sense danger and fear and malice, not just in people, but also in situations. Gunny grunted alarm, and Ace came back and sat by Bridget's side. She felt fear the moment she arrived at the first mystery station on her rosary. As it was Friday, she had been praying for understanding of the Sorrowful Mysteries, which first offer meditation of Jesus' Agony in the Garden. The cool winds turned, taking away Bridget's breath. She sensed that I would soon be in much danger. A shiver ran down her spine. She clutched her shillelagh close. Ace sensed Bridget's fear and nuzzled against her leg.

There was a powerful and mysterious trouble coming, and Bridget knew it. She could feel it. More, she could sense that there was nothing she could do to stop it.

Like a frightened animal, she retreated into her psychological safe corner. She drove through her rosary. But she shifted gears away from the Sorrowful Mysteries and prayed for a deeper understanding of the five Joyful Mysteries, at their respective stations on her rosary: God's Annunciation to Mary; Mary's Visitation; Jesus' Nativity; Jesus' Presentation in Jerusalem; and, finally, when Joseph and Mary found Jesus in the Temple.

Bridget knew our world soon would change. The hard way, with spilt blood.

# CHAPTER 7

# THE DIRTY JUDGE

It was six a.m. in Washington, DC. The shotgun felt good in his mouth, like it belonged there—a natural consequence of the crooked direction his life had blown. Nelson didn't experience a gag reflex any more. He swallowed the steel at least once a week.

For the past fourteen years.

Nelson's liver-spotted finger trembled on the front trigger of the double-barreled shotgun he tapped against his upper-molar crowns. He loved the antique. Its rosewood-scented gun oil filled the Justice's senses, carrying him back to a time when he was just a boy. He and his father had hunted pheasant and quail and rabbits with it, back in South Dakota when he was a lad. They nicknamed it the Swede. It had a beautiful bird's-eye-maple stock. He looked down both sides of the barrels, studying the round patterns in the polished wood as he studied his life.

Carefully.

The Chief Justice of the United States Supreme Court, Sydney Ignatius Nelson VI, rested his uvula dead center on the antique shotgun while he concentrated on his catechism. The part that prohibits Catholics committing suicide.

He argued with himself as he performed this morbid dance-with-death ritual in the pre-dawn hours of the morning. He sat in his cozy study, illuminated only by the green-shaded desk lamp and the dim glow from the coals of a once-bright fire in the marble fireplace. He was surrounded by the comfort and the curse of his floor-to-ceiling shelves of law books. Their pages and their progeny were infinite. The dusty, leather-bound volumes were filled with his judicial opinions. Opinions by which he solved every other human being's problems, except his own. But the only sense he could gather from those forgotten opinions was the smell of dust; nothing more.

Dust, to which he wished he would return. Nelson felt as though he were always the savior of man and never the saved. He had no one to turn to for comfort—except Noreen.

The judge of the world promised himself that this morning would be different because he wanted to end his suffering. He looked at his desk clock. He did not have time to dally. Nelson proclaimed to himself, as though it were an order to execute a prisoner: he must die by seven a.m., before his orderly, Rone, was scheduled to arrive.

Loneliness is everything it is cranked up to be. He was still lost without his dear Noreen. His wife had died almost twenty years ago. The poor, old guy was miserable in a prison of loneliness, even though he had an army of people to assist him in anything he desired. But all the power and pressure and his physical frailties were driving him crazy. He missed the way Noreen used to set him at ease with her gentle talk over supper, with the touch of her caring hand.

His Catholic faith would not let him commit suicide, so he could go see his Noreen.

He argued with himself. God had not saved his Noreen. It should have been him God took with the cancer, and not her. If he were a fair God. An equitable God. A God based on written laws. The laws of the Bible.

He wanted to believe there was a Heaven because that is where he desired to stay, forever with Noreen and their baby, Joan. Who lived outside the womb for only one hour. Little, innocent Joanie. But still infected with Catholic, original sin. Forever guilty, with no defense except the devotions of the living. Noreen prayed for baby Joan's soul every day until the day Noreen died. After they buried Joanie, Noreen seemed to shrivel up and die. But she kept saying the rosary for Joanie's soul, to keep her baby's soul out of Purgatory.

Nelson had given up on prayers. He was a lawyer. A jurist. He dealt only in hard facts, rung dry of emotion or sympathy. He reminded himself that he was the judge of the world.

Damn it.

CHAPTER 7

Catholic Purgatory. The middle kingdom in the dimension of death, where Catholics believe questionable souls might end because their sins were not bad enough to route them straight to Hell. The unfortunate souls of sinners of a thousand different sins would remain trapped there, perhaps forever. Hung up for infinity between Heaven and Hell, until redemption was earned by prayers. That's the way Chief Justice Nelson remembered his Catechism.

He pushed hard on the Swede's front trigger. Nothing happened.

He wished he had made more money during his lifetime. He was paid well. But not a mountain of money, like the other, less talented lawyers who practiced before him. For being America's highest jurist, he was ashamed he did not have anything of a monetary value to leave his two boys and their children. For "saving the whole, Goddamn country from the crazy, lawless bastards" is the way he put it in a recent speech given at the Ladies of The Potomac Breakfast Club. His chuckle echoed down the twin, twelve-gauge barrels as he remembered how he heard the silver forks dropping onto the ladies' fine china that morning. He had decided he would do what it would take to leave his boys dynastic wealth, when the opportunity arose. But his body told him he was running out of time. And he wanted to die anyway. Soon.

The Chief Justice pushed hard on the Swede's back trigger. He was disappointed—not a Goddamn thing happened.

The world came to him to solve their problems, and he could not even solve his own. He felt pathetic. He got angrier and more depressed. He was a human storm of bitterness.

But was he still Catholic? For God's sake, he hadn't been to mass or confession for more than a decade. It was a haunting voice from the past. His childhood catechism still rang loudly, like a church bell in his head. No suicide.

*Oh, what the Hell.*

He pushed on the back trigger. It was the trigger to the Swede's right barrel. Click. He still had his head.

He took his mouth off the business end of the shotgun. He broke down the gun. He hit the lever and opened its breach. No shells. The gun was empty, and he had the safety on, too. He shook his head. He knew he was a coward. Or just a depressed Catholic.

The ache in his heart made him sob, for missing Noreen and feeling lonely. A tear fell from his face and ran down the furrow between the shiny, black barrels of the Swede. He felt dejected. Defeated in his goal to kill himself. Defeated by his own values. It was an endless, Hell-on-Earth circle he ran, as a suicidal Catholic.

He hung the shotgun back on the wall above the fireplace and sat back down in his leather, wingback chair. He dozed off.

Twenty minutes later, Rone knocked on his door. He entered and administered to Nelson his morning medications for his heart and some pills for his depression and high blood pressure. He then helped Nelson down the hall for oatmeal and coffee.

Nelson secretly wished he could take his old buddy, the Swede, to work with him in the limousine so he could kill himself at his desk in the Supreme Court building, where a lot of people were sure to be.

He didn't want to die alone. He needed Noreen, and he wanted to see his daughter, Joanie.

# CHAPTER 8

# GET THE BUSINESS!

She was cursed with a conscience—the scourge of lawyers. Even though DeeDee's conscience was so slight it could fit into a thimble, it still bothered her. It nagged like a Sunday School lesson that she couldn't get out of her mind. But it wasn't the fear of a sin that would blacken her soul that had her so terribly worried. It was the thought of getting caught that troubled her day and night.

DeeDee was still doing her lay-on-the back cardio routine; the line of men outside the motor home's door was still long and loud. She thought they sounded like a pack of lonely coyotes, yipping and growling amongst each other waiting for their turns. But she took a break before she let in the next Hog Head union leader. Some time to think, without a beast taking her. She opened her purse and grabbed her chic, low-tar smokes. She looked at the fat balance in her bank account again, for the sixth time that day. Her money counting was interrupted by the RV's outside door bursting open.

Ajax, a gargantuan Greek, entered. He was one of the law firm runners, one of the non-lawyer men who ran out and signed up cases and worked on a ten percent commission paid out of the legal fee that the case eventually earned. He moonlighted by working the lobby security detail during the day. He stooped and turned sideways to make it through the door, and he kept his head down to clear the ceiling.

"Miss DeeDee, we gotta break camp immediately. We gotta hot one up in St. Martinsville. Big injury. Jet's waiting."

Sounded like big money. DeeDee stuffed her bank statement in her purse and got herself straightened out a bit. Ajax warmed up the RV for a quick exit. When she stepped out the door, the horny, union men saw a beautiful, dark-haired woman in a tight mini-skirt. They knew it was DeeDee, and they erupted in premature applause.

The union men celebrated their bestial nature as they clapped and chanted in unison, "Kegel Queen! Kegel Queen!"

DeeDee said, "Whew. Men, I'm done for the night." The men responded with a collective groan of disappointment. DeeDee worked her way down the line of C.U.R.T.I.S. union men. She gave each a genuine and breasty goodwill hug, with a kiss on the cheek and a rubbing of her bosoms, to leave her perfumed scent as a lingering reminder. The call girl extraordinaire stepped back up to the RV's doorway. She looked like a sailor shipping out to sea. DeeDee blew a kiss to the crowd and waved as Ajax drove the RV away to the waiting jet.

Ajax drove fast. The trip to the airport would take only half an hour, so DeeDee freshened up in the back. She was exhausted after her marketing workout with the union men.

After she had freshly showered, she combed her thick hair straight back, off and above her pretty face. She lay on the bed and stretched out her long legs. Some lawyers read dozens of pages of new case law each day to stay sharp and keep up to date in their profession. Not DeeDee. She did the important stuff that kept the business coming through the door. DeeDee did some of her ritual two thousand kegels per day. And it provided a good time to think. Besides, the case-law book on R.I.O., precedent was fairly thin. How to practice R.I.O. law was not taught in any law school in America. It was practiced by only a select few lawyers. DeeDee knew the most important rule of practicing lucrative R.I.O. law—get the R.I.O. cases, by hook or crook. Just get them.

She used greed-based logic to rationalize whoring to make exorbitant legal fees, just like she rationalized letting Felix take her when she was little more than a child. Money was her master. She said it out loud, like she had done when she was a teenager counting her secret, extra hundred dollars in allowance money Felix gave her for having sex with him.

"Money rules. Good girls drool."

Whoring and STD's were the least of DeeDee's worries. Her worst fear gnawed at her stomach so bad, she already had ulcers. It was those darned secret loans that worried her so. Not student loans. Loans she arranged for clients with the firm. Loans she knew were illegal as Hell. Loans she knew the I.R.S. would love to find out about.

What made things worse was, in her little panic fests, she couldn't shake the investigators that she imagined would eventually come knocking and asking lots of questions. No matter how much she smiled or flirted or flashed her cleavage at them, the fantasized investigators kept coming back to *those loans.* Each and every interview she conjured in her mind ended with DeeDee saying, "I need a lawyer."

DeeDee sat up with a startled feeling in her gut.

"Airport. Watch the bump," Ajax said, as they rumbled over a speed bump at the airport tarmac gate. She stepped down the steps of the RV and right up the steps of the firm's jet. This was DeeDee's life in the fast lane. The life of an R.I.O. Designated railroad injury attorney. A R.I.O. rainmaker.

Her stepfather Felix Falic was on the plane. He sat in for the co-pilot. DeeDee grabbed a blanket and settled into one of the plush, leather lounge chairs, pulling on a pair of eyeshades so she could take a much needed nap.

The jet was well stocked with liquor, food, changes of clothing, and photographic- and audio-recording equipment for taking statements of injury claimants or witnesses. But most important of all, the jet carried suitcases of money.

Cash.

Lots and lots of cash the I.R.S. knew nothing about. It was cash the firm obtained from a small bank it owned. Bank ownership allowed DeeDee's law firm to withdraw large sums of cash without a specific account number. Within a week, the firm's cash withdrawal would be covered up by moving enough money around to satisfy the banking regulators, who also did not know anything about Falic, Moore & DeVillay's bribery scheme. If a banking regulator made too much of a fuss about the cash irregularities, a phone call to Senator Moore would clear up the matter rather quickly. He was the firm's founder, as well as a member of the Senate Banking Committee. He would pull some strings.

Senator Moore was much like the proverbial fox guarding the henhouse. And he was a sly fox. He did not raise a lot of attention by taking too much, by eating all the hens. He just stole some eggs. American taxpayers and consumers were footing the bill for the R.I.O. bribery to the tune of a few billion dollars per year. Not enough to break the U.S. treasury. But sufficient to make it profitable enough to pay the high overhead peculiar to practicing law as an R.I.O. lawyer Designated by a railroad union.

Falic, Moore & DeVillay was the largest railroad injury firm in America. And they were Designated by all of the railroad unions. DeeDee's firm garnered its business according to the age-old eighty/twenty rule. Twenty percent of their business was obtained by giving railroad union men beefsteak dinners and booze, ballgame tickets and broads. But Felix Falic learned, thirty years before, that the most effective business getter was bribery. That was how his firm garnered about eighty percent of its more than one-hundred-million dollar per year attorneys' fees.

Even though his firm was Designated by the railroad union, there were twenty-three such law firms spread across the United States. The bribery was necessary because they engaged in cutthroat competition for railroad workers' injury cases.

With competition comes expense.

The firm kept four suitcases, with seventy-five thousand dollars in cash in each, stored in separate, secure lockers onboard the firm's jet. In the lid of each briefcase were flasks of Jack Daniels's whiskey, fine Russian vodka, and a small pad of paper and a pencil to keep track of who was paid how much in bribes and when. The line of union officials claiming to have referred the injury case got pretty long sometimes. That was because an additional ten percent, of the firm's final contingent fee, was paid to the union official who referred the case to a Designated attorney's law firm. Some union officials retired early.

"Which hospital we going to?" asked DeeDee, with a focused excitement about the possibility of signing up an "arm off." Lost appendage cases against the railroad were usually worth millions and a seven-figure attorneys' fee.

DeeDee assumed success in signing up the new client. "What is our client's name?"

"McAvoy. Billy McAvoy."

"What local?"

"Trackmen's Union Local 39 out of Statton."

"Statton?" said DeeDee. She was alarmed.

"I know, I know. That Local runs off the Santé Fe and is also damned near all sewed up by Van Killman's firm," said Falic.

DeeDee shook her head in bewilderment while Falic shrugged.

"Why are we even going on this wild goose chase to St. Martinsville to take a case that Big Dutch has all but sewed up? We haven't gotten a case out of that Local since I started with the firm two years ago."

Falic tried to interject a conciliatory remark, but was cut off.

"I know you want us to penetrate these other Locals, but Big Dutch has a jump on us."

DeeDee counted off reasons on her upheld fingers. "Big Dutch is on the ground. He's got a Local Union Chairmen who owns a three-thousand-acre ranch in Wyoming, totally stocked with buffalo, bought and paid for by Van Killman's 'litigation expenses.' And you know who Van Killman's investigator is?"

Falic knew. He nodded and acted as though he wanted to shut the cabin door, to relieve himself of DeeDee's lecture. It was impossible for him to get a word in edgewise.

"What's Van Killman's investigator's name?" She cocked her head to the side to feign ignorance. "Oh. Oh yeah, isn't it Knuckles? The half man, half Grizzly bear." DeeDee nodded her head to accentuate her extended pity party. "Yeah, yeah, that's the same Knuckles that played nose-guard for the '73 Oakland Raiders and did time in California for 'accidentally' stabbing his teammate. Got off with manslaughter. And he happens to be the same Knuckles Schultheiss who the California Parole Board, in their infinite wisdom, released to the care and supervision of Adolph 'Big Dutch' Van Killman, who makes a thumb-breaking loan shark look like a rehab nurse."

Sensing that DeeDee was just warming up for a tirade, Falic bowed his head and drew back into the safety of the cockpit.

DeeDee got out of her chair and started to pace the cabin, "I have no social life. Oh sure, I'm the Madame of a mobile bordello. A brothel that services horny railroad workers so we can get the first call when a serious injury occurs."

DeeDee sat back down and opened her book, *Lolita*, with an angry snap. "I guess I shouldn't complain. I did get my name on the door and junior partnership in the biggest railroad injury firm in America." DeeDee started to read in a steaming spirit of discontent.

DeeDee slapped her book closed. She spoke to the stale-smelling cabin air again, "Now I see why I should have gone to Yale's Business School instead of the Law School. I have become a ' sex supervisor.' It's all about making the union men happy, isn't it?"

She stewed over her plight for a few minutes before the pilot was brave enough to open his cabin door. He spoke to DeeDee. "Miss DeVillay, your nurse's scrubs are in locker number two. Put on your seatbelt after you change because we will be landing in nine minutes."

DeeDee threw in one last barb of smart-aleck frustration. "Landing? I thought this was going to be a low-altitude combat jump. I have my parachute."

The cockpit door was open, and Falic smiled at the pilot. They could sense that DeeDee's ranting and raving was just a show to blow off some steam and pump herself up to put on her game face.

DeeDee laughed and smiled a big "I'm-gonna-kick-ass" smile.

"I can smell the money."

CHAPTER 8

# CHAPTER 9

# THE CEMETERY

I ran into the black morning air to do what I did every morning at zero-dark-hundred. I ran to the National Cemetery hours before it opened to the public. Its high, stone wall was scaled easily, like I scaled the walls on the obstacle course at Quantico, where I had spent years as a hand-to-hand combat instructor. The faint smell of mowed grass, with a light, dew topping, tickled my gut instincts and produced a goose bump sense of patriotism and awe. I passed hundreds of rows of white tombstones before I arrived at a huge cedar tree marking the spot where I stopped. I looked at the stone with a leer and a loathing. It appeared like the other thousands of markers for graves of the brave. Except it was a special stone—a stone of guilt.

I took out my rosary and knelt on one knee in front of the stone. Guilt. Honor. Love. Duty. And a profound hope of receiving forgiveness. All fueled my prayers.

I use a rosary for prayer like a Marine uses a cadence for marching. A string of beads lets me get into a spiritual rhythm. The Catholic Church and the Marine Corps have something in common. Both help men and women find their souls. I knew where my soul was. It was full of a lot of holes that I was desperately trying to repair. God forbid that I got some help from a professional—that would require me formally to admit my weakness. I know. We men are weird and full of too much self-worth and honor. But those attributes got me up the hill in a lot of tough times as a Marine.

I said a full rosary, kneeling there in the dark in front of the stone. It being Friday, I also contemplated each of the five Sorrowful Mysteries, beginning with the agony Jesus endured in The Garden. But the cemetery security guard shined his car's spotlight my way causing me to lay low.

The light stopped on three deer only fifty yards away. But the searchlight abruptly went out, returning my place of worried worship to darkness. My mind stayed in the world and my attempt at meditation seemed only to bring me confusion. It did not get me anywhere but more anxiety and guilt and a goose bumps feeling up my arms and neck that things would soon change - for the better or worse.

I finished my prayers the usual way. I asked God to show me a way to redeem myself someway, somehow. I knew what I did was absolutely stupid. I was paying for it every day and every hour of my life. I crossed myself, stood up, stuck my rosary in my pocket, and looked around.

From the stone, you can see a thirty-mile stretch up and down the Mississippi River. The river seemed to me like the ebb of time. It appeared to narrow and slip into oblivion the further away it flowed. I looked upstream and saw the waters to come in the future. I looked downstream and viewed the water that had passed by. I looked down and saw my boots in the grass. They stood in the present, but in a cemetery where I remained stuck in a stagnant, guilt trip.

I was disgusted with myself. Even with all my praying, I had not yet figured out a way to get on with my life. Deep down, I knew the cause for all my worry. My sense of honor was keeping me from quickly shirking my shame in doing something stupid that I could never correct. And I continued to feel in my gut the instinct where the soul speaks to the heart. It told me I could be redeemed. But I just did not see how God could make that possible. I was a bit demoralized as I stood at attention and presented my good-bye salute to a rock.

I respectfully addressed the stone in a strong voice.

"Sir."

I did an about-face and ran and scaled the wall, out of the hallowed grounds, as a crimson sunrise bloomed over the river. I jogged along the top of the bluff and saw a long train wind its way downstream, along the riverbank. Like a huge snake that had swallowed prey, the train labored as it lugged a mile-long load of coal to the electric plant. The train was hauling the food that would fuel America's huge energy appetite. I thought of the millions of hardworking people who relied on that train and the black energy it transported. It all operated like a food-chain of politics and greed: one power feeding even greater power. I knew I was only a speck of sand in size compared to it all.

I ran home.

# CHAPTER 10

# THE DROP

Peace. Two fingers, set in the "Peace Sign," stuck out of the butcher-wrapped package wedged under Knuckles' arm. The ex-professional football player was still on the di-anabolic juice: fifty cc's in the buttocks once a week. He looked the size of a mobile home as he stood, waiting outside his sedan, watching the first rays of dawn pierce the South St. Martinsville skyline. The alley in which they stood smelled like what it was—a sewer used by transients as a toilet. Knuckles' partner, Davis, took a long drag on his cigarette and spoke through expelled smoke.

"Ain't like the old man to be late."

Knuckles grunted.

Davis eyed the package with a chuckle, "The sum bitch is giving' ya the peace sign." Davis motioned with his cigarette towards the two fingers sticking out of Knuckles' closely held package.

Knuckles grunted. He reached down and bent the dead, index finger. Knuckles then held up the morbid package to give Davis a middle-fingered "fuck off." Both sick bastards laughed.

"Since we are going halfzies on this, maybe we should have Big Dutch sign something; otherwise, one of us might get screwed," said Davis.

"Ain't signing shit."

Davis became indignant, "You trying to pimp me already? I mean we're splitting the ten percent finder's fee commission a runner usually gets 'cuz we worked this claim together, right? I mean, you needed me on that locomotive to get the boy set up just right, din'cha?"

Knuckles was perturbed and stood with his hands in his pants pockets, the package tucked tight under his left arm. The worn grip of his revolver peaked out of his under-arm shoulder holster. Knuckles looked at his watch. "We ain't gonna put nothing in writing. We ain't gonna sign nothing, and we ain't gonna talk about it to nobody, and when the time comes for us to get paid, we'll find out what we get paid because Big Dutch is gonna pay us whatever he damn well wants to. *Verstehen?*" Knuckles said.

But Davis did understand. He remembered that the last R.I.O. case runner Knuckles went halfsies with on a case ended up found in pieces over two different counties. Davis was only being practical.

"I just don't want one of us to get screwed 'cause an arm off is a big case and if we found an arm-off case for Big Dutch, we should be paid big," Davis said as he flipped his cigarette butt into the darkest shadows of the alley.

Knuckles turned and stepped in front of Davis. The red light from a flickering, neon sign advertising "Liquor" lit up Knuckles' back and became a shadow across Davis's face. "Now you're wanting to be paid ten percent each? Twenty percent? Big Dutch will cut off our balls before he pays his runners twenty percent. And you ain't no lawyer, you ain't no capper, that's for sure." Their squabble was interrupted.

Headlights from a smoke-gray Rolls Royce splashed down the brown, brick wall of the alley, spotlighting Knuckles and Davis. The chauffer killed his lights. Davis stayed towards the front of the Rolls Royce, by the huge silver grille, while Knuckles walked alongside the car to the back passenger door. A smoked-black window rolled down, smooth and soundless, wafting from it the unmistakable scent of success. Nothing smells like it, and every man knows it when it hits his nostrils.

A commanding voice called out from the dark backseat, "Do you have my package?" The chauffer kept one hand on the wheel, the motor running, and his right hand under his coat.

"Sure, Mr. Big Dutch, here's your package, real nice and neat." Knuckles handed the package to the huge hand that reached out the window. The two fingers stuck out of the package, again displaying a peace sign.

"What? You ran out of wrapping paper? Why even wrap the son-of-a-bitch if you're gonna leave fingers sticking out of it? *Sheisterkaumpf!*"

Knuckles had incurred the disgust of Big Dutch once or twice before. He thought he knew Dutch well enough to break the ice with a joke.

CHAPTER 10

"Yeah, Mr. Big Dutch, I didn't have any problems at the job site getting the package because your client gave me a hand."

Davis's face went taught. Big Dutch motioned for Knuckles to come closer. Knuckles leaned in towards the Rolls. Big Dutch grabbed Knuckles' tie and yanked his head through the open window. To Knuckles' horror, he saw a pair of pit bulls, one white, one black, on the floorboard of the Rolls. They were baring their fangs and growling.

Big Dutch said, "Press!"

Knuckles tried to pull back. But Big Dutch's grip was like an iron vice on his tie. It was a blink of an eye, and the pit bull had Knuckles' face and neck in their jaws, shaking him vigorously, fixing their fangs deep into his flesh. Knuckles screamed and tried to pull out, but could not because of the strength of the Hellish hounds and Big Dutch. After Knuckles' head was sufficiently tenderized, Big Dutch let go of Knuckles' tie and simultaneously yelled for the dogs to release. Knuckles fell backwards into the muddy puddle, his head covered in blood. He stood up with his trench coat dripping and came to Big Dutch's window. This time he did not lean in.

"You can cut my clients' arms and legs off, you can break their backs, you can even burn the sum-bitches, but don't you ever disrespect them," Big Dutch said, as he accentuated the lesson with a finger pointed at Knuckles.

"I expect you to be cleaned up and at the hospital within an hour, so we can get our client to sign the Rep Agreement."

Big Dutch's chauffeur, Otto, rolled down his window and dressed down Knuckles in low German. Otto also told him he was a *sheisterkaumpf*, a shithead, amongst a list of other black remarks. Otto ended the whole tongue-lashing with "Verstehen?"– a demeaning "Do you understand?" Knuckles nodded in pain. The Rolls Royce pulled off, leaving a stunned Knuckles pressing his handkerchief onto the bloody wounds left by the pit bulls.

Davis offered consolation to Knuckles as he pulled up his pants leg to reveal a fist-size chunk taken out of his right calf. "Big Dutch ain't got no sense of humor."

"Verstehen."

# CHAPTER II

# AN IMPATIENT MAN

I ran home from the cemetery, and I took a quick shower and shave. I put on my Old Spice cologne. I'm an old fashioned kind of guy. I still believe in opening doors for women, asking for a kiss on the second date, and only on the third date, a wet kiss. I dressed in my walk-in closet, where my U.S.M.C. uniform was hanging in plain sight. I carried a knife almost everywhere. That day I chose to wear leather knife scabbards, one behind-the-neck and one low-calf.

It was a habit from the Corps, where my job was in black ops. Secret Special Forces missions that were never divulged to the public, but ended up reported on the front page of world newspapers as movements of world resources. Oil. Coal. Water. Electricity. The list is as long as the necessities of man. As an assassin, I thought of myself at times as though I were a faucet that turned on and off the resources we fight wars about. I looked into my dresser mirror and silently reassured myself that I had saved lives by killing the defenseless most quietly. Enough self-examination, I thought. I did what I did, and I was comfortable in its bloody history.

I turned my back to the mirror on my dresser to see the scabbard as it hung below the base of my neck. I looked in the mirror and saw all the old war wounds blazoned on my back. There were knife and bullet and shrapnel souvenirs of missions from which I never should have returned. I used to be a target specialist, a fancy name for an assassin in the Marine Corps Force Recon. A killer angel. In a brief wave of self-examination, I wondered for a moment how many other divorce lawyers had those types of scars.

None.

I knew I didn't belong in the legal profession. I was like a fish out of water. It didn't matter that I had graduated from Harvard Law School. I still missed the reliability and the honor of the men I had known and fought beside in the Corps. It seemed the only thing I could rely on in the law was that I could not rely on anybody, except my law partner, Dalton. The whole profession seemed like it was built upon a foundation of lies, deceit, and greed. In an attempt to feel again the ancient honor of my prior profession as a warrior, I solemnly laid my hand on my old U.S.M.C. uniform for a moment. I felt a ripple of goose bumps from the *Semper Fidelis* spirit with which I had been imbued in the Corps. I then chose a gray, pin-striped suit. The unofficial lawyers' uniform.

I paused in midstream, wishing that I were back in the Corps, where life was simple, decided with steel by real men. But in a way, I felt at ease, like I was back in the jungle because as a lawyer, I was quick to learn that even a fellow lawyer will stab you in the back if it will serve his client. Practicing law was like going on special ops missions—trust no one but your team members.

In the daylight, my bedroom looked quite different. Large, wide windows on two walls allowed in light from a glorious sunrise. The open window allowed in the sweet, summer air. That morning, I had to go to court, so I was in a hurry. On my way to court, I had to give my sister Bridget a ride to her job at the Workshop for the Blind. I dressed quickly. I folded all my dirty clothes before I put them in the clothes hamper in neat alignment, just like I had as a Cadet at the Air Force Academy and for eight years in the Marine Corps.

As a last religious act before leaving my room, I went to look at my picture of the three wise men. I walked back into my closet and parted the shirts, hanging neatly in a row. Hidden behind all my hanging clothes was a twenty-year-old picture of the men I had relied on to lift my spirits for the previous two decades—Moe, Larry, and Curly. The Three Stooges. They made me laugh because they were the exact opposite of me, a member of MENSA. The high-I.Q. society. Those three crazy guys and their friend Shemp had helped me find some happiness and peace while I healed after suffering terrible injuries as a boy. They were zany. They were never serious. They were stupid cowards. But they made a seriously injured little boy smile.

I had had a number of broken bones, and my jaws were wired together. My doctor told me that I was not allowed to laugh hard or my jaws would not mend properly, so I watched the Three Stooges to lift my spirits. But I forced myself not to laugh, only to smile, to comply with the doctor's instructions. Later in life, my high-school girlfriend told me that we had been dating for two years and the only time she saw me smile was when I watched the Three Stooges. She told me they were dumb and anybody watching them must be an idiot and that if I continued to watch the stooges, she was going to give me my I.D. bracelet back and break up. She was history.

In my hyper-focused life, I need something that makes me smile. I met a man who spent five years as a prisoner of war in the infamous Hanoi Hilton. The North Vietnamese gave him the royal treatment. Daily beatings. A cell that allowed him a beautiful view of his excrement, front-row seating at the torture sessions of fellow pilots shot down over North Vietnam, and a starvation diet. He survived the horrible beating he received after he outsmarted them and sent a Morse-code message to the world: "T-O-R-T-U-R-E," using only blinks of his eyes while on camera. As a Marine Corps officer, I attended one of his speeches. The message I liked most from him was how he proudly wore a Mickey Mouse watch the rest of his life to remind him to smile. Life is short. It is not all work and horror. Smile when things are at their worst. Shine in darkness.

I gave my three wise men a thumbs-up and a big smile. They were my Saints Moe, Larry, and Curly and, of course, the alternate Shemp. They made me smile in my very serious world.

Even though I smiled, I moped on that day and felt sorry for myself internally. Self pity. There I was, caring for my challenged older sister in some form of guilt-trip duty. I couldn't leave Bridget, or I would feel I had deserted her, and it would break the oath I had made to my Father.

Downstairs, I adjusted my tie in the mirror of the foyer and saw, over my right shoulder, the eyes of a portrait locking onto me like a sniper. I turned and looked at the large portrait of my Father, Brigadier General Frank McRain, posed in a leather pilot's jacket. The beautiful portrait was painted upon Father's retirement. It even had a brass placard at the bottom of the frame that summed up my Father's beliefs: "Never Leave Your Wing Man." It was the Air Force's version of the Marine Corps motto, *Semper Fidelis*.

The portrait's eyes followed me everywhere. The General watched me tuck one of my throwing knives into my left combat boot. I was a lawyer, and I wore combat boots to court with pride. They were shiny, and they let my opponent know I was there to kick butt.

I looked at my watch and saw that we were running late. I walked to the bottom of the stairs and saw Ace at the top of the long, oak-banister staircase. Bridget dawdled; she would be late for her own funeral. "Come on, Bridgy, I know you can hear me. We're gonna be late. Ace, get her down here on the double."

As usual, Bridget was upstairs, praying feverishly with a rosary in each hand. She sat in her wing-back chair in front of her informal altar. It was made with masonry blocks and boards, covered by a menagerie of Celtic and Catholic religious relics and a dusty cello bow. Loud Irish-ballad music played on an old, scratchy-sounding phonograph. Incense of a light, oily scent burned in a small urn on the altar, and a toy, metal soldier stood on the lip of the urn. Ace came into his master's bedroom and barked. Bridget's fast lips stopped praying.

I was outside on the circle driveway, in my tricked-out, blue Mustang convertible. I listened to U.S.M.C. marching cadences on the stereo while I continued to rev-up the throaty, V-8, engine, waiting for Bridgy.

The cadence seemed to call me home to the camaraderie of my fellow Marines, marching, double-timing, running and chanting:

> Up from a sub 60 feet below.
> I scuba to the shore
> and I'm ready to go.
> A grease gun, K-Bar by my side.
> These are the tools that I live by.
>
> A Recon Ranger,
> Life a danger.
> A Recon Ranger,
> That's what I wanna be.

# CHAPTER 12

# THE CHAUFEUR

It was not easy for me—going from hanging around Harvard, where there are some pretty-brainy, articulate people and coming home to play nanny to my autistic sister. It got lonely because she didn't talk about anything except religion. Dawn had broken, and the warm daylight was wasting. I was outside on the driveway, sitting in my Mustang with the convertible roof down, waiting for Bridget to get in my car, so I could take her to work and get me to the courthouse. Judge Hardcastle penalizes your client if you are late.

I drive a nice, customized car because I like to feel good. Every knob in my Mustang had the Eagle, Globe, and Anchor of the Marine Corps on it, and so did the hub caps and each of the leather, bucket seats. The car was painted Marine, dress blue. A color mixture of Pacific-Ocean blue and Marine-Corps blood layered on top of Detroit steel and polished to a gloss so reflective, I could use it for a mirror. It was strack.

Patience is not one of my virtues. I revved the powerful Mustang engine to a roar and honked the horn. I saluted my bulldog, Gunny, who was sitting and panting in a neat attention, on a chain in front of his doghouse. I had fun with him.

"*Semper Fi*, Gunny."

Bridget came out the front door of the home, feeling the ground with her white shillelagh in one hand, her other hand on her grip harness for Ace. She was wearing three Miraculous Medals. The Catholic equivalent of the most blessed thing you can wear if you are not a priest. They represent miracles that happened in Christian faith. Bridget seemed to do everything in three. Ace led Bridgy across the porch and down the steps. When she approached my car, I pushed open the door and she got into my convertible.

"It's about time. Welcome aboard, Ace! Ooo-Rah! Force Recon!" I yelled over the loud cadences. The one playing offered a tale of woe about a "Dear John" letter received by a grunt.

Ace always enjoyed riding in my convertible with the top down. He nuzzled up, from his spot in the middle of the backseat, and licked my face. He always smelled good because Bridgey bathed the faithful dog every week with Dove soap. I roared the Mustang down the long driveway to the road. Our heads were thrown back when I laid a slick of tire rubber and took off onto Oak Street.

"Too loud!" Bridget said. Bridget reached for the stereo sound-control button, and her hand brushed over a Polaroid photo I had stuck into a crevice in the dashboard. I put it there to make sure it stayed in sight, so I would never forget. I wanted to feel damned guilty all the time.

I pushed her hand away from the stereo. "You got your music. I got my music."

Bridget argued back, "Not music. Too loud."

Bridget reached for the sound control again, and I slapped her hand off the knob. Being the vindictive older sister that she is, she snatched the Polaroid photo. She held it close while she fingered it all over, trying to read any Braille bumps on it. She even smelled it briefly. Then she held it, down and away from me, so I could not retrieve it.

"Put that back!" I said.

"What is it?"

"None of your Goddamned business."

I didn't need her getting in my business, and I reached for the photo. But she rammed me in the head with her shillelagh. Her shillelagh packs a wallop. It is what they call a "loaded" stick because it's custom made, with lead poured down the core of it. That makes it heavier and more painful when you get smacked with it. Growing up with six brothers, Bridget became a master at whacking skulls. In fact, she claimed that she could tell the difference between who she was whacking just by the vibration she felt in her shillelagh. It was Bridget's version of a divining rod.

CHAPTER 12

Bridget went back to praying her rosary. She started rocking back and forth in her seat, shaking her head in a spasm that she usually experienced only during her most feverish prayer.

"Cursing the Lord. Venial sin. Going to Hell. Going to Hell. Hail Mary, Full of Grace . . ."

Her prayers continued nonstop. She was still yammering the tail end of a Hail Mary when we pulled up to a red light, stopping next to a police car. I tried again to get the Polaroid while we were waiting for the traffic light to change. My hardheaded elder sister held it even closer against her bosom, where I couldn't reach, being her brother and all. Her thick, red hair was wild from the windy, convertible ride, and we were yelling at each other.

"Christ, Bridge, I said: Give it up!"

"No! Never! Sinner! Saint Ivo of Kermartin, save me."

I reached across the console to pry from under her arms, as a last-ditch effort to retrieve the Polaroid. But she clubbed me again with her shillelagh, which she was holding in her right hand. With her arms crossed over her chest, she clutched the Polaroid and a long, Franciscan rosary in her left hand. To make matters worse, Ace had a front paw on each of the front seats and was howling to the sky in protest.

That's when the police officer got in on the act. He rolled down his window, "What's the matter here, Lady? He giving you trouble?"

I could see my efforts were going nowhere fast. I gave up the tussle and grabbed the steering wheel with both hands. Bridget scowled and kept the Polaroid squirreled away. I looked straight ahead and fumed.

"She's no lady, officer; she's my sister."

The police officer shook his head and said, "The fightin' Irish." The light turned green, and we took off.

Bridget had been working at the same, sheltered workshop for the blind for the last ten years. She never missed a day of work. Ever. The workshop was only five miles from the house and enroute with my trip to the courthouse. I enjoyed taking her, even though she was a pain in the ass. I felt I had a duty as a brother, and as my Father's son, to take care of our own. But Bridget sure as Hell didn't make it easy.

We pulled into the drop-off area, past the sign that read: "St. Cecelia Workshop For The Blind." I stopped the car hard, which made Bridget brace herself on the dashboard, displaying the Polaroid for a second. I snatched it back from her. She was angry at me, and she got out of the car, with Ace, in a huff. Ace was usually my buddy.

"What now, Ace, no face-licky good-bye? I see who my friends are."

I looked at my watch. "Oops, late for court. Take the bus home, wouldja? Gotta work late."

Bridget shook her shillelagh at me as I pulled away.

"I pray for your soul."

Ace led Bridget inside while I hit the road. My 'Stang muscled up and laid rubber in all four gears.

CHAPTER 12

# CHAPTER 13

# LICENSED TO STEAL

There are over one million lawyers in the United States and not even one out of every thousand knew how the R.I.O. personal-injury racket was run. As with most professions, it is a minority of law firms that give the majority of firms a bad name. R.I.O. stood for the "Railwaymen's Injury and Occupation Act." It was a highly specialized area of the law that existed at the whim and fancy of the United States Senate Judiciary Committee. But I'm getting ahead of myself.

What made practicing R.I.O. law so special was the unique rights given to the R.I.O. lawyers—they held a license to steal. The United States Supreme Court allowed R.I.O. lawyers literally to chase cases. That was a right no other lawyer in America has ever held. But that special license to run after cases was kept on the hush-hush because it was the equivalent of having a goose that lays golden eggs. Secrecy surrounded the whole R.I.O. industry. It allowed taxpayer and consumer dollars to be wasted paying for the high costs of fat-cat, R.I.O. personal-injury lawyers jetting around the country to chase after personal injury cases and to buy whores and booze and pay bribes to union men; all so the R.I.O. lawyers could lasso injured railroad-worker, R.I.O. cases.

Felix Falic knew he ran a lucrative business that needed to be kept secret. He tried to keep as much as possible in the family to minimize that taxpayers and consumers might find out how they were paying for the highlife of his firm and the twenty-two other R.I.O. firms in America. The poor, bleeding taxpayers, and the earnest consumers, neither knew what hit them.

Before he and DeeDee got off the jet, Falic reminded DeeDee that they weren't doing anything unethical. And he added that the client loans were commonplace in railroad-injury law because R.I.O.-Designated railroad-injury lawyers were special. Theirs was only one of twenty-three firms in the U.S. that were Designated. DeeDee knew the whole nauseating story about how special it is to be Designated. She had heard it a hundred times. Falic would explain to her *ad nauseum* how R.I.O.-Designated railroad-injury lawyers are different because the United States Supreme Court allows them to chase the injury cases. She was sick of hearing it.

DeeDee swore to herself that she could smell death when she got too close to her stepfather, Felix Falic.

What DeeDee didn't know was that Big Dutch was about to march into the hospital, with Knuckles and Davis leading like blockers for a football running back. They were headed straight to Billy McAvoy's room to sign him up as a client for his arm-off "accident." Big Dutch knew that the vicious competition between Designated R.I.O. lawyers would cause a half dozen other R.I.O. firms' investigators and lawyers to be crawling all over any hospital that harbored an R.I.O. arm-off claim. They had to act fast, or someone would steal their case.

DeeDee was a pro. She had her hospital routine down to a practiced art. Once she got past the E.R., she worked as smooth as a surgeon at a tea party. DeeDee wore a surgical mask and scrubs, trying to blend in with the hospital staff as she helped push Falic, who was faking a heart attack, into the E.R. She quickly clipped her credit card, backwards, onto a surgical blouse, to fake a hospital I.D. badge. She then slipped into "Intensive Care," picking up a clipboard on the way. She pulled an attorney-client contract from under her shirt and slid it under the hospital documents already on the clipboard. She bluffed her way into one-armed Billy McAvoy's room. She waited for the attending nurse to finish with his I.V. and leave before she approached the semiconscious Billy.

DeeDee told Billy, "Just a few forms to sign. Relax. I can make it better for you . . ." She slipped her hand under his hospital bed sheets.

Fifteen minutes later, Billy's attending nurse came out of Billy's room and said, "You-all have got to come see this." A group of four nurses scurried into Billy's room.

"Man's got a flag pole and a shit-eatin' grin, and he's holding a wad of cash that'd choke a cow. And all he tells me: it was the 'head nurse' who worked on him . . . and he wants some more," said the attending nurse as she pointed at Billy. The staff nurses all laughed hard. But they stopped laughing when Big Dutch came into Billy's room. Knuckles had pushed them out of his way.

Dutch was surprised at the sight of Billy's elevated condition. "I'm Adolph Van Killman, attorney at law. Get out'a my client's room." But nobody left. The nurses just stared at Big Dutch in a go-to-Hell sort of way.

Billy's nurse looked through Billy's chart and then at Big Dutch. "I guess somebody beat you here because here is a medical-records request authorization from the Falic, Moore & DeVillay Law Firm." She grinned when she said, "So I guess he ain't your client and you better get yourself out." She put her fists on her hips to punctuate her order.

Out in the hallway of the hospital, Davis guarded the door. DeeDee walked up the hall to Davis with a sassy swing of her hips. She handed Davis a copy of the freshly inked attorney-client contract. She said, "Tell Big Dutch we need territories." DeeDee pulled down her mask for a moment and blew Davis a kiss-off. She then pulled her surgical mask back up and sashayed away with some more of her "kiss-my-ass" hip action. Davis didn't need to watch where DeeDee went because he knew he could follow her by the heavy perfume she trailed. Davis took the contract into Big Dutch.

Big Dutch roared, bulling his way out of the room into the hall in pursuit of DeeDee as he crumbled the contract into a ball. Big Dutch yelled, "Territories are for the weak."

DeeDee hurried away, pointing a security guard towards Big Dutch. The guard ran up and restrained Dutch and his henchmen. With his arm held behind his back, Big Dutch yelled as DeeDee scooted away down the hall, "You! You little bushwhacking bitch! You'd hump a dead man to get a case. I'll get even with you! Nobody takes food off my plate! You hear me? Nobody!"

DeeDee had stolen Big Dutch's meat right off his plate. Cold.

# CHAPTER 14

# TRAPPED

I suffered through a long day of professional babysitting and handholding, trying to work deals for my divorce clients, who had no intention of ever settling. They only wanted the usual high-strung, emotional bloodletting. That is what most of my divorce clients wanted to see: their spouses' blood on the wall. Figuratively speaking, of course. If there were some actual blood spilled, I suppose that would be okay with them, too. I was tired of practicing divorce law. And I had been a lawyer for only one year.

To me, divorce-law practice was like knife fighting with feathers, in matches that were postponed purposefully by opposing counsel, just so he could make more billable-hour money off an unsuspecting client. Some of my divorce-court adversaries were like vampires, keeping their victims—their clients—solvent enough just to allow them to pay more fees, an unethical divorce lawyer's form of extracted blood. There were plenty of times I wished we could just settle things the old-fashioned way. Maybe with clubs in a ring, like Ox Baker and Kurt Russell in *Escape from New York*. But we are a nation of laws. Laws written to help the lawyers.

I specialized in representing women—battered women; women whose husbands had cheated on them; women who had been threatened and beaten and run over with cars; women who had ten kids; women who cheated on their husbands; women who were just tired of making tuna casserole on Wednesday nights to please the old man; women who smelled like the drugs oozing from their pores; women who smelled like French whores; women who were battered and broken and lived in fear for their safety, for their children's safety; women who were alcoholics; women who were the spouses of alcoholics, drug addicts, gambling addicts, or sex addicts—or the converse, religious fanatics who were just as cruel as any drug addict or masochist, but tried to sell it to their spouse as a preordained fate, to be suffered just for being married. I felt like I had seen it all. And in such a short time, it jaded and bewildered me. The practice of law and these notions of marriage and divorce did not sit well with me. But I was a hopeless romantic. I still hoped that somehow life would treat me differently than all the other Joes I saw take it in the neck from their wives. I wanted to find my love, a soul mate, and settle down.

My Mustang rumbled, powerful and steady, down the road as I pondered the pitfalls of practicing law.

I couldn't figure out how some attorneys seemed to end up with all the business, no matter whether they achieved good trial results or not. I was a member of MENSA, but I didn't need to be a rocket scientist to figure it out. They had a fix in, a gimmick, a scheme. I wondered. *Pay-offs? Connections? Politics?* I figured there was some sort of invisible hand that pushed legal business towards the doors of the nation's wealthiest lawyers. One big rule I knew was that the canons of ethics for lawyers across America forbade us chasing business. We were allowed to advertise on T.V. and radio. But we sure as Hell couldn't call up the injured and sweet-talk them into our offices. You would lose your law license for that. I tried to figure out how the rich lawyers moved that invisible hand, as I downshifted, turning into the long driveway of the McRain family home.

The McRain family estate was called "Twenty-Three Oaks." I called it home. It had been built on two hundred forty acres, a full half-mile of Mississippi River shoreline. Over the years, land had been sold off, to where all that was left was a large, Victorian home and a carriage house, sitting on five acres of oak trees, ringed by a wrought-iron fence. Norman Rockwell could not have laid it out better.

The Marine Corps cadence played on my stereo with a strong beat, the clomping of a hundred boots in unison . . .

> I want to be a Recon Ranger,
> Live a life of sex and danger.
> Recon Ranger,
> Recon Ranger.

CHAPTER 14

Sex and danger,
Sex and danger.
I want to be a scuba diver.
Climb those mountains
higher, higher.

I tromped up the stairs to the wrap-around porch. My footsteps reverberated as I walked across the eight-foot by eight-foot, red-and-black chessboard painted on the porch. I walked past its three-foot-tall chess pieces. Bridget and I had been working on a game since the day before, and it was my move. Each of us would move only a few times per day, which meant that the games lasted pretty long. I lost more often than not because Bridget was a world-class chess player. There was something about her autistic mind that made her exceptionally adept at the chessboard. In her mind, Bridget would go through mathematical calculations for all her opponent's possible moves, coming up with the right move every single time. In our own unique way, Bridget and I were mental giants to one another. We complemented each other well.

I moved my black bishop to feign danger to Bridget's white queen. I smelled defeat lurking just around the corner. It was a move I knew would make Bridget laugh inside, since it could easily be countered and would actually put my own king in peril. Although I tried to win, I didn't care about beating Bridget because I felt like I was her nanny. I only wanted her to be happy. There was no sibling rivalry between us—not since childhood.

Bridget's autistic mind prevented her from communicating with me and the rest of the family the way we, the non-autistic, communicated with each other. But when she played chess and other games of the mind with me, I felt that I could talk with Bridget through indirect, intellectual ways that belied analysis. Those chess games gave me great comfort, knowing that I could touch my sister's life and she, mine, in a spiritual and endearing experience.

Many times, it kept us from cursing each other.

I slung my jacket over my shoulder. I smiled as I walked away from the chessboard, my boots clunking resoundingly on the porch's wooden planks. I knew that my older sister would imminently dispense with my king, leaving us soon to start all over. I was trapped by Bridget.

I was trapped by honor.

CHAPTER 14

# CHAPTER 15

# THE CODE

Up the long ladder,
And down the short rope.
To Hell with King Billy,
And God Bless the Pope.

If that doesn't do,
We'll tear him in two.
And send him to Hell,
In his red, white and blue.

> – Old Irish Ditty

I turned the key and pushed open the kitchen door. I was met by Gunny who woofed, real gruff, like bulldogs do. He danced around in a tight circle on the kitchen floor. He was happy to see me home, and he was ready for a post-dinner walk. Gunny would be disappointed; there would be no walk for him that evening. I was too tired from practicing divorce law. I had already learned that the practice of law will tire any man.

I headed through the kitchen, past the lingering smell of Bridge's burned macaroni and cheese, and out into the front foyer to the stairs. I heard the rhythmic beat of an Irish ballad performed by Tommy Mecum and the Clancy Brothers coming from the second floor. I put my car keys on the front-foyer table and placed my hand on the banister's hand carved newel. I started slowly to climb the stairs. But I stopped on the fifth step.

I stood there, and I looked at a large, gold-framed portrait of my father, the General, in a leather fighter-pilot's jacket. There was an inscription in brass at the base of the frame that read: "Never Leave Your Wing Man."

I spoke to the eyes of the portrait, to my father's eyes, in a hushed tone.

"Release me, Sir."

Then I directed my gaze up the stairs to the second floor and spoke loudly to Bridget.

"Up the long ladder."

In Bridget's bedroom, she lifted her head and stopped praying her rosaries. She stopped listening to the Irish ballad on her stereo. At the moment, it was being washed out by a garbled message from her 1970s-era television, set in a swing-door case, with no knob for the channel changer but a pair of vice grips attached instead, which produced a flickering, black and white picture of a Clint Eastwood western, "Two Mules For Sister Sarah." A large rabbit-ear antenna sat on top of her antique, cherry wood-cased television.

Bridget turned off the television using the one remaining porcelain knob and quieted the stereo, by lifting the needle off of the 33 1/3 vinyl and replied to me loud and clear.

"And down the short rope."

She could hear through her door, partially cracked open, that I was on the ninth step. It made its traditional, creaking sound just before I replied with the next line of the ditty. I had become like a piano player, the staircase's squeaking steps striking certain keys on cue with the lyrics of a song. Over time, we made it a code. It assured blind Bridget that I wasn't an intruder and that she was safe.

"To Hell with King Billy."

Bridget's face lit up in a gleeful way.

"And God bless the Pope."

I was almost at the top of the stairs. "If that doesn't do."

Bridget replied like a rifle shot. "We'll tear him in two."

I finished climbing the stairs. I held my tie in my hand as I peered through the partially opened door to Bridget's bedroom. I saw the characteristic arrangement of her large, red, wingback chair set in front of her makeshift altar of Catholic-Celtic religious paraphernalia. It held a myriad of saints, in clusters and positions that changed daily.

I saw Bridget standing with her back to me, oblivious to my stare, but fully conscious of my presence. I felt like a sidewalk organ grinder because I knew what my actions would prompt. I spurted the words, "And send him to Hell" through the crack in the doorway.

Bridget waved her white shillelagh back and forth. My older sister swung it around overhead, making Ace's eyes bounce with concern as he watched warily from behind her chair. Bridget started to move her feet in anticipation of the dance that would follow the final line of lyrics. I extended my arm and turned my thumb down, even though I knew Bridget could not see me do it as she culminated the ditty.

"In his red, white and blue."

She followed it with her persistent inquiry. "Did you file my taxes?"

"Uh, no, something kind of came up at the courthouse."

"But you promised!"

"I know, I know, I'll get it done."

Bridget snapped back on the television. She danced a light and fancy jig to the gay Irish music as she restarted the record player by feeling for and removing the dust that accumulated on the stereo's needle and then moving the needle back onto the black record that seemed to me to never stop spinning.

I shook my head and walked down the hall to my room. I couldn't understand why Bridget wanted me to file her income tax return for her. For Christ's sake, she would get a whopping refund of $2.14, since they didn't pay her much at the sheltered workshop.

I turned on the light switch at the wall and immediately saw the Polaroid of the tombstone fitted into the top of the light switch cover. I was tired and wanted rest. I disrobed and changed to my pajamas, laying my throwing knives and their scabbards neatly aligned on my dresser. I was drawn to the window and my telescope.

I was a voyeur of love. Not sex. Love.

I swiveled the telescope around on its tripod and examined life around the neighborhood as well as the openings between the tall oak trees would allow.

I saw against the shade of one home's window the silhouette of a man holding what appeared to be a crying child, as he patted the tot's back in consolation. There was another space through the trees where I could see a couple pushing a baby carriage down the street, proud grandparents. The sweet air of summer romance sneaked through my open window as a breeze pushed in and parted my lace curtains. I wondered when I would get on with my life, when I would end the professional babysitting routine I was acting out by living with Bridget.

I left the telescope and went to look at the worst thing of all. I looked at my dresser mirror, where, up high, I had tucked a photo of myself as a young boy. Over my right shoulder, I could see in the mirror the Polaroid of the tombstone tucked into the light-switch cover. In the walk-in closet to my right, my Marine Corps, dress uniform with my battle ribbons hung, facing me. Every object seemed to speak to me, telling me that I was a loser because I had failed so far in my life to grab the brass ring.

A family of my own.

I yearned for a loving wife, for the experience of the glow of fatherhood, and for people I could protect and provide for. These were earnest intentions to a lifestyle I had long ago promised to myself, as I sat for three days in a South American, crocodile-infested swamp, waiting for the right time to kill my unsuspecting target. I got him, and his three armed-to-the-teeth bodyguards. I figured if I waited long enough, I would get my dream girl, too.

A spider on the wall would have seen the battle scars on my back. They were the traditional marks of an assassin. One who did his job and was pursued. I had handled my deadly duties well in the Marine Corps. I had difficult, second thoughts about why I left the Corps to become a lawyer. The men I had killed in the Marine Corps—physically killed, by stabbing or shooting or garroting—those men I felt deserved it because my demigod, the C.I.A., had determined their fate. I long ago had accepted that I was only an instrument of fate. I felt no special remorse for the deaths of the men I assassinated, even though I had clearly seen the unfurling of their tongues as their throats were slit. What bothered me most from my past, what caused the cancer in my soul, was the breaking of an ancient promise.

I didn't feel like going downstairs to the kitchen. I didn't feel like leaving the secure cocoon of my room. As a boy, I would look out the window of my bedroom and daydream about manhood. I laughed out loud, knowing that the vision of manhood I formed as a boy did not fit the role of professional babysitter that I was now acting.

I broke open an M.R.E., meal ready to eat. Beef stew with crackers and an energy bar. I sat on my bed and ate it. I was so used to living in a jungle environment, away from everything else, that I actually enjoyed M.R.E.'s. More than Bridget's cooking, most of which had a distinctly scorched taste. I figured that was Bridget's way of knowing the food was done. She would smell it burning and turn off the flame on the stove. I split the stew and the crackers with Gunny and saved the energy bar for the morning.

I walked over to the wall switch and looked at the Polaroid of the tombstone. I turned out the light, and I knelt by my bed. I crossed myself and prayed for my sister; for her safety; for the poor; for my comrades in the Veterans' Administration hospitals, who would never know life outside those institutions. I prayed to them as I had prayed to the saints when I was in grade school. I asked them for courage and instruction. I prayed for one of the perpetual inhabitants of the Jefferson Barracks Veterans' Administration Hospital, where I visited every month. He was a Navy man, dying a slow agonizing death from exposure to Agent Orange. He was all jaundiced and yellow, due to liver failure. I affectionately called him "The Admiral," to give the sickly man a moment of glory and respect, even if he knew it was done tongue in cheek.

I recalled the advice of "The Admiral," who fell more sick and addled by the day. Every time "The Admiral" would see me, he would send me off with some wisdom. I would humor him, believing it was all just the gentle ramblings of a dying man.

Gunny sighed and laid his chin down on the U.S.M.C. rug at my bedside and watched me pray. I finished my prayers, crossed myself, and crawled into bed. I lay between the cool, cotton sheets of my antique, hand carved four-poster bed. It had been brought over from Ireland by my great-grandfather, Seamas Moghrain.

A well-intended induction clerk at Ellis Island converted "Moghrain" from its Celtic spelling to the Anglicized version—"McRain." Close enough.

The night was still, except for Bridget's music as it thumped a bawdy beat. The loud music kept me from falling asleep. After I had had enough, I reached over to my nightstand and grabbed a knife. I threw it into the heart of the silhouette target hanging on the wall. The knife sunk into the wood behind the target with a resounding thud.

The loud Celtic music stopped.

Bridget turned her head away from her makeshift altar, towards my room. A rosary-wrapped hand picked up a cork-stopped bottle made of thick, serrated glass. It was labeled "Holy Water." Bridget sprinkled drops as she worked the beads in her other hand.

She used a Gregorian pitch and rhythm to say, "Glory be."

My head hit the pillow.

I slept.

I dreamt.

CHAPTER 15

# CHAPTER 16

# THE ADMIRAL

My dreams became my prayers, and my prayers, my dreams.

*In my dream, I saw the great sailing ship appear again. Only now it was much closer to my island. It was flying the flag of Admiralty. I thought, inside my dream, that was odd because the ship was alone and it was quite rare for a ship of Admiralty to voyage unescorted. But if it did sail without a protector ship, it certainly never flew its Admiral's flag since that would be an unnecessary risk, an invitation for pirates to attack. It was well known that no Admiral left his port without his gold, and sometimes enough gold for the whole fleet. Yet there it was, an unescorted Admiral's heavy frigate. Sea spray from the waves on the beach spurted droplets of brine on my face, and the lovely smell of sailing enveloped me.*

*She was beautiful in her silent surging. The sails billowed full. The ship's bow was led by its flying lady, and she was headed directly for my tropical island. I could not tell if the ship brought me fortune or misfortune. My anxiety increased as the ship sailed closer.*

*The ship anchored with her stern to my island. She rolled up her sails and dropped anchor. She was "The Constitution." She drifted on her bow anchor to a broadside position, whereupon she dropped her stern anchor. In a short time, one of the gun portals opened and a cannon, a twenty-four pounder, fired at me. In that dream, I could see like I was superhuman. I watched the cannon ball streak towards me and stop, just inches from my face. The iron ball hung in midair. I stared at it, waiting for it to crush me. But it fell straight down to the surf at my feet.*

*The great ship anchored two hundred yards off shore. A skiff was lowered down the side of the great ship, manned by an officer and two burly oarsmen, who rowed, slow and steady, towards me through the surf. No one called "ahoy," not even me. As the frothy waves washed over my legs, chains and shackles appeared on my ankles. The crew pulled the kerry up into the surf and grabbed me. My feet were frozen. I couldn't run. The captain of the dragoons cuffed me with the butt end of his pistol and knocked me out. I rode out to the great ship, "The Constitution," lying in the bottom of a rowboat stinking of fish. I was hoisted aboard with a block and tackle, like livestock to feed the crew of hungry souls.*

The next thing I knew, I was kneeling on the deck, hearing the shrill piping of the boatswain blowing attention to all on deck. "Crew, square 'em up. The Honorable Lord of the Seas and of the Four Corners of the Earth, of Heaven and Hell, the Lord Almighty, Admiral J. G. Jaundice, brings his presence to be obeyed and honored by all. The protector of the faith, lord over land and sea, deity to all faiths, subjugator of heathens, claiming dominion over all men and souls as ruler of the Purgatory Seas. His Lordship is aboard." The boatswain clicked his heels, smart and proper. He stepped back from the gunwale and allowed a great and huge man to board through the port-side gate.

If this was a dream, it was too real. I looked skyward and saw limp sails. But as I looked back, I saw the biggest pair of shoes I'd seen in my life. One lifted and caught me square in the nose.

I was thrown onto my back by the blow. I tasted the blood from my nose. I looked up to see a huge, heavenly looking figure with hair that flowed like a woman's. He had the hawkish features of a man. He bellowed, and the seas started to swell and pitch. "So here we have our deserter. Run up the flag with the stone of the man he left, the flag of a deserter. Bring me the captain of the guard with his cat of nine tails."

I was dropped onto the deck, landing face down with a boot on the back of my neck. I heard the men about me speaking with a British, Old-English, sort of accent.

The Admiral strutted down the row of sailors, standing at attention in formation, inspecting them—for what I did not know because their uniforms did not match and there seemed to be little order about them, except they all feared the Admiral's presence. The Admiral's boots stopped before my face.

"You may lift your boot, Sergeant."

I braced myself to a kneeling, praying position. I peered down at Admiral Jaundice's boots, then up to his knees, his mid-section and his chest, and then I stood up and looked upon his face. I was startled, in horror because his face seemed normal and human in all other respects. But the place where his eyes would have been was just wrinkled skin. The Admiral had no eyes.

"How dare ye look me in the face? You are not worthy of such." Admiral Jaundice said as he struck me with the back of his hand, sending me down to the deck again. I saw my own blood on the oak planks.

"Who are you?"

Admiral Jaundice replied, "I am your worst nightmare." He kicked me in the ribs. "And the answers to your prayers."

CHAPTER 16

*I complained, "I didn't pray for this!"*

*"Oh, I can hear everything you say, Laddie. Up with him, mates." Two strong dragoons lifted me to my feet.*

*Admiral Jaundice began his indictment, "You are a deserter." His backhand across my face buckled my knees. The dragoons held me upright. "You left your wing man." The Admiral slapped me with his open hand across my face. "I tire of this. Ward Officer, flog him."*

*They stripped my shirt down to my waist. The Ward Officer worked a horrid flailing on my back with a cat of nine tails, opening up the flesh to a good bleed.*

*"You are a deserter, aren't you?"*

*I seemed to know exactly what the Admiral was talking about without any specifics being spoken. "I was doing my duty."*

*"Your duty was to your wing man, not to yourself. Douse him."*

*Some eager sailors ran forward with buckets of seawater and threw it on the open wounds on my back. I screamed in pain, and the dragoons dropped me to the deck, where I quivered.*

*"Mr. McRain, you have a mission to accomplish, a chance to redeem yourself."*

I woke in a terrible sweat that had thoroughly soaked my sheets. I knew I had been in a nightmare and I tried to shake it off as I stumbled down the hallway to the bathroom.

As I stood in front of the steaming water sink, lathering up my beard, I saw eyes over my shoulder, in the mirror. It was impossible; the fog from the steaming faucet had totally clouded the mirror. But the eyes were as real as if they sat a clear two feet from my face. I spun around, and nothing was there.

I bolted from the bathroom. I darn near knocked over Bridge, who was just outside the bathroom door.

It had been over six months, and I had thought they were gone for good. But the eyes were back. The eyes of the man I had deserted.

# CHAPTER 17

# THE ORGANIZER

Jake Casteel pissed off the wrong people for the right reason. He told his union men the truth. The C.I.A.; the Continental American Railroad's Board of Directors; Big Oil; the Hog Head Union executive board; the Pentagon; and, worst of all, the Lawyer's Mafia. They all wanted a piece of Casteel because he told the truth.

Jake looked back at what had gone terribly wrong. His family had been destroyed by the trials and all the legal wrangling. He wondered what he could have done differently to avoid going to prison. He figured he should have applied a lesson from what happened to the famous U.S. Presidential candidate, Ross Perot. Perot became famous for brandishing a voodoo stick and telling the American electorate the way it really was—the truth. And Perot's predictions and warnings eventually turned out to be true. Right on the money. But he lost the election *because* he told American voters the bitter truth. The sore lesson that Jake Casteel learned, too late, was that the powers that run this country do not want you telling the plain truth. And if you do tell that truth, they will make you pay for it.

If Jake Casteel had not been a believer in the better side of people, he could have seen just how far telling the truth would get him in the politics of running the most powerful union in the world. Nada. Hindsight is perfect vision.

It's not that Jake would have lied to his men. But if he had it to do all over again, he thought he might not have told them anything about how the lawyer's mafia was stealing them and the rest of America blind. Jake would have just kept quiet. At least, maybe then he would still have his family together.

Jake missed his children. He missed the trust between man and wife. He missed a lot about his early life as a father. He was isolated and angry in his gut for all his travails. All his sacrifices for his union men that seemed to go unappreciated and ended for naught. He was frustrated. The damned railroad was winning, just like it did in the 1800s, when it took what it wanted from whomever it pleased.

Again.

Jake could feel it in his bones. It was all happening again. The robber barons were taking, and the American people did not suspect a thing. It would be more than a decade in the future before history would reveal her secrets, about the way hundreds of billions of dollars were being stolen right out from under the noses of Americans.

The C.I.A. watched and recorded the speeches and the deal making Casteel participated in to strike the whole country. After all, the railroads were trying to starve out the union men. But the world's biggest and deadliest surveillance organization watched Jake closely for good reasons. Jake pissed off the wrong people when he threatened to put the lawyer mafia out of business.

It was a move so brazen, secretive, and far reaching that it got C.I.A.'s immediate, high-level attention and concern. The men who worked in the shadows, moving the invisible hand across our economy, decided something had to be done. The President, a Texas oilman, concluded that Casteel had to go. As he lit up a huge, Cuban cigar, he offered an interesting analogy to support his desire. With a voice as heavy as his stogie's aroma, the President said, "We have to cut this rogue bull from the rest of the herd before he causes a stampede, a rail labor strike."

Jake was destined to meet the same fate as the famous labor leaders Eugene Debs and Jimmy Hoffa.

History repeats itself.

CHAPTER 17

# CHAPTER 18

# THE LAST SUPPER

The people came in alone mostly. But sometimes as couples. Looking and acting like regular folks just passing through. Some even struck up a conversation with her. Right friendly types. Mabel Jean did not know they were agents of the United States Department of Defense. They had been frequenting her eatery to place electronic, eavesdropping bugs throughout her squeaky clean, little diner. Even in the bathrooms. With her diner situated directly next to the South Saline railyards, Mabel Jean's restaurant enjoyed the patronage of men from all the railroad crafts.

The diner had a fresh, bleached smell, from Old Dutch cleanser rubbed over lots of chrome and over white porcelain floors and walls. The scent of strong, fresh-brewed coffee made its way out the door, beckoning the railroaders inside. It was the unofficial meeting place and a speakeasy for railroaders from coast to coast, especially for Hog Heads Union, Local 1101. The Department of Defense, and the CIA, and the Department of Labor, and the N.S.A., and the railroad's Board of Directors were all very interested in what Jacob Casteel had to say. When Jake spoke, they listened—with a big, electronic ear.

On July 29, 1995, Jake came to visit Hog Head Local 1101. The men who didn't know him well treated him with equal parts of awe and distrust because he was such a learned man in their rank and file. Most of them wondered, *"Why would a man with all his brains want to help us?"'* And since they did not understand what made Jake tick, they didn't trust him. After the men got to know Jake, he had an ally for life.

Casteel felt some angst of his own, too. He gave polished legal advice to uneducated men, most of whom had barely graduated from high school. Jake compared it to throwing pearls to swine. It was hardly appreciated because another large block of men didn't trust Jake, simply because he was a lawyer. They were accustomed to union leaders who had no college education and had the morals of a snake. Birds of a feather flock together. Jake was on the outside, just for being bright and educated and honest.

Nevertheless, Jake tried to get through to the men that they could do much better, raise their standard of living, by being more aggressive in their labor-contract negotiations.

With his union constituents around him, Jake held the equivalent of a royal court in that small diner. The men were his subjects. He had a jester, who tried to impress him by laughing at all of his jokes, even the horrid ones. He had a prince, who tried to be the man giving only accurate facts about how they were being treated. This man was usually the local's chairman. And, of course, no regal court would be complete without one or two dark figures plotting to kill off the king. They, too, sat at Jake's table, acting as his faithful disciples.

His meetings were conducted strictly by "Robert's Rules of Order." The guy named Bob ordered his food first. After that, there were no rules. That day, Jake was talking a bit of treason. A possible nationwide strike to break the five-year dry spell of working with no contract. The visit with his union; constituents in Local 1101, and a standard practice for Jake. He visited locals throughout the country, as the duly elected International President of the Conglomerated Union Rail Transportation International System, C.U.R.T.I.S, for short. Most just referred to the union as C.U.R.T.I.S. And its members were affectionately referred to as Hog Heads.

Jacob H. Casteel, Attorney at Law, Marine Corps veteran, a sergeant with three tours in Vietnam, was as tough as a leatherneck when he represented his union men and their families. He had no pretenses, and he had no secret agendas to pad his own pockets. He had only the welfare of his men in his heart. He also had a hatred for the railroad in the pit of his stomach, twenty-four, seven. And triply so on Sundays. He treated the railroad executives like they were robber barons.

Damn it.

Up front in a window overlooking the railyard, a neon sign flickered a spasmodic: "Eat." Jake rolled up his sleeves, and he put his elbows on the table. He made no attempt to hide the large tattoo on his massive right forearm. It was a dandy, created by the best tattoo artist in Thailand, where

Jake enjoyed two months' R&R between his first and second tours in 'Nam. It spoke volumes about the man who wore it—a growling British bulldog, with "U-S-M-C" linked together to form its collar.

Casteel explained the intricacies of labor law to his brethren, who all looked perplexed. The majority of the ears listening to Casteel's law lecture belonged to brains ranked average in I.Q., which caused their respective eyes to glaze over with disinterest. They were common men with common sense.

His royal court was completed by Jake's queen, Mabel Jean Juttenhausen, who owned the diner. She took orders, washed dishes, flipped hamburgers, bussed tables, and, most importantly, served piping-hot, stick-to-the-ribs food with an enthusiasm matched only by her broad smile and a work ethic that made assembly line workers look lazy. She *was* the entertainment. While the jukebox played its country and western selections, Mabel Jean amused most everyone who frequented her 1950s art-deco-decorated café with her unapologetic advice on everything from "A to Z." Unsolicited suggestions about your love life were her specialty, slung at you from clear across the room so everyone could hear. They hit close to home often, and you were left with the impression that she was a clairvoyant.

Mabel Jean's laugh was a gulping, high pitch, punctuated with a snort. Just hearing her laugh was infectious and made you want to laugh with her. She was the salt of the earth. That is why so many railroaders liked to frequent her café. Her sincerity and maternal friendship made the railroaders feel better. Visiting her was home away from home.

She was everybody's mother. And her counter, full of flower bouquets that she received every Mothers' Day from railroaders all around the country, served as a testament to the mutual friendship between husky, no-bullshit men and the hardworking lady who doted on them in her oasis on the rail.

Mabel Jean pushed three tables together to accommodate the baker's dozen of union men gathered for Jake's meeting. They all knew Jake was the only licensed attorney in the entire 100,000-strong rank-and-file membership of C.U.R.T.I.S. Their union ran the most important cog in America's economy—the railroads. But the men didn't understand why they had to be so careful when dealing with the railroad and why they had to listen to Jake's horror stories of how different union brothers got the shaft.

They were like trusting sheep, and Jake was their shepherd. Their German Shepherd.

Jake had something eating at him, too. He held back a secret from his men that a unique mafia was stealing not only from them, but also stealing billions from the American people every year. But Casteel couldn't advertise what he knew. Not yet. The secret ate at him so much so that he wound his speech for a strike around a promise to get rid of "the cancer in our midst." Casteel, as a lawyer, was uniquely qualified to advise his men about the perils of giving too much information to the railroad and signing up with a Designated lawyer when injured.

"It's a barrel of snakes. A big, old, Goddamn barrel of snakes."

That was probably the nicest thing he could say about the whole railroad, R.I.O., injury system. But he went on to explain about how the injured workers are taken advantage of by a lot of the Designated lawyers.

The R.I.O. railroad-injury law did not require the railroad to pay their injured workers for time off when they incurred a work injury, unlike all the other employers in America, who had to pay their injured workers temporary injury benefits. The Designated lawyers took full advantage of that glitch in the law by offering special, secret, and highly illegal loans to the injured workers in return for the workers' promise not to run to some other railroad-injury attorney. These things Jake could tell his men. But he couldn't tell them the whole truth.

"They will suck you in by promising you the moon. And get you on the take so that when it comes time to try the case or settle it, they will be able to squeeze you, and make their legal fee bigger."

Casteel explained in detail about how the unscrupulous railroad-injury lawyers would entice the men with the loans to pay for their mortgages, the food on their tables, and the shoes on the their children's feet. And when it came time for settlement, the Designated lawyers hid the loan repayment and fees in the client's closing statement so that it appeared as litigation expenses. The bottom line was a shrunken line of numbers. The workers received such a small amount, after all the deductions, that the workers wondered why they had ever begun to work for the railroad in the first place. It appeared that the union men were worse off after they got paid for their injury than beforehand.

CHAPTER 18

And after most settlements, the union workers no longer had a job. The settlement money spent fast and they found themselves on welfare before too long.

Tommy Ray Luechtenfelder was Casteel's jester for the day. He pestered Mabel Jean in a soft drawl that dripped of a land a bit more old South and of a familiarity gained by innumerable days spent at her diner's counter.

"Mabel Jean, you settle up a little bet we boys took up 'bout what makes for a good relationship with a woman. We all think it's sex, but I bet you can learn us something on that, wood'ja?"

Mabel Jean, scooping up plates to clear the table, shot from the hip with advice for the heart. "Three things for a great relationship: keep your arguments short, always follow a slow song with a fast song, and never give up your boot knife."

The last bit of advice brought snickers and chuckles from the table and begged Jake's inquiry.

"What do you need a boot knife for if you are in love?"

Mabel Jean balanced a soup bowl under a tray filled with salad plates, glasses, and silverware, but she didn't miss a beat.

"That's so's when the time comes to move on, you can cut it off."

The table of men laughed hard.

"Cut what off?" said Jake.

The whole diner roared with belly-shaking laughter. And most of the men were still holding their sides from the hilarious moment when one of their union brothers flung open the well-worn screen door and rushed in. He marched quickly across the room and stopped next to Casteel. Snaggle Tooth was an old timer, whose false teeth corrected the real reason he got his nickname years before. He used to have a nasty-looking mouth full of green, crooked teeth. Everybody on the rail had a nickname, and his was shortened to Snags.

Snags looked like a wrinkled-up derelict, from a long career on the rail and the job hazards it brings: oceans of whiskey and beer; whores waiting at each lay-over; road food; cigarettes for boredom; and, thanks to the callous railroad barons always looking at profits instead of safety, asbestos vented right into his locomotive cabs for thirty years. He was a sorry-looking excuse for a man. And he looked even worse on the inside.

"There's some F.B.I. agents up at the yard asking where you're at, Jake. Said they want to talk to you." Before Jake could even stand up, two F.B.I. agents and three huge, U.S. Marshall' s deputies barged in and headed straight for Jake.

"Mr. Jacob Casteel, we are putting you under arrest."

Jake did not struggle, but his men stood up for him and asked in unison, "What for?"

"Orders from Federal District Judge Lackey because you lost your appeal."

"I've never been told I lost my appeal, and, besides, I've got a bond." Jake said, defiant to the insult of handcuffs and a surprise arrest. F.B.I. agent Stemp, a guy who looked like he couldn't punch his way out of a wet, paper bag said, "Judge Lackey revoked your bond because he thought you were a flight risk."

Casteel grimaced as he extended his wrists to the shackles. A thin grin drew across the deputy's mouth as he pinched the handcuffs tight.

"You sure it isn't because Judge Lackey's friends just don't like the strike speeches I've been making? Or maybe it's the Designated lawyers who don't want their golden-goose system changed?" Jake said to agent Stemp, as the gorilla-sized deputies yanked Jake out the door.

Jake was led across the gravel parking lot next to the rail yard. They shoved him into a black, Chevy Suburban in the middle of a convoy of three Suburbans that spun their tires and threw rocks at the union men as they took off in a cloud of dust from the gravel parking lot of "EAT."

Tommy Ray turned to Snags and leveled his own indictment.

"They follow you here, or did you lead 'em?"

Snags shot Tommy a sideways how-dare-you-think-that kind of look, but made no reply. Snaggle Tooth left right away.

Fifty yards to the east, a three-locomotive consist was struggling to build up speed to haul ten thousand tons of Wyoming, low-sulfur coal to the local, electric-power plant. Plumes of black smoke shot out of the tops of the locomotives. The lead locomotive's brassy horn blasted two times.

# CHAPTER 19

# A THOUSAND PIKES

Ace lay next to Bridget's chair. His golden-coated chin rested on the Persian rug as Bridget prayed. He only moved his brown eyes to watch her dabble with her Irish-Catholic figures and objects of ancient religious worship. Her hand was characteristically wrapped in a rosary. The only time it was not was when she entered the bathroom. Otherwise, she got dressed, and she cooked, and she even strung beads onto rosaries, in her job at St. Cecelia's Sheltered Workshop for the Blind, with a rosary wrapped about her hand and fingers. Bridget practiced her Catholicism and its manual ceremonies at all waking hours. They were a psychological security blanket for her powerful intellect, which flew, at a screaming fast speed, in ten different directions.

Bridget Mary had a method to her madness, as far as I could see. There were good episodes, when she spoke in a clear voice and she did not sound as though she were challenged at all. Then there were most other times, when she seemed to speak in endless gibberish, punctuated only by the words of standard prayers like the "Hail, Mary;" the "Our Father;" the "Glory Be;" and the Mysteries for all the stations of the rosary. She used the rosary and the prayers to Jesus and his saints as navigational polestars to move around inside her star-guided, mental universe.

Bridget had never had a boyfriend. She had never known lust. But she knew all about love. Real love. The caring type of love everyone wants at the most important times of life—when things are at their worst. Bridget Mary McRain knew all about that timeless sort of love. And she cultivated it with every bead she pushed and each time she crossed herself. She was pure in heart. She had the biggest heart in the world. But she swung one hell of a mean stick if you messed with her or her little brother.

She was blind-sighted to the world. But she had an inward sight like an eagle. She suffered the most difficulty in expressing herself, her ideas and her thoughts, to those around her. She would stumble and mumble and fidget, hem and haw, and stutter and repeat herself, over and over like a record that was skipping. But she would persist. If she didn't get her thought across on one day, it might be a week or a month later that she finally was able to get her tongue to cooperate with her mind. Then a statement would come flying out, with no context, and it was unexpected by anyone around her.

That evening, Bridget was in a feverish prayer, rocking frontward and backward in her bedroom's prayer chair. Her head was cocked up and to the side, while her eyes bounced around under her eyelids like an old-fashioned, percolating coffeepot. She shook some sweet-spice holy water on her altar's menagerie for the day.

Some people close to the family claim that Bridget's prayers worked because when she prayed for the sick or the challenged, or prayed for a good result in a terrible situation, it seemed, much more often than not, that her prayers were promptly answered. Some said her prayers were actually celestial given that she was born challenged with autism and without sight—supposedly making her soul pure and untainted by the world.

Our mother believed Bridget enjoyed a spiritually perfect form that was free from the inescapable original sin that the Papacy instructed that all humans were born with and could never shirk as mortals. She claimed Bridget possessed a direct channel to God because she was pure in heart. Mother was a God-fearing Catholic. And she had the spiritual strength of a dozen women. But she remained most jovial and fun-loving in her spiritual life. Bridget did not fall far from her mother's tree. She inherited everything but the joviality. Bridget was serious about everything. It appeared that God had not equipped her with a sense of humor. Or at least one that I could understand. My sister would have made a wonderful U.S.M.C. drill sergeant.

Bridget had been praying hard for me. She had heard the anxiety in my voice, and she sensed my desire to leave her. I wanted to get on with my life. I wanted a family of my own and all the joy a family can bring. But she also sensed that the days soon to come were dark and foreboding, with challenges the likes of which neither of us had ever seen.

CHAPTER 19

That is what she felt in her soul. I began to feel the same in my gut.

She was rocking back and forth. Her nose came close to a shelf of her altar where two, toy, tin soldiers stood, about three inches high. They were painted like the Royal Guard. The aromatic smoke from the incense she was burning smelled like lavender. It wafted amongst and around the tin soldiers. She raised a bottle labeled: "Holy Water." She sprinkled it on the two soldiers, quite sparing but sure.

"Glory be," she whispered. She set down the holy water and continued saying rosaries two-handed, to a cadence from our Celtic bloodline. Her old stereo played a hearty rendition of "By the Risin' O' the Moon." It was an ancient battle cry older than the legend of King Brian Boru and it was sung by Bridget's favorite Irish singers, Tommy Mecum and The Clancy Brothers:

> "By the risin' O' the moon,
> By the risin' O' the moon,
> They'r'll be a thousand pikes a' flashin',
> By the risin' O' the moon. . ."

Bridget Mary's little brother slept while she prayed. She called on the saints in the name of her Lord. She used all her spiritual cunning. She pushed the envelope almost to shamanry, to make Michael's journey safe from the evil that waited for him. Bridget burned some sweet, apple incense and breathed her prayers rhythmically in and out.

# CHAPTER 20

# THE INJURY CLIENT

*"I cannot blow the horn,*
*I cannot clang the bell,*
*But if this train jumps the track,*
*Guess who catches Hell."*

***An Ancient Railroad Worker Lamentation***

"My God, where's my arm?" Billy McAvoy cried out to the world every time he woke up when his pain medication wore off. It had only been two days since he had his little "accident." But the Designated lawyers from DeeDee's law firm had already been warning Billy that if he persisted in telling everyone that some horrible man made him cut off his arm with the train, he would not receive a single penny from his injury claim against the railroad. Billy was told his lawyers would be alleging the sill-step he was allegedly standing on had been defective. And the storyline continued, to include that that was why he slipped off and ended under the train, where he got his right arm lopped off.

But Billy didn't like it. He was out an arm. And now he was going to be losing his honor, too, by telling and retelling the lie the lawyers were selling to him.

Under oath.

The lawyers did not like Billy's version. It was the truth. A truth that would not allow them to collect a legal fee.

He got some more pain medicine from the friendly nurse and slipped back into his self-induced coma of despair, where he tried to dream up a way an honorable railroader might lose his arm and not his honor.

By the time the painkillers wore off again, Billy was half believing his dreams that his arm had been cut off in a derailment. Delusional. He didn't remember anything about Knuckles or putting his arm under the wheel. But he wasn't talking about it. Not to the railroad dicks. Not to anybody. Not even to his wife.

Paranoia struck Billy every time he felt his stump. He hated his stump. When he smelled it, it smelled like carrion—rotting meat. Smelling it made him almost vomit.

After Billy would not stop screaming about a huge man forcing him to cut off his arm, Billy was transferred to the Psych Ward at St. Mary's. He kept telling the psychiatrist that he had had his arm cut off by a thug out on the rail. But the police told the doctor Billy's story was he fell and got run over. DeeDee's firm gave the police Billy's *official* statement about what happened.

Billy received lots of visits from his Designated lawyers. The ones from DeeDee's firm. He liked DeeDee a whole lot. One time someone came from Big Dutch's firm. Knuckles came and just stood out in the waiting room, saying he was Billy's Uncle George and needed to talk with him. Billy didn't go out to see Knuckles. He told the nurse he didn't have an Uncle George. Billy didn't see any more of Knuckles after that. Kinda like Knuckles dropped off the earth.

Then Billy's real uncle came to visit. Uncle Fergus.

Fergus McDaniels was Billy's uncle on his mother's side. Fergus worked for the railroad, too, and ended up a left-armed amputee. He stopped by to see Billy at the hospital, and Fergus told Billy the story of how he had lost his arm.

Billy told Fergus about Knuckles and the night Billy lost his arm. Billy explained *he wasn't given a chance to look for his arm.* Fergus was angry, but not surprised. Fergus was livid that the lawyer mafia took an arm from one of his family members to feed their greed. He offered Billy a minor consolation, "I got injured honest, and, I guess, in the devil's way, you did, too. You had no choice in the matter, lad."

Uncle Fergus warned Billy to stay away from Big Dutch's firm. He called that whole firm, "a bunch of back-stabbing, thieving bastards." He told Billy not to take any loans from the Designated lawyers. It's a goddamned lawyers' mafia, and you don't want to be anywhere near it when the ballyhoo starts flying." Fergus referred to the old Tennessee Ernie Ford song, *"Sixteen Tons"* as his final advice. "Besides, you'd be better off not owing the company store everything when your case does settle. Else you'll be left with a pittance."

Billy did not tell his uncle that he was already into the Designated lawyers for loans to pay the mortgage and the children's school lunch money and shoes for the kids and meat on the kitchen table and the like that nickels and dimes every family. Billy that he did not receive injured-on-the-job paycheck replacement checks like his neighbor, Bob, did when Bob broke his arm at the local auto assembly plant. From the day a one thousand pound engine fell on Bob's arm to the day he returned to work, he was paid a check for being injured and unable to work, just like all the other workers in America. It's the law for all of America's workers except the railroad workers who were required to labor under R.I.O. to keep the fat injury lawyers fat. That is the way Billy saw it after Fergus told him so. Lucky Bob did not have to pay back any loans like Billy had to. Billy felt like a genuine sucker. Like he was being used by greedy lawyers.

Those damned loans. Fergus told Billy the bad news that DeeDee left out when she got him on the dole, taking secret loans. Uncle Fergus explained in painful detail how Billy was, unwittingly, covering up a fraud on the I.R.S., by not claiming the monies he received as cash. By the way Billy figured it, he would have to pay DeeDee's law firm back for loans they gave him under the table, that were going to accumulate to such a large pay-back amount that he would not be left with near what he would have received, if he had been hurt at Bob's assembly plant. He realized that he was stuck in a system designed to feed lawyers a feast on every R.I.O. client.

"Hell, the R.I.O. lawyers even take their fee out of the cost of your future medical bills," Fergus said, which meant Billy would not be able to afford continually better prosthesis as medical science improved like the amputees from Bob's plant were provided. "The R.I.O. system is a sham. And it won't ever stop as long as you got those damned Designated lawyers bribing the union officers and the politicians," said Fergus. "R.I.O. has been around for one hundred years, not because it's good for the union men; no, it is still on the books because the son-of-a-bitchin' Senate Judiciary Committee has never let it leave the committee for a 'repeal R.I.O.' vote on the floor of the Senate. That's what the Designated lawyers told us at a local union meeting. You betcha. There was two of them assholes there at the meeting, you've seen 'em. One handing out hats with their phone number on them and the other giving a speech about how they'z our saviors cuz R.I.O. workers aren't allowed to get injured-on-the-job payments and how's they'll take care of us with the money we need for our families bullshit you know?. That dadgummed loan bullshit. They're milkin' us like dairy cows cuz if they don't make ya have an accident like yours, they're telling us we gotta get cut on by their sawbones surgeons to make their case value and fees go higher."

Billy interrupted his uncle. "Goddamn." And he shook his head in woeful disbelief. "Buncha punk-assed crooks." And Billy nodded his head that he'd seen those Designated lawyers, or some a lot like them, at local union meetings before. Uncle Fergus had his Irish up and was red faced and continued his bluster. "And he's just a'strutting up in front like the top cock of the henhouse." Fergus shook his head for the shame of the R.I.O. system and he rubbed together the ends of the fingers on his remaining hand. And Billy understood the politicians were all bought off.

Billy stewed on it all: the damned illegal loans, the forced amputation, the goddamned lawyers telling him to lie so he could collect money for something that was no accident, and the way the lawyers all talked to him like they were his friend. *"Friends my ass,"* he thought.

"Bunch a goddamned coyotes scavenging for their next carcass, their next R.I.O. case victim, is what they are."

Fergus left after they shook hands – left-handed.

"Bunch of yipping coyote bastards," he said out loud to the blanched, sterile hospital walls. Billy curled up in his bed like a little lost lamb, without his mother.

Billy wanted God to grant him biblical justice; he wanted an eye for an eye. He rubbed his stump and his mind kept raging. He swore to himself an oath before God, praying for sinful violence, some revenge, or maybe a change in the law to something that favored the little guy, some type of social justice. *Somewhere, sometime, someone will pay for what they did to me. I swear to God.*

CHAPTER 20

# CHAPTER 21

# THE TABERNACLE OF TORTS

I never saw anything that extravagant and gaudy in my life. And I've seen the Louvre and the Taj Mahal. These lawyers had money to burn. Wall Street executives looked like misers compared to the egotistical excesses of these secret lawyers. They were *Designated*.

They sued railroads exclusively and built a shrine with their captured booty. It was a grand tabernacle for the practice of torts: a house of inspired legal prayers for special remedies to right statutory wrongs. Only the divine tort was practiced there—R.I.O. injury lawsuits for railroad workers. R.I.O. personal-injury cases were prayed to courts across the land. They were prosecuted and adored like pagan idols. Each arm-off or leg-off or buy-out case achieved a separate respect, as though the case itself, and not the injured man, was exalted and adored like a false idol, a golden calf.

The builders and keepers of the tabernacle were partners—Felix Falic, Bratford Moore, and Delilah "DeeDee" DeVillay, attorneys at law. Powerful Senator Moore was listed on their letterhead as "Of Counsel." They elevated the practice of R.I.O. law to a fundamental religion. It was plainly a worship of money. In the Tabernacle of Torts, they did not practice law. They practiced their own religion—Greed. And their high priest was U.S. Senator Moore, who they all worshipped like a demigod.

This was obvious to anyone who was close to them or their firm, Falic, Moore & DeVillay. The firm boasted satellite offices in Washington, D.C., Biloxi, Boca Raton, San Francisco, Provo, Denver, and, of course, their home office in St. Martinsville.

The Tabernacle of Torts was in downtown St. Martinsville at the corner of Jordan and Bass. It filled half a city block, and it was an architectural marvel. An open, museum-sized atrium lobby comprised much of the Tabernacle of Torts' square footage. The longest glass wall faced east, rising eleven stories to swallow the morning sun. Office space went up seven stories, and the remaining stories were all glass. Spectacular. Bold architecture for bold lawyers.

Their license to steal was proudly displayed in a prominent place in a ten-foot-tall obelisk standing in the very center of the majestic lobby. The gold-framed, glass-fronted display panels each showed a separate page of the U.S. Supreme Court opinion, "Hog Heads Union v. West Virginia Bar". All the pages were displayed, except the scathing dissent by three justices that called the R.I.O.-Designated-lawyers system an ethical train wreck waiting to happen. Those three justices, who were all conservative, strict constructionists would look like swamis before the story would all be told.

The Tabernacle of Torts, as Falic, Moore & DeVillay employees referred to it, was the recipient of no less than six architectural awards for the striking views inside and out. In a nightscape view, the building looked like a lit-up candle because the top four stories and a sloped half-story atrium shone like a flame. But the inside joke in the St. Martinsville Bar Association was that the Tabernacle looked like a huge phallic symbol. That seems like merely envious jabs from lawyers who wished they knew Falic's secret for getting business. But it was a harbinger of what to expect by doing business with that law firm. And it was true. At night, the Tabernacle of Torts did resemble a huge phallic symbol. Warning: Deal with these lawyers and you will get screwed.

The firm's doorman was Ajax. He looked as if someone had put a suit coat on a fifty-five gallon drum with legs. He was big like a bear. He stood sentry by the door, next to the bronze statue memorializing railroad laborers who had given their lives in building and running America's railroads. Joe the Conductor was Ajax's coworker in the lobby.

Joe the Conductor seemed to have a smell of diesel fumes about him permanently. Probably due to breathing them in as a Hog Head for thirty-three years on the Cotton Belt rail line. Joe the Conductor dressed in the old-style railroad conductor's uniform, complete all the way down to his stovepipe-billed hat. He pulled a silver, engraved watch by its chain from his vest pocket, to check the time every three minutes, to make sure his holographic trains ran on time. Security was paramount at Falic, Moore & DeVillay, so it was Ajax, and only Ajax, who allowed you admittance onto the elevator.

Displayed on the marble walls of the granite-floored lobby were photographic portraits of Falic, Moore & DeVillay with some of the clients they had represented in negotiating huge settlements or winning mega sized jury verdicts for their R.I.O. injury claims.

One such portrait's brass announcement plate read: "T. H. Edison: $4.5 million."

The portrait photo was blown up to twenty by thirty inches and showed Delilah DeVillay with her hand on Mr. Falic's shoulder in a care-taking sort of way. Tommy Edison looked pleased—about as happy as a photographer could make him look. After all, he lost a foot. There were thirty-three of those portraits around the huge lobby, separated by massive urns spouting colorful flora. For every multi-million dollar settlement advertised in the lobby, they had hundreds more like them. Thousands of cases settled in the low- to mid-six figures. Their success was nothing short of phenomenal. And they never ran out of business.

In that smaller, roped area, and set into the wall was a beautiful, polished-brass encasement. In that case, behind bulletproof glass, were two documents displayed with prominence, as though they were as important as the United States "Constitution" and "The Declaration of Independence." Both documents were set against fancy red velvet. Beyond all the flowery legalese, the proclamation stated that because Jake Casteel was the only lawyer in the whole C.U.R.T.I.S. union, Jake Casteel had been officially "Designated." The other document was Jake's proxy, his official loan, of his Designation to DeeDee's law firm.

Jake Casteel never had to bribe anyone to get his Designation. He'd earned it, and that made the rest of the Designated lawyers furious. For Casteel loaned the Designation to DeeDee's firm for free.

DeeDee was Jake's niece.

Outside on the sidewalk, Joseph bellowed, "All aboard! The San Francisco-Charlotte Meteor Express bound for Denver leaves in three minutes! All aboard!"

Passersby looked quizzically at Joe the Conductor. Those who knew grinned. And the curious stepped into the lobby. Two minutes and fifty-five seconds later, Conductor Joe was in the lobby and hollered, "Make clear! The Meteor is pullin' out!"

As if by magic, a full-sized holographic replica of the once-famous "Meteor" steam locomotive appeared in the cavernous lobby. Ghostlike in its transparency, it chugged, while standing still in the large, roped-off area in the lobby. Those who never saw it before had wide eyes and gaping mouths.

The Meteor's steam-driven pistons turned huge, sixty-inch-high drive wheels under a strain. Special gadgets released steam and smoke scents to make the illusion even more real. A bearded engineer wearing a cap waved his arm out the locomotive's window, signaling their departure. After a short while, his arm came in the window and he pulled the whistle cord. A shrill whistle echoed up, down, and all around in the atrium. It was heard even into the farthest reaches of the offices. It had an eerie sound, like a banshee seeking solace.

Right after the whistle sound rang out of the audience's ears, a Johnny Cash song, "Folsom Prison Blues," gained volume from speakers behind the urns, and the Man in Black appeared in a wispy, transparent form and he started singing about trains, and Momma and prison and a life of killing, in front of the Meteor.

Joe the Conductor acted as a tour guide and gave information about the different locomotives and the recording artists who sang about trains. He informed them that Falic, Moore & DeVillay hired the retired Director of Hologram Works at Mouse World in Florida to build their lobby's holographic theatre. The firm exhibited, as holographs, a revolving stock of memorable, antique locomotives that arrived exactly on the schedule each particular locomotive once kept. After Johnny Cash finished his song, Joseph told everyone they could leave or stay to browse the lobby. But, either way, the holographic show was over.

The holographic train was a million-dollar toy for Falic. They deducted it as a business expense, even though they didn't need it to get the business. The firm's vanity bred even more vanity and an "untouchable" attitude towards the law and all its well-intended rules of ethics.

CHAPTER 21

In the beginning, Casteel saw R.I.O. cases and the great amount of money they cost the railroad as a way to stick his thumb in the eye of the railroad. Jake fought with the railroad every day, and any discomfort he could cause them, he encouraged. But Jake never took any kickbacks or fee splits on any of the cases his Designation brought into DeeDee's law firm. And he could have become a multi-millionaire with all the fees he refused. Jake Casteel was satisfied just working for his men and their families to bring them a better way of life.

Far above the lobby, Felix was looking at the Meteor and scheming up how to use Senator Moore to wrangle another union's Designation. His appetite for money was insatiable. Felix Falic stopped watching the hologram below and stepped away from the balcony. He walked back to his desk twenty yards away. His secretary, Sam, hailed him over the intercom.

"Mr. Falic?"

"What do you need?"

"Sir, I just got a call from Gary Boyd. There is a derailment in Addyville that a friend picked up on a police scanner."

"A derailment? How bad?"

"He said it sounded pretty bad, with a lot of collateral damage. It happened right in town, in Addyville."

"Get DeeDee on the phone for me ASAP."

Fifty-three seconds later, Sam came back, "Sir, here's DeeDee; I got her on her car phone."

"DeeDee, you there?" said Falic.

"Yeah, Daddy. What's up? I'm just coming back from Court. I argued that Vandover motion."

"Well, you can tell me how it went later on. I got big news. There's been a derailment out in Addyville. A bad one. You know where that is?"

"I know exactly where it is. C.A.R.'s line runs right through it."

Falic listened for a few seconds and heard nothing. DeeDee said no more.

"DeeDee? Dee, Dee! Oh, Hell, she hung up on me. Go get 'em, girl!"

He threw his hands up in the air in pleasant wonderment that *his girl* was that money hungry. He was a proud Papa, proud that his step-daughter was the best damned capper in the United States, (capper was railroad lingo for a rainmaker in a union Designated law firm). Falic stayed at the Tabernacle of Torts to oversee the derailment-injury client capture like a general when he sends out his troops and stays behind the lines.

Falic walked back to the balcony and pushed a large button labeled: "Man in Peril." Instantly, the Meteor holographic train reappeared below. Hank, the faceless engineer, blew Meteor's steam whistle—five long wails, signaling to the whole building a derailment had occurred. Ajax responded in a practiced protocol, hailing two chauffeured SUV's for the firm's investigative crew. Junior attorneys stopped in the middle of depositions, or telephone conferences with judges, and bolted for the door, with little or no explanation, leaving their professional secretaries to mend any hard feelings. The firm held the unique right to chase personal-injury cases. And they took it seriously.

Their life's blood was not litigation. Their whole existence depended on getting more cases: lucrative strict-liability R.I.O. tort cases that damn near tried themselves.

The thin calf of a Gucci goddess wore a diamond-studded anklet as it pressed down on the accelerator. Three-hundred-thirty horses harnessed to her two-door, Mercedes convertible chariot responded, wild and furious. DeeDee flew almost like Mercury to the train derailment site.

Falic, Moore & DeVillay possessed unheard-of powers that were envied by every lawyer in America. They were Designated. They were above the law. Untouchable. Unholy.

They were the Tort Gods.

CHAPTER 21

# CHAPTER 22

# CAPTAIN CARION

I was ignorant. The black, tenuous thread of honor among thieves was woven throughout their scheme. It was a conspiracy hatched against me and a client I did not yet know was to be mine. And I had no idea I was soon to be ambushed by the ruthless bastards.

To make it worse, my dreams were like my life. They went from bad to worse. They were ongoing nightmares.

*I found myself onboard the Constitution again, sailing through the choppy seas of Purgatory. On a ship that smelled of lost dreams of heaven, of ancient sins long forgotten, but never forgiven. It stunk of all of human weakness. I was in chains, kneeling on the wood-planked deck. The ship was engulfed in a white fog as thick as cotton. I smelled the salty sea air and felt the great ship pitch to and fro.*

*A funny little man with a bright red nose, dressed in Irish green, white, and orange, squatted down beside me and said, "We will be taking on a new commander, Mr. McRain, and I don't like a bit of it."*

*I raised my face and looked into his, but I couldn't speak.*

*"And don't be thinking you can reason with him. He'll send you to Hell just as soon as look at you, just for the sport of it, just to watch you burning in the unholy waters."*

*He jumped up in fear at the sound of the boatswain's voice. "Mr. Troubles, you shouldn't be talking with the prisoner. If the Admiral caught you, he'd throw you in the waters of Hell himself."*

*"Just tell'n him the rules of decorum and protocol, Mr. Fetid."*

*The wind shifted, and I was downwind of the boatswain, Mr. Fetid. I retched from the horrible stench of him. The terrible smell buckled Mr. Trouble's knees, and he scurried off with a kerchief over his nose. Fetid bent from at the waist to look me in the face. I held my breath; otherwise, I could not have looked upon him without throwing up.*

*"I've been sailing these seas since the Black Plague. I don't quite know how we will earn our redemption with you on board. No, sir. Not on this voyage."*

Mr. Fetid walked away and blew his boatswain's whistle for muster. All fell in, sailors of many sorts: Chinese in short jackets and barefoot, Germans in World War I and II uniforms, Brittish in their Royal Navy blues, Russians, Dutch, Argentinean, French and others too numerous to list. It seemed there was a representative from almost every navy that ever floated ship or skow. I pegged the Americans and I sought to move toward them, but I was stopped by a sudden bright light.

The Admiral appeared upon his announcement like he had been beamed from the heavens. He addressed the crew, "You will be receiving a new commander for this voyage: Captain Carion." The crew drew a collective gasp. Two fainted. One crazed soul, a Portuguese sailor, ran and threw himself overboard into the waters, where he was eaten by the insatiable sins of man. They devoured their spiritual prey like piranhas strip a body of its meat—all the way down to the naked bone, leaving only a black, inedible soul to sink to the crushing bottom, where it would remain, in stark isolation, for eternity.

Mr. Troubles ran front and center and threw himself, on his knees, at the feet of Admiral Jaundice.

"Admiral, we cannot use Captain Carion for this mission, sir. You know what a mess he made at Pearl Harbor."

Admiral Jaundice bellowed, "Yes, but he got the ultimate mission done. He's coming aboard now."

All the crew was fearful and sought places to hide below decks. Everyone except Mr. Troubles. He hid behind the flowing, great coat of Admiral Jaundice.

A beast of a man marched onboard, to rule our destinies. He was scarred across his nose and wore a patch over his left eye. A terrified whisper from the crew behind me rumored that Carion wore the patch, and actually switched it from side to side now and then, just so he could turn his gaze away from the truth when it suited him best. Mr. Fetid followed closely behind Carion, tucking a worm back into his ear as Carion stopped with his fists on his hips, sizing up the slowly returning crew. Carion walked over to Admiral Jaundice and saluted him.

"Captain Carion at your service, my Lord."

Admiral Jaundice did not bother to return the salute. The Admiral spoke, resonant and strong, raising the waves around the ship. "This is your mission," Admiral Jaundice handed Captain Carion a rolled-up parchment, with ribbon and a seal. "This is your subject," Admiral Jaundice gestured towards me, still on my knees awaiting my fate.

CHAPTER 22

Before the Admiral exited the ship, he motioned for Mr. Troubles to step to the side. Admiral Jaundice counseled Troubles quietly, "Troubles, you are to stay on board and be my eyes in my absence."

"Your service is my destiny, my Lord." Troubles watched Admiral Jaundice become ethereal as he vanished into the thin air.

Captain Carion stomped towards me, looking down on me from his great height.

"The first thing we must do, Mr. McRain, is open up a direct line of communication."

Carion kicked me in the stomach and then punched me, a black ring on his finger opening a large wound on my face.

"Why do I deserve this? These chains? This beating?"

"What you did, Laddie, was a mortal sin. You'll have to be earning your way off o' this ship. This is the place ya learnt about in Catechism—the ship of the dead and forgotten souls."

"Purgatory?"

"Ah, you're a bright lad, aren't ya?"

The Captain spoke to the crew.

"It seems nobody knows what the mission is, so we have to remind Mr. McRain that he must complete an impossible mission to earn his redemption."

Mr. Fetid chimed in, his stench-filled breath in my face, "You have to succeed or ye will be serving with me for the next three hundred years."

Carion threatened, "Or maybe I'll send you overboard to the bottom, straight to Hell."

Carion snatched a large, leather-bound law book, as thick a tome as ever existed, and dropped it in front of me.

"Here you be, Harvard boy. I'm going to teach you everything about the law you need to know. We are going to take all the skullduggery you learned at Harvard law school and burn it out of your brain."

The huge law book began to vaporize before my eyes, into dancing blue flames that jumped up and disappeared into the air. It became fine ashes that floated across my face. Carion smeared the soot over my eyes.

"Laddie, the law is war. You are nothing if you do not win. To the victor goes the spoils. Just so you don't forget, you're a Dragoon. A Marine. Lead, damn it! Take command of the mission and kick some legal arses. Now I'm gonna leave you with a little reminder."

*Captain Carion reached out and grabbed a white-hot poker that Mr. Fetid heated in the ship's smoke box. Eight men held me down as Carion branded the letters "L-A-W-A-R" deep into my chest. Fetid then threw seawater across my new wound. I screamed, but I could not hear my screaming.*

I woke up in my bed, with Gunny's sharp nails poking me in the chest. He was licking my face to wake me. My revelry alarm had not gone off. I was late for the blasted day.

# CHAPTER 23

# THE CIA'S PEOPLE

Location: 308th Transportation Command, Fort Eustus, Virginia

She was certainly pretty enough to be a professional model. If she had been back on the streets of New York, she would be turning heads with her strutting march. Black and beautiful. Her head was held high atop ramrod-straight posture. Her gait was broken only by a slight and very sexy swing of her hips, wrapped tight and right in a G.I.-green skirt. Her wrist wore a snug handcuff, attached to a metallic briefcase. The biting cuff reminded her of her simple mission. Sergeant Clorece Butler was delivering hyper-secret documents to her new boss, Colonel Dirk Durant. She wore her Army greens with pride. She couldn't help the strut. It was a by-product of long legs, firm hips, and a head full of confidence.

A long string of florescent lights blared impersonal blinding white light everywhere she walked, underground at Fort Eustis. Her heavy-healed footsteps echoed as she marched down a long hallway that smelled of institutional-strength disinfectant. Its white-tiled floor was buffed to a lustrous glow. She arrived at a security checkpoint before a riveted, steel door. A large M.P. supervised her iris scan. The same old routine. She stepped through the automated door and didn't look back to see the M.P. checking her out, from the floor up, as she continued on her delivery route. She arrived at the door and knocked and announced herself.

"Sergeant Butler. Under direct orders of Lieutenant General Crowe to deliver sensitive documents, Sir."

She entered, and Colonel Dirk Durant stood up from his desk chair.

"Come in, Sergeant, and let me see the documents."

Sergeant Butler dropped her salute. She walked in and put the steel briefcase on one of the two chairs in front of Durant's desk. The room was subterranean. It had no windows. It smelled of mold, second-rate coffee, and Durant's sickening musk cologne. He wore his hair high and tight in a butch flat-top. Colonel Durant returned to his desk chair and flipped a switchblade knife into the air, catching it by the handle, trying to impress Butler.

She turned her back to Durant and bent over to the briefcase. She entered her share of the digital code required to open the briefcase. The Colonel undressed her with his eyes and imagined all sorts of things might go on if this assignment lasted more than a few days. Hell. He hoped he'd get lucky that night. And if not, he decided he sure as Hell would lean on her with his full-bird Colonel rank until she acquiesced.

Colonel Durant was married and divorced—three times—with a daughter born from each marriage. He hated to see a beautiful body like Sergeant Butler's get rusty from lack of use. Sergeant Butler turned around, and Colonel Durant saw what looked like a wedding ring on her hand. He became even more interested at the prospect of a short, tawdry affair with no emotional strings attached.

He punched his five-digit code into the top of the steel briefcase and heard the sound of a vacuum release from the latch. Butler turned her back to him again in order to extract the contents. Durant leaned back in his chair with his arms across his chest, wagging his head back and forth, looking at her hiney. He could smell her sexy confidence. Colonel Durant wondered what it is like to go to bed and lie next to a body like Sergeant Butler's every night. He thought she was damn good looking.

Durant was hailed back from the jungles of Central America, where he had been the Commander of a Green Beret, Psychological Warfare (Psy-War) Unit. He had been playing with the minds of revolutionaries who were fomenting unrest in a country that was a political ally of the U.S. The rebels had been destroying equipment owned by large oil companies. He had been sent down there to put an end to Big Oil losing big money. It made him feel like a glorified Pinkerton. He was combat-dropped into hot zones just to protect the assets of multi-national companies that happened to contribute to the campaigns of the right politicians.

CHAPTER 23

Durant was proud to be a mercenary. A hired gun who dealt in black ops, no written records, so he was interested to see the paper files for this mission. Durant had been pitching the knife into the air, almost the height of the ceiling, and catching it by its handle. But this time, he threw the knife high, then quickly put his hand palm down on the table and let it fall and stick into the desktop between his index and middle fingers. Sergeant Butler was impressed for about one second. She pegged him to have the emotional maturity of a teenage boy. In her mind, he didn't stand a chance with her.

"Colonel, here are your files."

She held up a four-inch-diameter disc of plastic with a half-inch hole in the middle.

Durant knew what it was, but played dumb in hopes of getting mercy sex. It was 1995. He had been crawling on his belly through jungles the past ten years. He was not yet a full citizen of the digital world. His blank face prompted the Sergeant to explain.

"Colonel, this is our newest technology. The information is loaded on this 'C.D.'" The pretty and professional Sergeant held up the CD for the Colonel, as a shield from his stare. He had been focused on her perky breasts.

Butler walked around the side of the Colonel's World War II era, wooden desk with dents and scratches all over it. Durant's knife gouges on its top only gave the desk more character. Butler flipped open what looked like a large plastic book to Durant. "This is a laptop computer." She popped open the bay for the C.D. and slid it in. "This is how you put it in, Colonel."

Durant thought he'd take his shot, "I thought you'd never show me how to stick it in, what with that wedding ring." Sergeant Butler smiled, big and warm. She had great teeth and bobbled her head back and forth like she thought the comment was cute. She gave no response. She was busy moving the little icon around on the screen, using some type of touch pad the Colonel had never seen before. She looked at the screen while she instructed him on how to run the computer.

"I hate computers. I never liked them back at West Point when we had to write our programs on punch cards. And I hate them now. They are no more user-friendly than an anvil. Give me a K-Bar and an M-16 and I'm good."

She looked out of the corner of her eye and bobbled her head again. "Colonel, I should advise you that this room is under constant video surveillance, although they do not have audio. These are all the files you must review by 1300 hours tomorrow, when General Crowe will be expecting a briefing from you."

Durant looked at the screen of only a dozen files. "This shouldn't take too long." Sergeant Butler started back around to the other side of the desk. "Each one of these files contains approximately two thousand pages of documents, except the last file." She showed him the summary, where all the other documents are boiled down to one hundred pages for a quick read.

"Well, I guess we should put on a big, ol' pot of coffee if we are gonna get through all this tonight."

"Sir, I've read every one of the documents. It is you who is going to be up late, Sir."

"By the way, where is the camera in the room?"

Butler snapped to attention with a sharp salute, "It's at my back, sir."

He took his eyes off her tight mid-section and raised them to look at her face. He stood to salute her in return and saw her stick her tongue slightly out between her pretty, white teeth in a sexy flicker. To a guy who had been in the jungle too long, it looked like an invitation. She did an about-face and walked away as Durant watched her stride at hip level. As she opened the door to leave, she thought to herself, *"Pretty big ego. But damned cute."*

Butler also thought to herself that, this time, it might be fun to play babysitter for C.I.A. Durant was hard and athletic. He was not like those chubby generals she was usually assigned to shadow and to stay on top of.

"I'll get your coffee, sir."

"Black, Sergeant, hot and black."

CHAPTER 23

# CHAPTER 24

# THE DIVORCE LAWYER

The St. Martinsville courtroom of the Honorable Judge Philip Hardcastle was of typical institutional design. An over-abundance of fluorescent lighting washed out whatever charm the architect had intended, using dark woods for the jury box and the Judge's bench. And in what appeared to be a modernistic-justice movement, there was no rail between the gallery and the counsel tables. I guess it was to make justice appear more accessible to the public. A musty smell told all who entered, the worn carpet needed cleaning. But Judge Hardcastle would not have it, claiming to all who complained, "I don't want my courtroom smelling like a Goddamn hospital. I spent six months in a V.A. hospital, and I don't want to go near another one, ever again."

The Bailiff chomped on an unlit cigar. By the telltale smell of the air, it was lit during off hours. My law partner, Dalton Boyle, and I were seated on each side of our client, Mrs. Allen. Opposing counsel sat across the huge six-foot-wide counsel table with his client, the ex-husband, Mr. Allen. We were there for a divorce case and, more specifically, for Mrs. Allen's three years of back child-support and spousal maintenance. Mr. Allen had avoided paying the money under the excuse that he had no job. We submitted the fruits of our investigation, presenting ample evidence he had been plying his trade as a plumber, for cash, many times over. He was hiding his money to avoid paying what was his duty under the law.

Mr. Allen wore his dark, thick hair in a pompadour, and he chewed gum like a cow chews its cud. He leaned over and whispered something in his counsel's ear. Mr. Allen smiled. His counsel's eyes darted back and forth behind horn rimmed glasses. But he kept his ferret face straight as a poker player's. He revealed nothing, except that he was a cold, hired gun. Because Mr. Allen didn't pay any child support, Mrs. Allen and her three young children had had to move out of their secure, middle-class, white-picket-fence neighborhood to a rural county. They lived in a rented, single-wide trailer that smelled like it had been used as a kennel, no matter how many times Mrs. Allen cleaned it.

Yet Mr. Allen had his girlfriends. And plenty of them. This plumber was good at "plumbing," you might say. But it was not his philandering that caused the argument between the parties. We were there to hear the Judge's determination. After four years of divorced separation, three of it without any financial support, the divorce court file had grown to be a foot thick, from motions and pleadings and forms and depositions that relayed a tale of sorrow.

We were there to bring home the bacon for Mrs. Allen and, hopefully, get a fee. Mrs. Allen had walked into our office three years before with only a fifty-dollar retainer that she had scratched, scrounged, and saved by working three jobs. No one else would represent her. No one else cared. No one would provide justice for the innocent in an unjust world. Dalton and I took way too many of these bleeding-heart cases. Even though we were conservative by nature, we still felt an innate need to help the helpless.

Dalton and I looked at the situation with a "can do" attitude. In the practice of law, that means you are gonna do a Hell of a lot of work and research and probably never get paid for it.

At meetings in chambers with Judge Hardcastle, my Lilliputian opposing counsel came off as a fee-generating twerp who was not there to settle the issues or try the case, but only to keep the case going to allow him to milk his client for more fees. To stall. To keep the court chasing after justice like a dog chasing its tail, with no intent of ever attaining justice. Dalton and I, on the other hand, came off as a couple of street brawlers. We filed emergency motions to avert Mrs. Allen and her three children being evicted from their dilapidated single-wide trailer. We did something different from all the other cookie-cutter motions and pleadings used by divorce counsel in the state. We sharpened an old, forgotten knife— the abandonment statute.

CHAPTER 24

To the Judge, an ex-Marine, it appeared we had figuratively fixed our bayonets and prepared for a down-and-dirty, fight-to-the-finish battle against that first-class scalawag, Mr. Allen, and his pinstriped mouthpiece.

Hardcastle read all the briefs in chambers and, after hearing our oral arguments in court, retired to his chambers to contemplate his result. Hardcastle, as opposed to the majority of other judges, liked to decide his cases immediately, rather than sit on them to let them gather dust and inflate the legal importance of the issues at hand.

We took a short break and walked outside with Mrs. Allen, who was a smoker. We allayed her fears and assured her that the money *should be* forthcoming, that her children and she *should not be* cast out onto the street. Her fears, though, were well founded. Mothers and children being put out on the street was a harsh result that occurred in divorce court every day in every state in America.

We went back inside to await the Judge's ruling. As I looked across the counsel table, I caught the darting eye of opposing counsel. And I saw it. The thing all warriors know when they see it—fear. Then I looked at Mr. Allen. He was white and clammy, like he was waiting on a possible death sentence. Their briefs had recited the same case law for the past two years, and the facts had grown worse and worse as time went by. They had thought they could outlast Mrs. Allen, who didn't have any money for attorney fees to begin with. They had thought we'd ditch our client, since we had not been paid for a couple of years.

They figured wrong.

The Bailiff swung open the door, and announced the entry of the Judge, and commanded that all stand in his presence. Hardcastle, with black robes flowing, ascended the bench. His Bailiff ordered all to take their seats.

Hardcastle made his ruling like a Marine attacks. He delivered it loud and clear, "Mr. Allen, you are ordered to attend Anger Management Classes." Then he got to the best part, "I am ruling in favor of Mrs. Allen for all of the $60,000.00, three years' back child support and spousal maintenance, *plus* $16,000.00 attorneys' fees. All of this will be paid for by Mr. Allen out of the sale of his thirty-five-foot Scarab racing boat."

The gavel never sounded louder to my opposition.

Dalton was the first to jump up, then Mrs. Allen, then me. We had justice. As I hugged Mrs. Allen, I looked at the faces of opposing counsel and his client. They were the faces of drowning men.

CHAPTER 24

# CHAPTER 25

# LIES

I ran a short rhyme through my head. *The shoemaker toils with leather and laces, the blacksmith hammers steel upon steel, and the lawyer sews truth over lies, to tailor his client's deal.* I had constructed that little poem to remind me that dealing with lying was a fact-of-life for a lawyer. After I began practicing law, I realized the worst part of the lying is not when the other side doesn't tell the truth, it is when my own client was lying to the judge and me.

Dalton and I walked to the elevator with a little bit of a swagger. We won! It felt good. We reveled in our success.

"Hell of an argument there, counselor. That spousal abandonment statute hasn't been used for thirty years. Stopped hubby's lawyer cold."

We turned the corner into the fifth-floor elevator bay.

"Old laws are like old knives. You just gotta sharpen 'em and know how to throw them," I said.

"Yeah, but Harvard Law didn't teach you to throw knives. The Marine Corps did."

"Ooo-Rah."

Dalton was making reference to my career in the Marine Corps, which included a stint as a knife-fighting instructor at the Marine Corps base located in Quantico, Virginia. I longed for the days when I could trust a blade of steel. In the jungle, like in the practice of law, you must watch your 360-degree perimeter to make sure someone wasn't going to take you from behind. But in the Marine Corps, when you did meet the enemy, you knew what to do and you took care of business. In practicing law, everything is conducted on the pretense of civility. Our adversarial system of justice presumes lying, cheating, and stealing and builds in a number of procedures, devices, and rules of evidence that address that recurrent problem.

People lie. We are the only species that lies. The judicial system deals with our worst side—as liars. People lied ten thousand years ago, and they will lie in the future. But it bothered me that we, as lawyers and as truth seekers, could not trust each other. Not all of us. It made me jaded about why I chose to become a lawyer and leave the honor of the Marine Corps.

*I wondered.*

*Are both parties to a lawsuit telling the truth? Maybe both are lying in order to find the truth that lies between.*

I was stuck in an industry based on lies.

CHAPTER 25

# CHAPTER 26

# GET A LIFE

Our little victory party moved out into the courthouse's main hallway. It looked like a nondescript walkway, with the courtrooms along either side. The fourth-floor elevator foyer was in an alcove down the hall and to the right.

During the hearing, I saw Dalton now and then dart flirting looks towards the young, sexy court reporter. She was busy working the keys of her stenographer's machine. As we walked out, Dalton again tried to catch her eye as she folded up her machinery and walked back to her office. No dice.

Mrs. Allen had no intention of riding the elevator down with her ex-husband, so she stalled and grabbed my sleeve to slow our walk towards the elevator. She thanked Dalton for believing in her and for being charitable enough to take her case on a pittance of a retainer. She explained, were it not for Dalton, she and her children would be destitute and only another statistic of the long list of homeless.

Mrs. Allen then turned her thanks and comments to me. She looked at me and tugged on my sleeve as her tears began to flow. She smiled through her tears of joy.

"I will never forget the first time I came to the office and you counseled me about my case. You threw those knives into the wall at a target, and it scared the holy Hell out of me."

We all laughed about my infamous counseling techniques. I employed them because I had been trained in the Marine Corps in rescue situations. The person you were rescuing was usually so traumatized that he did not understand what you were saying to him. So we Marines were taught to show non-verbal signs of what should be done. They leave a much more effective impact, so to say. And they create the action needed to get a client moving and believing in herself and her case.

I knew, as a divorce lawyer, I should do much the same thing because the women we represented were the equivalent of hostages or prisoners of war, who had been battered, bankrupted, psychologically traumatized, brainwashed, and physically, mentally, and spiritually violated by despotic men with no honor. America's own little multitude of Saddam Husseins and Mohamar Khaddafis. These were women who had been ruled by terror and fear, and they had the courage to walk into our office for help.

Sure, I could see their eyes bug out. And some even grabbed their purse handles and started for the door after they saw me take the knives, lined up neatly on my desk top, and throw them, one by one, into precise areas of the silhouette target on my law office wall.

In Mrs. Allen's instance, I counseled her, "I understand you and your children have a lot of emotional pain." I threw a knife into the red heart painted on the black silhouette. "You came to the right place because we know the law." I whipped the same-sized knife into the top of the head of the silhouette.

Laughter is important to combat troops, to juries, and as a way of developing a rapport with your client. "I reviewed the file, and your husband's case is weak." I purposefully selected a tiny knife, only about three inches long from tip of blade to end of hilt. I threw it directly into the crotch of the silhouette. It stuck out and downward from the target, at a impotent angle. Mrs. Allen's mouth dropped open in astonishment. She knew I was either nuttier than a rabid raccoon or I was her savior. Her white knight, who would ride into battle and defeat her enemy to save her children.

I ended the nonverbal reinforcement with a long-bladed, red-handled knife. I flung it into a white pocket chalked onto the target. "And don't worry about the legal fees, ma'am, we're gonna hit him where it hurts."

Ms. Allen laughed so hard, she bent over and slapped her knee. She loved my knife throwing. It gave her confidence. I know it's a strange way for a lawyer to advise his client. But it works for me. That is the way I practice law.

CHAPTER 26

We said our good-byes and hugged Ms. Allen again. It was a true victory to celebrate. In divorce law, you have your wins and your losses, and you get paid so seldom that the emotional celebration helps. Dalton and I found ourselves at the elevator lobby where I stabbed my finger into the down button. Right as the perky and pretty court reporter walked past us. Dalton picked up the scent of her pheromones and left my side like a love-seeking missile that had just been launched.

"Oh, gee whiz, Mike, I forgot to get a copy of the Judge's order. I'll catch you back at the office."

"Don't give me that bullshit. I saw you making googly eyes at the court reporter. Go ask her out and do what young studs do."

Dalton chased after the leggy brunette. But he stopped and turned back to look at me.

"But, uh, hey, Mike-o, why don't I see if she's got a friend. Maybe we could double date?" Dalton scrunched the shoulders of his dark-blue, striped, two thousand-dollar Brooks Brothers suit coat. The same suit his parents bought him as a law-school-graduation present.

Dalton had known me my whole life. We grew up boyhood friends, and there wasn't a stream, a meadow, a forest, a ball field, a dance hall, or even a library in a five-mile radius that he and I had not frequented together. In fact, Dalton taught me one of the greatest lessons of life: how to pick up a crawfish without getting pinched.

We never lied to each other. No matter if the truth hurt and cut to the bone. We had learned that it did no good to point the finger at each other when, as boys, our baseball went through Mrs. Leonard's front, picture window.

"I mean you gotta get a life, Mike-O, you gotta get out."

I knew immediately what he was referring to. My sister Bridget, and me staying home with her. Over the past year, it had progressed to the point where I left the house only for work, grocery shopping, or exercise. And it had been that snoring, boring existence ever since I came home from Boston. Fresh out of law school and right before Father died. A whole year of babysitting is how it felt to me.

Dalton celebrated his bachelorhood with unmatched pride. He made it his duty to date as many different girls as possible. There were some weeks when he was booked for four different girls. All of them pre-qualified for good looks and good jobs. I watched his galloping through girls' hearts with fraternal admiration. And I endured his constant ribbing to "get a life," taking it all with a grain of salt. But Dalton saw in me what I did not. I was playing up my own pity party. It allowed me to stay at home and lick my figurative wounds.

I waved Dalton off like he was speaking nonsense, "Nah, you know I promised Father I'd look after Bridget."

"Look after doesn't mean wiping her nose twenty four, seven." The truthfulness between the two of us was quite often brutal. Dalton poured more salt on my emotional wounds.

"Hey, you remember I have a degree in clinical psychology."

While I was marching around at the Air Force Academy, Dalton had been at Stanford, picking up a Bachelor's and a Master's in psychology. He then changed careers for a reason that he traced to a mishap with his live-in girlfriend, Sharon. She left Dalton for an assistant professor of paleontology, who offered her a two-year stint on her hands and knees, sifting through the mud of Mesopotamia, searching for some long-lost archeological secret of our roots. Dalton was devastated. But being the trained clinical psychologist he was, he performed psychoanalysis and counseling on himself. His result? Law school and a new career would solve everything.

I played along with his fifty-cent opinion about how ball bearings bounced around between the ears of my jar head.

He put down his brief case and started counting off reasons one by one, holding his fingers up to my face and closing in for the kill like a trial lawyer making the strongest points to a jury.

"My diagnosis is you are hyper-responsible, a hopeless caretaker, juggling guilt feelings, all bound up neat and tidy into a psychological, strangling spasm of overriding maternal instincts. Combined, it has you tied like a horse to the emotional post you call home—your sister, Bridget."

"What's all that mean, Dr. Freud?"

"It means you need Bridget more than she needs you. You gotta let her go, Mike. You gotta let her go, McRain."

The elevator doors opened, and I tried to evade Dalton's unwanted message by climbing aboard and pressing the button to go down. Dalton yelled into the narrowing gap as the doors closed, "You're not doing her or yourself any favors by hanging around, acting like a professional babysitter. She's a big girl and you gotta let her go. Mike-O, you gotta let Bridget go."

I stood inside the elevator, holding my briefcase with both hands in front of me. I shook my head while the elevator doors shuttered out Dalton's harping advice.

The air in the elevator smelled like burnt machine oil. And I wondered if it would make the trip. I thought to myself as I rode down, *"What the Hell? Let the damned elevator fall. It would make it easier than facing up to the reality of Dalton's words."*

I shook my head in disbelief and spoke out loud to the empty elevator.

"Let her go? Overriding maternal instincts?"

# CHAPTER 27

# A GOOD IRISH FIGHT

The elevator stopped at the third floor on its way down. The doors slid open to a scene I never would have expected. A huge house of a man had his back to the elevator's open door. He held what appeared to be a knife up to the throat of a woman he was restraining and dragging into the elevator. It looked to me like I got to the party a little late. And there I was—a party crasher.

It seems that someone on the F.B.I.'s team transporting an infamous serial murderer had forgotten to give Robert Pells his meds. Robert "The Slasher" Pells made big-time media notoriety by pleading guilty to murdering no less than eleven women. He didn't like guns. He was afraid of them. Instead, he used large butchers' knives to slash the nice ladies' throats. He was caught, up in Montana, living in the woods, his victims' bones pushed through his earlobes in a mirrored behavior—he really wanted to be a girl. But according to Pells, his parents denied him his birthright. Pells should have taken a look in the mirror and concluded his six-foot-eight-inch, three-hundred-twenty-pound frame, that bench pressed four hundred pounds, was not intended by God to bear children.

Nevertheless, Pells' frustration mounted on successive trips to the state penitentiary for rape and assaults against women. And for one attack against a man in prison who looked like a woman. But when Pells got out of prison the third time, he decided he'd had enough. He thought up a plan. Take the hair and fingernails from his victims and a bone or two here and there and sort of dress up to try to gain a feminine persona.

In a crime spree that lasted three and a half years and stretched throughout twelve states, Pells plied his trade of butchery in pursuit of finding his inner woman. They caught Mr. Pells alive by shooting him with a gun the state of Montana used to tranquilize bears for transport. He was big. He was powerful. He was mean to the point of evil. And due to his borderline personality disorder, he really did not have any appreciation for manners or any other societal custom.

He was brought to the St. Martinsville Courthouse for extradition proceedings, to officially arraign him after a long journey, courtesy of the good folks of Montana. He admitted to the F.B.I. that he murdered one of his victims in St. Martinsville. She was a prostitute who he befriended at the corner of Washington and Twentieth. The police found her dead body, without ears or hands, in high weeds on a vacant lot three blocks from where he met her. Pells admitted he took her ears because he liked her turquoise earrings. There had been no fingerprints or I.D. on the corpse for investigators to go on. And Pells liked her long fingers—the skin was so soft on his face, reminiscent of his mother's. Jane Doe #17, as the homicide detectives labeled her, was a young freelancer who had a clean record and a blank trail to follow. No pimp to question. She had been written off as an unsolved case. But with the capture of "The Slasher" and his frank admission, it was removed from the cold-case filing cabinet and prosecuted to the hilt. Jane Doe #17 found justice.

Two minutes before I got on the elevator, Robert Pells was leaning his gargantuan frame against the bench of Judge Hilton Summers. Pells motioned the judge to lean forward. The big man was talking in whispers, and he motioned towards his throat as though he was having trouble speaking. After the judge leaned in too close, Pells finally whispered, "I have nothing to lose." He lurched up with his manacled hands and wrapped the chains around Summers' neck. He braced his feet against the dais and immediately snapped the judge's neck with a loud crunch. He broke the chain of the handcuff by slamming it down on the corner of the stenographer's banister.

Slasher Pells seemed to have a natural flair for the dramatic. He was onstage.

Slasher threw off the guards trying to subdue him. He grabbed a tazer from a guard who was about to shoot him and shot it into another guard. He broke a third guard's arm and punched out two more. He bolted for the door as quick as his leg manacles would allow. Due to the established, ill-conceived policy of the St. Martinsville Courts, none of the guards had a firearm in the courtroom. A simple twelve-gauge pump shotgun with double-aught shot would have prevented the whole mishap. But I'm digressing.

CHAPTER 27

All this was happening when Dalton and I were in the elevator foyer. One floor up, waiting to ride the elevator down. Down on the Slasher's floor was a beautiful woman with a two-associate entourage behind her. Her name was DeeDee DeVillay.

"The Slasher" bolted out of the courtroom right when DeeDee was walking past the courtroom's doors. She was filing her nails, inattentive. Slasher grabbed DeeDee and the steel nail file and took her hostage. "The Slasher" held the steel blade of the file against DeeDee's jugular vein. He quickly pressed the button for the elevator, threatening to kill DeeDee. He swore.

"I'll kill her; I swear to God I will kill her. Quick as I killed the others! Back off!" "The Slasher" said.

The doors of the elevator opened, and the Slasher backed in towards me. I grabbed the Slasher by the hair and, using an Aikido hold, pulled the Slasher's hand holding the nail file away from DeeDee's throat. I pulled the Slasher's arm around and down, so that the nail file stuck into his thigh. He howled like an animal.

After Slasher loosened his hold on DeeDee, I put my foot on her butt and shoved her out of the elevator. Her broad-brimmed, black designer hat fell from her head and into the elevator.

DeeDee looked back into the elevator. For just a moment, our eyes met. I saw she was a beauty. The elevator doors closed.

I figured first things first: Slasher needed a lesson in who was boss. I feigned sensitivity and worry: two courtesies I had always had trouble extending to violent criminals.

"Oh, dear. We have a problem child here," I said.

Outside the elevator in the lobby, the security guards were in a panic.

"The elevator is stuck!" said a guard named Pete, who was trying the doors.

The guards pried the doors apart to reveal the elevator was gone. They looked down and saw the elevator, stuck between two floors. Howls from an indiscernible voice were heard, pleading for mercy, for help, amid a blue streak of curse words.

Pete, a worried deputy, said, "We gotta get down there. It sounds like the Slasher is tearing him limb from limb."

An older deputy, Orville, chewed on a cigar and thought about how this particular hostage scenario had never before presented itself in the thirty-three years he served as a protector of the St. Martinsville justice system. Chief Courthouse Deputy Orville Dweekins was well trained and erred on the side of caution.

His eyes lit with excitement at the thought of strack, paramilitary, gung-ho bastards crawling all over his courthouse. He got into it. He smiled. Orville bit harder on the butt of his three-day-old domestic cigar and said, "Call S.W.A.T."

Thirty minutes later, a T.V. reporter was standing on the courthouse steps reporting the situation. "We have an apparent hostage situation. Recent information indicates that local attorney Michael O'Brien McRain is stuck in an elevator with admitted serial murderer Robert Pells a/k/a "The Slasher." We fear the Slasher might have another victim, as howls and screams have been heard coming from the elevator. The S.W.A.T. team is trying to get into the elevator as we speak."

The S.W.A.T. team descended by rappelling onto the elevator. They inserted a thin, camera cable into the elevator. It showed on a small screen what was happening in the elevator. The S.W.A.T. Team members started to laugh.

Orville had been a deputy at the courthouse a long time. He had never seen anything like it. Orville looked down the elevator shaft. He couldn't figure out what the S.W.A.T. team was laughing about. He shrugged his shoulders and said to Deputy Pete, "Those S.W.A.T. boys are sadistic bastards. They are laughing while the Slasher cuts up a lawyer."

At dusk, the reporter continued her coverage with a news flash, "We have breaking news that the hostage situation has ended. The elevator is moving, and demands have been made for the release of the hostage. We anticipate the release to be soon."

As the elevator doors opened, dozens of policemen were standing there, their weapons drawn and pointed at the door. I came off the elevator, riding on the back of the Slasher, using my belt as a reign and wearing Dee Dee's broad-brimmed hat, like a cowboy riding a bull. I waved to the crowd. Then I dismounted and let the Slasher stand up. Slasher's face was all puffy and bruised. And plenty bloody.

CHAPTER 27

I walked past the police chief, "He's all yours, Chief."

"Mr. Pells, don't you have an apology to make?" I said.

Pells acknowledged by holding up his hand. It sported two disjointed fingers. "Uh- yeah, I'm sorry for holding the nail file to that nice lady's throat. It won't happen again."

I asked a policeman where the lady was who I had saved. He said, "She left with another lawyer about ten minutes after you saved her."

"She didn't stay to see how it turned out?"

"No, she and the other lawyer were talking about a derailment he wanted her to go to up in Wyoming."

"Wyoming?"

The policeman nodded, "She's a lawyer. Her name is DeeDee DeVillay. She left with her partner, Felix Falic."

The policeman saw I was not well informed.

"They're the richest lawyers in the state."

I was incredulous that DeeDee was so wrapped up in her law career that she couldn't wait around to thank me. The man who saved her life. But I didn't save her to get a pat on the back. There was a hostage situation. I just reacted the way I was trained. I was more surprised than hurt by DeeDee leaving. I smiled a knowing smile at the cop while my mind flashed my conclusion about DeeDee and her partner.

*Warning. Greed. Shallow people alert.*

I met up with Dalton, who patiently waited for me to finish with the police. We walked towards the exit and exchanged notes in a low tone of voice. Dalton knew I had been in worse scrapes than that.

He laughed at the Slasher's weapon. "A nail file?"

I nodded and laughed, too. Dalton knew how I felt about bullies. Pells was a murderer. That only made him an even bigger, more villainous, bully to me. A murderer—the ultimate bully. Dalton couldn't wait for me to give him all the juicy details about how I destroyed a serial murderer. And I got to do it without anybody seeing me, or so I *thought* nobody had seen me, give Pells my special, Marine Corps, crash course in manners.

Another policeman stopped me at the door. He wanted to ask questions. I said, "You can ask me any question you want. You know where I live. Otherwise, speak to my lawyer." I pointed my thumb towards Dalton.

The policeman said, "Just one thing. What happened in there?"

I turned around and said, "We set up some direct lines of communications." I was evasive. I shrugged my shoulders. "We had a meeting of the minds."

Dalton and I walked out of the courthouse towards my car. I didn't tell the police what I told my confidant, Dalton: that if you cut off the air supply to a man's lungs, he becomes very compliant. The Slasher reacted like a typical bully. He was a problem student in M.O.M.'s Marine Corps school of decorum and etiquette. But after I made a slight change to his oxygen supply, the Slasher understood I was there to teach him some manners.

Dalton and I got into my convertible Mustang. I was pumped up and had to cool down. I turned on the stereo to a U.S.M.C. marching cadence and roared off into the night. I made Dalton suffer and listen to my way of life:

A one, two, three, four,
Marine Corps!
One, two, three, four,
Marine Corps!
The Army, Navy was not for me,
Air Force was just too easy.
What I need was a little bit more,
I need a life that is hard core.


Paris Island where it all began,
A little rock with a lots of sand.
I can't talk about Hollywood,
San Diego and it's all good.
PT drills all day long,
Doing them from dusk till dawn.
A one, two, three, four,
Marine Corps!

# CHAPTER 28

# DESERTER!

The hectic day took a heavy toll on me, sapping my energy down to nil. It was against my nature to be that tired. I had been a Special Forces operative, able to stay awake for a week at a time, during combat or just to wait for the right moment to ambush an adversary. But practicing law was different. And I was learning that the concentration required to maintain a vigilant look-out was not the same concentration required to analyze complex theories of law when I had not slept for three days. I was reading a daily dose of lengthy legal opinions that were much less exciting than the Sears catalogue. Such is the life of a lawyer. Conducting a cross-examination in trial is the closest thing to ambushing an opponent a lawyer will ever see.

I was accustomed to high-stress days as divorce lawyer. But that day was especially demanding, with the Slasher escapade and dodging the media hounds. It was uncharacteristic for me to be in bed early—by midnight.

I knelt next to my bed, crossed myself, bowed my head, and said a quick "Hail Mary," an "Our Father," and a "Glory Be." Not much more than a token offering to God, given my sleepy stupor. Gunny stood guard on his bedside rug while I crawled into bed. I lay in a cocoon of deep and restful sleep, oblivious to the world.

*As soon as I fell asleep, I found myself back on "The Constitution." Captain Carion wasted no time. He immediately subjected me to a flogging with a cat-of-nine-tails swung by the gray bony hand of Mr. Fetid. The fish hooks on the end of each tail maximized the pain and tore of my flesh. The pain seemed real but I did not wake up in my bed even while Captain Carion spewed a diatribe of accusations already well known to my soul.*

*"You are a deserter, you will always be a deserter. I wish I could kill you. But I can't. The Admiral won't let me. Not yet. I'm your only chance for redemption, McRain, but you have an impossible task. Nobody has ever been acquitted of Perjury on Admiralty for over three hundred years. So you have to find another way to win, McRain."*

*He kicked me hard in the ribs and had the dragoons douse me with seawater after Carion gave me another twenty lashes. My face was pushed into the deck, where all I could see was the murky mixture of a Marine's blood and seawater. I was being dominated, and I hated it.*

I woke up with my face in a puddle of coffee at our kitchen table. I was so fatigued from sleep deprivation that I had no recollection of getting out of bed and walking downstairs to the kitchen. I leapt to my feet and used a dishtowel to mop up the pool of coffee.

Bridget tapped into the kitchen with Ace by her side.

"No sleep last night?"

"Yeah, Bridge, how'd you know?"

"Michael, I went into your room. Things lying all over the floor. Big mess.

You okay?"

I was embarrassed. "I guess I have not been able to sleep. It's kind of like somebody is pushing me on."

Bridget started getting eggs and bacon out of the refrigerator. I did not see the devious smirk on her face as I stumbled back to my room for a brief nap at 6:00 a.m. My older sister was pushing my buttons and playing me like one of her chess pieces. I went back to sleep wondering about my dream. And what in the heck is "Perjury on Admiralty".

# CHAPTER 29

# JIMMY HOFFA'S ANNIVERSARY

I woke to the smell of honey-cured bacon burning on the stove and the sound of Bridget's shrieks in the kitchen. I raced downstairs and found Bridget with a pile of pots and skillets already in the sink, her burned and disastrous experiments at cooking. Her present attempt was a trio of sunny-side-up eggs with toast, all of which were smoldering. She pushed the same toast down into the toaster for the sixth time. She was cooking the eggs on an ungreased, cast-iron skillet, producing three round, black objects that were supposed to be eggs, although they looked more like hockey pucks. I took control of the situation over Bridget's belligerent objection, just to save the house from burning down.

"What the Hell are you doin', Bridget? "

"I cook. I cook. Move. I cook."

She reached for her shillelagh. The Equalizer. I saw she was going to try to hit me with the shillelagh, and I quickly grabbed it from her hand. I walked to the back door and pitched it out into the backyard. Whereupon Bridget clipped me in the back with a rolling pin. I swore and snatched the rolling pin from Bridget. I threw that in the backyard, too.

Old habits die hard. "Bridgy, you gotta learn. Ya can't fix everything by whacking people with that goddamned white stick of yours. Might does not make right." I knew I was being a hypocrite, remembering my Force Recon days.

Bridget took hold of her grip harness for Ace and stomped up the stairs, snorting a litany of saints' names associated with cooking. "Saint Zita, help me with my cooking. Saint John Bosco, help me change my little brother." She stormed from the kitchen to her bedroom. She slammed the door and found her seat in front of her altar.

Bridget grabbed her bottle of holy water. She shook blessed water on the tin soldier and on a small model of a four-mast sailing ship.

I was downstairs in the kitchen, waiting for Bridget's anticipated descent from upstairs. I cursed my situation. But I still resigned myself to prison life—to taking care of my sister the rest of my life. While the coffee was brewing, I stepped out onto the porch. I walked to the chessboard. The time had come. I moved my knight to put Bridget's king in check.

Back inside, I was scrubbing scorched pots and pans when a newscast came over the television. The newswoman was talking about July 30, 1995, the twentieth anniversary of the disappearance of legendary labor leader, James Riddle Hoffa.

The talking head on CNN rattled off a number of theories for Hoffa's disappearance and an equal number of possible locations where his body might have been disposed of. I poured myself some coffee and chuckled to myself about the ridiculous notion that someone might discover what actually happened to Hoffa. I thought the answer was obvious.

As in chess, power checks and neutralizes power. Organized pawns can neutralize a king if the pawns are moved by a practiced hand.

I figured it this way. History taught me that whoever did in Hoffa had to be an organization so powerful that it could cover up murdering the most popular labor leader in the history of the United States. A man to whom some United States presidents owed their positions and who had called Hoffa "Sir." And it had to be an organization with enough internal discipline to keep a lid on the whole affair. Tight.

In my head, my analysis generated a very short list of the deadly powerful. To me, the "Why" of the whole Hoffa disappearance didn't matter. And it did not seem to concern the rest of America. The forty-hour work week; retirement you could count on not being stolen by corporate raiders; health care, both for the working and the retired; and jobs for Americans—true, red–blooded Americans—were long foregone conclusions by over-confident Americans with short memories. Much like the victorious heroes of World

War II, Hoffa's gutsy victories for the working man were forgotten, too soon. And it angered me that all that Hoffa was being remembered for were cocktail-party jokes and stand-up comedians on T.V., making money dissing the man: how he died and where he was buried.

He was a leader who fought for the little man to put real food in real people's mouths—millions and millions of them, and their children, and their grandchildren. Hundreds of millions of them worldwide.

I tried to lure Bridget downstairs for breakfast by bribing Ace. I yelled upstairs, "Ace, I got some treats for you." Bridget's door made a creaking sound. Perhaps we could coexist, but for how long? It would have to be a truce for the time being.

I got back to thinking about Jimmy Hoffa. I shook my head and took another slug of coffee. I thought to myself, *"There is no way any one will ever know what happened in the most intriguing, missing-person, cold case in American history. What really happened to Jimmy Hoffa?"*

# CHAPTER 30

# A GUILTY CONSCIENCE

DeeDee set an all-time record for her firm signing up new clients. It was a Hellish three-day marathon of in-house doctors' examinations of asbestosis and silicosis, Hog-Head- Union claimants. Fresh meat. At least, the doctors worked twelve-hour shifts. But DeeDee had to stay through it all, for fear a claimant would walk away to another Designated lawyer. "Client capture" is what the firm's accounting department labeled signing up new R.I.O. clients. They used those numbers to calculate her bonuses, which were tied to the number of new clients she brought into the firm. Two hours of sleep in the past seventy-two had siphoned away all her strength.

She stumbled into her penthouse, exhausted and feeling like her innards had been sucked out. It was that damned Texas habanera chili the local and general rail-union chairmen had pushed on her the night before. That and the tequila. DeeDee could still see the worm at the bottom of the bottle disappear. She shook her head at the things she did for money. She thought she should have offered them an extra thousand apiece in bribe money just so she didn't have to eat the chili.

The satchel of cash wasn't her money anyway. It was all funny money that got reported to the I.R.S. as entertainment and travel expenses. She tried to visualize an I.R.S. prosecutor leaning on the railing of a jury box at her trial, if she ever got caught. A trial she hoped would never come. He'd say something that inflamed the jury's senses, *"Imagine that: a law firm that spends over 1.3 million dollars per year on entertainment."*

A jury, sitting in judgment of lying lawyers, would be much too anxious for a guilty verdict. Then the court could drag DeeDee into the penalty phase of the trial. The sentencing. The prosecutor DeeDee's imagination had conjured would refer to the long line of witnesses. Union men, who had received immunity, and testified that they received bribes to send railroad personal-injury cases to her firm.

In DeeDee's mind, "*Guilty*" would be the verdict for sure. That is, *only if she got caught.*

# CHAPTER 31

# CIA'S LITTLE SECRET

On August 2, a bright, full moon shone high in the Virginia sky, unbeknownst to Colonel Dirk Durant. In his underground office, he waded through the thousands of documents and reports regarding the Hoffa Protocol. This was a mission, the likes of which he had never imagined. He wondered, *"Why am I at the Transportation Command?"* After graduating from West Point, he had gone into the Airborne Rangers and became a Green Beret. Army Sniper School followed. And, as a natural progression from that, he served a two-year stint crawling around on his belly throughout the Central and South American jungles, blowing away third-world revolutionaries, drug lords, and unwanted dictators. He kept America safe from folks you would not want to invite to Thanksgiving dinner.

A sniper spends weeks alone in hostile territory, absolutely quiet; you move, then sit and wait. It gives you time to think. Sniper duty is awfully tough on a marriage. You can't talk about your job with your better half, *"Yeah, honey, I had a rough day. Had to put a 7.66 mm round through a drug lord's head. And I caught a round in my right calf on my way out. Just like Friday night traffic on the Beltway, I got delayed; the damned extract was late and at the wrong landing zone. Sorry, I'll be home late for dinner."* Snipers, like sailors, go six months or longer without seeing their spouses.

About the time that Durant's second wife was killed and his second-born was one year old, he decided he wanted to provide a more stable environment for his children. Bright and articulate Durant decided on a career in psychology. The Army paid for his schooling with a secret agenda in mind. Colonel Durant earned a Master's Degree in Psychology from Vanderbilt. He had eight years remaining before he could draw a full pension, and, as a result, the Army decided to put him in the Psychological Warfare Unit stationed at Fort Campbell, Kentucky. In Psy-War, he was able to conduct mass hysteria and fear campaigns on third-world countries and revolutionary organizations Uncle Sam wanted to intimidate and dissuade from fighting.

Durant became a master at screwing with people's heads. His previous assignment had been in the jungles of Colombia where he served as an "advisor" to the Colombian government. Durant taught them how best to intimidate the cocaine drug lords to stop the flow of cocaine into America. He enjoyed that assignment, even the killing of a Catholic priest who had been suspected of harboring the drug lords' cadre. That one was tough. He had to supervise the Colombian Army throwing open the doors of a quaint, little Catholic church, nestled in the Andes mountains, and march down the center aisle to shoot and kill the priest with a machine gun as he was giving Mass. Colonel Durant figured the priest's violent death would make a bigger impact on the general population if there were hundreds of witnesses. Word would spread fast not to cooperate with the drug lords.

Dirk Durant certainly had a flare for the dramatic. So it was a big surprise when he read something on the algae-green screen that made him leap to his feet in astonishment.

"That's who killed Jimmy Hoffa? Jimmy fuckin' Hoffa? No fucking way!"

Colonel Durant said it out loud, to an empty room. Durant put his hands on either side of his head and massaged his temples because he couldn't believe what he was reading.

"They are funded by who? No way. That's impossible. How could they keep this secret?" He stabbed his switchblade knife into the top of his desk and forcefully blinked, shaking his head back and forth. He could not believe the magnitude of this secret. It was the answer to the biggest, cold-case murder in American history.

*"Why? How was it set up? Who decided to neutralize Hoffa?"* His mind was spinning because he had been in the assassin business for years, and he was never given a hint of any of this information. He had a keen interest in the art of killing. He wanted to know more. He read on.

CHAPTER 31

"Their organization is big. Huge. Why haven't I heard of these people?" Durant stood up from his seat and paced back and forth while he looked at the laptop.

A commanding voice came from behind him. "That's because it's secret. And it was a mistake." Durant turned quickly. He was astonished that someone could get into the room without him knowing it.

Colonel Durant sprang into a full-brace salute. Lieutenant-General Crowe walked in and tossed his hat on Durant's knife stabbed into the top of the desk.

"At ease. I mean, killing Jimmy Hoffa was a mistake. The rest was planned."

General Crowe walked around the desk and shook Durant's hand.

"I think with all your reading, you must have learned about our little Hoffa Protocol."

"Sir, I was advised the briefing wasn't until 1300 hours. You are early."

"I know, Colonel. Standard procedure for a Field Commander. I needed to see how seriously you would take this assignment since it is a bit different from your typical, combat jump-into-a-jungle circle jerk."

"Field Commander? This is a desk job. I am trained to be in a jungle, neutralizing terrorists and third-world revolutionaries."

"No, Colonel. As bland as it looks, the Transportation Command is the most important one in the D.O.D. Take a look."

Lieutenant-General Crowe reached under the ancient, battered desktop and pressed a button. A whole wall slowly dropped down. A floor-to-ceiling window was revealed. It overlooked a room the size of a football field. The far wall had T.V. monitors showing strategic harbors, highways, railways, and airports from coast to coast. The floor was full of desks topped with computer monitors. Uniformed personnel whizzed around the room. Durant looked on in amazement.

"This is bigger than N.O.R.A.D.'s nuclear-missile monitor bank at Cheyenne Mountain, Colorado."

"So I guess when they gave you a tour of Cheyenne Mountain's nuclear-missile center, they didn't show you the back door to the mountain, where we have an duplicate of this Ops Center?"

"You're kidding?"

"No, and after I explain this to you, you will understand why we've been more concerned with the Jimmy Hoffas of the world than we have been worrying about nuclear war."

CHAPTER 31

# CHAPTER 32

# THE HOFFA PROTOCOL

Colonel Durant's world exploded. He was trained in war and how to deal with shady leaders on foreign soil in order to mount insurrections and rebellions. Some of his best work had been with the Afghani insurgents against the mighty Soviet Army. They won that one. And not just because they intimidated the Soviet Union. The C.I.A.-backed rebels demoralized Ivan with guerrilla tactics, using roadside bombs. U.S. shoulder-fired missiles shot down Russian Hind helicopters by scores.

The Afghanis ran Ivan out of their country by taking away Russia's ability to move its men and war machines on the ground. Logistics. Everything that matters in the world boils down to logistics—the ability to move goods from one point in the world to the location where they are needed. In America, Wal-Mart built its retail empire by being better at logistics than its competition. In Afghanistan, the Afghanis cut off the roads with ambushes and bombs so as to put a tourniquet on the Soviet Union's logistical artery. Russia simply could not airlift into Afghanistan everything needed to wage war.

Durant was ashamed that he never thought of the logistics inside the United States the same way. The whole country would come to a stop, *everything*, if someone shut down the railroad trains.

Durant pointed to the far corner of the massive control room. "Why is that screen black?"

"Train derailment in Wyoming. We leave one live screen on and black out another screen to show to the whole floor of personnel how severe the problem is in that region. Derailments and collapsed rail bridges are the highest priority. But then, again, *anything* that will stop a train from moving is our top priority. And that includes striking rail unions."

General Crowe waved his arms, showing stoppage and the seriousness of losing train service for America. "Railroads keep the refineries and the majority of electricity running. Without fuel, nothing moves. This is all C.I.A.'s secret love child," said Crowe.

"C.I.A.?"

"Yeah, but we carry it on the Pentagon's meteorology budget." Crowe pushed the button under the desk again, and the wall closed. "Listen, Colonel, you were handpicked by the President. He reminded me, in no uncertain terms, that not one U.S. President has ever been reelected, in the past fifty years, after there has been a prolonged rail strike."

Crowe sat on the desk corner. "Your mission is to get rid of the most serious security threat to America since Fidel Castro parked nukes ninety miles off our shores."

"Arab? Chinese? Communists?"

General Crowe pushed a file, with photos of Jake Casteel, across the desk to Durant and handed him a three-page document. "This is the speech President Truman gave to a joint session of Congress on May 24, 1947. The President directed me to order you to read that speech because it says everything about how serious this situation is." Durant glanced down at the speech and started to read through it.

"But, first, Colonel, I need you to understand who our target is. He's not a foreign spy. He's Jake Casteel, an American, an Eagle Scout, a Boy Scout Troop Leader, a national- champion swimmer, and a highly decorated vet."

Durant saw the file photos of Casteel in a Marine Corps uniform—a sergeant, no less. The highest functional rank in the Marine Corps, according to General Chesty Puller.

General Crowe stood and walked around the room, pacing with his arms across his chest. He explained to Durant that Casteel was the President of C.U.R.T.I.S., the International Rail Union. Casteel had promised to shut down the whole country with a primary strike if the Hog Head Union did not get a good contract. Apparently, the railroad workers had been working five years without a contract, and C.A.R.'s C.E.O., Sewill, was the Secretary of Transportation and the President's presidential campaign manager.

CHAPTER 32

Clearly, C.A.R. was trying to break the union. "So, Mr. Goody-two-shoes isn't a team player?" Durant said.

"Casteel seems to be an honest man. And everything he is doing is absolutely Constitutional. However, we have an economy to run and keep secure. If our economy is not running, the whole world's economy collapses."

Colonel Durant interrupted the General, "So we are going to do the dirty work in the union-busting war for Secretary Sewill and try to keep the world safe at the same time?"

"No. We are simply going to keep the trains running on time. You see, Casteel has to be stopped. But C.I.A. dictates we must follow the Hoffa Protocol. We can't kill him."

"And that's the theory that says if we kill a transportation union leader, it will spook the unions into wildcat strikes that can't be predicted or controlled. And those rail strikes will shut down the country much more than if Saddam Hussein set off a nuclear device in New York City?"

"Very good, Colonel. Economics 101. Logistics, logistics, logistics. I see you've been studying."

Colonel Durant looked at the photo of Casteel, giving a speech to railroad union men from the bed of a pick-up truck in Sacramento, California.

"Your resources will come from the railroad," said Lieutenant-General Crowe.

Crowe said, "They will be coordinated through our union operative, the lawyers' mafia boss, Adolph "Big Dutch" Van Killman. Durant looked at a photograph of Big Dutch Van Killman. Graying temples and a dapper dresser; he was an overconfident, organized-crime, rail oligarch, right smack dab in the middle of good-old, capitalistic America.

Colonel Durant dropped the photograph of Big Dutch on the desk. "I nsever knew America had a lawyer's mafia."

Crowe laughed. He said, "They don't advertise on the back of the phone book, if you know what I mean, but they are real. They have been our eyes and ears inside the rail union for the past fifty years."

Colonel Durant stood up and looked directly at General Crowe. "My experience with mafias tells me that we should just off Casteel and be done with it."

"Colonel. Transportation unions are touchier than land mines. Damned near anything can set them off. Follow the Hoffa Protocol." He pointed directly at Durant.

"That's an order."

Durant sat down and did not stir. He kept his eyes directly on Lieutenant-General Crowe. Crowe leaned across the desk and tapped Durant's shoulder, on the eagle signifying his Colonel's rank. "If you want a nice, shiny star, do not kill Casteel. Get Casteel convicted of perjury so he can't hold union office. That is your mission—plain and simple."

Lieutenant-General Wallace Crowe started to walk out, but stopped and turned around. "Remember when you are dealing with the lawyers' mafia, you must assert that you are the alpha male. Otherwise, they'll piss all over you and the whole goddamn operation."

"I'll tie my knots early, Sir," Durant said.

They broke their briefing with salutes.

CHAPTER 32

# CHAPTER 33

# OLD MEMORIES - OLD SCARS

She was a saint and a she-devil. She moved me, and she crushed me. She infuriated me on a daily basis with her mothering and her demeaning, know-it-all orders she dictated to me like she was the Mother Superior of her own convent. Bridget claimed she was my elder, and I had to obey her. Our relationship was yin and yang. I loved her, and I hated her. She was my sister. Blood. And I would forever protect her with all my being. But I had not realized, until I was eleven years old, that my blind, autistic sister, Bridget, was simultaneously an inescapable anchor around my neck and powerful fins on my back. I had long ago accepted that it was God and God alone who would be the only force that determined if I were to sink or swim, for my influence on Bridgey was minimal.

On a warm June day in 1969, Bridget and I were at the local park, just hanging out. Sort of babysitting each other. A no-good, scraggly bunch of young men piled out of a '68 Chevy Malibu, all jacked up in the back. They were ruffians I had never seen before. They strutted and stumbled into the park. And they claimed one of the picnic tables as their own territory. A brown bag was passed amongst them. The gang eventually saw Bridget walking by the pond with a rosary, saying prayers to herself. She was feeling her way around the bank with her red-tipped cane. The punks started calling across the water at Bridget, making fun of the "retard." They taunted her. They mocked how Bridget walked with a flimsy, white cane. She had no dog to protect her and no fluent tongue to tell them to go to Hell when they blocked her, circling around her, chanting "Retard! Retard! Retard!" My frail sister held up her hands and forearms in front of her face like she was a boxer on the ropes of a boxing ring, as though it would stop the blows, the nasty words, from assaulting her innocent ears.

Then the leader snatched Bridget's white cane from her and started playing with it. He wasn't the tallest of the gang, but he was muscled up pretty well. He looked kind of wild eyed. Like he was strung out on something. He cruelly broke Bridget's plastic cane, fashioning it into something that looked like a rooftop T.V. antenna. The jerk wore it on his head, claiming reference to a popular T.V. show of the day. "Look, 'My Favorite Martian.' Retard!" The gang laughed. Bridget cried. She was only thirteen.

It all probably just would have ended with the bullies getting a few laughs at the expense of the defenseless. Nothing new to the planet. But unknown to the bullies, I jumped off the jungle gym and ran straight for them, like a streaking arrow. I tackled the leader so hard, we ended up in the pond. He was fully grown and much stronger, and he soon got the best of me. He held my head under water while I thrashed around, trying to find air. I went limp. Being dishonorable, they dragged me out, coughing and gasping, and proceeded to kick me in the face and chest to revive me. I suppose I would have died if Bridget hadn't been screaming so loud, flailing and kicking at them. The bullies retreated in their car, leaving me with a crown—Bridget's cane, wrapped around my head.

They never caught the bastards. Not a one. It was a plain injustice.

I lost my two front teeth standing up for Bridget on that playground. Although the dentist did a marvelous job giving me permanent replacements. I learned a lot about myself when I defended my older sister. I felt the difference deep down in my heart the rest of my life. I learned I was a natural-born fighter, like my fighter-pilot father, the General, Dad, the Legend.

In my first eleven years of life, I heard countless stories, repeated countless times by countless admirers of my Father about his World War II exploits flying a P-51 fighter plane, beyond its intended capabilities and into the record books, as the most decorated fighter pilot in the U.S.A.F.

The one story that kept coming back to me as I mended from my beating was the episode that earned Father a Silver Star for heroism in aerial combat. It was when he flew like a madman and attacked a group of fifty battle-hardened German fighters, with only his faithful wing man, who stayed with him, protecting his back. He was a faithful wingman who did not bailout, did not dessert his leader, and hung in through the terrible heat of aerial battle, while huge, white-hot bullets blasted into his airplane and past his cockpit. Father shot down three, and his wing man got one, too. They lived to tell the tale. And they learned what legends they had become. A lesson learned. Pilot and wing man. A legend of doing the right thing no matter the odds of success or failure.

A legend of faithfulness.

Never leave your wing man.

Always faithful.

I learned that I was Bridget's protector. At least, I came to believe that was what God sent me to do on the planet. But it was a lot like war and combat. It was an unwanted task I had to remind myself of daily. For a while, I wondered if I was her guardian angel. It was a notion I eventually discarded because it made me depressed. It sounded too much like eternity, a life sentence in prison; Bridget was no easy person to live with.

After the day of the beating, Father bought Bridget a shillelagh. Father drilled a hole in its center and filled it with lead. Bridget painted the top white, and I painted the bottom tip a bright, Protestant orange. She learned to swing it hard, like Mickey Mantle, both left- and right-handed.

I worshiped my Father for his strong and kind ways. But I was worried that Father might think I wasn't a warrior, too, seeing how I couldn't defend my sister and myself from the thugs who beat me and taunted her to tears. I never told him or Mom that I feared they would think I was less of a man. I was raised as the baby in a family full of boys. Expressing feelings was met with ridicule from my brothers. I just kept my fears about what Mother and Father might think of me to myself. I handled it by sobbing into my pillow at night, hoping that some day, I would be given a chance to prove my worth as a man, as Bridget's protector, to my father.

I convalesced at home. I was away from school for two months to heal my body and my ego. I didn't realize it, but during that time, a malignant cancer grew within me. I could feel it twisting inside me like a woman feels her baby grow in her womb. Mine was no ordinary cancer. It was a cancer of the spirit. Of the soul.

I learned to hate.

I learned to hate bullies and injustice so bad, it boiled and rolled and grew deep inside me, worse than the physical injuries the thugs gave me. Bridget would bring pureed food into my room, where I sat by a window, looking out on a beautiful world. It was the world where I painfully learned there hid many dangers. I thanked Bridget through clenched teeth, wired together. My jaw, amongst other bones, was broken in the fight with the bullies.

I realized I sounded a lot like Bridget when she tried to speak. My words came out unintelligible. I had to repeat myself many times when I knew I was saying the right words. But people didn't take the time to listen real close so they could understand me. I began to understand Bridget in a whole new way. When I was alone, I cried for my sister. I knew my bones would heal. The doctor told me that. But Bridget would be broken and trapped forever. It made me sad for her. I would become angry all over again about the fight, and about bullies, and about the unfair things that just didn't belong. If God was a fair God.

I learned to hate real well.

I drank my meals through a straw. I sucked them through the hole left by my missing front teeth. I thought long and hard during those youthful times, as I licked my psychological wounds. Jesus' teaching to turn the other cheek was lost on me, a victim of violent crime. Eventually, I came to peace with violence and, especially, with the violence required in self-defense. I looked at it as a natural force. And that peace was a freak of human nature—only a temporary wrinkle in a universe flat full of greed. I figured it was natural to break peace and use violence to defend yourself. I knew we'd keep finding greedy people everywhere. People who wanted to take something from you. Something they didn't have. Your money. Your body. But worst of all, your honor.

I was just a boy. But as I sat on that windowsill with my broken jaw wired together, I swore to myself an oath of vengeance against the oppressors in life. All of them. I came to realize that the bullies actually did me a favor. The beating they gave me taught me how to hate the wrongs in life. That hatred wasn't enough. Action and preparation were required to right the wrongs. I decided I would never be anybody's punching bag again. I became a boy, and then a man, bent on justice.

My whole family, we all changed that day, the day the innocent learned that bad things can happen to good people. We grew in limitless dimensions. Forever.

# CHAPTER 34

# I WANT TO BE SOMEBODY

I was putting breakfast dishes away and trying to get Bridget out the door. "Come on, Bridgey, we can't be late for your doctor's appointment."

My sister did not want to think about her trip to see her psychiatrist. She wanted to focus on her status as a bona-fide contributor to our national treasury.

"You gonna file my taxes today?"

Before I could answer, she continued.

"Saint Matthew, Patron Saint of the tax collector, please help Michael file my taxes."

I stepped into Bridget's danger zone and interrupted her praying.

"Why? Why would you want to file a tax return to get back two bucks? I tell you what, I'll give you five dollars to forget about it."

"Taxpayers are somebody. Taxpayers have a life of their own."

"You already have a job."

"I want a life of my own, Michael."

I tried to console her and teach her that her social security number was not what makes her a person. I added that neither does filing your taxes to receive only a measly two dollar and fourteen cent refund from the United Sates Treasury.

"Bridgey, you are already somebody. You don't need to file a tax return to be somebody. Besides, you already paid the taxes because St. Cecelia's Workshop for the Blind withheld your taxes and sent them to Uncle Sam. I mean, the I.R.S."

As bright as she was, Bridget took things literally. She could not distinguish a metaphor like "Uncle Sam" from our real relatives. I did not know it at the time, but one of the symptoms of her Asperger Syndrome denied her the ability to understand the double meanings of metaphors.

When we were teenagers, I told her I was "browbeaten" by my teacher quizzing me in an oral exam. She thought the teacher physically hit me on the head. Bridgy still did not understand the distinction twenty years later. Such was her prison of the mind.

Once Bridget fixed a notion in her mind, she treated it like Gunny with a soup bone. She never let up on it. Currently, she wanted to chew on the taxman's leg—she wanted her refund. Now! Her current focus was becoming a person by receiving a tax refund. Only in Bridget's mind would such silliness be tolerated.

I patronized her instead of dashing her hopes of becoming a full-fledged human. I then saw the horrible scene in my mind. Twenty-years later, Bridget would be confronting me like Marlon Brando assailed his brother, Johnny, in *"On the Waterfront."* Bridget would be complaining to me that it was all my fault she never attained her full potential, "Michael, I couldha been a taxpayha. I couldha been somebody."

Bridget dealt in reality and to Hell with the metaphors. When she browbeat someone, she gave them a knockin' on the noggin.

Bridget raised her shillelagh and acted as though she was going to club me with it.

"File my taxes." She swung at me, and I ducked getting hit.

"Why? The envelope and postage will cost about what you'll get back."

"I'll have proof."

"Proof of what?"

"Proof that I'm somebody, Michael! You get to go to college and be a big lawyer and a Marine man, and I'm . . . I'm just Bridget. I ain't nobody. Nobody knows Bridget 'cuz Bridget's a nobody. I hear them call me a freak and a retard, Michael."

She was crying.

"I want something to show off to people. My refund."

I could not argue with her logic. Especially with her pursuing me through the foyer, past Father's portrait and up the stairs, as I retreated to the safety of my room.

CHAPTER 34

"O.K., O.K., O.K.! I'll file your damn taxes! For Criminea's sake. Stop your browbeatin', wouldja," I said as I shut my bedroom door.

I gave up. Bridget "The Bull" McRain won the bout on a T.K.O. As usual, I threw in the towel. If I had been inclined to call for help, the police report would have stated that Bridget browbeat her little brother. No, really. It was not a metaphor. It was hard, and it hurt. She literally browbeat me with her shillelagh.

# CHAPTER 35

# SURROUNDED!

"Goin' to the doctor, goin' to the doctor, pray for us."

Bridget was jabbering her prayer-speaking and rocking at the kitchen table, waiting for me to finish the lunch dishes. I came home from work midday to take Bridget to her psychiatrist's appointment. It would be the first time she allowed me to accompany her to talk with her doctor. I was anxious to find out the doctor's diagnosis. I hoped I could ask a few questions, too.

Bridget Mary McRain was pushing for some independence lately. I needed to know her psychiatrist's thoughts about Bridget maybe someday living on her own. I fantasized, *"And maybe then I can get on with my life."* But I was also being overprotective. I wanted to be there for Bridget, to keep her safe forever. Long before, I came to accept I could not have it both ways. I could not protect her and have my own life, too. I prayed the night before, hoping the doctor would give me some good answers. Something I wanted to hear.

I opened the front door to walk out. But I was confronted by journalists with cameras, notepads, and recorders—all clambering for an interview.

They hit me with an avalanche of questions about my fight in the elevator with Slasher. A newspaper reporter from the "Globe Demagogue" asked, "Mr. McRain, how long have you been torturing people?"

"I didn't torture anyone. Hey, what's all this about?"

I was cut off in mid-sentence when the CNN reporter started to run the fight footage. A tech held up a portable T.V. monitor for me to look at. The elevator fight footage showed me putting the Slasher in a martial arts, submissive hold while I "instructed" Slasher on good manners.

I called time out.

I shut the door quickly. Ace and Gunny were barking through the door at the small crowd of media hounds.

Bridget was curious. "Who's that? What are they saying? Saints be gore. They say you beat a man?"

"It's nothing, Bridgey, let's go out the back."

The slow beginning of a curdled howl began to well up in Bridget's chest and throat. She clutched her shillelagh. The phone rang, and I walked back to the kitchen to answer it.

Bridget said to herself, *"Oh, they are coming for my little Michael?"*

Louder this time, "Who are they, Michael? They say you beat a man? Are they here to beat you?"

As I walked towards the phone, I told her, "Don't worry about them. They are just protesting me taking a bully to the woodshed."

Apparently, the ring of the telephone drowned out some of what I said. Bridget heard the words "protest," "worry," "taking," and "me." Her mind spun those words around, and it came out in a five-foot-two vortex of violence named Bridget the Protector. She intended to perpetuate the ancient, blood feud between the orange and the green of Ireland. An old, old, bloody vendetta.

Bridge said to herself, *"Protest? Protestant? Protestants! Are here to take away my little brother for beating a man?"*

She mistakenly believed that *"The Troubles,"* the ancient warring between Protestants, backed by the British Crown, and militant Irish Catholics, spearheaded by the I.R.A., now darkened her American doorstep. Bridge flung open the front door and brandished her white shillelagh in one hand, holding Ace's lead in the other.

"Be gone, you bloody rabble. In the name of the Pope and the blessed saints, be gone, you heathens."

She swung her shillelagh at the journalists, believing they were Protestants there to lynch me. A television journalist hollered to his cameraman, "Get this on tape!" The cameraman filmed Bridget's attack as he retreated. He turned and ran as Bridget heard his voice and, like a sonar guided torpedo, locked her blind audio fix on him. She rushed towards the fleeing cameraman, swinging her shillelagh.

"You will take my little brother over my dead body!"

CHAPTER 35

Bridget kissed the crucifix on the emerald-green, beaded rosary that hung around her neck, that she'd received all the way from the Poor Clare nuns' cloistered convent on an island close by Dublin, Ireland.

The journalists backed away, quickly. They ran from the crazy lady. Bridget was not eloquent, but she was quite persuasive.

"And you will not be destroying my house, you bloody heathen bastards."

The cameras kept rolling.

"You'll have to bring more of the King's men to take this holy home." She spit into each hand. She rubbed them together and gripped her shillelagh, like Willie Mays held a baseball bat.

The telephone call was from a reporter for "Newsweek," asking questions about the Casteel case and its details. When I heard the big commotion, I ran out onto the porch. I grabbed Bridget and calmed her down. We said a *"Glory Be"* prayer together, three times, as I walked her down the porch. I eased her into her Adirondack chair by the chessboard. Most times, a prayer is the only thing that will calm down the poor girl. She did have the redheaded Irish temper now and then.

The reporters, being opportunists by necessity, crept back onto the porch to try to interview me. They reminded me of jackals creeping up to what they believed to be a defenseless carcass to pick it clean of its flesh, its story.

Bridget started to rock on the edge of her chair, and she twitched and rubbed the Celtic cross atop her shillelagh as she chanted. Ace had seen that behavior in Bridget before. She was irritated, and she was warming up for something. Prior C.T. scans of Bridget's brain showed she had a portion of her brain that did not function well. It was the area that is responsible for her emotions. Ace covered his face with his paws. She was in the calm before her intermittent, explosive- disorder storm.

"Going doctor. Hail, Mary, full of Grace. Going doctor. Hail, Mary, full of Grace."

I looked again at the small T.V. monitor. It showed the S.W.A.T. team's audio-video footage, obtained through a Freedom of Information Act request by CNN. In the footage, the elevator fight was playing back what I said and did on the elevator with the Slasher: *"Think you're so tough, taking a knife to a woman, huh?"* said onscreen, amongst many other comments, steeped in salty language. At the time, I was also bending the Slasher's right-hand middle finger out of joint, and my boot was on his crotch. Was it torture? *Me thinks not.* Was it an attitude adjuster? *Yes.* It was just one of a few dozen standard, Marine Corps, instruction protocols reserved for those disrespectful men who purposefully put themselves on the outside of the learning curve. Bullies. Shit disturbers. Serial rapists. Butchering murderers. Take your pick. They are all problem students craving my attention.

Slasher screamed in pain.

"Well, I'm your M.O.M. . . Yeah, that's my initials," I said, without any knowledge that my little colloquy with the serial murderer was being recorded by the remote S.W.A.T. camera.

Slasher whimpered.

"Michael O'Brien McRain. So don't sass your M.O.M., boy."

Slasher pleaded for mercy. I showed him little.

"Yeah, that's what the recruits in the Corps called me— M.O.M.–'cuz I taught 'em everything they needed to know . . ."

I asked the reporters, "They released that to the public?" Three journalists said, "Yes," in unison. I waved off any further questions from the reporters. "No more questions. No more questions."

The reporter, being a reporter, suffered from selective hearing. He continued to stick the monitor in my face. But in my peripheral vision, I saw another reporter wandering down the porch, moving one of the chess pieces on the porch chessboard.

"Don't mess with that," I said.

The reporter disregarded me and moved one of Bridget's chess pieces.

"I said leave it alone."

The reporter hammed it up. He danced with Bridget's white chess queen. I warned him again.

"Buddy, believe me, you don't want to mess with . . . "

Bridget clobbered the reporter upside the head with her shillelagh. She drew blood.

"I blind. You deaf," she said to the prostrate journalist.

I sprinted down to Bridget and caught her stick before it came down again on the bleeding man's skull. I tried to restrain all 105 pounds of her as the reporters stampeded off the porch and jumped in their vehicles. She still wanted a piece of him for messing with her chess game.

More likely, I think, with the unfriendly crowd around me, she snapped and flashed back to our childhood attack, when I was severely beaten in the course of protecting her. The girl just dropped into full battle mode, in the blink of an eye.

We waited for the reporters to leave before we got in my Mustang and left, fast. Maybe the psychiatrist would give us some answers.

I was not looking forward to watching the evening news.

# CHAPTER 36

# MIKE'S SECRET

I love driving my U.S.M.C. custom-detailed Mustang—hard and fast. I shifted, with deliberate malice to the clutch. Bridget's head snapped back as I left a scratch of rubber in third gear. The weather was beautiful, and the convertible top was down. It made the Polaroid, tucked into a crack in the dashboard, flap in the breeze. My mind wandered to my Marine Corps days, as a marching cadence roared out of my stereo:

> I want to be a Recon Ranger.
> Live a life of sex and danger.
> Sex and danger, sex and danger.
> Recon Ranger, Recon Ranger.

The cadences gave me a beat. A consistent timing for my life. It offered something exactly opposite to the shifting sands of practicing law. I had come to observe that the law was a profession premised on society's human penchant for lying to win. If a lawyer does not know the truth, he has no choice but to pass on the lies of his client. My Harvard professors did not need to teach me one of the tenets of practicing law.

Greed is the fuel of lying.

Bridget was her usual self. She rocked in the bucket seat as much as the seatbelt harness would allow.

"Going doctor. Hail, Mary, full of Grace. Going doctor. Hail, Mary, full of Grace. Going doctor. Saint Hermes of the psychotic, Hail, Mary, full of Grace, the Lord is with thee . . ." Bridget then seasoned her spiritual stew with some Gaelic. "Need *fírinne*, need *fírinne*, praise Saint Patrick in the blessed blood of Jesus the *fírinne*." Bridget was saying she wanted the truth, *fírinne*, in the Gaelic-Irish tongue. My older sister was intent on discovering something. Something of which I was presently clueless, but that I surely soon would regret. Oftentimes, she spoke Gaelic when she was in a trance-like state—into which I never dared intrude.

I looked at the Polaroid and then at Bridget, whose long, red hair was whipping upward in the strong wind and waving like the serpents of Medusa. Bridget held her shillelagh in her right hand like a scepter. Upright, with the bottom tip on the floorboard so that the Celtic cross on top appeared almost regal above the windshield.

"Hey, didn't I take you to the psychiatrist two weeks ago?"

Bridget disregarded my question and continued with her prayers.

"Saint Dymphna, patron saint of mental ill, mental ill. For Thine is the kingdom and the power . . ."

I looked back and forth between Bridget and the road. I was angered by the lack of communication with Bridget.

"Well, isn't that normal? Nothing has changed in the past thirty years. All I get from you is religious babble."

Bridget continued to bob her head, attempting to rock. But she looked like a turkey in a strut. I shook my head as I turned the car onto St. Anthony's Hospital parking lot.

Bridget kept her face stoic, in a trance of mumbled prayers. I got out of the car and walked around to the other side to open the door for my sister. While I was not looking, Bridget grabbed the Polaroid out of the dashboard. She stuffed it into her purse before I opened the door.

Minutes later, Bridget, Ace, and I were seated in Dr. Sarah Ardden's office. I sat in the waiting room reading a "Field and Stream" article about how some hermit in the Alaskan woods fought off a Kodiak bear with only a Swiss Army knife and a roll of toilet paper. I empathized with the victim of the story as I compared Bridget to the bear, in my mind. The receptionist opened the frosted-glass window and asked me to step into the doctor's office.

Dr. Sarah Ardden looked a little sexy in her white coat. And her office had a sweet smell of cinnamon apple. But before my male brain could turn that into some kind of Garden of Eden fantasy, she spoke.

"Mr. McRain, during my session with your sister, she requested that you be informed about her medical condition." I looked at Bridget, then back at the doctor, and nodded.

CHAPTER 36

"As you know, she has a mild form of autism called Asperger Syndrome," said the doctor.

"Whatever she's got, she's had it her whole life."

Dr. Ardden explained, "Asperger manifests itself in a lot of different ways. In Bridget's case, it presents in a sporadic speech pattern, anti-social behavior, constant prayer, and rocking in her seat." Dr. Ardden caught my attention. My eyebrows rose as she crossed her legs. Bridget rocked and prayed. "Her neuro-psych evaluation indicates she is a genius. Her I.Q. is above 160. But her mind is going so fast, her tongue can't catch up.

"No cure?" said I.

"No, there isn't." The doctor paused and seemed to gather her thoughts or her courage, while she fidgeted with a paperclip. "But there is something else she asked me to discuss with you."

Up to that point, I was thinking about asking Dr. Ardden out on a date. Not just because she was pretty and intelligent and seemed to be cool. It was because I thought it would be impossible for Bridget to raise her shillelagh and chase Dr. Ardden out of the house, like she had done to a number of dates that I had brought home previously. She'd run them out while she called to the heavens for help from Saint Margaret of Cortona, Saint Afra and Saint Mary Magdalene, the patron saints of fallen women.

I was interrupted by the Polaroid of the tombstone, spinning face-up as it slid across the desk. It ended up about one inch from the edge. My face went grim as I picked up the photo.

"Where'd you get this?"

"Bridget gave it to me, but the picture is so grainy, you cannot read the name on the stone."

"The Polaroid is of my father's tombstone."

I sat in front of Dr. Ardden's desk as a convicted criminal. Dr. Ardden scribbled on a prescription pad and handed it to me. I turned to look at Bridget scornfully, as the finked on would look at the finker. A rare shiver of emotional nakedness ran down my spine. I could feel my face grow cold and taut. My eyes froze into an icy glaze. The truth spoken aloud is often quite scary.

The *firinne*, the truth, is just that. It never lies. It is a universal constant. But lawyers, like Catholic priests, are forbidden from disclosing the truth revealed by a confessor of a crime, perhaps even a murder. And therefore, the truth becomes inert and emotionless and meaningless, and it rests like a beast in a cage, imprisoned and segregated in our souls, to growl at our conscience which pokes sticks into the cage to enrage the beast to test the strength of the prison, the ethics of not revealing the truth to the world; which in a round-about way, causes that truth to become tame and less damning. But through time and inattention that beast of damning truth becomes forgotten and cured and is never discovered by the world. It remains a sacred secret between the lawyer and the confessor and God. Caged and quarantined forever.

The truth, about my relationship with my father, was boiling in my heart and it scalded me; no different than if Doctor Ardden had thrown a pot of steaming water on my lap.

I jumped up from my chair. I put my hand underneath Bridget's arm, and I damned near lifted her out of the chair. It was a quiet, but obvious move of great strength. I hoped it would send a nonverbal message to the doctor and to Bridget that they were treading on the forbidden, hallowed ground between a father and a son. But the doctor was not impressed or intimidated.

"You can run, but you can't hide from whatever ghost is chasing you, Mike."

If my head had been a pressure cooker, steam would have been coming out of my ears. My jaw was tight.

"That so?"

Bridget gave her little brother a wide berth, sensing that I was under too much pressure and might blow at any second. She knew me very well. Although I remained cold, I maintained a professional and deliberate decorum as I moved with Bridget and Ace towards the door.

"That prescription is not for your sister, Mr. McRain. It's for you."

My hand hesitated over the doorknob.

"It's something to help you relax. Maybe then we can talk about your issues next week."

CHAPTER 36

"Issues? I don't have any issues," I said in a flat tone. I looked the doctor in the eye.

Dr. Ardden rose to her feet. She walked around the side of her desk and sat on the front corner, crossing her arms over her chest. Confident and direct.

"Mr. McRain, I think anyone carrying around a Polaroid of his father's tombstone and fighting his blind, autistic sister for it has issues. Maybe they are issues you feel comfortable with. Maybe they are issues you want to get rid of. Maybe they are issues that will chase you for the rest of your life and turn you into a broken, hollow man who can't move emotionally. Perhaps you feel more secure in a shell of shame or guilt. Like a turtle, afraid to face the emotions and repercussions of the outside world. You strike me as being a lot more courageous than that, Mr. McRain. Especially since your sister shared with me that you are a highly decorated Marine Corps officer. Is that true?"

I didn't take her bait. I looked at my watch and said, "Sorry, I'd love to sit on your couch, but I have to get to court."

I damned near dragged Bridget out of the hospital building to my car. "That's great. I take my sister to a head doctor and I get the prescription."

Bridget became indignant when we got to my Mustang. I let go of her elbow and was lucky to see, out of the corner of my eye, Bridget's shillelagh on a collision course with my head. With the reaction time and training of a Marine Corps martial arts instructor, I deflected the blow, grabbed the shillelagh, and raised my hand to strike Bridget. But I held it there in a petrified state, unable to strike a woman. Even my pain-in-the-ass, nosy, overbearing older sister. I restrained myself as an officer and a gentleman.

My conscience brought me back to earth. I realized what I was doing. I further realized that I was probably on the surveillance camera, so I faked as though I was scratching my neck with my raised hand. Then I smiled and opened the car door for Bridget and Ace to enter.

We slowly rumbled off the parking lot. My car stereo played the Marine Corps Hymn louder than if twenty Marines sang it in person:

From the Halls of Montezuma
To the shores of Tripoli,

We fight our country's battles
In the air, on land and sea.

First to fight for right and freedom,
And to keep our honor clean,
We are proud to claim the title
Of United States Marine...

No one told me that the toughest battle of my life was yet to come. A battle fought, between my ears, over my heart and soul. I was muttering to myself as I shifted with disgust and fury about the whole Dr. Ardden situation. Bridget's hair started to float back and forth, on end like a nest of dancing cobras. I punched the steering wheel and yelled.

"I take my sister to the frickin' head doctor, and I get the script."

Traffic stopped as we watched a slow-moving freight train cross our path. It carried the lifeblood of our society and our economy. I determined that I needed something to get my life off the slippery slope that was sending me down to an obscure existence as a chauffeur and orderly for my holy, older sister.

Bridget blurted out a quick psych profile, "You crazy, Michael."

I yelled back at my older sister, "I'm crazy? I'm crazy?"

I pled guilty. "Yeah, well, maybe I am crazy. You betcha. God made me crazy, so I could do his dirty work."

The traffic jam caused by the train cleared. We were scooting along, and I wanted to get Bridget to shut up. I skipped third gear when I downshifted and let out the clutch with malice. It made Bridget's head snap forward. She backhanded me with her shillelagh to return the affection. She became angry and quiet. Brother-sister love.

That night, I sank down into my mattress like an anchor finds the sandy bottom of the ocean. I believed that my prayers asking God to release me from my bondage fell on deaf ears. But I said them anyway. Gunny had first watch, with my explicit instructions that he should bite anyone invading the perimeter. I faux-saluted Gunny, "Carry on, Gunny, Ooo-Rah. Oh, and if you see an unfriendly carrying a white stick, attack."

Gunny wasn't worth a damn in a foxhole. He fell asleep before I did.

*Firinne.*

CHAPTER 36

# CHAPTER 37

# MY MISSION

On the 3rd of August, I pulled up to the East St. Martinsville Federal Courthouse. A low-standing building that looked like it was designed to comport with 1970s-era, boring, institutional, architectural guidelines. I thought this was going to be a simple trip. All I had to do was go in the courtroom, wait in line, and get a discovery-by-consent order signed by the federal judge. I'd be out in twenty, maybe thirty minutes, maximum. On a piercing-blue-skied day, I approached the base of the courthouse steps. I navigated my way through a crowd of thirty burly, union men, dressed like railroad engineers. Some carried signs: "Railroaded," "Free Casteel," and "Conviction Conspiracy." It was some form of protest.

The union men chanted. "Hog Heads forever," while they picketed.

Now and then, fate deals most of us a terrible hand. But it must be played. I was there to get an order signed by the bankruptcy judge regarding a divorce in which a husband had filed for bankruptcy, trying to discharge his duty to pay child support. As fate would have it, the court clerk told me that the bankruptcy judge was gone, for gall bladder surgery. She directed me down the hall to District Judge Lackey. He was addressing all orders for the bankruptcy judge immediately after he finished a criminal hearing. I hurried down the hall. But I was stopped by the guards stationed outside Judge Lackey's courtroom.

"The courtroom is closed. The judge has got Jake Casteel in there. The next Jimmy Hoffa," said the bigger of the two guards, the one standing to the right of the huge, ten-foot-high, oak-paneled, double doors. The guard went on to explain that the reporters and union men in the courtroom were packed like sardines and there wasn't any more room, for non-lawyers or lawyers. Nobody.

I explained to the guard that I had an emergency order to be signed and that the bankruptcy court clerk had sent me down there. I was supposed to have access to Judge Lackey. Neither of the guards was impressed. They stood close together to block my entry. I remembered an old saying Father taught me about dealing with people to get what you want. "People do things for only three reasons. They know you. They like you. Or they trust you."

I went for the like or trust part of the advice. I talked guy talk with them. Guns.

"I see you guys are carrying Glocks. In the Marine Corps, I was a knife and firearms instructor. What do you guys think about the Beretta compared to those Glocks you are strapping?" We proceeded to exchange ballistic notes for a few minutes.

Voila.

The advice Father gave me about how to handle people was the most useful that I could apply to practicing law. In order to get things done in a courthouse, you had to schmooze people. Get to know them. Then they will bend over backwards to help you if they knew you, liked you, or trusted you. Simple.

One hundred thirty-seven seconds after exchanging personal preferences for different weapons in different situations, the double doors of the courtroom were opened—one by each guard—as though I was Moses parting the sea.

"Standing room only." The six-foot, four-inch guard said as I entered the courtroom.

The opening of both doors simultaneously raised the attention of the judge, who looked up from the paperwork he was referring to while addressing the prisoner in front of him. The act of the judge in raising his head to see my entry caused all the guards, the bailiff, and the gallery to turn to look at who deserved to have both doors opened for him. I walked into Judge Lackey's courtroom with a look of embarrassment.

The judge's clerk, a Miss Annaleah Eves, who was infamous in St. Martinsville legal circles for being a shrew, and proud of it, kept her beady eyes on me like she was watching a shoplifter. Alas, her once (rumored) smiling face had been botoxed so many times that she could no longer even spare a grin. Her perpetually arching eyebrows made her look like a surprised demon all the time. The poor lady's mouth stayed in such a continuous pout, and her forehead wrinkled so, she appeared to be passing a kidney stone – every minute of every day. She continued her glare toward me, which I gathered I was suffering for having the gall to enter her courtroom.

Miss Annaleah must have felt negative vibes from my entry; she started to nervously bounce her crossed legs and then she rubbed and scratched at the large wart on her chin. It was an unseemly, black-haired growth of the type that you see on a Halloween witch's mask. From all the way across the courtroom I could tell she did not like me. It made me want to find a hole and crawl into it. But not because I was afraid of her, heavens no. I knew how self-important and extra officious some court clerks can act. I was just worried that she might think of some nonsense excuse to deny me an audience with Judge Lackey. And I needed my court order signed.

I was in the spotlight, and I didn't like it. I looked around for a seat and found none. I was stranded out in the middle of the aisle, like a sheep with no flock. Slowly, I walked up and down the middle aisle, looking for an opening to sit down. The judge addressed the prisoner standing in shackles in front of him while I searched for a seat, under the painful stare of the judge's gatekeeper, Clerk Annaleah The Terrible.

Jake Casteel was flanked by huge corrections officers wearing blue blazers. Casteel preferred the orange jumpsuit of the jailhouse resident as his outfit of the day. Due to the large union turnout and the possibility of some disorderly conduct, Judge Lackey had ordered four large deputies, who looked like they had played defensive line for the Minnesota Vikings, to stand between the courtroom gallery and the bar area of the courtroom.

Judge Lackey addressed Jake Casteel. "Mr. Casteel, you realize you have been convicted of Perjury on Admiralty and you just lost your first appeal?"

When I heard the phrase, "Perjury on Admiralty," my ears perked up like I had recently heard it somewhere before, forgetting my recent dream. I dismissed the notion, as a figment of my imagination.

Jake Casteel stood tall and erect, with his hands shackled in front of him. The chain between his ankles lay on the institutional carpet. Even at his age of fifty-five, Casteel looked powerful. He possessed thick forearms and a bullish neck. He had a strong jaw beneath incisive, dark eyes and a thick head of black hair. It looked like a razor had not been dragged across his face in a week. His gray temples and salted beard were the only signs of his true age. In every other respect, he looked like the Marine Corps sergeant who had stepped out of the jungles of Vietnam with not one, not two, but three Navy Crosses for extreme heroism in bloody combat. Casteel spoke like an educated man, a lawyer with a timbre of unwavering confidence. It was how an innocent man would speak.

"Your Honor, I was set up. I am innocent, and I intend to appeal this to the United States Supreme Court."

"Yes, Mr. Casteel, you only have that one appeal left. As a criminal defendant, you have about a one in a half million chance of winning at the Supreme Court. Do you understand that?"

"I did not lie, Your Honor. I want my appeal."

Lackey toyed with Casteel as though he was trying to while away the time. "You just informed the Court that you are now bankrupt and can't afford a lawyer, so you want me to appoint you a lawyer to handle your appeal to the Supreme Court?"

"Yes, Sir. I'm innocent."

"But I have never appointed a lawyer to represent a criminal defendant in the Supreme Court before. Why should I do it for you?"

"Because, sir, I am innocent," Casteel said.

A scruffy looking blond-headed union man stood up in the gallery and shouted, "You're darn right he's innocent. He's railroaded 'cuz he's too good of a leader. You can't bribe Jake Casteel. Damned kangaroo court." The Judge made a hand motion for the deputy to work, quickly. The protestor was collared and dragged out of the courtroom, kicking and screaming—right past me.

I saw the open spot vacated by the protestor, and I attempted to occupy it in the confusion. I started to move down the row of big men, who were still on their feet, watching their comrade being removed.

CHAPTER 37

"The problem is it's hard to find a lawyer certified to practice in the Supreme Court," Lackey said, and raised his hand to illustrate the directive that followed.

"All the lawyers certified to practice in the United States Supreme Court, please raise your hands."

I froze in my tracks. I was belly to belly with a locomotive engineer and only two steps from the open spot I intended to take. I reluctantly raised my right arm, turning around slowly. I hoped there were a good number of other lawyers with their hands raised.

There were none.

I was the only lawyer in the courtroom who raised his hand. I never felt more naked. "Well, lo and behold, we got lucky. Please step forward and state your name, young man," Judge Lackey said.

I looked at the Judge like a deer looks when it's caught in the headlights of a train. I froze. I'd never handled a criminal case, and I didn't want to represent a criminal. Innocent or not. I'd gathered my conservative opinions about crime and punishment at a young age, on an afternoon when I had a duty to protect my sister, Bridget, from a carload of hooligans.

That horrible day happened over twenty years before. It had been my burning source of energy to become the physical specimen that I was now, to make sure I could win any future fight with criminals. I absolutely hated criminals, especially those who committed acts of violence against innocent people. In the Marine Corps, I volunteered for suicide duty to rescue hostages. U.S. citizens held by terrorists in unknown, unpublicized incidents around the world. I did it just so I could deal justice to the types of people who had caused me to miss months of grade school and lie in bed wondering, *"Why?"*

Intellectually, I knew my innermost fears were dead wrong, but psychologically I put all criminals at arm's distance. I thoroughly understood the difference between innocent until proven guilty and actual guilt. But I was a childhood victim of violent crime. It did not matter to me, emotionally, whether or not the person was accused or convicted; they were all criminals to me. All of my fears and prejudices shot through me like a lightning bolt of electricity. It made me freeze like an inarticulate boob. I looked at Judge

Lackey and gave him the look, "Who, me?" Lackey immediately nodded his head and motioned with his finger for me to approach the bench.

Forthwith.

"Counselor, what is your name?"

"Michael O'Brien McRain," I said from the gallery. For a moment, I felt even more naked. Like a streaker running across a football field at half-time during the Super Bowl. I started to walk towards Judge Lackey's bench as one of the guards standing next to Casteel said to the other, "That's Psycho Mike-O." The other guard said in response, "Yeah. Throws knives at his clients."

Jake Casteel's eyes bugged out as I continued my walk up to the bench, "Psycho Mike-O? Throws knives?"

"You are so screwed," the first guard said, as I stopped next to Casteel. I stood to Casteel's right, between Casteel and the joking corrections officer.

I knew I did not have much time to get out of this one, so I took the offensive, "Your Honor, I am not a criminal defense lawyer. I only handle divorces."

Jake Casteel chimed in with his similar sentiments. "Your Honor, I don't want this lawyer. They call him 'Psycho Mike-O'."

"Now, don't believe everything you hear, Mr. Casteel. I'm sure Mr. McRain has some redeeming qualities," said Judge Lackey.

"Yeah, well, how long you been practicin' law?" Casteel asked me.

"About a year, but . . ."

Casteel was collared by the corrections officer for raising his shackled hands above his head in protest. News of how the Slasher killed a judge traveled fast in the criminal justice system.

"A year? You are lucky you could find the courthouse, son."

Jake lowered his hands and turned to address Judge Lackey. "Your Honor, this is not the experienced appellate lawyer I need to fight for me in the Supreme Court."

"I don't know about that, Mr. Casteel. What law school you go to, Mr. McRain?"

"Harvard, Your Honor."

CHAPTER 37

Miss Annaleah scoffed and tried to give Judge Lackey a troubled look, which Lackey disregarded, partly out of his superior attitude, but moreso because he could not see any change in his stretch-skinned clerk's continually alarmed appearance.

"Harvard man?  Well, that settles it.  Meet your new lawyer, Mr. Casteel."  Judge Lackey brought his hands together, in a loud, resounding clap at mid-chest.  "I'm appointing him without pay.  Expedited Supreme Court brief is due in thirty days."

Judge Lackey struck his gavel, hard.  The sound echoed in my ears, even more than the first time I heard mortar fire.  I turned and looked at my new client.  Jake shared an equally astonished look of surprise.

I said to the judge, "Thirty days?  No pay?"  Judge Lackey put his hand over his microphone and whispered.

"You'll be done real quick, won't you?"

I shook my head in disbelief, as though I was shaking off a hard right cross to the jaw.

What the judge said next brought me out of my disbelief.

"Now you two are kind of married," Judge Lackey motioned to my new client, Jake Casteel, and me.

Casteel and I looked bewildered and surprised.  We each looked each other in the eye.

"Till death do us part," Jake Casteel said to me in protest.

I saw Casteel's U.S.M.C. "*Semper Fi*" and bulldog tattoo on his arm, as we shook hands.  I said, "*Semper Fi*.  I'm your best friend and your worst enemy."

"You a Devil Dog, too?"

"Ooo-Rah."

Judge Lackey looked back and forth between Casteel and me, thinking we were both nuts.

"I got a Marine.  I got a chance," said Casteel.

I could only watch as the powerful correction officers hooked Casteel under the arms and dragged him out of the courtroom.  His shoes left dual scuff tracks all the way to the door.

"I've been set up, kid.  It's gonna be a long fight.  Better pack a lunch," said Casteel as the door closed him off from his new attorney.

# CHAPTER 38

# BEHIND CLOSED DOORS

After Jake Casteel was dragged out the back door of the courtroom, Judge Lackey stood to leave. Like a boxer given smelling salts, I snapped out of it—been knocked out on my feet. I remembered the reason I came to the courtroom. I asked the Judge to sign the Bankruptcy Court Order.

"So, you only practice divorce law. Is that right, Mr. McRain?"

"That's right, Your Honor. Never handled a criminal case in my life. I only got my certification to practice in the Supreme Court because I thought it would look cool, hanging on my office wall."

"By the time you get to the end of this case, Mr. McRain, you'll have a different kind of skin to tack to the wall."

"How's that, your Honor?"

"You'll be able to say you've represented the most powerful and dangerous union leader in the country. At least, since Jimmy Hoffa. And all the way through the United States Supreme Court, at that."

I thought about playing my ace in the hole. That I had to care for my challenged sister. That I'd been a victim of violent crime and could not be impartial, and unbiased, and zealous in my representation of Jake Casteel. All of which, the Rules of Ethics require. But, for some reason, I jammed my hand into my right-hand, suit-coat pocket and groped for a pen. When I pulled my hand out, I held a Polaroid of the stone. I couldn't believe it. I couldn't believe that I had been appointed to represent a criminal. Or to be technically accurate, someone who had been accused of a crime. But any way you looked at it, I was going to be representing someone I, professionally, did not believe I should be representing.

I had an ethical duty to tell the court all of my misgivings about representing Jake Casteel. But as I looked at the photo of the stone, right there in front of the judge, I also could not believe that I had actually pulled out the photo. It was a thing highly private and personal. I hoped no one else had seen what I had been looking at because I knew they would think I was a nut, keeping a picture of a tombstone in my pocket.

It was the same damned photo Dr. Ardden had slid across her desk. The one Dr. Ardden used to indict my psyche. Exhibit A in my basket case of lunacy. Lackey signed the Bankruptcy Order with his usual flare: a spaghetti-bowlful of scribble ending with a long strike, all the way off the paper and onto the blotter. "Good luck," said Lackey, who immediately rose to exit the bench, as the bailiff shouted, "All rise."

I stood there, stunned. I wondered if anyone had gotten the number of the train that just hit me. I stood, rooted in place, wondering what had stopped me. Why had looking at the photo of the tombstone stopped me from trying to get disqualified as Casteel's lawyer? The newspaper reporters filed out. The throng of union men marched out. The Bailiff herded them along, like a cowboy moves cattle. All the while, I stood in front of the Judge's bench, acting like I was looking at the Bankruptcy Order, when I was really peeking at the Polaroid hidden behind the Order.

I heard the Bailiff say, "Mr. McRain, you gonna leave?"

Unknown to me at the time, a secret meeting was being conducted in Judge Lackey's chambers. Lackey entertained a most unusual guest, who sat in one of the visitor's chairs across from the Judge's large desk. The Judge still wore his black robe, his own confidence builder. His psychological shield from his visitor.

Judge Lackey's Court Clerk, Annaleah, sat at her desk outside the closed door to Judge Lackey's chambers and she listened in on the judge's conversation with Durant using the intercom. There was absolutely nothing that happened in her courthouse that she did not know all about. A control freak with a bullish, condescending personality.

Lackey knew he wasn't just blurring the line between the Constitution's separation of powers. He was driving a bulldozer over the Constitution. It was a simple *quid pro quo*—you scratch my back, and I'll scratch yours.

"Well, you couldn't have drawn a better lawyer for what you want, Mr. Durant."

CHAPTER 38

Colonel Durant sat back in the leather chair. He ventured a smile.

Judge Lackey added, "You lucked out. Casteel is now represented by a terribly inexperienced lawyer. He is certified in the U.S. Supreme Court. But he has never handled a criminal case in his life. Not even a traffic ticket."

Lackey thought lustfully about the appointment to the Court of Appeals he had been promised for cooperating with the C.I.A. and D.O.D. A much-coveted promotion, of sorts, for federal judges. The framers of the Constitution had not envisioned the greed for promotion when they gave federal judges lifetime appointments. This was a simple deal. Lackey did the back-door, dirty work, and he was rewarded with one of the few things Federal Judges care about—a higher-court appointment.

"A greenhorn, huh?" Colonel Durant said.

"Yeah, and a divorce lawyer on top of it."

They both laughed, good, hard laughs. Durant even rubbed his hands together, in anticipation of a general's star. He heard the commotion outside, from all the protestors chanting. However, he stayed ever mindful that his deal with Judge Lackey was secret. It was also extremely illegal. He did not dare go near the windows to see me as I exited the courthouse.

Annaleah could see the scheme between Judge Lackey and Colonel Durant play out like a movie in her mind, all to my destruction. And at the ultimate expense of my client, Jake Casteel. The price of vanity; she tried to grin but the Botox would not allow it. Her eyes squinted into a smirk. Annaleah was excited, the trap was set. And, like a rube, I was walking straight into it.

But Annaleah got a bad feeling that things might not go as planned. The plan was too perfect and this new guy, Michael McRain, was an unknown factor. He was a Marine and so was the target. And she hated Marines. They had backbones. Judge Lackey never dared stand up to her. She had him trained to put his tail between his legs and she was angry that he did not pick up on her tacit objection to picking a Harvard educated lawyer to defend Casteel. And now they had to fight not one, but two Marines. And both lawyers. She did not like a bit of it.

Annaleah's gut instinct was screaming at her. She rubbed her witchy wart. It seems that every courthouse has one like Annaleah. She was a know-it-all and just plain wicked. Durant would have her that night if it was up to her; any which way he wanted it. Birds of a feather flock together. She took out her mirror and combed her raven black hair and put on some "pump me" red lipstick. Colonel Durant had treated her like the dirt on his shoes before he went in to meet the judge. That excited her. She primped the few hairs she had remaining on her eyebrows as she waited for the Colonel to come out of the judge's chambers. Annaleah fantasized about how she would do him. Which hotel. Which position. Which excuse she would tell her husband.

CHAPTER 38

# CHAPTER 39

# DAZED AND CONFUSED

I walked out of the courthouse, into a new world. It was the 6th of August, and the air was hot and sticky, and I was not prepared for camera flashes or camera crews or any sniping journalists. They assaulted my senses as I pushed open the doors. I strode down the marble steps, while Jake Casteel's faithful union men chanted, "Hog Heads forever." They raised their picket signs, waving them in angry protest at Judge Lackey's decision to give Jake and me so little time to prepare for the Supreme Court.

A microphone was shoved into my face by an aggressive, female T.V. reporter. "Mr. McRain, can you tell us why the Judge chose you to defend the most powerful union leader in America?"

"Lucky, I guess. I'm just real lucky." I pushed through the crowd of union men, who seemed to stick to me like I was the tar baby.

One union protester shouted, "Look. Here's Casteel's new lawyer. Psycho Mike-O McRain." The union men were about two hundred in number. They began to chant, "Hip hip hurray, hip hip hurray." Upon a command from one of their cheerleading cohorts, they switched back, "Hog Heads forever."

I bulled my way through the crowd. It seemed to tighten upon me as I progressed. The protestors sensed their savior, Jake Casteel, was getting a screwing. The angry union men became a morass of testosterone and emotion. They were frustrated, fighting for their jobs and their way of life in a land that had promised the protection of all. But their gut instincts told them something sinister was secretly working against them.

I saw the protestor who had been dragged out of the courthouse. He had not been charged with contempt of court. He merely had been ejected from the courthouse and denied re-admittance.

I extended my hand in friendship, "You a friend of Jake Casteel's?" I asked.

The man nodded.

I could not hold back my suspense any longer. "What's a Hog Head?"

CHAPTER 39

# CHAPTER 40

# MISSION IMPOSSIBLE

I walked back to my Mustang. I sat in my car in shock, trying to absorb what had happened. I tried to get a grip on where my hectic life was going. It all hit me like a tsunami.

I had a terrible, internal conflict. A violence in my heart. I wrestled with the honor of a Marine Corps officer and with the ethics of representing a very powerful man in strange circumstances. My new client was a lawyer, accused of lying. I felt the battle raging in my soul. I saw the rosary hanging from my rearview mirror. I rubbed my Savior's cross in quiet, deep meditation. I slipped into a daydream as thick as fog.

*"Old Ironsides" lay steady on the calm Sea of Purgatory. Down in the bowels of the "Constitution," in Captain Carion's quarters, Mr. Fetid and Mr. Troubles counseled a callous Carion. Troubles stood before the Captain's desk, with his feet planted apart and his hands folded behind him at parade rest. He gripped his tri-cornered hat.*

*"Captain, I have serious doubts about this mission."*

*"Oh, really?"*

*Troubles held his nose as Mr. Fetid crossed in front of Mr. Troubles to seek a secure place beside the captain's good ear.*

*"Mr. Captain, Sir. We got Michael O'Brien McRain appointed to defend a lawyer who is charged with lying. That's an impossible case to defend. Lawyers lie when they open their mouths. It's like trying to defend a fish for swimming."*

*"So?" said Captain Carion.*

*"You are forcing McRain to get Jake Casteel acquitted when Chief Justice Nelson is going to convict him, no matter what?"*

*Mr. Fetid whispered something to Carion, who seemed not to be affected by the stench from Fetid. Over the centuries, he had built up a tolerance to his first mate. Carion had grown jaded. Injustice no longer moved him.*

*"What is your point, Mr. Troubles?"*

"You see, sir, if the fix is in and McRain is up against the railroad assassins, he doesn't have a chance."

Mr. Fetid walked over and looked closely into Mr. Troubles' face. Troubles covered his nose with his kerchief.

"I knew you was trouble when you first came aboard there, Mr. Troubles. Never seen an Irishman that didn't cry on about injustice," Fetid said. "Next, you'll be achin' your belly about a lion eating a lamb."

"Sir, I don't mean to be rocking the boat, so to speak. But Mike McRain is doomed to fail."

Captain Carion hammered his huge fist onto the desk and shouted, "Balderdash! You are talking nonsense."

Mr. Troubles dug in his heels, taking a stand. "It is not nonsense, sir. Admiral Jaundice would want to know about it. And he would know, if his conscience wasn't all occupied, what with the Avian Flu killing all those nice people in Asia. This mission will fail. It will fail badly. The Admiral will have my head because he wasn't told about it. I'm his legally appointed liaison for this mission. And I'm going to go tell him now."

Mr. Troubles turned to march out of the Captain's quarters. As Troubles neared the door, Captain Carion grabbed a sword hanging on the wall. He threw it, like a javelin, into Mr. Troubles' back. The sword impaled Mr. Troubles to the Captain's door. Troubles' belly stuck flat against the inside face of the door, and the point of the sword protruded from the other side. The skewered Mr. Troubles squawked and screamed, flopping like a speared fish, as Captain Carion and Mr. Fetid swung open the door, with Troubles suspended there, wiggling to get free.

Mr. Troubles' face was pressed hard against the dark wood of the door. The Captain fixed his mouth against Troubles' ear and spoke, clear and resolute.

"The mission stands, Mr. Troubles. Our man is going in."

As Carion and Fetid walked out, Mr. Fetid bent the end of the sword on the opposite side of the door, so Troubles could not push himself free so easily.

Troubles shouted loudly, up to the heavens, "This is treasonous. I have to tell the Admiral; he will have your heads."

Mr. Fetid stopped and turned. He removed his head. He held it at arm's length for Troubles to observe as his talking head spoke.

CHAPTER 40

Fetid's head said, "Don't be havin' such a long face there, Troubles. The Admiral's had my head a hundred times." Fetid moved his talking head in closer. It made Troubles ever more nauseous. "The winds of fate do change. You never know, now, do ya? Perhaps they'll fill our Mr. McRain's sails. Put him on a nice tack across the seas. Onto victory. Maybe even anchor our crew in Purgatory Cay."

Troubles persisted in being a naysayer, "Purgatory Cay? The salvation at Purgatory Cay? Huh! More likely, capsize Michael and our ship with a typhoon to Hell."

Mr. Fetid swaggered away, his head perched backward on his right shoulder, parroting Mr. Troubles' threats to tell Admiral Jaundice. "I'm going to tell Admiral Jaundice; I'm going to tell Admiral Jaundice; I'm going to tell Admiral Jaundice."

Carion's loud, sinister laugh could be heard as he shoved away Mr. Beelzebub, punched open the hatch, and climbed on deck, followed by Fetid. Mr. Troubles swung back and forth against the Captain's door. He pulled a calendar out of his pocket. And he spoke, aloud to himself, "Thirty days? To do the work of a legion? Why, it takes a staff of six lawyers at least ninety days to do a good job of it. Laddie, you'll be like Hercules, cleaning the stables of King Augaeas . But your task is twice as smelly, if the truth be said."

When the security guard for the federal courthouse swung open the door to my Mustang, I snapped out of my anxiety-filled trance.

"Hey, buddy, you all right? We gotta clear the parking lot. I was knocking on your window, and you didn't hear me. Who you talking to in there?

THE REDEEMER: IT IS WRITTEN

# CHAPTER 41

# WOMAN ABOARD

Back at the office, I was pacing up and down the client foyer. I stopped at the frosted glass door with the stenciled sign: *McRain and Boyle, Attorneys at Law.* My fist shook at the air as I shouted through the door.

"I told you reporters fifty thousand times, I have no comment; now, go away."

My arms waved in disgust as I turned to face Dalton. He was seated in a client chair in the foyer, watching T.V. news. The broadcast showed me coming out of the courthouse, into the crowd.

I protested, "I don't know why our secretary had to up and quit on a day like this."

"Probably the last straw, after all your 'Yes, sir, no, sir' bullshit and white-glove inspections."

Dalton pointed at the T.V. while I paced back and forth. "Hey, they just said the locomotive engineers are called the 'Hog Heads' because they ran the trains in the 1850s, sitting on a hog-head barrel of whisky."

"A shot or two of whisky sounds pretty good right now," I said.

Someone banged loud on the door. I flung it open, ready to paste whoever it was right across the chops. I even had my fist pulled back, ready to punch. I saw the crowd of reporters, in a flurry of questions. Seven men, with stenographer's pads and flashing cameras, tried to rush in. But a shorter figure darted into the office, just under my arm. I shut the door, preferring to deal with just one of them, instead of all. Perhaps give this one a good thrashing and then send him out, an example of what not to do when dealing with Mike McRain.

I turned to see a slender woman. I was stunned for a moment. She had the face of a goddess. Her dark hair shone. It was pulled back to reveal a face of timeless beauty. High forehead and beautiful, big brown eyes. She wore a flattering, black, business suit and a white blouse. Three-inch-heeled, black pumps adorned the ends of her shapely legs. I saw the throng of reporters had made it rough for her in the hallway. The way she clutched her purse tight, she looked like a scared child who had just seen a horror movie. But she had backbone.

She barked at the reporters, "You oughta stick those cameras where the sun don't shine." I shut the door. Flustered, she turned and spoke to me, "They are a bunch of rude bastards." She put her hand up over her mouth, embarrassed that she had cursed in front of Dalton and me.

I admit it. I was smitten from the very first moment.

I stepped between her and the door. I extended my hand to introduce myself, "Hi, I'm Mike McRain." She reacted like she preferred to get back to the throng of reporters.

"Whoa, you're that Psycho Mike-O."

I stalled for time. "You must be the girl the temp agency sent?" I got no response. "How long you been out there? What is your name?"

Ann felt trapped, and she made the best of it. She stuck her hand out and introduced herself, "Ann. Ann Parsons. I was out there long enough to learn that one of my new bosses is Psycho Mike-O. The lawyer for the most powerful union leader since Jimmy Hoffa. You don't look psycho."

I took a deep breath, as though I was getting ready to defend my reputation. Dalton came to my rescue, "He isn't psycho. He's just a gung-ho Marine, trapped in a lawyer's suit."

"The temp agency didn't tell me about Psycho Mike-O. I think I'd better leave." Ann looked frightened. She put her hand on the doorknob to walk out.

She stopped when I used the magic word, "Please. You came all this way. Why don't you stay and visit with us. I promise we don't bite."

Ann took her hand off the knob, "Okay. But I'm not promising anything. My Daddy's a Marine. I know how crazy you guys get."

I gently led Ann through our lobby: a waiting room with our secretary station at the end of the room, away from the door.

"Besides, you can't leave with those crazies out there. Please, let's sit down and talk." I motioned for Ann to step into my office. I insisted on shaking Ann's hand again before we took seats. I was definitely in a swoon over her.

"So you are our new secretary," said Dalton, more a statement than a question. He was trying to overcome her reluctance to take the position by subtly assuming she had already done so.

Dalton shook Ann's hand, then motioned behind Ann's back to me—in a classic, Three Stooges gesture of finger biting— that Ann was so pretty, he was going to faint. He started doing the "Curly" shuffle behind Ann's back. I began to laugh. My chuckle made Ann turn to look at Dalton. He acted like he was picking something up off the floor. Ann looked back at me, expecting an explanation. I gave her none because there is no explanation for Dalton, except that there isn't a serious bone in the man's body.

I pulled out a chair for Ann. The three of us sat around my desk.

I tried to disregard Dalton as I reached over my desk and shook Ann's hand for the third time, "I think you'll do just great." Trying not to reveal how nervous I was.

I liked Ann's hair pulled straight back. She had it knotted in a bun. It allowed a plain view of her greatest assets. Large, olive shaped eyes. Sophia Loren's kind of eyes. I was the biggest dork in the world, the way I was gushing over her.

"My name is Michael McRain. Most people just call me Mike."

I did not let go of her hand until she made a point of it.

"Uh, my hand?"

"I think we could certainly use someone with your experience."

"Experience? In what?" Ann asked.

"In handling crowds. You did a good job out there."

I had tunnel vision. My eyes were fixed on Ann's lips. It was worse than I thought. First, I was indicted for psychological guilt by a psychiatrist. Next, I was appointed to represent the most dangerous union leader in America on a criminal case in the U.S. Supreme Court. Then I met a woman who impressed me so much I was in a swoon. I felt embarrassed inside. But I went with the flow. It was like when I went through the Marine Corps Assault Course with my butt too high in the air, and I almost got my ass shot off. I gathered my composure and came down to hug the ground real quick.

"Why, thank you." Ann said.

I shook off my lover's eyes. "We just practice divorce law here."

"Satisfaction or *your honey* back." Dalton said.

Dalton had been corny his whole life. His favorite shtick was developing a rapport with woman through humor. Preferably beautiful women. He was great at it. He walked out of more bars than he could count, with a woman on his arm, just by being funny and approachable. I was always in awe how easily he accomplished it. I never could pull it off. Ever. I wrote it up as that we all have talents in life. It's not all bad that my best friend is a great pickup artist.

Ann and Dalton laughed, while I shook my head. Ann giggled at Dalton's corny humor and pushed Dalton hard with one hand. Dalton played the clown, well enough for an Academy Award. He fell off his chair and feigned injury. He drew even more laughter from Ann.

"You know a good lawyer? I want to sue." Dalton said.

My stone face reflected my intolerance for Dalton's show-off humor. Actually, I was getting jealous. I was red-faced over a girl I had met only ten minutes ago.

"You're a riot," Ann said, while Dalton acted like a dying cockroach, with his feet wiggling in the air. "I think it will be a lot of fun working for lawyers. I'm a country girl, but I've got a million lawyer jokes."

I sat at my desk, with my arms crossed in strained amusement as Ann and Dalton had their own little party, oblivious to me. I attempted to inject a serious tone over the meeting, but the jokesters did not pay any attention to me.

"Oh, yeah, oh, yeah. What do you call five hundred lawyers on the bottom of the ocean?" Dalton asked.

"A start," Ann said.

Dalton and Ann broke into uproarious laughter. Ann slapped her knee and punched Dalton on the shoulder. She tagged him good. I shook my head at the two clowns in front of me. Dalton signaled to me that Ann punched hard and might be a force to be reckoned with.

"Why are lawyers bottle fed when they are babies?" Ann said.

Dalton stole Ann's thunder. "Because their mothers don't even trust 'em.'"

Ann's mouth dropped open. She was astonished that Dalton knew the scandalous joke. Ann and Dalton laughed out loud, for stealing each other's punch lines. My jealousy grew.

"Okay, you're hired. Now can we get some work done?" I interjected above the boisterous banter growing between Ann and Dalton.

Ann and Dalton looked at each other. They got up and walked out of my office. Dalton winked at me over his shoulder as he pulled the door shut, leaving me to my own pity party.

"We'll take care of ol' starchy pants later. Now, where was I . . ."

Dalton showed Ann around the office and went over general procedures. Ann assured Dalton she had plenty of experience working in law offices. She promised to keep the hours we needed. But she explained she needed off, right at 5 p.m., on the button. She had to pick up her eight-year-old daughter Kylee from daycare. She was a single mother, fresh from a nasty divorce.

Ann showed us she was a worker. She rolled up her sleeves and dove right in. In about three minutes, she had the filing system figured out. She entered Dalton's office to deliver a pile of files for his week's court appearances. She looked at pictures on the wall in his office as Dalton sat at his desk, reviewing documents.

"Boy, there's sure a lot of pictures of you and Mike. You all grow up together?"

"Partners in crime, our whole lives."

Dalton got up and walked over to point out particular photos to Ann. Pictures of Dalton and me in high school baseball, football, and boxing uniforms.

"Mike has always been my best friend, since we were kids. The man can throw anything." Dalton pointed to the baseball photo and then at other photos, "All-State pitcher, All-State quarterback, and he threw a Hell of a right as a Golden Gloves boxer." Dalton faked a boxer's feint, drawing Ann's smile. "I was his catcher. His tight-end. And his sparring partner. There isn't anything that man can't throw."

"Sounds like my ex. He used to throw me into walls."

Dalton raised his hands to indicate the negative. "No, no, no, Mike is nothing like that. He wouldn't harm a fly; I mean, not if it wasn't deserved. It's just something that goes back. Way back to when he was a kid. Crime victim and all that,"

Dalton said. "If you get past his tough bark, he's the biggest clown in the world."

"He sounds like fun," Ann said.

"He's been a bit of a recluse since his Dad died." Dalton turned and walked to his desk. He picked up some papers and took a seat as he addressed Ann. "He was a knife fighting instructor, firearms instructor, hand-to-hand combat instructor, counter-intelligence instructor, and sniper instructor in the Marine Corps." Dalton acted as though he was thinking, "Did I leave anything out? I wouldn't want to have any other man next to me if I had to march through the gates of Hell. He's the best man on the planet." Ann nodded her understanding and turned to walk out of the office.

"But, oh, I forgot. Beware; knock real loud before you enter Mike's office. He has a target on the back side of the door that he throws knives into." Dalton moved his hand across his hair as though he were creasing it. "Parted one secretary's hair."

Ann raised her eyebrows in amazed fear and surprise that a learned man like Mike, who had a law degree from Harvard, would still be such a man's man, a macho man. The exact opposite of the wimpy lawyers portrayed on T.V. She knew she had misjudged him at first blush. "Thanks for the warning," Ann said. She walked out of the office with the files and smiled a friendly smile at Dalton as she shut the door behind her. Dalton shook his head and cursed his dilemma, being the boss of a beautiful and available woman.

"*Mercy*," he thought, "*Angels really do live on Earth.*"

CHAPTER 41

# CHAPTER 42

# ESCAPE

The phone was ringing off the hook at the small, law office of McRain and Boyle. It was something that Dalton and I were not accustomed to. Ann was swamped, trying to field the calls to shield us from prying reporters. I spent most of my day trying to understand how the media seldom sought the truth, but instead tried to create a good story. "I told you for the fifteenth time I have no comment. You need me to spell it out for you?" I paused to listen to the biting voice in the phone, and I railed back at it.

"Yes, I think it would be professionally irresponsible for you to run headlines 'Psycho Mike-O Represents Lying Lawyer.'" What? No. Not because lying lawyer would be redundant. Yes, I was a Marine Corps officer in charge of training drill instructors. Should I call you maggot? Hello? Hello?"

I was fuming. I slammed down the phone. I opened my desk drawer to see a Polaroid of the tombstone: the stone. My mind was in a dither, and my head was shaking, back and forth, when Ann knocked on the door three times, loudly and forcefully. It sounded like she was one of the ancients, hammering on the gates to my fortress: my refuge from the world, which was being invaded by impertinent journalists who pursued not the truth, but the story.

I looked up and I saw her——her head peeking in the door. I motioned her in. She marched up to my desk in a comical way. She presented with a bright smile, an exaggerated snap to military attention, and a non-regulation salute, "Sir, I mean Mr. McRain, I've finished all that filing. I checked, and the reporters are still out in the hall. But there are even more of them, now that they've found out that you represent that labor boss, Jake Casteel."

"Too bad I don't have a frag grenade to clear 'em out."

Ann relaxed and pointed at the sword hanging on the wall in my office. "My Daddy has a Marine Corps sword just like that one."

I was immediately intrigued, "Oh, really?"

"Yes, Sir. He keeps it above the fireplace, crossed over the old, double-barrel shotgun. It's real pretty, like yours."

"When was your Father in the Corps?"

"World War II. He doesn't talk about it much. He has a big Medal of Honor hanging on the hilt of his sword, for the fight they gave the Japs at Iwo Jima."

I knew at that point I was hopelessly in love with Ann. I sat there, gape mouthed. Not because her Father was a highly decorated Marine. But because she had been *raised* by a Marine.

I felt I could trust her to understand me, like a Marine. Most women could not understand how my drive and my sense of honor affected my approach to life. They thought I was a dork for shaking their hands when I walked them to the door at the end of a first date, instead of trying to steal a kiss or bed them.

Ann regarded my blank stare. It passed straight through her. She thought I was just daydreaming about my legal work. "Yes, Sir, and, oh, I forgot to tell you earlier, I need to get let off work at four o'clock today, please. I'm divorced, and I have to pick up my little girl, Kylee, from the babysitter in order to get her to a doctor's appointment. That okay, Sir?"

"That will be fine, Miss Ann." Ann turned to walk away after a quick thank you.

"I'd rather land at Iwo Jima than answer all their questions out there," I said to Ann's back.

Ann stopped. She turned around, "Wanna hear my plan to get you two outa here, past those jackals?"

I perked up, "You've got an evasion plan?"

Fifteen minutes later, Dalton and I were looking out the second-story window at the rear of our law office. Ann pulled her baby-blue, '66 Chevy pick-up truck beneath. She was using Daddy's truck. It had a big, chrome cattle-guard across the front grill. Dalton and I swung out the window, lowered ourselves down onto the roof of the pick-up's cab, and climbed down onto the bed of the truck. Dalton and I lay in the back of the pick-up truck, to avoid being seen by the reporters. Ann gunned it and took off, around to the front of the building, past the throng of reporters lying in ambush for Dalton and me.

Ann got us to my car and stopped. We jumped off the truck bed. I walked to Ann's driver-side window.

"Thanks for the lift, "I said.

"Lighten up. Don't let the journalists get to you. Daddy always says, he may have left his leg on Iwo Jima, but he'd a died without a sense of humor," Ann said. Her fudge-brown eyes were kind to me. Dalton sensed the chemistry between us. He gave me a wide berth, to work my backwards, "aw shucks" mojo.

"I hope to meet your Daddy some day. He sounds like a good man."

"I don't know if I'm gonna tell him about this Bonnie and Clyde, escape routine. He's gonna give me enough trouble just knowing that I am back to working for lawyers."

"Lawyers?"

I forgot to ask her work history. I had been tripping all over my tongue when I first met her. I was about to ask her who she had worked for, but Ann nodded her head and smiled. She put the truck in gear, and the truck jumped off about as fast as the its slow, granny gear would go. Ann waved good-bye.

"Good luck with your jailbird." Ann repeated her wave as she looked at Dalton and me in the large, side-view mirror.

"A woman and an old blue truck," I said, as I watched Ann's truck slowly pull out, onto the main drag.

Dalton punched my shoulder. I didn't flinch. I didn't even feel it. "What are you doing? You can't hit on your secretary. It's immoral."

I snapped out of my daydream of Ann and me, somewhere down the road, hitting it off. I wondered if I enjoyed that daydream more because I had a real life in the dream or because it included Ann. "What you talkin' about. I was admiring that '66 Chevy's tailgate."

"Sure, checking out her tailgate now. Do I have to worry about a sexual harassment claim against the firm some day? Yeah, she's real pretty, but Catholic, like you and me."

"What does that have to do with anything?"

"Dontcha see, Mike-O? Beautiful and Catholic? She'll frustrate you to Hell and back. She's a Catholic Miller-Lite girl."

"Ok. Whatza Catholic Miller-Lite Girl?"

"Tastes great. Less willing."

I almost hit Dalton for that one. Always the joker. But he came by it naturally. Dalton had been cracking those kinds of jokes in the back of catechism class, at St. Mary the Immaculate Parish, since before our first communion. He was the best friend I could possibly have. I was the serious one. He was the jester. Together, we made a pretty good team. We laughed as we got into my Mustang and made fast tracks towards the jail.

Neither of us knew many details about Jake Casteel.

"They say this Casteel guy is a lawyer, a real hard ass. But a great labor organizer."

"I don't know about Casteel. We gotta meet him and see what we can shake free. I have a bad feeling about this one. Kinda like I used to get when my C.O. would volunteer me for a suicide mission."

CHAPTER 42

# CHAPTER 43

# INTERROGATION

It seemed we went over the facts a dozen times with our new client, Jake Casteel. But no progress. I leaned back in my chair. My face turned towards the drab concrete ceiling of the St. Martinsville Jail's client-interview room. It was a typical, client-interview room: small and dusty, with a steel table, steel chairs, and hardass attitudes. Dalton stuck a whittled-down pencil behind his ear. He clasped his hands together and gave me a look, like he thought Casteel was hiding something.

"We've been here a couple hours, and we're running in circles," I said.

"We've been over this ten times," Casteel said, as he sat, his powerful forearms resting on the table in a typical, jailhouse "protect my food" posture.

Persistence is one of my faults. "And one more time. You were dragged in front of a grand jury investigating how R.I.O. cases kept going to the Falic, Moore and DeVillay law firm, and the Assistant U.S. Attorney asked you 337 questions in 120 minutes. And they warned you forty times to answer "Yes" or "No" with no explanation, by you, allowed. The legal wet boys from Washington picked out two 'No, Sir' answers that were actually true, but sounded technically wrong, so they charged you with Perjury on Admiralty, which of course denies you a right to a trial by a jury of your peers. Judge Lackey was hand-picked by the Department of Justice. And he slam dunked you guilty before you could find out what you were actually charged with. Trial by ambush."

Jake nodded his head in melodramatic fashion. He was insulting me by giving me obvious, nonverbal responses, indicating that my interview techniques were unnecessary and droll. I had not yet earned his respect. And without his respect I knew I would not be worth a damn as his lawyer. I decided to think outside the box and play directly to my audience — a battle

-tempered Marine. I had to forget that Jake Casteel was also a lawyer, in order to get through the thick skull of a jar head. It was about time to stop talking legal theory and use some body language. But I was patient, in spite of my growling stomach.

"And I told the truth," Casteel said, in defiance. He wanted out of the interview room. He wanted us to turn some kind of miracle. Jake was a lawyer. He knew we couldn't just wave a magic wand to make it all go away, like they do in Hollywood. Somehow, he wanted us to exonerate him, without talking about the facts. He knew better than that. I could feel it in my gut. Casteel was hiding something.

"I believe you," I said. "You get railroaded through your trial and your appeal in Chicago. We are back to square one. But why would the Feds be worried about you referring railroad-injury cases to lawyers? I mean, what business is that of the government?"

"It's all too complicated. Can't we just appeal the truthfulness of my answers, without getting into all this other stuff?" Casteel's evasiveness was beginning really to piss me off.

"There's supposed to be an open line of communication between attorney and client, based upon a relationship of trust. If you can't tell me everything, then who *can* you tell everything?" Casteel was being too cute with Dalton and me. He gave us a brush-off look.

I stood up. I leaned over the table and got in Casteel's face. "I think this 'other stuff' is something you and I know is important. If I'm gonna be your lawyer, I gotta know all of it."

Little did I know that Colonel Durant was outside, listening to the whole interview with a couple of techs in a surveillance van.

The bare, concrete walls of the interview room were cold to the touch. As our interview progressed, they seemed to close in and wrap around us, like a polar freeze. It gave us an up-close and personal feeling, without the ambiance. I could smell Casteel's coffee- and starch-laced, jailhouse breath, so strong, it almost crawled across the table. Like Marine chow line breath, only heavier. I stroked my chin as I thought. I put one foot up on the chair and placed my hand on the table. He could see I was getting comfortable. I wasn't going anywhere soon. Finally, Casteel started to flap his lips.

"Let me tell you when the shit hit the fan,"

"Bring it."

"I dropped a bomb. Really, two bombs. Big ones. I threatened a nationwide strike. As the international president for the rail union, I can call a strike at any time. That is why they put my ass in here."

So far, we were just getting a civics lesson and a history of the American labor movement that sounded much like the life story of the second, most famous labor leader, Eugene Debs.

I got the sneaky suspicion that history was trying to repeat itself. It sounded like my client might be following in the sad footsteps of America's largest labor legend. Bigger than Jimmy-Hoffa big.

Eugene Victor Debs was a railroad union labor organizer who, like Jimmy Hoffa, was also railroaded into prison. But Debs was so popular amongst the manual laborers, those who earn their livings honestly, that he received almost one million votes in the 1920 United States Presidential election, while he still sat in prison!

A fleeting image flashed through my mind, that the government might try to do the same thing to my client that it did to Eugene Debs. A set-up. Debs and Casteel were both leaders of powerful railroad unions. And both were prosecuted, using very suspicious and ancient laws that cut off a man's ability to defend himself in court: against Debs, the then U.S. Attorney General, who sat on the railroad's board of directors, used the old Espionage Act of 1917 that prohibited uttering anything against the U.S. President. And against Casteel, the government chose to employ the Perjury On Admiralty Act, which prohibited a trial by jury and prevented any effective defense by allowing the prosecutors to change the charges against the accused after the Defendant could no longer speak on his own behalf.

I went to Harvard Law School. But I drew the majority of my life experience from being in the Marine Corps' elite commando unit, Force Recon. One of the first things they teach you in Force Recon is to follow your gut instincts. They teach you to look for things in your fighting environment that have a connection. I was receiving double signals about my client, Casteel. My gut instinct was screaming at me. There was a connection between Jake Casteel and those earlier labor leaders, somewhere in this case. I did not know back then how prophetic my gut instinct was.

I tried to keep things on track. The interview was drawing on much too long. And somehow I had to gain my client's total respect.

"A nationwide rail strike is the Pentagon's worst nightmare. Can't move their tanks and trucks, food and fuel. I'm surprised they didn't off you," I said.

"I am, too. I kept my boot knife," said Casteel, as he slapped his lower, right ankle, as though he were reaching for a knife tucked in his boot. It was only a charade because he was wearing the jail-issue, slip-on deck shoes.

"What's the other bomb you dropped?"

Casteel lowered his head and examined his hands. He picked at calluses he'd developed from holding onto the bars of the jail cell to do stretching and isometric exercises. He was a typical "A" personality in jail: a caged animal.

"I told the mafia we weren't gonna do business with them any more."

"Come again?" Dalton and I shook our heads at the notion of a mafia.

"You just mentioned a mafia," I said.

Casteel froze and would no longer speak.

"We've been here three hours and once we hear 'mafia,' the cat's got your tongue," Dalton said, in indictment of our client.

"It's nothing," Casteel said.

He was weaseling on us. "It's nothin'? You hear that man? It's nothin'. Well, row-dee-dow, idn't that a kicker?" I said. I felt that we weren't really developing a chummy type of relationship with Casteel. I saw the Marine bulldog tattooed on Casteel's left arm. It displayed "*Semper Fi*" in faded blue ink. We had been playing ring-around-the-rosie for hours and I wanted the truth. I realized that there was but one thing that would make Jake respect me as a man, as a Marine, and only then, as his lawyer.

I was a professional educated at Harvard, but I was trained by U.S.M.C. Devil Dogs. The man was lying to me and acting flip about a mafia; exposing

CHAPTER 43

Dalton and me to danger. I made a risky, command decision. Action was required. I could feel my client drifting away with a disgusted lack of respect for me. But I had to win his case; for Casteel, sure, but more so to square-up with my demons of the dead. I decided I was not going to leave that jail empty handed, without the truth.

Forget the professional demeanor between two lawyers, when both of them are Marines, and one of them is lying and pulling the other's chain. Things get squared away quickly. Also, there is a little known Rule of Attorney Ethics that provides that when one Marine is representing another Marine and the client Marine is clearly lying and evasive, you are allowed to kick his ass to get the truth.

"We are both lawyers, but I can't help using my nose. I smell a rat. You're leading me right onto a damned minefield aren't you?"

"Hell no. Nothin' you should be concerned about."

"Zat so?" I studied Casteel. His eyes were averting mine. And we had a protocol for these type situations in the Corps. Clear, linear communication. I spoke to my client in  a language I knew he would understand, marine-speak, with a violent purpose.

"Mr. Casteel, you're an old, Marine sergeant. Tell Dalton here what N.R.A. means in the Corps."

"Yeah . . ." Casteel hesitated. "N.R.A.," he said to Dalton, "means 'No Rank . . .'"

"Asshole," I said.

I threw a punch, like a cannonball, across the table to Casteel's jaw. I struck him so hard, he fell off the back of his chair, ass over ankles. I ran around the table to finish the job.

I had hit him hard and square. Right on the chops. It could have knocked out a horse. But Casteel was a battle-hardened Marine. He had been thrown into the air by explosions and shrapnel in the merciless heat of war. He came up, swinging, and landed a right uppercut on me that about took me off my feet. Dalton jumped in and tried to break up the fight. I got around Dalton, behind Casteel, and put Jake in a chokehold. Dalton's attempts to get me off Casteel were in vain.

"You son-of-a-bitch. You're holdin' out!" I squeezed his throat harder, "Who is it? Who's got your gonads?"

I was either going to get my hard-ass client's respect and a three-course meal of the truth or I was going to push away from the table and get rid of this client. I squeezed him like a python. I lightened up, right before his larynx would have collapsed, "Who?" I cursed him, hard and mean, with the vile words Marines stab into others, when they are at their very worst and their very best. "Who?" Jake struggled through the choke. I relented enough to allow a hoarse whisper to escape his blue lips.

"*Di Trina.*"

"*Di Trina?* You ever heard of *Di Trina?*" I said to Dalton, who had been pounding on my back the whole time, bouncing a couple dozen knuckles off my head, trying to get me to let go of our client.

Dalton was finally successful in separating the two of us. Casteel staggered back to the table. We had it now, respect between two Marines who just happened to be lawyers. I wiped my bloody lip on the back of my hand.

"My Italian's a bit rusty, but I think it means, 'the train,'" Dalton said, as he handed Casteel a handkerchief for his nosebleed. We watched Jake dab blood from his nose, simultaneously attempting to massage his throat back into a speaking condition.

Before the interview, I told Dalton how I wanted to conduct our first meeting with Casteel. Use some roleplaying. Good cop. Bad cop. Now it appeared Dalton had shifted roles. He was aggressive and more than a little pissed off. Dalton yanked the reigns of the interview from me. I was impressed.

Good cop gone bad.

CHAPTER 43

# CHAPTER 44

# EAVSDROPPERS

The back of my skull started to throb from the peppering my law partner had given me with his fist, trying to peel me off our client. Dalton attacked Casteel with his own questions.

"Tell us somethin' makes sense. What's this mafia bullshit? You're talkin' like you're crazy."

"I trust you," Casteel whispered, as he made a circular motion above his head. "But the air has ears."

"We're bein' bugged?" Dalton said.

I had the feeling that the mafia that Jake was referring to was not the mafia of wise guys, machine guns, and drug trafficking. Black markets are everywhere. They always precede legitimate markets, and they outlast them, too. There is organized crime in every country in the world, and each organization is different. Some are more violent than others, and some are almost without violence, run in a somewhat genteel way, where violence is reserved for only the rarest circumstances. At F.B.I., they say, "The Italian mob plays Bocce ball, and the Russian mob plays chess." But the Russian mob is a lot more vicious than the Italian.

As a Special Forces operative who had conducted numerous G.B.G.– "Get the Bad Guy"–missions for C.I.A. around the world, I knew that much of our country's intelligence is gathered from organized-crime sources from across the planet. When the foreign mafia was being killed by secret, Special Forces troops, who made it look like rival mobsters did the killing, the reluctant Mafioso's became cooperative and sang like canaries. Once they understood that Uncle Sam was not there to convict them or put them in prison, the mafia relaxed a bit. Squeezing them for information after that was usually pretty easy. Now, I wanted more information from Casteel. We were both Marines, and we would communicate the way we knew best—face to face and nose to nose.

I was all ears, as Casteel nodded that he believed someone was listening to our sacred, attorney-client interview. I didn't believe it myself, but I did a quick recon of the room for bugs. There it was. Dead center, under the client table. I picked it off and crushed it under my heel. I knew the old rule of electronic surveillance they taught me at Fort Meade. If they went to the trouble to place one bug, there were probably two or three more that were better hidden.

~~~~~~~~~~~~~~~~~~~~~~~~~~~~~~~~~~~~~~~~~~~~~~~~~~~~~

Out in the surveillance van, the lead technician was miffed, due to a sudden loss of audio. "Lost sound, Sir. Switching to alternate frequency," he said to Colonel Durant, who was finishing a knife-point etching in the paint on the inside of the van. A cute, little picture of a stick-figure man, pissing on flowers.

"Break up the party," said Durant.

~~~~~~~~~~~~~~~~~~~~~~~~~~~~~~~~~~~~~~~~~~~~~~~~~~~~~

In the jail's interview room, we pressed on, despite my doubts we could make a clean sweep of the electronic bugs.

"I'm a union officer. I'm under a Masonic oath of secrecy to keep it on the square. I've told you too much," said Casteel.

"I can't help you if you don't help me," I said. I took back the reins of the client interview from Dalton, with nothing said between us. I was angry, and Dalton got out of my way.

"Gotta keep it on the square. They threatened my family. My niece, DeeDee, the one you saved."

"DeeDee?"

What a small, small world it just had become. The picture was becoming clearer as I began to connect some dots.

CHAPTER 44

"Look, if they were gonna kill you and your family, they would have done it by now."

I knew my audience. And I used slang and vernacular, as they were called for. Casteel was defiant. He did not understand my expertise in these matters.

"How do you know that?" Casteel said.

"Let's just say I was a 'Force Recon'. I used to be in the business."

Matter of fact, between attorney and client. That's the way I liked it. But then I got hit with an epiphany. I stood and pointed my finger upward, as though I had come up with the invention of fire.

"If we can find out why they haven't killed you, we're going to find out why they convicted you on some bullshit perjury charge."

"What's '*Di Trina*?'" Dalton said.

"The railroad finances *Di Trina* because the mafia runs the railroad," Casteel said.

"What's the mafia's angle?"

"It's not so much the mafia as it is the government. C.I.A. has the mafia come by and drop money on the union men and the pollies."

"C.I.A.? Now I know you're bull shittin'. The C.I.A. has no domestic jurisdiction. They are strictly international," I said.

"C.I.A. has been claiming jurisdiction on every international union operating inside the U.S. since the "Red Scare," Harvard boy. Welcome to Economics 101," Casteel said.

Casteel looked to the door, as the C.O. barged in with reinforcements. "Interview's over, gentlemen." The first C.O. said, showing a billy club.

"You can't do this. We get as much time as we need," Dalton said.

"Not for Casteel, you don't," said the first C.O.

The C.O.'s reinforcements grabbed Casteel and started to drag him out of the room. Dalton tried to stop them. That earned him and Casteel each a billy club to the stomach. Casteel moaned, and Dalton bent over.

"Stay away from them. Too powerful," Casteel said, as he was pushed out of the room.

I tended to Dalton, who was doubled over in pain.

"I suppose that was an interview technique Harvard taught you? Missed that course in law school-—advanced chokeholds for the problem client. Who was your professor? Dick the Bruiser?" Dalton said, as he recuperated in a chair.

I stood him up, dusted him off, and pointed him towards the door, as I picked up our briefcases. We needed more intel.

"Come on. Let's take a ride."

# CHAPTER 45

# ALPHA MALE

Big Dutch Van Killman was seated in a large, leather chair at his huge desk. His face was battered. His left eye was swollen shut, and it was starting to color. Dutch's left, pinky finger displayed a gold ring with an inlaid, golden spike.

A knife was stabbed into the back of Big Dutch's left hand, trapping it palm down on the top of the desk, next to his phone. Blood trickled down, pooling on either side of Dutch's hand and between his fingers.

Knuckles sat in one of Big Dutch's leather, client chairs, with his back to Colonel Durant, who stood at the door. Durant was dressed in civvies and he sucked the contents from a packet of Taco Bell hot sauce. He looked at Big Dutch.

"Remember that personnel change will be done by morning, or I'll be back and I'll debate you, too."

Big Dutch swore vengeance. "The President will obliterate your world, mister. Who do you think you are, coming in here and . . ."

Durant interrupted Big Dutch, "I killed your white dog, so I could deal exclusively with your dark side. Don't spoil it and go weak on me now."

In the corner, Big Dutch's black pit bull was lying on the floor, with a bullet through its hips. It was licking the head of its dead, white brother, which had a knife stuck into its throat.

Durant looked at Knuckles' back. "What's wrong, Knuckles, cat got your tongue?"

Knuckles was unresponsive. Durant laughed.

"Don't feel bad. I was captain of the debate team at West Point."

"And thanks for your backhanded advice, Dutchie. How did you phrase that? 'I don't let nothing or nobody get in my way making a profit.

Nothing.' That's a good one. I'll remember that when I get out of the Army and go into business for myself."

"You are a crazy bastard. You know that, don't you?" Big Dutch said.

"And you are a greedy bastard."

Durant opened the door.

"I think we'll work well together."

Durant left.

As the door shut, it allowed Dutch a view of Davis, sitting on the floor behind the door Durant had exited. Davis's eyes were still open, even though he had a nine-millimeter hole in the middle of his forehead.

Knuckles made a futile struggle. Both his forearms were nailed to the arms of the client chair with K-Bar knives. A gold letter opener, with an emblem on its hilt identical to the one on Big Dutch's ring, was stabbed into Knuckles' throat. The emblem was the symbol of *Di Trina*. Knuckles could only gurgle as he drowned on his own blood.

Big Dutch stared at Knuckles in disbelief. He struggled to reach across his own body with his free, right hand. He picked up the receiver of the phone, sitting to the left of his impaled hand, and put it to his ear. Angry, trembling fingers stabbed at the numbers on the phone and he put the receiver to his ear.

"Get me Senator Moore. No. I don't care that it's three a.m. in Switzerland." Big Dutch drummed the fingers of his impaled hand on the desktop. Impatient. He could feel his tendon twitch against the knife blade.

"Just tell him it's railroad business. He'll get his ass out of bed if he wants to get reelected."

CHAPTER 45

# CHAPTER 46

*"The best place to steal is in the U.S. Senate;*
*no watch dogs."*
—Bridget

United States Senator Joseph Youngstown Moore was chairman of the United States Senate Judiciary Committee. A four-term senator running for reelection found that voter polls in his home state were up. So much so that the other party had not even offered a candidate to oppose him. Reelection would be a cakewalk.

Moore was a shrewd politician. A pure politician. Every nice thing Senator Moore did for his constituents had a price extracted for his benefit. He championed many conservative causes, including a blistering attack on the plaintiff's bar and the personal-injury tort system. Surprisingly, that attack exempted the R.I.O. railroad personal-injury system.

It was a family cluster-grab. Even though his son, Bratford Moore; his stepson Felix Falic; and his stepson's stepdaughter, DeeDee DeVillay, were milking the R.I.O. system for tens of millions of dollars per year, no journalist ever picked up on Senator Moore's profound conflict of interest. Moore supported all that benefited his family. How Senator Moore, who was an ordained minister, could so zealously preach from his tabernacle for the damnation of tort lawyers, on one hand, and remain the savior of railroad-injury, tort lawyers, on the other, was a perplexing question. That would seem irreconcilable unless you understood a little of Moore's family business. And applied President Harry Truman's Teapot Dome Scandal rule for investigating complex thievery.

Follow the money.

The scalawags were putting the huge contingent legal fees, that they made on railroad injury cases, into small banks that they controlled or out-right owned. Whenever they needed a large withdrawal of cash for bribes, they just took it and filled out fraudulent forms filed with the banking regulators. Simple. But illegal as Hell. Big time money laundering.

Felix Falic and Bratford Moore were the two, most senior partners in the largest, railroad-injury firm in America, Falic, Moore & DeVillay. DeeDee was the junior partner. Senator Moore was simply keeping the riches of the railroad-injury system in the family. As with all large systems that generate mountains of cash, there must be some sharing and cooperation with others. Law firms. Lawyers. Politicians. Judges. Reliable bag men to deliver money. Prostitutes to do what they do best – make the union men compliant and happy. And, most importantly, greasing the palms of the union men and their officers. They were all necessary to make the system work.

Senator Moore had the whole system down to a science.

Secretly, Senator Moore siphoned off millions of dollars, of personal injury legal fees to himself, under the table from his family's R.I.O. law practice, where he was listed on the letterhead as "Of Counsel."

The in-house payments of cash were always delivered in brown-leather satchels. The payola destined for the Senator's Cayman Island accounts was picked up by Senator Moore personally, behind closed doors in the sanctity of Falic, Moore & DeVillay's building in downtown St. Martinsville. Accordingly, the cash payments were commonly referred to by the firm's core conspirators—the lawyers and the firm runners who went and fetched the money—as "brown bags." It was a secret, cash-money, drop system that had worked for decades.

The big risk with Moore's tort referral system was that Moore had little control over the Department of the Treasury. To put it pure and simple, what he and his law firm were doing was tax evasion. Senator Moore saw no need to let Treasury in on his little scheme. And the threat of an I.R.S. audit was a wonderful way to keep the union conspirators quiet, since none of them wanted the I.R.S. knocking on their doors, asking the railroaders how much in cash payments they took under the table from Moore's law firm and why they did not list those payoffs on their tax returns.

CHAPTER 46

DeeDee was cursed by something that spared Felix. DeeDee had a conscience, the scourge of lawyers. On more than one occasion, DeeDee asked her step-step-grandfather, Senator Moore, if what they were doing was tax evasion and money laundering. His standard response was, "Keep your mouth shut. We have been doing this for decades. Nobody's rocked the boat yet. Treasury doesn't need to know." The one that twisted her stomach the most, "You wouldn't look good in one of those orange, prison uniforms." But DeeDee knew the truth. She did not need Senator Moore to tell her the obvious.

*It was illegal as Hell.*

Senator Moore and all the other R.I.O. lawyers in America knew it was criminal. But they believed they had the keys to the perfect crime. It seemed to work sort of like a Monopoly game Get-Out-Of-Jail-Free card. The Senate Judiciary Committee had oversight for the whole Department of Justice. That included America's primary watchdog, the F.B.I. Nothing moved inside F.B.I. without Senator Moore knowing about it. He made sure the people he placed in jobs in the D.O.J. reported any activity about R.I.O. directly to his office.

Plainly, Senator Moore, as Chairman of the Senate Judiciary Committee, was thieving at the expense of the American people. But no journalist picked up on the story because Senator Moore's office made any explanation so convoluted that no journalist—and no lawyer who was not in on the scheme—could understand how the system milked America for a couple of billion dollars per year.

A decade later, the public would find out that making a simple thing complex would allow the world's economy to be washed away. The worthless, trillion-dollar hedge-fund dealings discovered much too late, marking the beginning of The Great Collapse, were akin to the white-collared criminality of the R.I.O. lawyers scheme. There was a striking similarity between the R.I.O. racketeering and the use of hedge funds with derivatives—almost all the trickery was conducted in plain sight. This reinforces the old circus huckster's claim that the best place to hide an elephant is on the front porch. But journalists had not fully figured out either scheme.

DeeDee knew that what they represented to the inquisitive was like the scene in "*The Wizard of Oz*," "Pay no attention to the man behind the curtain." But none of the journalists ever did what Dorothy's little dog, Toto, had done. They never pulled back the curtain to expose the truth.

Senator Moore's secret, money machine worked like a goose that laid golden eggs because nobody on the inside of the scheme ever talked. Every single one of the lawyers in the firm was required to make brown-bag drops. At first, they were not told what was in the brown satchel. After they had delivered "documents" a few times, they were told the truth. By then, they were participants in the ongoing scheme to pay bribes and kickbacks to union leaders, judges, and politicians. They didn't talk because if they did, after they knew about the scheme and participated in it, they were headed for prison, like all the others. But Moore had another way to keep people from spilling the beans about R.I.O.

*Di Trina.* His own little, lawyers' mafia. If somebody's lips got too loose, you never heard from them again. They went swimming with the fishes in the muddy Mississippi River.

CHAPTER 46

# CHAPTER 47

# PROTECTION MONEY

DeeDee was too smart for her own good. DeeDee knew it was Senator Moore's iron-gloved command of the Senate Judiciary Committee that kept the whole system alive. R.I.O. was a relatively unknown federal statute that the railroads had been halfheartedly lobbying to have it repealed for the previous thirty years.

Or so went the story.

It was only by means of Senator Moore's heavy politicking and sleight of hand, in the form of brown-bag payoffs to compliant politicians, that the Senate Judiciary Committee kept the railroad's "Repeal R.I.O." bills off the Senate floor.

It was the bribes paid to high-level and local union officials that kept the working man's voice out of the halls of Congress. And it kept the trains running on time, by not allowing union leadership to call a strike.

The R.I.O. bribery and kickback system had morphed over the years into what was now a mafia protection racket. It required the railroad to pay "Protection Money" to the Designated lawyers, to keep their trains running on time. If they didn't pay the protection money, the union would call a small strike. Then, if that did not get the railroad's attention, the international—union president would order a primary strike that would shut down the whole United States.

The railroads begrudgingly allowed R.I.O. to stay alive, so the R.I.O. lawyers could make their billions in profits. From which they would then turn around and pay their own protection tax to the politicians who kept the R.I.O. system on the book of laws. The runners, the men carrying the brown bags full of money, worked for the Designated law firms. They were kept quite busy on Capitol Hill, delivering bribes to the politicians and the railroad-union leaders, who kept the railroads running.

The end result was no rail strikes.

The scheme had a perfect, circular logic, fueled by money paid by the unsuspecting American consumers and taxpayers. The secret, lawyer mafia tax. As a result, Moore and his brothers and sisters in crime milked America, like a dairy cow, for billions over the decades. There were few rail-union strikes that crippled the economy. The trains ran on time. And Senator Moore and his cronies raked in the dough.

The worst part of it all was its effect on the average American family. John Q. Public, his wife, Jane, and their three children were being drained, like victims of Count Dracula. They paid more for every single thing they bought because the cost of rail transportation was artificially higher, to pay for all the bribes and kickbacks the R.I.O. system required. Even the cost of their electricity was higher because of *Di Trina*. Railroads transported fuel to the majority of America's power plants.

The taxpayers were paying for the crooked R.I.O. system, too. The government was paying enormous amounts for transporting millions of tons of government materials and for coal generated electricity; coal delivered by rail transportation. Thanks to Senator Moore, Uncle Sam passed along the huge cost of the R.I.O. system's bribery, waste, and corruption to unwitting American taxpayers. If the secret lawyer mafia tax had been divulged to the public, the National Taxpayers Conglomeration would have yelled, "Taxation without representation!"

But the gigantic R.I.O. system could tiptoe through America only so long before, eventually, the giant would make some noise. The most noise came from the rumbling in DeeDee's stomach, as she fretted over a life in prison. She had ulcers and she kept big jars of antacids in her office and on her bedside table. DeeDee knew her stepfather's stepfather, Senator Moore, was a first-rate scalawag. But she still loved him. And she loved her money. Such love was inseparable, in her gold-lined heart.

It was an expensive and complicated system. But it worked. Two billion dollars, of suspicious fees per year, went into lawyers' pockets. And then an honest man, Jake Casteel, took office as International President of C.U.R.T.I.S. He was elected on a "Reform the System" ticket that promised to straighten out the crooked R.I.O. personal-injury system. Casteel pissed off the wrong people for the right reason. And now there would be blood to pay.

CHAPTER 47

# CHAPTER 48

# THE INTIMIDATOR

Dalton and I were angry and tired. After we left the jail, we tried to analyze the conflicting stories given by our client. The night road had been cooled by a fresh rain, now stopped, that left the roads slick. I stayed off the main drags since I knew we now had Big Brother watching us. My mind raced over the facts we had gleaned from our interview with Jake Casteel. The biggest fact was that this case was like no other.

*We'd found an electronic bug in the client interview room.*

I knew our opponents were powerful, or they would not have put electronic eavesdropping bugs in a client interview room. A room that is so sacred, it cannot be invaded—short of a war. I didn't know Uncle Sam considered my client an economic terrorist, no different from Saddam Hussein.

My Mustang's 351-Cleveland engine was showing off its V-8 muscle. The glow of the glass dashboard lit our faces, like the glow in a Huey helicopter had lit my face hundreds of times when I was a Recon Marine.

"Our client's freakin' nuts," Dalton said, disgusted. He still nursed his ego, hurt from getting busted in the belly with a billy club. "The mafia, the Masons, the C.I.A.—what a freakin' loony."

I looked in the rearview mirror for the tenth time since we left the jail.

"We got a tail."

"A tail? Sure. Now you sound as paranoid as our crazy client."

We were on an isolated stretch of road. The car behind us raced up, tailgating us. A bullet exploded through the back window and exited the front. It took my rearview mirror with it. Glass splattered on Dalton and me. I dropped into third gear and romped on the accelerator.

"Paranoid is good." Dalton turned around to see who was shooting at us.

"Stay down," I ordered Dalton.

Another shot knocked off Dalton's passenger-side mirror. Dalton offered driving tips. "Do your Earnhardt shit, man."

I developed a good distance between the chase car and us. I shut off my lights. I slammed on my brakes and put the car into a power slide, that turned us around to face the assailing car streaking towards us. We headed straight down the middle of the road towards the would-be assassins.

Dalton seemed more afraid of me than of our pursuers. "You're not gonna'?"

"Oh, yeah, 'the intimidator.'"

I clucked like a chicken as we blasted towards the other car. We flew, closer and closer to colliding. Another bullet ripped through the middle of the windshield. I threw it into fourth gear, crushed the accelerator, and unleashed the power clutch. In this game of chicken, the other driver blinked. He steered off the road, careening into a three-foot-thick oak tree.

I wheeled the Mustang around and pulled back to the accident scene. Dalton and I jumped out. We ran up to the car and found both of the hit men dead. One had gone through the windshield. The other had had the steering column rammed through his chest. I said, "What dumb shits. To think that we would actually pull over after they shot at us." They were either stupid or desperate.

I grabbed the I.D. of one, and Dalton grabbed the other's. "Department of the Army?" I said.

"No, I gotta Navy Intel guy over here," Dalton said, before he added, "It's smellin' mighty fishy."

"Yeah, and this ain't Denmark."

We ran back to my 'Stang when we caught sight of the headlights of a car coming towards us. My spinning tires threw gravel over the dead men as we peeled out of there.

I knew just where we were heading. For a big bowl of spaghetti and a bellyful of information.

CHAPTER 48

# CHAPTER 49

# LITTLE ITALY

Dalton and I made a beeline away from the two, dead troublemakers. It seemed like Saint Larry of the Stooges was trying to speak to me, in a little voice inside my head. He sounded like a good Boy Scout, telling me that I should stay and wait for the cops. But I knew that was crazy because they would certainly bring in the Feds, who would arrest us for some trumped-up charge, like the one they hit Casteel with. And, of course, I disregarded advice from one of the three stooges. I had too much street smarts for that. It doesn't pay to be on scout's honor all the time.

We could have, and maybe should have, stayed at the accident scene. But we would have been only consoling the dead. And we would have been lining up for the undertaker if we'd waited for their pals to show up. Prudence and my counter-intelligence training gave me a strong, gut-level message to get the Hell out of there. I also knew that, by then, they had to have put military-grade G.P.S., homing devices on all our cars. I had to get this next meeting done, pronto.

St. Martinsville has a large and private Italian neighborhood up on a hill, the highest point in the city. It hosts some of the finest Italian cooking in America, with toasted ravioli one of the unique dishes served only in St. Martinsville. I should have been born Italian, with all the fine food they make. I'm Irish. A potato head. Stuck with cuisine that makes up the world's shortest cookbook, "Potatoes."

I knew this part of the "Hill" area very well. The Italians in this part of town kept a tight rein on the safety of their streets, so to speak. There were some public streets that you just weren't allowed to drive down after dark. A few too many drive-by, machine-gun shootings over the years. Old habits die hard.

I turned onto Spring Street, but was flagged down by a muscled-up, young stud, who appeared suddenly from between two cars. I knew the procedure. I told him where I was going. That was good enough for me to proceed to the second stop. I pulled up in front of the large, green awning over the front of a well-appointed brick building. It was an Italian Ristaurante with an old-fashioned, two-sided neon sign advertising, "The Couch."

The valet ran up and took my car. But when we approached the front door, two refrigerators wearing finely tailored Italian suits stopped us. One man's hand covered half my chest. He spoke softly, with a voice that sounded like it came from the bottom of a deep bucket, full of gravel. I had to lean in close to hear him, and his musk cologne was overpowering. I assumed he poured it on by the quart.

"Closed," he said, while the other walking refrigerator sized up Dalton.

"I'm here to see the Doc."

"Oh, yeah? You got sumpin' to show?" I pulled out the card of psychiatrist, Dr. Marco Falcone. I pressed it into the big man's hand. He turned it over and read the Italian, *"Miglione Amico"* (my best friend) written on the back. It also bore the signature of the good doctor.

Both guards raised their eyebrows and escorted Dalton and me inside. We slipped to the back of the restaurant, where the one who resembled a single-wide Frigidaire gave three sharp raps on the door. A peephole opened, large enough to reveal two dark eyes and a Roman nose. A conversation in Sicilian took place. Then the doctor's business card was handed in.

The door opened, like magic. The guards patted down Dalton and me. They put our personal items in a basket. From me, they fished a Polaroid photo of the stone, a gun, two knives, my wallet, and a wire strung with two nails. Off Dalton, they plucked a Bic pen, a wallet, and two condoms.

Dalton seemed a little defensive about the condoms.

"Hey, I was a Boy Scout—always prepared."

The guards didn't pick up on Dalton's humor.

"Dat everything?"

I didn't mean to embarrass the man, so I let him in on my undiscovered weapons.

CHAPTER 49

"You missed a few."

I unsheathed my short knife from my behind-the-neck scabbard. I pulled a nice, Hibben, medium length from my left boot. Both of the guards' eyebrows rose in terror that they had missed two knives.

"Due'?"

I nodded.

"Grazie."

As we were led in, I briefed Dalton.

"You don't see anything, capisce?"

Dalton nodded, and the double-wide guard nodded to another man standing at a second door with a peep hole. Dalton later told me that he thought he had walked through the gates of bachelor heaven. Bare-breasted women performed erotic routines on swings and danced around poles. A buxom contortionist made a table of old men smile and shake their heads, stuffing money under the young lady's string. Topless ladies floated, like naughty little angels, through thick clouds of cigar smoke, serving expensive drinks and even more expensive attentions. It was a shameless and gracious, naked hospitality to an all-male clientele.

Strictly no skin on skin.

I should have been born Italian. The Romans did everything with class. Even nudity. They hadn't slacked off at all in the five hundred years since Michelangelo's sculpture of Venus. I don't know what amount of lust is in other men's souls. But my mother was an artist. From a young age, I watched her draw and paint portraits of naked people. It left me with a genuine appreciation for the beauty of the human body that is not all about sex. The women were exquisite, true assets to their gender. I think I even recognized a few faces I had seen on television the last time I'd watched the local, professional football team play—with their sexy cheerleaders shaking pompoms. But I knew everything was "hands off." After all, I was a good, Catholic boy. Mostly.

We stopped as Dr. Marco Falcone approached us. Most women would describe Marco as a beautiful man. He carried machismo like a gracious king. Even his eyeglasses were cool. He had more charisma than any other man on the planet. And I knew, because he had been my roommate for three years at the United States Air Force Academy. He had an innate air of innocence and sincerity that made you want to believe everything he said. His handshake was rock hard.

Marco embraced me and kissed me on each cheek. The Italian custom between friends. He extended only a handshake to Dalton.

Marco took the basket of weapons and dismissed the guards. His voice was as smooth as single-malt, scotch whiskey. He handed back our personal items.

"Still playing with your Marine toys?"

I smiled and introduced Dalton to Marco.

"It is my pleasure to meet you. And I express my sympathies to you for having to put up with my friend. Mike is too stressed. You agree?" Marco said.

"Twenty-four, seven, Doc; he never stops."

Marco threw back his head gently and laughed to the clouded ceiling.

"Then you know him well. Come, please."

Marco motioned for us to move to a corner booth. Dalton's eyes were bugging out at the sight of the girls. We made our way across the floor and through the tables, where power brokers smoked big cigars and spoke in hushed tones.

Marco motioned to one of his lovely staffers to set us up with drinks, as Dalton started with small talk.

"What type of doctor are you?"

"I'm a psychiatrist. I pared my practice to a select, few clients when I took over the family business after Papa passed away."

A round of Uzzo was served by a voluptuous girl, who gave me a wink. I returned it with a smile. She placed the bottle in the middle of the table and stroked her hand along its neck in a very polite sign of platonic affection. She left with a sultry smile that would have raised a dead man.

Marco lifted his tiny glass of Uzzo towards the tin-plated ceiling.

"Salute. To the Air Force Academy."

"And friendships forged," I said.

CHAPTER 49

We all raised and clinked our shot glasses together, "Salute." Then we threw the sweet liquor down the hatch.

"So what brings my paeseno to me this evening? You are usually home with Bridget."

"Well, besides the lovely scenery . . ."

Marco shrugged his shoulders in modesty, "I feed the male ego."

Dalton added, "A smorgasbord."

We all laughed, as Marco shrugged that Italian shrug that only he could do. I'd never got it right. No matter how much I had practiced, in our room in front of the mirror, with Marco coaching me at the Academy. But it never worked for me. I always ended up looking like a guy lifting weights. I'm a Mick. I do not have the suave, Italian blood.

We dropped more Uzzo.

"I need information about an outfit called *Di Trina.*"

Marco leaned back in his seat. He poured another round at arm's length.

"Of this, I can help." Marco beckoned one of his staff with a snap of his fingers. He whispered something to her, making her float away.

"'The Thumb' will know. After Papa died, Uncle Tony came over from the old country. He tells me he runs our quality control. But I just think he likes to sample."

The messenger approached Tony "Two Thumbs" Falcone from behind as he was standing at the bar in the cigar lounge. He had each of his thumbless hands on a thong-adorned, naked bottom. A redhead on his left and a curly-haired brunette on his right. Uncle Tony leaned to hear the whispered message.

# CHAPTER 50

## *DI TRINA*

Tony "Two Thumbs" slapped his two, thumbless hands on our table. Marco introduced us.

"Gentlemen, this is Uncle Tony."

Tony shook hands like royalty. Fingers only. He respectfully nodded to each of us. I was grateful Tony was not put off by Dalton's amazement at his thumbless hands.

"He knows all about *Di Trina*," Marco said.

Tony's eyes opened wide when Marco mentioned *Di Trina*. Marco motioned for Two Thumbs to sit down. Dalton broke polite protocol and poured himself another shot. He threw it down before Tony hit the seat. Tony established himself in the booth next to Marco. Marco spoke to Tony in Sicilian at first. He told his uncle he could trust these men with any secret that he would trust to the Mother Mary herself.

Two Thumbs spoke in broken English. He said, *"Il Silencio Di Trina."* He offered his palms to the sky with a shrug that spoke paragraphs. "The 'Silent Train'. This is the strongest syndicate in the world." Marco nodded in agreement. A reciprocal shrug.

"Because its muscle is the F.B.I. The whole government," Tony said.

"Who runs *Il Silencio Di Trina?*" I asked.

"The Capo? The head of *Di Trina?*"

I nodded, and I looked him in the eye. Tony waved his hands to answer in Sicilian first. Nonverbally. Then, in English.

"The most secret . . . fat, railroad personal-injury lawyers."

Marco looked at his Uncle Tony "Two Thumbs" like he was crazy.

"Don't be a fool. These men are serious; don't waste their time with your jokes," said Marco.

Tony "Two Thumbs" made gestures with both hands over his heart. He pulled a rosary from his breast pocket. Kissed it and raised it briefly, for some type of a celestial blessing, up into the air, thick with cigar smoke and the gentle aromas of garlic, and oregano, and fine cheeses.

"I swear on the honor of the Virgin Mother. They are real. Capisce?"

Tony slapped his hand, still holding the rosary, on the table and pointed at Marco.

"*Di Trina* lawyers. They had a deal with Jimmy Hoffa."

Dalton dragged his eyes from chasing thongs and planted them squarely on Tony "Two Thumbs." He exchanged looks with me—"Wow." My jaw tightened, and I squinted at "Two Thumbs."

"You are telling us this *Di Trina* outfit, this mafia . . ."

"Two Thumbs" cocked a disapproving eye at my choice of words.

"You're saying this 'ring' of crooked injury lawyers had a special deal with Jimmy Hoffa?"

I pounded my pointed finger on the top of the beautiful, Italian-leather topped table. And "Two Thumbs" nodded his head slowly and deliberately at the same time that he grabbed all four of our glasses. He put them together, one by one, in the middle of the table, to represent airplanes and trucks and boats and trains. He explained at length how Hoffa tried to merge the transportation unions for power. He made a fist, indicating consolidation.

"Da planes, and da trucks, and da boats, and da trinas."

He moved the glasses one at a time.

"But den the Government say, 'Jimmy, you're too strong,' so they make up some bullshit to convict him so he can't run the Teamsters and bring together all the power of transportation into one union."

Dalton, Marco, and I were rapt. We leaned in closer, hanging on every hushed word.

Dalton hurriedly poured himself another round in the glasses "Two Thumbs" had gathered at the table's center. He picked up his glass, which had represented the airplanes, and made the Uzzo fly down his throat.

"President Nixon's pardon forbade Hoffa from running the Teamsters. What did *Di Trina* have to offer that would fix that?" I asked.

CHAPTER 50

Tony "Two Thumbs" offered a simple shrug in explanation.

"Jimmy's replacement was screwing up bad. Embarrassing the government so much, they thought, better the devil we had than this new guy, Fitz. Uncle Sam offered Jimmy be the boss. The Capo over all these unions."

He waved his hand over all the glasses.

"So Jimmy doesn't violate his pardon by being in the Teamsters or running for Teamsters" Office."

"And *Di Trina* gets all the injury cases across the country."

"No rail strikes," said Dalton.

"The trains keep on rolling," said Marco.

Two Thumbs clapped his hands together. He nodded his head and pointed at us that we got it right.

"But whatever happened to this deal between Hoffa and *Di Trina?*" I asked.

Two Thumbs shrugged. He had a knowing glint in his eyes.

"I would die for such a racket. *Di Trina* lawyers use the six 'Bs' to get injury cases."

"Six 'Bs'?" Dalton asked.

"Booze, broads, beef, ballgames, bribes, . . ." Marco said.

"And butchery," "Two Thumbs" said, in a flat, matter-of-fact tone. His eyes looked like sharks' eyes. Black. Cold. Hungry. He shrugged again and gestured, holding both of his four-digit hands level over the table to indicate this was the solid truth. Tony was an unassailable expert on amputations. Dalton's eyebrows looked like mountain peaks.

"Lawyers keep an eye on the rail unions for the government. It's an old Pentagon game. Lucky Luciano did it for the U.S. Navy in World War II shipyards," "Two Thumbs" said.

"But the lawyers' mafia doesn't work for free," I said.

"Two Thumbs" nodded and kissed his fingertips, raising them to heaven in a form of blessing,

"The rail injury cases are very lucrative. Many millions every year." Tony leaned in, pointing to his pinky finger.

"They even wear special rings on their little finger. Black, with a gold spike in a white circle."

He shrugged his broad shoulders. They were the strong shoulders of a working man, and they were followed by his thick hands. His eyes changed, back to sharks', as he made motions like a garroting, produced guttural sounds, and motioned his fingers to signify a lot of money.

"Is it all about money?" Dalton asked.

"Two Thumbs" reached across the table and poured Dalton another glass of Uzzo.

"No rail strikes in America. The world is happy."

Tony pantomimed spitting. He raised his angry, thumbless hands.

"Mussolini cut off my thumbs because I didn't run a *di trina* on time," He waved his hands in the air. "Fifty years, nothing changed."

Dalton and I couldn't believe what we were hearing. But we believed every word.

"Are any local law firms in *Di Trina*?"

Tony held up two fingers.

"Due."

Two hours later, Dalton was drunk, as we walked out of "The Couch." Marco gave Dalton and me the customary Italian good-bye, a ceremonial kiss on each cheek. The valet drove up in my Mustang. Dalton walked to the car door, opened by the valet, and got in. Marco pulled a Polaroid out of his pocket. He tapped it down into my breast pocket. Then he spoke to me.

My dear friend, Dr. Falcone, looked me in the eyes.

"You were supposed to get rid of this months ago, Paeseno. You need couch time. Tell me your feelings."

Marco took in my Mustang's bullet ridden windows.

"You have ventilation problems?"

"Hey, fugget about it . . ."

We grinned, and we each shrugged, before I hopped in my car and motored off, with a toot of the horn and a wave.

Dalton leaned his seat back.

"Love that man's hospitality."

CHAPTER 50

# CHAPTER 51

# MAFIA RETIREMENT

The attendant watched one of Chicago's finest pull in front of his parking lot's tollbooth, at the base of the multi-story parking garage. The burly cop got out of the black-and-white, slipping his billy club into his weapons belt.

"What ya got?"

"I dunno, officer. I called it in because I got a big-shot lawyer been there a coupl'a hours. He won't respond."

"Let's have a look-see."

They walked up two levels, to a Mercedes idling in a reserved parking space. The car was the long, sedan type that belonged to people with too much money. The patrolman and the parking attendant tried to open the car doors to look into the car. They couldn't see inside because the windows were tinted black. The cop banged on the driver's side window, to no avail.

"Stand back." The policeman reared back with his billy club. He brought it down onto the window, shattering it into hundreds of pieces. The broken window revealed the lawyer, sitting with both hands on the steering wheel. His eyes were wide open. He was motionless.

A black-onyx pinky ring, identical to Big Dutch's and Dee Dee's, was on the pinky finger of his left hand. The cop reached in and shook the lawyer's shoulder.

"Hey, mister, you all right?"

The lawyer's head fell off to the side. Only one spinal ligament prevented it rolling onto the floorboard. It had been a clean cut. A garrote line stretched neatly across his neck. The cop jumped backward grabbing his own chest.

"Jesus."

Clear across the country, more skullduggery was happening in California.

Big Dutch's west-coast squad moved in with equal efficiency. The San Francisco Police Department found the most prominent railroad-injury lawyer on the west coast spread eagled on top of a BMW's crushed roof, face up to the sky. The dead lawyer stunk of gin.

They categorized it a suicide. The accident reconstruction report stated it had been a direct fall from a broken-out ninth story office window. The evidence bag held a ring removed from the corpse's left, pinky finger. It hadn't been given a second look by investigators—black onyx within a circle of Exodus white, with a tiny, gold, railroad spike in the middle.

*Di Trina* had some retirees.

CHAPTER 51

# CHAPTER 52

# TICK – TICK - TICK

DeeDee dropped the keys to her Mercedes Roadster right next to the Tiffany lamp on her baroque, foyer table. She was dog tired. She did not waste time listening to phone messages. Since her whole life was wrapped around the firm, she knew that if they called her at home, they didn't know her well enough to know that she lived her job, only responding to her pager and cell phone. She staggered through her professionally decorated penthouse overlooking historic World's Fair park. She headed to bed for some much-needed sleep.

At least the place smelled like the scent of the cleanser she insisted her maid use: lavender, with a hint of lemon. It had been a long week of long days for DeeDee, chasing railroad injury cases from Spokane to Atlanta. But that was what she'd been hired to do. She was a rainmaker. The most valuable of all persons in every law firm. She brought in the business. And lots, tons, of it. In the solitude of a bathroom bigger than most people's parlors, DeeDee laughed to herself as she took off her make-up. She had no real love life. No boyfriend. Not even a cat. She hated the bar scenes. It was worthless to start a relationship. DeeDee had such crazy hours that dating someone would amount only to a meaningless fling with some guy who would remain only a stranger. She wouldn't be able to spend enough time with him to find out if they were compatible.

Her biological clock was ticking.

She could feel it—going off, like an alarm, to make babies. To settle down. But she never woke up to face facts. She kept hitting the snooze button on her life, to allow herself a little more money, a little more time in the glamorous lifestyle of a Designated, railroad-injury lawyer. She knew she could not have both a family and the money. Something had to give.

She was not happy. But she was rich. For a brief moment, she actually wished the Feds would bust her firm, just so she would not have to make a choice between money earned with bribes and an honest trade. She defaulted to the dough and the fashionable status it provided.

All her relatives and her old classmates stood in awe of all the material things she had accumulated in such a short time after law school. They all presumed that, since she had lots of money, she was a great lawyer. The fact was, she had not even tried one case.

Ever.

Her emotional overloads would always come back to the money, the money, the money. But the ill-gotten lucre in her bank account didn't help her sleep. She knew *Di Trina* and Senator Moore and his Judiciary Committee had no control over the Treasury Department. DeeDee knew she would be dead meat if the I.R.S. and the Department of the Treasury offered immunity and amnesty to all the railroad union men who received cash bribes from her firm. They might testify against the lawyers who milked the R.I.O. injury system. She and the whole *Di Trina* lawyers' mafia would be destroyed.

She rolled over in bed for the umpteenth time. DeeDee stared out her window, wondering what the view was like from a federal prison bunk.

Most nights, DeeDee just lay in bed for hours on end, thinking of worst-case scenarios. She pictured a federal investigator, the F.B.I., the Department of the Treasury, or maybe a guy from Labor, sitting in her office, asking her lots of questions about the unique way her firm practiced law. He would explain it was just a little something he needed for the grand jury.

She saw the lawyers in her business as kind of like cowboys. They lassoed clients and kept them in a corral, until their claims could be cashed in for a huge fee. The corral kept the clients from going to honest lawyers. The fence of the corral was built with the loans hanging over the heads of the clients. It was a perfect scheme, that had worked for decades before DeeDee arrived at her stepfather's law firm.

DeeDee could not understand why she could not be contrite over business as usual. It was the law firm her step-stepfather, U.S. Senator Joseph Youngstown Moore, had founded and built into an economic powerhouse.

CHAPTER 52

The biggest R.I.O. firm in the country. They relied on a secret ruling of the United States Supreme Court, that allowed union-Designated lawyers a privilege no other lawyers in America were allowed— the right to chase R.I.O. railroad, personal-injury cases.

It was the stuff she was not authorized to do that kept her buying antacids in the economy-size jars. She shook her head every time she remembered she had had a gastro-enterologist to treat her for stomach ulcers before she was thirty.

In her nightmarish musings, DeeDee visualized the investigator's stony face. He'd scratch his head like Lieutenant Columbo, before he stopped beating around the bush and lowered the boom. With a cocky smile, he'd lean forward, in one of her Corinthian-leather, client chairs, and get around to the juicy stuff.

The lose-your-law-license-for-life stuff. The thing that made the whole, six-billion dollar a year, railroad-injury industry work for just a handful of lawyers. The reason the union-Designated lawyers enjoyed their monopoly. Client loans.

*"I'm here to ask more questions about some suspicious loans, Ms. DeVillay."*

Each and every interview played in her devious mind ended with her crossing her legs and saying, "I need a lawyer."

She was a survivor. A snake. A lawyer. She stayed awake, curled up in the middle of her king-sized bed, under perfumed, three-hundred-count, combed cotton sheets imported from Egypt. A Gloria Vanderbilt comforter. DeeDee calculated how she could cut herself a deal with Uncle Sam. Usually, by the time she'd rung herself dry of emotion and energy, her cell phone would ring, bringing news of another railroad injury, requiring her to race off, like a fireman to a fire, to chase those R.I.O. injury cases.

She knew she was in danger. She didn't know how to get away. She fantasized quite often that some day, after she made as much money as possible and right before the prosecutors got their hooks into her, a white knight would come galloping to her rescue. Just like in the movies. DeeDee decided she would then become a stay-at-home mother.

Tick, tick, tick, went DeeDee's clock.

# CHAPTER 53

# BAD TIMING

He was dead to the world. I damn near had to carry Dalton in when I dropped him off at his apartment. He'd let the housekeeping go too long. The place smelled like the stale beer cans sitting on top of most of the level surfaces. He collapsed onto the couch and started snoring immediately. It had been a long night, full of surprises. A mafia of lawyers, two dead bodies, a bellyful of Uzzo, and a piece to the puzzle that was the biggest, unsolved crime in American history—who killed Jimmy Hoffa.

I shook off images of our hot, serving girls. As opposed to what my law partner, Dalton, believed, I thought about women all the time. I longed for the company of a woman every night. I just couldn't get around the fact that I was there to take care of my challenged sister. I couldn't move on. I was trapped—emotionally, psychologically, and, worst of all, spiritually. Every night of my life, since I'd been beaten by thugs as a child, I used a beaded rosary or, my favorite in the field, a ten-pointed Celtic rosary, every night of my life.

My rosary was my armor.

I am, sure as Hell, no angel. I had had women on every continent in the world. I cannot repeat the things I did at Subic Bay, Philippines, during a three-week layover. It was debauchery, twenty-four, seven. But, through it all, I hit my knees at night and prayed. Prayer was more than a means of centering. It was an element of my being a man in awe of a greater power. There were many times I prayed the rosary when it wasn't religious. At least, it didn't feel that way. I was a better Marine than I was a Catholic.

The Uzzo made me hurry through my ritualistic kneeling and praying before sleep. I admit it. I was in a lonely, self-centered kind of mood. I prayed for Casteel and Bridget and my mother's and father's souls. I prayed to have a woman in my bunk—Ann. I slid into the sheets as morning dawned. Thank God it was a Saturday morning. I nodded off quickly.

In my sleep, I was swept back into Purgatory upon the great ship.

*A sense of misfortune gripped me, as I found myself imprisoned aboard the Constitution. The great ship sat, dead in the water, gripped by an icy, iridescent fog bank. Its sails hung limp.*

*I was beaten, and beaten, and beaten by Mr. Fetid, until my flesh was ripped and torn, on my back, and my chest, and my arms. After each beating, they doused me with buckets of saltwater, to torture my nerve endings. I felt the scream in my throat.*

I woke up in a pool of sweat. It smelled like the Uzzo, seeping from my pours. I could have sworn I smelled a hint of brine.

From what I remembered of the nasty dream, Captain Carion had raged on and on with only one message, loud and clear:

"No women on board. They're bad luck."

I knew it. The life of a litigating lawyer is a lot like a Marine in the field. You are cut off from the people you love. I was forbidden from seriously courting Ann until the mission was complete, until Jake Casteel was free. I was depressed. I couldn't bring Ann and her daughter into my life. Not yet.

I got out of bed and stumbled to the bathroom. I dropped my razor when I saw the eyes. The eyes from which I had run. They were there, over my right shoulder in the fogged mirror, as I lifted my razor to shave. I was shocked. I could not believe that Father's eyes had reappeared when he had been gone for over a year.

A year of sitting on Dr. Falcone's couch. A year of self-analysis. A year-long road to nowhere. I was right back where I had started. Guilt was my middle name. And not one man would step up to speak for me. No one human.

I wished I could shed the wet blanket of my shame and get on with my life. I tried to get Ann out of my mind. But she struck through my conscience, like an arrow through my jar head. She was my secretary. And I was on a mission.

Ann was forbidden.

CHAPTER 53

# CHAPTER 54

# THE CALM

My days and nights went by quickly, in a sleepless grind of legal research and brief writing. Trying to write a Supreme Court brief in thirty days and research all the issues with no online, research capabilities—on a case you know nothing about, is like trying to cram an elephant through a keyhole. A lot will be lost in the process: your sleep, your health, the quality of the brief, and your sanity.

Bridget thought I was a ghost. I almost never slept. She was starting to do a lot of things on her own. She was even taking care of Gunny. I just did not have the time to take care of him, pulling twenty-hour days, seven days a week. It got so bad, one night a cop pulled me over at three a.m. I had the top down. He saw me slapping myself to stay awake. He thought I was nuts, or drunk, or both. He saw my "OOO-RAH" license plates. He followed me home, as a courtesy to a fellow Marine. The good, old *Semper Fi* brotherhood.

One night, I came home early, at eleven p.m., with an armload of cases to read. I shuffled through the kitchen. Bridget had already eaten. The distinct smell of burnt pasta hung in the air. I poured myself a glass of milk and went upstairs.

Bridget and I went through the "Up the long ladder" ditty we use as a welcome-home code. I opened the door to Bridget's bedroom. She threw some white dust onto a candle. It caused a puff of smoke to rise into the air.

"Jesus Christ! What are you doin'? You are gonna burn down the house."

Bridget seemed to be oblivious to me. Ace and Gunny were curled up on the rug under her prayer chair. They looked contented. Bridget chanted the names of some the saints, rapid fire. She said the Memorare before she tried to tap into a little energy from the miracle of Lourdes. I knew I was in the presence of a master. The world's most prolific, Catholic prayer maker. She finalized her swoop through the world of the miraculous with a deft plea to Our Lady of Guadalupe, the Mother of the Americas, at the tail end of the rosary on her right hand. It was like I was at the Catholic Olympics. I had just seen Mary Lou Retten stick a perfect-ten dismount. I almost applauded.

Then I heard her pray, "Dear God, keep Michael safe. Please help Michael save Mr. Jake." She immediately broke away, fast and strong, like Walter Peyton turning the corner on a power sweep and running all the way down the sidelines for a touchdown. Her tongue laid down a litany of dual-speak, where she recited "Hail Mary"'s in a cascading falsetto. It was breathtaking, if you knew what you were listening to.

In Special Forces, nothing beat a good, rear, security man covering your extraction route. I knew Bridget had my back.

"Goodnight, Bridget." I closed Bridget's door. I smiled as I walked to my room.

Bridget spoke loud enough to be heard through the door, "Good night, Michael. Love you. Sweet dreams, don't let the bedbugs bite. And Saint Vitus, patron saint of sleep, and Saint Michael the Archangel, patron saint of the warrior, please help Michael. He has to fight tomorrow."

I stopped. I turned around and walked back to Bridget's door and opened it. "What do you know about a fight tomorrow?"

Bridget did not turn to look at me. She held a rosary in her right hand, murmuring prayers, while she held a small, black-robed figure in her left hand. I could not tell if it was a priest or a judge. She circled her hand in the air above the burning candle, as she grasped the black-robed figure.

My sister had her mojo going.

I was bewildered. I turned and walked back to my room. I opened the door, turned on the light switch, and looked directly at the Polaroid of the stone. I held it, and I looked at the picture of a lonely piece of marble. I shook my head in disgust and put it back, tucking it into the corner of the light switch cover. I kicked and punched the body bag. I took two knives out of my wall target. I walked five paces away, wheeled around, and threw one right-handed and one left-handed. One knife stuck above the picture of Jesus Christ, and the other stuck above the picture of Marine Corps General Chesty Puller. A little spackle will fix the holes.

"Ooo-Rah."

Outside the house, in a surveillance van, the government's monkeys stayed on top of me with their electronic eavsdropping.

~~~~~~~~~~~~~~~~~~~~~~~~~~~~~~~~~~~~~~~~~~~~~~~~~~~~~~~

Surveillance Tech 1 said, "This guy is nuts."
Surveillance Tech 2 said, "Crazy like a fox."

~~~~~~~~~~~~~~~~~~~~~~~~~~~~~~~~~~~~~~~~~~~~~~~~~~~~~~~

My bedroom lights were out. Moonlight shone through my window. I knelt by my bed and said my prayers. I forgot what I was praying for. Was it for God to set Jake free or for God to set me free? I prayed for both. I also prayed for hungry children in the Third World. Innocent souls, starved of food, who had a natural bravery that reached beyond their terrible poverty and squalid quarters. They were my heroes for the evening. They kept hope and the courage to keep on going when they had nothing, absolutely nothing, in their bellies or in the pot. Saints by birth. Terrorists by their upbringing. But each and every one, a soul.

I said my old black Celtic ten-point-star rosary for my client. I figured it would be best to meditate on the Glorious Mysteries at the five meditation stations on the normal, string-beaded rosary: The Resurrection (Jake really needed this); The Ascension; The Descent of The Holy Spirit; The Assumption of Mary; and Mary's Coronation. But as I prayed for Jake, with the circular Celtic rosary, I found that I could only concentrate on The Resurrection of Jesus from the dead, the first meditation station. And so I visualized Jake being resurrected from prison, where he said he felt like his spirit had died. I set my mind to make it a nightly practice to pray a rosary for the resurrection of Jake's spirit as a man, as a Christian, as an innocent man, until Jake Casteel was exonerated. Even as tired as I was, that praying on my knees for Jake felt quite good, and natural, and sweetly satisfying, in a way that left me believing it would certainly bear fruit. My prayers became a meditation on justice, real justice, justice for Jake.

Faith in God. A rosary. *Semper Fidelis.* Always faithful. Internal peace. Confidence in God to give you abilities in your time of need. A man and his faith become one, and he finds his soul in the mixture of life's desires and God's will. Driven by Marine Corps persistence and elbow grease for God helps those who help themselves.

I crawled into bed. I fell asleep, clutching my Celtic rosary.

I do not know why God did not vector me that night to the Purgatory Sea for my regular flogging of guilt. He let me stay in port. I was a landlubber for the night.

I slept peacefully and dreamt of Ann.

CHAPTER 54

# CHAPTER 55

# DIRTY JUDGE – DIRTY DEALING

Durant sat in the office of the most powerful judge in the world. The United States Supreme Court's Chief Justice, Sidney Ignatius Nelson. Durant looked around while he waited for the old fart to get there. The office needed some more color. Something with earth tones. Perhaps with some flashy or showpiece items hung on the wall across from the desk. Something that speaks, I'm a man, thought Colonel Durant. Or, at least, that was what he thought his latest ex, the third, would have said. She was an interior decorator, bound and determined to spend his inheritance. He had wanted to kill her for it. Years ago, he had the safety off, his finger on the trigger, and the nine-millimeter against her temple. Then he realized, "Who's gonna watch the kids?"

The scouting report on Nelson was that he could not delegate anything, not even wiping his nose. But, recently, the old codger had relented and let an orderly do that. The man ran the Supreme Court with an iron fist. Nelson had his nose and fingers in every little conspiracy or plan to use legal mumbo jumbo, smoke and mirrors, sleight of hand, and back-door dealing to get the results he desired.

Lady Justice wore no blindfold in Nelson's chambers.

Durant smiled because he could see this was an office where women were not allowed admission, including Lady Justice. He read the sign on Nelson's desk, carrying a Dickens' line: "WOE TO ALL WHO SEEK COMPASSION HERE." He looked across the long desk and saw a 1950s-era picture of Noreen, the Chief Justice's late wife, her white-stone rosary hung over the upper, right side of the picture frame.

The first to enter Nelson's chambers was the Chief Justice's orderly. He was a slender, almost girlish-looking man, the Chief Justice simply called "Rone." The Chief Justice then entered, slow and shaky, in three parts. One part was his cane, topped by his liver-spotted hand, like a magician's hand. It stuck out of a black, judicial robe, which revealed not arm, or feet, or shoes because of the short train dragging along the floor.

Next, his head, the middle of the procession. It had a stone face, wrinkled and hairless. Like a farmer leaves the field after the harvest.

Finally, the end of the procession. The hump on the Judge's back. Justice Nelson had stood a healthy six-foot-two-inches tall when he took the bench upon the appointment of President Eisenhower in 1956. Almost forty years later, he was whittled down to a five-foot-seven-inch, stooped, shuffling shadow of a man. Perhaps it was the weight of the world that caused that hump. His opinions, the Court's opinions, the opinions he allowed the other justices to issue had shifted national and world policy. They affected financial markets around the world. And they defined the way everyday people lived their lives. When the United States Supreme Court spoke, it had a ripple effect upon every nation in the world.

Durant stood as Justice Nelson entered the room. He walked up to greet the Judge. Nelson's handshake was still firm. His word was still good. Durant knew that would be very important to this operation. He would be the glue to keep together the secret deal he had with Nelson. There could be nothing in writing to record their agreement.

Nelson eased into his large, leather, high-backed desk chair. Rone scurried away, shutting the door behind him. Durant just sat there and waited for the judge to speak. Partially out of respect, and partially because he knew that, nine times out of ten, the first person to speak at a deal is the one who loses. There was a long, awkward silence that Durant used to pick at his fingernails. He avoided eye contact. Perhaps you could say he was just letting the aged Justice gather himself before he addressed Durant. Nonetheless, Durant won.

Justice Nelson spoke first, "Colonel, I wasn't expecting you so soon."

Durant leaned back in his seat, not appearing overanxious or intimidating as he said, "I came to remind you of our deal. I got the Chicago and California *Di Trina* men to step aside, so your two sons can become Designated lawyers."

CHAPTER 55

Chief Justice Nelson rocked back in his chair and shook his head back and forth in disapproval.

"You remember our little deal about Mr. Casteel?" said Durant.

"Yes, I remember the deal, Colonel. But it didn't include killing anyone. Word travels fast. Those men didn't actually step aside, as you put it."

This was Durant's operation, and he wasn't going to let some old judge who was full of himself ruin his success. "Mr. Chief Justice, your job is to play games with legal words that nobody cares about. I deal in action. Getting things done. I delivered on my end. Your two sons will make tens of millions of dollars, over and over again, as Designated counsel for California and Chicago. And I can certainly find another Chief Justice. . ."

Nelson interrupted him, "No. You cannot, you dolt. Don't you know there is only one Chief Justice of the Supreme Court?"

There was a knock at the door that interrupted their discussion. It was Rone, carrying a cup of water and a small, prescription, plastic cup containing pills. He gave it to Nelson, "Your medicine, Sir."

"Ah, got to keep the ticker pumping."

Durant wanted to shake his head at the pitiful way the most powerful judicial officer in the world took his medicine. With the orderly inching it gingerly into Nelson's mouth. Placing it on the tongue of an orator who had shaken the world with his legal opinions. The Judge couldn't even drink water. Rone held a rag under the Judge's chin as he attempted to get enough into his mouth to wash down the pill. The Judge took a blood thinner for his heart, that beat only because of a pacemaker. The feeble, old man existed in an artificial state, like a prune-skinned doll. Rone left, with a subservient head nod, as he backed out of the room, shutting the door.

Nelson rekindled the conversation about conspiracy. "Now we were saying. . ."

Durant seemed to concede the Judge's point. "Yes Sir, Article III judges enjoy a lifetime appointment."

Chief Justice Nelson acted his characteristic, pompous self as he nodded. "Exactly, so you're stuck with me 'til I die."

Durant opened one of the Taco Bell hot-sauce packets he carried in his coat pocket and sucked some of it out while he stood. He leaned over Justice

Nelson's huge desk and dropped the hot sauce packet on Nelson's beautiful, white, desk blotter. It left a trail of deep red.

"Precisely. Let's see. In the big picture of things, which is more important to society: an ancient judge who twists and contorts the reality he's given— the facts and the law—into the result that he wanted or worldwide, economic collapse?"

Durant acted as though he was actually contemplating the two options. He extended his hands to either side, like he was the scales of justice. "No. When you're gone, Mr. Chief Justice, many qualified lawyers will want to take your place. C.I.A. will make sure it ends up being a judge who is just as cooperative, if not more cooperative, than you. Why don't you make your decision and choose the right option. Keep all the money in your family."

Nelson fumed, and his lip quivered as Durant walked towards the door.

Durant stopped, and turned around, and said, "You are going to give me a better F.I.S.A. judge. That F.I.S.A. Judge Cavanaugh wouldn't sign an order letting us surveil and tail a labor leader. You know what that communist bastard told me? Just because Casteel is in an international union leader does not mean we can spy on him." Durant spoke, tongue in cheek. "That's a fine way to run a dictatorship." Durant pointed at Nelson. "From now on, you'll sign the Federal Intelligence Security orders."

Durant walked towards the door.

Nelson shook his head in disagreement. "I can't just fire Judge Cavanaugh. He's appointed to F.I.S.A. until next year."

"I know. That's why I'm telling you not to expect Judge Cavanaugh to be reporting to work this morning. He had a little accident last night."

"Accident?"

Colonel Durant smiled and acted with a false naiveté.

"Oh, they didn't tell you yet, this morning? Yeah. Seems that a dump truck ran a red light and T-boned Cavanaugh's car. Squashed him like a bug. Dump truck driver got out and ran. Never caught the guy."

Chief Justice Nelson pointed towards the door with his cane.

"You sonofabitch. Get the Hell out of my office."

CHAPTER 55

# CHAPTER 56

# ANN'S DARK PAST

Working for McRain and Boyle, Attorneys at Law, turned out to be a pretty good gig for Ann. She lived in a small town in Chakateptkee County, out on a farm, past the woods and past anywhere someone could see from the state highway. She and her daughter, Kylee, lived in a small farmhouse on the back acreage of her Daddy's three-hundred-acre spread.

Corn, soybeans, wheat, and tilled dirt was her yard, which changed with the seasons. She had no garage. She parked her truck under a stand of pecan trees. It was a farm, work truck, named "Old Blue." A '66 Chevy that wore an intimidating cattle guard across the front, like a huge, tubular-steel brassiere. It was not impressive or chic by any stretch of the imagination. Old Blue was a loaner from her Daddy. It was reliable. It got her to and from work, seventy miles every day. It topped out at sixty miles per hour. But it was plenty strong. On the weekends, Daddy used it to pull stumps with a logging chain, setting it in its low, granny gear.

She liked the men she was working for. Ann felt they were fair. Mike and Dalton were fun and did not try to use her for some ulterior motive, like the last law firm she had been. She was still ashamed of the things that she'd stooped to, in order to keep her child and her job and keep food on her table. But she reminded herself that she'd at least kept the custody of her child, Kylee. Ann remembered that painful patch in her life much too well and all too often.

Back then, Ann was working for DeeDee's law firm. Ann was going through a nasty divorce. Her ex-husband, Sammy Beaux, was a man who decided, after Ann got pregnant with Kylee, that he was just the sperm donor. The fact that he had married her held little importance to him. According to Sammy Beaux, everything that had gone wrong in his life had been Ann's fault. He liked to use her as a punching bag during his drunken rages against "The Man."

Sammy believed "The Man," or some inexplicable, invisible, vindictive force held him back, keeping him from getting ahead in life. Not giving him a chance by making life so rough for him, he couldn't even get to and from a decent job. In his mind, it certainly wasn't his fault he'd racked up five D.U.I.'s and lost his driver's license for five years. Quite a stretch of bad luck. Her husband, Sammy Beaux Bullford, cursed into the business end of whiskey bottles. In his mind, his curse was punctuated by an exclamation mark that looked like his wife. Ann.

Ann worked for DeeDee's powerful R.I.O. personal-injury law firm, that seemed to have an endless supply of injured clients. She was a paralegal, putting herself through night school while her supportive mother and father watched her baby daughter grow up.

After she worked at the Falic, Moore & DeVillay firm for about six months, she caught the eye of the young partner, Bratford Moore. He was the blood son of U.S. Senator Moore. The firm's founder. Bratford already had bedded every woman at the firm, except the seventy-year-old cleaning lady. He offered Ann an option. Sleep with him and get custody of her daughter in her divorce case, or refuse him and take her chances of losing her daughter. Bratford explained to Ann that her divorce judge was a good friend of his. The judge would probably find Ann to be an unfit mother if Bratford were to lie under oath that he'd fired her for stealing. Something Bratford was prepared to swear to, with his hand on a Bible, if she said no.

The lying, little bastard.

Bratford Moore ended the threat on an up beat. He told Ann, he felt, deep down in his heart, that they "belonged" together. She knew that was a line he used on every paralegal in the firm. He had already paid for two abortions. He looked at her long legs, gave her an unwanted squeeze just above the knee, and offered her *a bonus* of two thousand dollars if she could make it for a whole weekend at his lake-home retreat. Ann shook her head almost every day of that weekend getaway, with a man she felt nothing for and pleasured just to keep her child, just to feed her child, just to survive.

CHAPTER 56

And being a survival-minded person, Ann thought long and hard about how to make sure she would never get fired if she said no to Bratford.

Bratford didn't know what Ann took from him, from the firm, to settle the score. Sensitive stuff. Copies of clients' closing statements. The statements showed the firm had falsified accountings for their clients, about the deductions taken out of the clients' big R.I.O. personal-injury awards. Ann knew it was real damning stuff. She learned in paralegal school that lawyers are forbidden to loan money to personal-injury clients. But Falic, Moore & DeVillay made loans to hundreds of its R.I.O. clients. Bratford explained to Ann that the firm gave the loans because, if they didn't, the client would go to a firm that had better financial backing. It all came down to financing cases and tricking the new clients to start taking loans to keep them from running off to another lawyer.

Working with Mike was different. It was the absence of sexual intimidation and harassment that Ann enjoyed about McRain and Boyle. Mike and Dalton were cute. But Dalton had a string of women chasing him. A couple of different ones called, asking for him, almost every week. Dalton would tell Ann to tell them he was in a client conference. Mike, on the other hand, was a diamond in the rough. He would need a lot of work. Ann found it amusing that Bridget would call the office at four p.m. sharp, every day, and give Ann a shopping list for Mike to pick up on the way home. One day, Ann said half of a rosary on the phone with Bridget. They became fast friends.

Ann was beautiful. She could see, out of the corner of her eye, when Mike or Dalton was looking her up and down. They tried to be discreet, of course, but they were definitely checking her out. Those looks from men flattered her. She had dealt with that her whole life. She enjoyed being treated like a lady. Mike never made any sexual innuendos or moves towards her.

On one dreary day, Ann was alone at the office. Her bosses were in court, arguing for a divorce-seeking women. The big task she had given herself that morning was to organize the many cardboard boxes, piled haphazardly around the office, into an organized mess. Ann was going through the boxes. She stacked them and put them in their proper order. She came across a box marked "Mike's Medical Records." She opened it to determine its rightful place in the office. And she read the police report and medical records. After she'd read for five minutes, she put her hand over her mouth.

"Oh dear . . . no wonder . . ."

# CHAPTER 57

*"I hate big companies
and big unions."*
−President Harry S. Truman

Colonel Durant returned to his Washington, D.C., hotel room. He was tired. He changed and tried to rest. He was expecting a female visitor. A lady he'd ordered in by phone. He asked that she be a Swedish blonde, wearing fishnet stockings. But who knew. It all boiled down to how much she wanted to impress him. He lay down on his bed, wearing only a towel, wrapped around his waist. Durant started to read the 1946 Truman Rail Strike speech Lieutenant-General Crowe had ordered him to read at the request of the President. It was supposed to give Durant a feel for the magnitude of a rail-strike situation.

He thought it was amusing that he might do her *before* the intellectual foreplay. Then take a rest to talk geo-political economic issues. Sort of a warm-up to a climax already in the past. After they got all hot and bothered, talking Keynesian economic theories, he'd do her again. He always had a plan B. Dirk thought about disciplining her. Strong and hard. If she had a hankering for that sort of thing. Wild. The man had a plan.

On the cool side of devious, Colonel Durant settled into reading President Truman's 1946 rail-strike speech before his date showed up. Over the previous few years, he had had some problems with his lower unit. So to speak, Colonel Durant had been unable to come to full attention. He took a little, blue pill in anticipation of his visitor.

He read the historic words. They still rang true, almost fifty years later.

President Truman's speech, May 24, 1946, given to members of the Congress of the United States:

"*I desire to thank you for this privilege of appearing before you in order to urge legislation which I deem essential to the welfare of our country.*

*For the past two days the nation has been in the grip of a railroad strike which threatens to paralyze all our industrial, agricultural, commercial, and social life.*

*Last night I tried to point out to the American people the bleak picture which we faced at home and abroad if the strike is permitted to continue.*

*The disaster will spare no one.  It will bear equally upon businessmen, workers, farmers and upon every citizen of the United States.  Food, raw materials, fuel, shipping, housing, the public health, the public safety—all will be dangerously affected.  Hundreds of thousands of liberated people of Europe and Asia will die who could be saved if the railroads were not now tied up.*

*As I stated last night, unless the railroads are manned by returning strikers I shall immediately undertake to run them by the Army of the United States.*

*{The Congress applauded.}*

*I assure you that I do not take this action lightly.  But there is no alternative.  This is no longer a dispute between labor and management.  It has now become a strike against the Government of the United States itself.*

*{The Congress applauded more.}*

*That kind of strike can never be tolerated.*

*{The Congress applauded again.}*

*If allowed to continue, the government will break down.  Strikes against the government must stop.*

*I appear before you to request immediate legislation designed to help stop them.*

*The benefits which labor has gained in the last thirteen years must be preserved.  I voted for all these benefits while I was a member of the Congress.  As President of the United States,*

*I have repeatedly urged not only their retention but their improvement. I shall continue to do so.*

*However, what we are dealing with here is not labor as a whole. We are dealing with a handful of men who are striking against their own government and against every one of their fellow citizens, and against themselves. We are dealing with a handful of men who have it within their power to cripple the entire economy of the nation.*

*I request temporary legislation to take care of this immediate crisis. I request permanent legislation leading to the formulation of a long-range labor policy designed to prevent the recurrence of such crises and generally to reduce the stoppages of work in all industries for the future.*

*The legislation should provide that, after the government has taken over an industry and has directed men to remain at work or to return to work, the wage scale be fixed either by negotiation or by arbitrators appointed by the President, and when so fixed, it shall be retroactive.*

*This legislation must be used in a way that is fair to capital and to labor alike. The President will not permit either side—industry or workers—to use it to further their own selfish interests or to foist upon the government the carrying out of their selfish aims.*

*Net profits of government operation, if any, should go to the Treasury of the United States. As a part of this temporary emergency legislation I request the Congress immediately to authorize the president to draft into the armed forces of the United States all workers who are on strike against their government.*

*{The Congress stood and applauded even more.}*

*{Whereupon, there was a note passed to President Truman, by the Secretary of the Senate Biffle.}*

*Word has just been received that the rail strike has been settled on terms proposed by the President.*

*These measures may appear to you to be drastic. They are. I repeat that I recommend them only as temporary emergency expedients and only in cases where workers are striking against the government.*

THE REDEEMER: IT IS WRITTEN

*I believe that the time has come to adopt a comprehensive labor policy which will tend to reduce the number of stoppages of work and other acts which injure labor, capital, and the whole population.*

*The general right of workers to strike against private employers must be preserved. I am sure, however, that adequate study and consideration can produce permanent long-range legislation which will reduce the number of occasions where that ultimate remedy has to be adopted. The whole subject of labor relations should be studied afresh.*

*I make these recommendations for temporary and long range legislation with the same emphasis on each. They should both be part of one program designed to maintain our American system of free enterprise with fairness and justice to all the American citizens who contribute to it. I thank you."*

*{The Congress resoundingly applauded.}*

Starving children and hospitals without electricity? The stakes could never be higher. Durant laid the speech on his nightstand. He knew that the long-term legislation President Truman requested ended up being the formation of the C.I.A. And the C.I.A. was the agency that kept the trains running, by bending and breaking every law in the books with the Hoffa Protocol. But it worked. *Di Trina* would pay off the union officials, and, rain or snow, America's trains ran on time. The economy stayed strong like a bull.

He turned out the lamp and panned through scandalous images in his mind. But he then remembered the business advice he'd received from Big Dutch before they'd started their little fracas— their debate. Before Durant kicked some ass and settled who was alpha male. The motto of a mafia Don.

*"Never let nothing or nobody get in your way of making a profit."*

Durant got up and paced anxiously and mulled over how he could make a mountain of money using the Hoffa Protocol, while he waited for his sugar-date.

CHAPTER 57

# CHAPTER 58

# WHO'S ZOOMING WHO?

It was hot in mid-August, as Colonel Durant looked out his hotel room window, overlooking the Capitol Building in Washington, D.C. The town was washed with lights and Colonel Durant's sugar-date was now very late. Durant took another blue pill, just in case. He was thinking. He got a good laugh, deep down inside, about how nervous and worried Justice Nelson had been during their meeting that day. He had his own ideas about why our forefathers created a tripartite of government. All separated and of equal strength.

To Durant, the country was going to Hell because the legal beagles didn't have the balls to do the killing. They were cowards who chose to destroy a man from the inside, by cross-examining him on the witness stand. They weren't man enough to do the same thing with weapons. He had little respect for the judicial branch and even less for the defense lawyers, who, he thought, were bottom-feeding, scum suckers. They just twisted words and the law into shapes that the framers of the Constitution never intended. He longed for martial law, where you could catch a man stealing and shoot him on the spot. Or torture the poor S.O.B. until he told you what you wanted to hear. A double tap to the back of the head with a gun, and the interrogation's over. Efficient investigation. Save the taxpayer on police and prison expense. If only *he* ran the country.

"The General will now speak with you, Colonel," said Lieutenant-General Crowe's assistant, as she patched Durant through to Crowe.

General Crowe was the head of Air Force Intelligence. He was up to his neck in alligators. That day, he was dealing with a defector from North Korea, who walked right onto Ramstein Air Force Base in Germany. He was full of good intelligence. But Crowe had to fly to Germany immediately, to make sure the defector wasn't planted as a double agent to spy on the United

States. Crowe wanted to get to brass tacks with Durant and get off the line. His jet sat fired up and waiting on the tarmac at Andrews A.F.B.

"Everything is going as planned, General. Just tying up a few loose ends here in D.C. Yes, Sir. My report will be on your desk in the morning, Sir."

Durant visualized millions of dollars in his own Swiss bank safe-deposit box as the General hung up without saying good-bye. His pondering and scheming for dynastic wealth ended as abruptly as his phone call.

"Hot Damn!"

Colonel Durant's groin pulsed after the sound of French-manicured fingernails playfully scratch-scratching at his hotel room door.

His date announced her feral mating call.

"Meow."

Expecting a female guest, but always careful, he put his hand over the peephole first, in case someone wanted to shoot through the door, when the peephole went dark. After he waited a few seconds, he peered through the security peephole before he opened the door. It was who he expected. He opened the door eagerly.

There stood a tall, platinum-blonde woman, wearing four-inch-high stilettos, shiny black. Large, Jackie-O sunglasses covered her eyes. She was wrapped in a skintight, leopard-print mini-skirt, beneath a skimpy, white, low-cut blouse. Mauve, fishnet stockings seemed barely to capture the long, sexy legs of the woman. She leaned on the doorjamb while she chewed a golf-ball-sized wad of gum. She carried her clutch under her arm, like a football running back, as she entered, leaving a trail of bordello-grade perfume that some might mistake for use in mosquito fogging.

"I asked for a Swedish Blonde." The long legs strutted past Durant with attitude. "But I guess platinum will do. First let me check your I.D.," Durant said, as he shut the door.

From Sergeant Butler's vantage point across the road, she could see everything. *"What a dumb-assed twit you are, Durant."* She wasn't thinking about how Durant was going to be screwing a hooker. She couldn't believe that Durant was so dumb and brazen as to leave the curtains open. *"Sloppy, sloppy,*

*sloppy,*" were Butler's thoughts. It had nothing to do with Durant's sexual techniques and that of the woman he was taking.

Butler tapped N.S.A.'s cameraman on the shoulder, "Now don't watch this and get any bright ideas, Leroy."

"I'm always ready to learn," said Leroy.

"Yeah, well, you won't learn much from Durant. He's so stupid, he left the drapes open, and he's working this girl over like she's a mare in the pasture."

Durant was taking the hooker seven ways to Sunday. She still wore her tiger-stripped bra, fishnet nylons a la garter, and polished, high heels; with the sex servant's feet in the air, she recognized the style was unmistakably Prada, even with a grainy surveillance picture. Butler watched through the high-powered lens. She was trained in how to use sex as a weapon and a snare. Her present assignment was to keep close tabs on Durant for C.I.A. Sergeant Butler had a Master's Degree in Political Science from George Washington University. She became close to Durant during his short stays at Fort Eustis, during her late-night "document courier" visits to the Colonel's hotel room.

Durant was bright. But the Sergeant believed he had no suspicion that C.I.A. and N.S.A. were using him to try to catch much bigger fish than Casteel.

Terrorists. Economic terrorists.

Butler watched Durant and the woman fall into the bed, finished. She looked at the monitor of the closed-circuit T.V. camera, fitted into the smoke detector in the hotel room. The picture was grainy. You could see what the bodies were doing, but you just couldn't identify anybody if you had to swear an oath in a court of law.

Durant was naked, lying next to the woman, caressing her hair again and again. He was calling her "the Kegel Queen." He pulled off her wig. He rolled her over onto her back. It was DeeDee DeVillay. But Sergeant Butler could not clearly identify her from the telescopic camera across the street or from the video camera in the room. She still wasn't quite sure what went on after Durant turned off the lights. She had not installed a low-light camera in the room.

Back at Langley, Butler listened to the audio of Durant's sexual escapade over and over again. The last thing she heard Durant's voice say was, "Now that I got laid, you get made."

Try as they may, the techs couldn't clear up the rest of the audio file. Seventeen minutes of whispers, with Durant's bedside clock radio playing rock and roll at 103 decibels in the background. Sammy Hagar, The Stones, Led Zeppelin, Queen, and Twisted Sister, all came through loud and clear.

Seventeen minutes of whispers. That bugged C.I.A. operative, Sergeant Butler. And it really bugged her bosses, who were trying to snare some wanna-be terrorists, who were hiding behind diplomatic immunity. Butler's woman's intuition kicked in. Hookers don't wear polished shoes, especially not Prada.

Butler wondered. *Who's zooming who?*

# CHAPTER 59

# A SECRET OATH

C.A.R.'s corporate, mansion getaway sat high on the banks of the Mississippi River, on the opposite river bank from Twenty-Three Oaks and five miles down stream. Eighty acres, surrounded by an eight-foot-high, barbed-wire-topped fence. It was patrolled by two security units, assisted by canines. The corporate helicopters had been busy ferrying the *Di Trina* lawyers onto the estate for the last hour.

In the huge, dark-paneled great room, a ritual was unfolding. A fire roared in the eight-foot-wide and six-foot-high fireplace. Big Dutch and twelve other *Di Trina* mafia lawyers stood as a group, exchanging notes and commiserating. A tuxedo-attired butler opened the sliding parlor door. Felix Falic stepped in. "Mr. Falic, as you requested, Sir."

Big Dutch greeted Falic by kissing his *Di Trina* golden-spike ring. Falic returned the gesture.

"My Capo, we live in extraordinary times," Falic said.

"I know. I've seen the fury of Colonel Durant, and I know he doesn't quibble. But does he know we have never gained admission to two lawyers from the same firm, or to any woman?"

*Di Trina*'s Cleveland Designated attorney was a nondescript man with shallow eyes and a slouch. He said, "We saw what Durant did with Freemont in San Francisco. And Schultz in Chicago. We don't like it, but we can't bite the hand that feeds us."

"True. I agree. This will take more money out of my pocket than any of yours, but I realize Durant's alternative," said Falic.

"Mr. Falic, do you have a proposal?" asked Big Dutch.

"Mr. Chairman, I move we induct a new member to further our cause of justice."

"All opposed, 'Nay.'" The room was silent. "Then it's settled."

The heavy, parlor door slid open silently, and DeeDee gained admittance. She was dressed in a conservative black, dress suit, a white blouse, and black pumps. She chose to bow instead of curtsy, as she kissed all of the rings of the *Di Trina* lawyers.

The room smelled of the wood-smoke fire and a strong trace of cinnamon the house staff had sprayed, using old-fashioned pump sprayers before the meeting. The cinnamon was part of their ritual, to lend some sacredness to an unholy affair.

"Are you the candidate for induction?"

DeeDee answered. She was anxious, but did not appear so.

"Yes, my Capo."

A security man with big shoulders and a close-shaved beard brought Big Dutch a red, velvet cloth. Big Dutch unwrapped it to reveal a silver knife and a picture of Saint Thomas More. The fireplace burned in the background, as DeeDee lifted the Saint Thomas More picture with her right hand. She extended her left hand to Big Dutch. Big Dutch cut one of DeeDee's fingers and squeezed some of her blood onto Saint Thomas More's picture.

Then Big Dutch took from the fire a burning stick of Dogwood and used it to light the saint's picture while DeeDee held it. "If you drop the Saint, your oath is worthless. You will not be one of us." DeeDee winced in pain, from the fire burning her fingers. She began her oath of allegiance to *Di Trina*.

"I am sacred counsel. If I should betray *Di Trina*, my flesh will burn like this Saint. If I lie to my brethren, my tongue will be cut out. I will be faithful to *Di Trina* in all of my dealings, until consumed by my grave."

*Omerta* – the mafia's secret oath of faithfulness and silence.

DeeDee repeated the oath over and over. She rolled the picture in her hands while reciting the oath, until, at last, it was all ashes. Finally, Saint Thomas More's picture sifted through her scorched fingers. The Designated lawyers each picked up bits of the ash and rubbed it into their *Di Trina* rings.

"We identify each other by our rings. Locomotive black in a circle of Exodus white, containing a golden spike."

Big Dutch slipped the black onyx ring with the golden spike onto Dee Dee's left, little finger. *Di Trina* had a new member.

"We are one. And one for all," Big Dutch said.

CHAPTER 59

# CHAPTER 60

# A BREAK

---

It was Friday, August 18, 1995. The thick summer air and hot sun of St. Martinsville had me driving with my convertible's top down almost every day. The Federal courthouse was almost vacant, except for essential staff. The usual, hard-ass, unsmiling security detail at the metal detectors gave me uncharacteristic well wishes for the weekend.

One recognized me as Jake Casteel's new lawyer, "Is it true you throw knives at clients?" the Deputy Marshal asked me, with a grin.

"No. I mean, no comment." I was catching onto the media game pretty quick. I walked down the hall to the clerk's office. I was on a mission based on a hunch.

I opened the tall, federal-wide door, and I found a pleasant looking, elderly lady behind the court clerk's counter. She appeared to be the only one in the office. Soft and cheerful music played from the radio on her desk, further back in the room. I approached the counter, where the clerk was standing. I greeted her kindly and asked to see the "United States versus Jake Casteel" file.

Elvina Ethra Tibbins was a virtual fixture at that federal courthouse. She had worked there for over forty-three years. Her thin lips stretched wide as she touched her face, indicating her exasperation, "Why, that file has been looked at five hundred times, young man," she said.

I leaned into the counter and smiled at Elvina. I looked her straight in the eyes.

"I need your help, Miss." Dalton, the ladies' man, taught me it was always best to refer to a woman as "Miss." It is always flattering, never insulting. "I was hoping you wouldn't have figured out that it was just an excuse for me to come by to see you."

Elvina's face brightened at my overt flirting.

"You an attorney?"

"Yes, I am, Miss." There I went, with "Miss" again. Earnest and sincere. Elvina located the file. It was so thick and heavy, she brought it to me on a cart. I hung my coat on the office's coat tree, and I took the cart into the attorney's anteroom to review Jake Casteel's thick files. Elvina watched me closely.

Two and a half hours later, not long before closing time, I emerged from the anteroom, after having reviewed the minutes and the foot-thick folders of pleadings, motions, appellate briefs, writs, and orders in the file. I reviewed it in a cursory way, to get the lay of the land and a feel for the file and the charges against Jake Casteel.

The case looked to me like it had been a set-up. Casteel was railroaded into prison. I was damn sure of it.

The government's theory of prosecution wasn't divulged until the closing argument at trial. Wicked. And Judge Lackey let the government lawyers, some wet boys from D.C., get away with it, over strenuous objections from Jake Casteel himself. Certainly not from his lackluster trial counsel, who seemed to be glued, or paid off to stay, in his chair. I'd thought that was a tactic reserved for close-in fighting. Ambush at the last second. Element of surprise. But in a way, I sort of respected it. Military tactics in the courtroom. Impressive.

"Excuse me, Elvina." We were now on a first-name basis. "There is something very wrong here. It appears that there are a lot of entries in the court minutes that have been deleted from this computer-generated record."

"Oh, Mike, that's that dang-blasted, new computer system they have. I used to type those by myself on that old typewriter over there. Now, they want us to enter all of the court proceedings into the computer. So we got rid of the old, manually typed, court-file minute sheets."

"Well, there are all these entries on what happened in the file in that are missing." I pointed at the missing entries. A whole block of documents that looked as though they had been erased because the remaining documents retained the original sequence of numbers they had been assigned as the case progressed. The entries looked suspicious; they jumped over a blank of numbers, here and there, with no pattern. "Miss. Elvina, do you know where all those records are now?"

"You would have to get the originals and . . . now, wait a minute. I think I saw them somewhere else." Elvina thought for a moment and said, "Let me check in the back."

Elvina shuffled off, trying to tuck her rear end in as much as possible. She was hoping that Mike might be looking. He was pretty darn cute, even if she was thirty years his senior. It was that smile and his dark hair, and he dripped with confidence. Nothing sexier than a confident man, she mused as she made her way to the back rooms. She went all the way to the vault. That was where they kept the sensitive filings ordered sealed by the judges, when the judges thought it was necessary to protect the public from the truth about what went on in the taxpayers' courthouse. She returned with a big smile.

"Looks like it's your lucky day."

"You got something good?"

"These are all the original minutes to the file." Elvina pointed at the legal documents. "They were sitting back by the shredder, with a note on the pile, saying that it was an order from the United States Supreme Court they be shredded. I don't see why because they are just the minute sheets I typed up personally. They can't be secret."

Elvina pointed out, in the computer-generated record, where it referenced that the Supreme Court ordered some of the documents destroyed after Casteel lost his first appeal to the Seventh Circuit Court of Appeals in Chicago. Extremely unusual. *Destroying official documents before a man's final appeal was complete?* Very fishy, indeed.

"Miss Elvina, do you think I could get a copy of those, please?"

Miss Elvina took care of me.

"I suppose so, since you are so nice. You're the only customer I've had most all day."

I made a quick review of the documents Elvina saved from the shredder. She was now Saint Elvina.

I'd hit gold.

It was a whole treasure chest of valuable documents that were meant to be destroyed, to cover up how Jacob Casteel had been railroaded into the penitentiary. Just like the legendary rail-union leader, Eugene Debs, had been set up, over sixty years before. History repeated itself.

I said to myself, *"Whoa! I can't believe this. This is why I never got to read the record of this case. I can't believe they deleted it off the computer. The audacity."*

"You okay?" Elvina asked because I looked spaced-out at my luck.

"Miss, please give me six copies; certify all of them."

Elvina gave me certified copies of the documents that were supposed to be destroyed. But someone had been lazy and put off the document shredding until tomorrow. Saint Elvina gave me certified copies of all the documents of the court-file sheet, that should have been shredded, and a certified copy of the new, computerized version, that showed the huge gap left by the missing documents. I thanked Elvina for her help. I wished her well, wrapping my warm hand around her cold fingers in a genuine handshake.

"Elvina, there's a star in heaven for you."

I was so excited, I seemed to float out of the clerk's office. I could not believe it. I was just given copies of documents that showed that the government had met with Judge Lackey, the trial judge, *ex parte*, in secret, without Jake Casteel's trial attorneys ever knowing about it. Secret meetings with the other side are strictly forbidden under the law. Judge Lackey knew better than to do that. Thank God Judge Lackey's clerk was honest, recording that a meeting had occurred and the general subject matter of that meeting.

There were entries that reflected Lackey met with the government attorneys and government agents. They didn't meet about the law, or about the facts, or about any charges brought against Jake Casteel. They'd met about trying to avert a railroad strike.

The documents lined up quite well with the information "Two Thumbs" had shared with Dalton and me.

Elvina Ethra didn't have to stick her neck out and snatch from destruction some court documents that were supposed to be shredded. But she did. She did it, partially because she believed in the system of justice. But she had another more human and honest motive.

CHAPTER 60

"It was nice meeting you, Elvina. Very nice, indeed," I said, as a final send-off to Elvina. I bobbed my head in an abbreviated, southern-style bow, as was customary in polite circles, prior to leaving the company of a lady. They were circles Elvina still lived in.

I slung my jacket over my shoulder and I swung the federal-wide door open, enough for me to clear the armful of documents I had just obtained. Inadvertently, I gave Elvina one last glimpse of what she thought might be my better side. I was excited that I now had a sharp weapon to use in Casteel's defense. But Elvina enjoyed a different excitement.

She thought back to how she might have looked at things forty years ago, before she was married and then widowed. She marveled in a short fantasy, with her throw-back big band music playing.

She said under her breath, "Nice butt."

# CHAPTER 61

# DOUBLE AGENT

Durant knew he was being watched. Making a "secret" connection with his mission operative, DeeDee, was part of his plan. How he handled his field crew was his damned business, as far as he was concerned. He left his hotel-room curtains wide open so that the camera crew, Sergeant Butler, or whoever else wanted to see him screwing could see it. He even put on a good show for them. He did it with his butt facing the window, just so they got a nice, clear shot of his ass, where he wanted them to put their lips. They could kiss his rear-end.

Durant let them think he was a bit sloppy, leaving open the curtains. But he knew the people watching never fought in the jungle, where you might be right up next to your enemy and not know it. It was an ancient tactic, as old as the Trojan horse. Faking an injury, to draw an opponent in close, within striking distance of your dagger. In war, in the law, as in all things of action, you gain a tremendous advantage if you can make your opponent *think* you are sloppy. They lower their guard. Then you attack with *your* plan.

Colonel Durant was smug. When he was done, all of them, the whole country, the whole world would pay. No one would be spared the effects of his plan.

He had a Plan B.

Colonel Durant left his room and took the stairwell down to the hotel's underground parking garage. Along the way, he put on a disguise: glasses; a fake mustache, thick and black like Groucho Marx; and a hat with a curly-haired wig. He turned his shirt, and pants, and belt—all reversible—inside out. He changed his gait, making it shorter and slower. And he stooped, like a shriveled, old man with a bad back.

He shuffled into the underground parking garage, past the BMWs and Mercedes, to a beat-up, plumber's van, bearing stolen license plates. The driver was a thick-necked, Middle-Easterner, wearing wraparound shades. Durant slipped in the back door. They left the garage and drove around D.C., to make sure they were not followed.

Ten minutes later, the van pulled through the gates of the Afghan Embassy and into the garage. The driver walked to the back of the van, and, as if on cue, opened the van's back door, just in time for two guards with submachine guns and the Afghan Ambassador to approach. Durant stepped out of the van. He removed his facial disguise.

"The quality of your information is quite good, Colonel. I have been authorized to accept your offer."

The ambassador handed Durant a C.D.

"Here's your de-crypted disc. It was most informative. I was surprised it was only an 8-bit encryption. Your people, your experts, are a bit sloppy, yes?"

They discussed the two things most important to any deal: timing and money. Durant slipped the reformatted C.D. into a black, carrying case. He shoved it into a cargo pocket in his dungarees, a civilian version of Army fatigues. The ambassador's assistant, a swarthy man with beady eyes, handed Durant two steel briefcases.

"Do I have to count this?"

"You are dealing with the son of a camel trader."

Durant smiled. Honor among thieves. He had a deal. And a huge down payment.

CHAPTER 61

# CHAPTER 62

# A SLIP OF THE TONGUE

Ann pounded so hard, it hurt her fist. She pushed open my office door. It had a coat-tree of knives stuck into the other side. I was struggling with a mountain of legal research I had copied at the law library and brought back for analysis. I paced back and forth, looking at copies of opinions from federal appellate courts from around the land. I threw some papers in the air in frustration as Ann came in.

My back was to Ann as I said, "Casteel's trial judge had it all wrong, according to these cases." I held up my right hand, full of papers. "All these say Perjury on Admiralty is unconstitutional and denies the Defendant a jury trial." Then I raised my left hand, with still more papers, "And all these cases say it's only proper in the military, in a court martial."

Ann felt compelled to interject, "Mike, I was wondering if you were going to need me to type again late tonight, for the deadline. I gotta get someone to baby-sit Kylee."

I was preoccupied in thought, bent over, looking at one of thirty-five different piles of papers I had stacked on my office floor. Each pile represented the case law on a different legal issue. They all had to be analyzed and indexed so they could be referred to when writing the many parts of the Supreme Court brief. The deadline loomed large. It was only a few days away.

"I'm sorry, Annie, dear, I really need you tonight." I spoke before I'd thought. I had never before called Ann, "Annie." I had never called Ann "dear" before, and I never told her, "I really need you tonight."

Freudian? Maybe. Embarrassing? Yes. Did I want her for my own? You bet I did.

My slip of the tongue sounded bad, just by itself. Ann put her hands on her hips, cocking one eyebrow upward. She did not know how to take what I said. Was it an invitation? Was it a directive? Was it a come-on? Was it sexual harassment? Ann parroted back to me what I had just said to her. She put her hands on her hips, and an incredulous look stretched across her face.

"I'm sorry, Annie, dear. I really need you tonight?"

It didn't help that big-ears Dalton chimed in, hollering from his office, "Sounds like a Freudian slip to me, counselor."

I was dumbfounded, embarrassed that I would say something like that to Ann. My employee. I hadn't meant to word it that way. When I said it, I had been deep in thought about the schism between the circuit courts of appeal on the main issue we had been researching—the unconstitutional nature of allowing conviction of a criminal defendant without a full, jury verdict. Casteel's trial judge had sat as the fact finder, the jury, to determine some of the elements of the offense. It was a complicated issue. And further complicated by the fact that eight of the eleven courts of appeal had eight different ways of handling prosecutions under the Perjury on Admiralty Statute of 1807.

But the most complicating issue of all was my inescapable attraction to Ann. I thought I hid it well by keeping things all business between the two of us. Ann did not know I thought of her quite often, inside and outside the office.

I struggled to respond to Ann's inquiry. Especially since it was true. I secretly adored her. It was a true, Freudian slip. I was a lonely man, sitting at home. I ate M.R.E.'s in my bedroom, listening to the steady beat of Irish ballads that strummed through the plastered walls from Bridget's room. I chauffeured my challenged sister about town, while everyone else got to get on with their lives. Their lives were full, with a loving spouse and children. Even though all that was true, I sure as Hell couldn't tell it to Ann or anyone else.

She was my employee. Asking Ann out, putting a move on her, creating a personal relationship, a boyfriend, girlfriend kind of thing, was strictly forbidden, as far as I was concerned.

CHAPTER 62

Boss dating secretary. I knew the rest of society would look upon our relationship as dishonorable. I had a rule I *tried* to live by: "Only with Honor."

I struggled for a response to Ann. "I said that?"

Ann nodded her head, with a sexy smirk. Dalton continued to play the smart-ass. "Ayup," resounded from Dalton's office.

I shifted gears, like I was driving my Mustang. I kept the wheels straight, and I just dropped it into a lower gear. I became more direct.

"Could you, please, work tonight?"

Ann looked like she expected a different response. She was speechless. *How dare he? He blew right past an obvious, romantic overture, like it never happened.* She even shook her head, back and forth, like she couldn't believe what had just happened. Ann looked a bit disappointed that I had not been forthcoming with my feelings. She sensed I had been expressing a hidden desire when I first addressed her.

She turned and walked out. "Sure."

I turned around and watched her walk away, with her bewildered nose in the air. I felt like an ass. I went back to reading the boring case law. The Casteel case had nothing to do with falling in love and starting a family or raising children. It had everything to do with duty, for a payback so secret I could tell no one.

I yelled into the next room for Ann's to hear, "And I am going to pay all your babysitting costs, too, you hear?"

I was in trouble. I was in love.

# CHAPTER 63

# THE PIRATES OF PURGATORY

I was surprised how easily sleep came to me that night. It was 0200 hours when my head dove into the six-inch-deep piles of papers on my office desk. My legal-research papers had begun to resemble something like a haphazard raft, strung together by the shipwrecked. The piles of research became a huge, hodge-podge collection of legal cases of the damned, the poor, innocent souls convicted of Perjury on Admiralty. I read them to make sense out of a crazy prosecution under an ancient, punitive law used to convict enemies of the State because they could present no effective defense. Casteel's case had been a sham. It became painfully clear to me that my defense in the Supreme Court was going to make some very big people, very vindictive people, very powerful people, very angry. If we won, my legal career would be over. I was planning on putting my head between my knees and kissing my rear end good-bye.

Right before I fell asleep at my desk, I thought about the life of a lawyer. We get paid to piss off the other side. Kind of like if a surgeon went into another surgeon's operating room and tried to bump the surgeon's elbow when he was using a scalpel on his patient. Practicing law is a ruthless business, only for those with the strongest of stomachs. It is a true adversarial system.

My dreams washed over me, with my face smashed into the stack of case-law papers.

I drifted away from the shores of the mortal.

*I was lying on the deck of the great ship. The Seas of Purgatory were surprisingly placid. The calm before the storm. There was a great cantilever extended over the port gunwale. I was hog-tied. My ankles and hands were tied tightly behind my back. The dirty bastards hung me upside down from a rope, strung off the end of the cantilever boom, like a captured fish on* display. They were getting their merry jollies, dunking me into the ocean, where shark fins cut the water. The crew was laughing at my terrified expense.

Captain Carion was up on the quarterdeck, quaffing a pint of the black. He ordered the crew to hoist me up and down, in and out of the Hellish waters. Carion would wait until the last second to avert my being eaten by the sharks of Original Sin. The creatures of Hell clacked their sharp teeth together, wanting my tasty flesh of Honor. Mr. Fetid was encouraging the crewmen, who were manning the ship's boom. They all shouted contradictory jeers and cheers as I went up and down. I was dunked in and hoisted out, again and again, until Carion could laugh no more.

"Okay, McRain, tell us all again why you are helping Casteel," Carion said. I tried to respond, while I hung upside down, struggling at the end of the rope, hanging over the water, made frothy white by the hungry sharks.

"I'm trying to be a Good Samaritan."

Captain Carion indicated with a down turned thumb that I should be dunked again, whilst the sharks swam at me like torpedoes.

"Now!" Carion yelled.

The boisterous crew quickly lifted up the cantilever and snatched me away, at the last second, from jaws filled with rows of razor- sharp teeth. A shark gashed my shoulder, instead of swallowing my head. My blood dripped into the water. Massive sharks churned the waters more and more.

"McRain, you are a liar. You are no Good Samaritan. You are like the rest of us—semi-damned. We sail in a world of limbo, victims of where the winds of Fate shall blow us, for centuries on end. Oh, boohoo. Admit it, you bastard. You are just a selfish soul, doing whatever you got to do to be redeemed. Carion did not wait for my response. He continued my indictment.

You know why else you ain't no Good Samaritan? Mr. Michael O'Brien McRain. Ya bloody Irishman. Its 'cuz a Good Samaritan actually helps people. You've been doing nothing, but lose. I'm tired of it. You are a loser and a deserter. I've had enough of you."

Carion gave a thumbs down, to drop me into a certain death. But at the most fortuitous moment, Mr. Troubles cut one of the counterweight ropes holding the cantilever, and the contraption swung me, like a catapult, onto the deck. Troubles was as quick as a cat. He ran to my rescue, cutting the ropes that bound me. He bravely held off the crew with his sword as they screamed for my blood.

CHAPTER 63

*We escaped and found refuge in the upper riggings. Up in the crow's nest. Not the best place to be as a storm, full of green, powerful clouds, bore down on us.*

*Mr. Troubles' advice was delivered in a hurry, with his crooked finger poked into my shoulder. "McRain, seems the Cap'n got into the Celestial Rum. He's on a tear. He's an ol' pirate in the King's name is what he is. And Mr. Fetid's plottin' your demise 'cuz he likes to see the suffering of the righteous. They've both given up hope of getting their salvation to get off this boat and up to the Admiral's territories. To top it off, Carion hates deserters. You are gonna have to drop Judge Lackey in the first round. Else, I think the Captain will kill you, for sure, the next time you board. It will be the waters of Hell for you if you don't next succeed."*

*A front of storm clouds gathered above and sent a bolt of lightning that jolted me out of my shoes. I was stunned. My spirit seemed just to hang there, waiting for some bodily response in the eternity of that split second.*

# CHAPTER 64

# LOVE

I snored like a buzz saw. I was asleep, sitting at my desk, with my head sunk into the raft of legal-research papers. A darkly clad figure entered the office and approached me, with a device on a pole that emitted intermittent, electrical arcs. It was a cattle prod, the kind farmers use to move uncooperative cows. The figure got closer and closer. It loomed next to me, illuminated only by the faint glow of my green-shaded banker's lamp. When the figure got close enough, the electric device arced and was thrust into my shoulder. Jolted by 50,000 volts of electricity, I leaped to my feet. The dark figure was Ann delivering my requested wakeup service. She jumped back, in fear of my response to being shocked by her Daddy's cattle prodder.

"Whoa. Feelin' good. Let's do the obstacle course again. Ooo-Rah," I said, while I ran in place, warming up.

"Mike, you're not on the obstacle course. This is St. Martinsville. You are in your law office, and you are doing legal research at 2:00 a.m."

"Working on the Supreme Court brief," I said, loud and clear, **as** though I was doing it for a drill sergeant. Ann was standing with her hands on her hips.

"Of course, it's the Supreme Court brief. It's the only thing you've **been** working on for the past two weeks. You never sleep."

"Sleep is for wussies." I sat down, and my head started to bob from fatigue.

"I swear you are trying to kill yourself. I can't do this anymore." Ann threw the cattle prodder on my desk. It spilled a cup of coffee over the six inches of papers on my desk. Ann was in a huff, on her way out.

"My Momma's been watching my little girl most every night so I can type late for you. Plus, I brought Daddy's cattle prod in like you asked.

And, over my objections, I've been sparkin' it on you so you can make your damned deadline. But enough is enough. Do it yourself, Mr. Tough Guy."

I gave up trying to blot up the spilled coffee, and I ran after Ann. I grabbed her elbow and twirled her around. "Don't go, I need you . . . I mean. . . I've got a deadline."

"You've got a deadline for the undertaker is what you've got," Ann said, as she leveled her hand, swiping the air like a sideways karate chop, back at me.

Exhausted and demoralized, I fell back in my chair. "Annie, I think they chose us to represent Casteel 'cuz they knew we didn't have the resources to do the impossible."

Ann was exasperated. She waved her hands in the air. "Duh. You had to go all the way to Harvard to get the brains to figger that one out? I can type ninety words a minute. But it's a different draft every day."

I gave a reason to obtain mercy for my idiocy. "Ann, it's a complicated case . . ."

"And you got a complicated life."

Ann stepped forward, closer to me, and held onto the back of a client chair, as I sat on the other side of my desk, looking at her. I marveled at how beautiful she was and how her eyes burned when she was angry. Like a fire, deep down inside her.

"You know, I read your whole box of medical records."

My head cocked to the side, like a wrestler who'd had a half-nelson put on him. Ann gripped the back of the chair harder with her fingernails. She was being defensive, right in the middle of a good offense.

"When that gang of men beat you half to death in 1969."

My eyes glazed over. Half from fatigue and half from the stupor I'd entered when Ann sucker-punched me with my medical records. It was private. My personal pain, that I didn't have to share with the rest of the world, like the goofballs spilling their guts on the talk shows. I had my own personal cross to carry. I did it by myself. I was incensed and hurt that my privacy had been invaded and my internal pain, my weakness, had been exposed. I looked at the ceiling in exasperation.

CHAPTER 64

Ann continued, "Yeah, all of them. The box was sitting out and open. I think the plastic surgeon did a nice job." She raised her voice, from the lower assertive to a higher, consoling tone. "Nine surgeries. I saw the police report, where the dirty bastards were out for good times—just out to get drunk. High and joy-riding around, beating up children."

I was quick to add another layer of bandaging to explain the new-found emotional wound Ann had uncovered.

I said, "And they never caught 'em. I was just eleven. Just a boy . . . You think I'm crazy?"

"If courage is crazy, you're nuttier'n Carter's peanut farm."

I turned my back to Ann and looked out the window. Ann stood, with her arms across her chest, behind me. She was ashamed she cut me so deep. She thought she might have struck to the bone. Ann thought how bad my emotional hemorrhage might be. She took a step closer to me. Into the spotlight of a full, summer moon shining through the office window.

Ann could feel the awkward tension, "I don't mean anything by it. You are just the bravest man I ever met."

I spoke then, of the beating I'd received when I tried to protect my blind and autistic sister, Bridget, and of the lifelong effect it had had on me, as a boy and as a man.

"That's when I lost my innocence." Ann covered her gasp with her hand, "That's the day I learned how to hate. I learned to hate real good."

Ann sidled up to me and pressed her supple breasts into my back. I could feel her body's warmth. She laid her hands on my shoulders and slid them down and around my waist. I turned around to face her, with a tear in my eye. Ann leaned into me and hung on my neck. She looked up into my eyes.

"It's time I learnt ya somethin' else."

We kissed and slid down the wall slowly, on to the floor, and across the U.S.M.C. rug under my desk. We were entwined. Two lonely and earnest hearts, chaperoned only by a tolerant moon. Our restraint and waiting were over. Neither of us were virgins. And neither of us wanted sex. It was love we desired. We surrendered our restraint and sacrificed ourselves to each other. Our mouths, our lips, combined and remained together even as we spoke words of affection, and of heartfelt longing, between us. We made love, as those in love do.

An open drawer of my desk revealed a Polaroid of the stone. The picture looked black and white in the bleaching moonlight. My shadow reached up and pushed the drawer shut.

CHAPTER 64

# CHAPTER 65

# INVITATION TO THE LION'S DEN

The next morning, I bumped into a Federal Express courier as I entered the office. I wondered, with reluctant anticipation, who was the lucky recipient. I told myself it was probably another deadline in the making. Loose papers flapped under my arm as I balanced a week's worth of legal research in a precarious compilation of files.

"Well, it's too early for Valentine's Day; what did you get?" I said to Ann.

"It's not me, it's for you. I never get anything," Ann said, as she noted my hair getting a bit longer. It now touched my ears, and I could comb the top across. No more straight-up, butch cut.

I set my slipshod collection of files and papers on the corner of Ann's desk. It soon became an avalanche, spilling onto the floor. Ann jumped up and came around to the other side to help me pick up the papers. "Darn legal research I just copied at the law library." I was frustrated.

"What is it? Something from a judge?"

"No, it's an invitation to a Masquerade Ball at the Falic Firm."

I sensed something was wrong in the way Ann said, "The Falic Firm." But I thought it best to let it slide, since I was down on my hands and knees, trying to reach papers that had floated underneath chairs in the waiting-room area of the office.

"DeeDee's firm?" I said, with my head under a chair.

Ann had a view of my rear end. She begrudged me with a long sigh, "Yes." But she really wanted to make a wise-ass comment about my butt. Ann turned cold at my response.

"Great. Order us some costumes."

Dalton stuck his head out his door, "Falic? Masquerade Ball? Boy, we're coming up in the world. Gonna be lots a judges and politicians . . . Better make my costume 'The Exorcist.'"

"Order me whatever. I got too much work between now and then," I said, while I tried to balance the stack of papers as we picked them up. Ann was still on her hands and knees, trying to retrieve a case that had sneaked behind the wastebasket. I thought she looked a bit pitiful, kind of like a Cinderella.

"Ann, order yourself a costume. We can go as a trio."

"Is that an order?"

"Why, don't you want to go? I mean, it is the richest law firm in the whole state."

"Oh, its nothing. I don't know what to wear."

Dalton, being a man, visualized the unclothed version of Ann in that position. He was a shameless dog. Wise-acre Dalton said, "Sure, maybe a Playboy Bunny outfit. Or dress like Lady Godiva; then you could tell everyone at the party, 'I just couldn't drown all the puppies, so I saved these two with brown noses."

Ann's face went red. She looked like a N.A.S.A. moon shot, about to launch. Her mouth dropped open. As she got up to kick Dalton's ass, I saved the day.

"No, I think she'd look better hiding in a nun's habit."

Ann lowered her fist. "Oh, I'm Catholic enough to wear a nun's habit. But you don't think I could fit into a Playboy Bunny's outfit?"

I knew there was no good exit from the huge hole we had dug for ourselves. I employed traditional, military tactics when I found myself in an impossible situation.

Retreat.

I offered to Ann, "Dalton and I will both be priests. Order whatever costume you want." I did not want to ask Ann why she sounded like she shunned the Falic, Moore & DeVillay law firm. I steered Dalton towards the hallway door for a quick exit.

"Lunch time."

CHAPTER 65

# CHAPTER 66

# KNOW THY ENEMY

In the process of sizing me up as his enemy, Colonel Durant interviewed some of Mike's former military commanders to get a feel for his character. He wanted to find out some of Mike's weaknesses so that he could exploit them, to better implement the Hoffa Protocol mission. The contest of the Casteel litigation was one he refused to lose, and he wanted every possible advantage on his side.

One of these interviews took Durant to the Marine Corps' Twenty-Nine Palms base in the Southern California desert. On a remote section of the base, in a Quonset hut containing two chairs and a desk, sat Colonel Durant and Mike's last, Marine Corps, commanding officer. Lieutenant-General Frederick "Bull" Baker had a little, man-to-man talk with the Colonel about what made Michael O'Brien McRain tick. It went like this.

"This better be damned good, Mr. Durant. I'm missing my granddaughter's piano recital," said General Baker.

"I'll pass along a good word for you to the Secretary of Defense and Joint Chiefs."

Bull Baker was not consoled in the least. He wanted to get to brass tacks.

"I've been told to cooperate with you in every way by the Intel boys. What'cha got?"

Durant dropped the file of Michael O'Brien McRain onto the general's desk. General Baker bristled at the sight of Mike's name.

"Mike-O?"

Durant was surprised, "So you know him by his nickname?"

"Affirmative. Mike-O McRain was not one of my best Recon operatives in Force Recon. He was THE best operative I ever had. Why you interested in him?"

"Sorry, General, that is on a need-to-know only, Sir."

General Baker turned his bad side to Durant. It was the side of his face that was burned in a secret combat, on the wrong side of the Russian border, that the rest of the world would never know about. Skin grafts, three surgeries to remove shrapnel, and a year's worth of recovery at Walter Reed made Bull Baker a very impatient man.

"Tell me this. What weaknesses does McRain have?"

"Besides the usual human ones, you know, family and all, none. Because his only weakness is dead. Let me tell you a story that came straight from the mouth of the three-star Superintendent of the United States Air Force Academy."

General Baker spun Durant a tale, repeated over and over, since the beginning of time. Only the names change over the centuries—a domineering father tries to run the life of his strong son.

It seems that, in his senior year at the Academy, Mike McRain declared that he would take his commission in the Marine Corps, instead of the more obvious choice, made by almost all his classmates, the Air Force. As both Durant and Baker knew, being West Point and Naval Academy grads, respectively, it was all perfectly proper. Every service academy cadet is required by his senior year to declare in what arm of the service he wanted to serve upon graduation. But what made this choice even more strange was that Mike McRain was number one in his class at U.S.A.F.A. Worse yet, Mike was the son of the legendary Brigadier-General Frank "Bubbles" McRain, who was the highest-decorated fighter pilot in Air Force history. General McRain's picture hung in a place of high honor in the Academy's Fighter Ace Wall of Fame, reserved for the greatest fighter aces.

Durant interrupted for a brief moment. "I read the full file on General McRain. He was one Hell of a pilot and an even better tactician. The best."

General Baker nodded. "You're damn right. And Mike was a chip off the old block. Damn near a clone. And that was the rub. The biggest problem in Mike's life was his old man."

CHAPTER 66

Baker continued, explaining to Colonel Durant how the Air Force Academy had its first duel between father and son.

General McRain was livid when he heard Mike would take his commission in the Marine Corps and not the Air Force. He immediately flew up to Peterson Field in Colorado Springs, commandeered a vehicle, and raced up to the Academy. He stormed into Vandenberg Hall, where Mike had a room as a member of Sixth Squadron. It overlooked the athletic fields, set against the background of the breathtaking eastern slope of the Rockies Rampart Range. Mike was Cadet Wing Commander and had just finished leading the whole cadet wing to midday meal in Mitchell Hall. Mike walked into his room, his Cadet Wing Commander's sword and scabbard in his hand.

He told others, later on, he didn't know what hit him.

General McRain cold-cocked Mike in an ambush. Mike reeled from the blow. But he kept his feet. The two of them wrestled to a Mexican stand-off. They broke, and Mike kept the general at bay long enough to find out why he was being attacked.

"You are gonna be a Marine over my damn body," the general said.

They started shouting at each other. That drew a crowd outside the door.

The squadron commander, Major Estes, tried to get into the room, but General McRain, who was not an active- duty officer, ordered him out. The M.P.'s were not called— yet. However, General Solomon, the Academy's three-star Superintendent, was called, and he ran all the way to Sixth Squadron.

When General Solomon got there, he opened the door to Mike's room, to hear General McRain yell, "Please, General, this is a private conversation, between father and son. It seems Mike here declared he wants to be a Marine Corps bullet sponge. Apparently, from some type of delusional affliction. I'm just trying to knock some Air Force sense into his head."

Durant interrupted again, "None of this was in any file I read."

"And you won't find it in a file because it's a legend."

Baker continued: Lieutenant-General Solomon laid down a unique law.

He told the McRains that he would accept a decision about Mike's commission from the next man to walk out of Mike's room. Then he shut the door. He immediately placed a bet, on the old man, with Major Estes, who took Mike to walk out in fifteen minutes. Estes had inside information that he thought the General had probably forgotten. Mike was an All-American wrestler, and he'd set the U.S.A.F.A. push-up record. One hundred and nine strict ones in sixty seconds.

Nobody actually saw the fight that followed, between Mike and his father. But the witnesses, who, by then, numbered about twenty— some upper-class cadets and two light colonels, stood out in the hall, not counting the little, fourth-class plebes, with their doors ajar. All listened to a two-man brawl that sounded like the gods of Mount Olympus at war.

Mike yelled he wanted to be his own man. And the old man, who had fought on the same fight card as the legendary, world- champion boxer, Joe Louis, fired back that he'd die first. The yelling and fighting went on and on, behind the closed door.

The duel lasted for over an hour.

The door to Mike's room never opened from the inside. Nobody in the hallway moved. Not even when the M.P.'s showed up on a rumor that there was an altercation in Sixth Squadron. General Solomon shooed them away. There was silence in Mike's room for about ten minutes, before General Solomon opened the door, thinking the two, crazy bastards might have killed each other.

What he found was amazing. Mike and his father were lying on the floor, holding each other in crushing headlocks, that would melt momentarily into loose grapples, but re-tighten whenever the other would move. It was a perpetual lock of deep respect between father and son. Neither could let the other go, for fear of sacrificing the other's honor. Neither was trying to win; they were trying to save the other from losing honor by not winning. General Solomon just observed for a minute or two before he broke them up. He recalled the words of Father and Son.

"I can't let go of you, Father."

CHAPTER 66

"I can't let you kill yourself, son."

"I gotta be my own man."

"The Marine Corps will set your ass on a beach to get it shot off. I flew fighter cover over Omaha Beach. I saw the dead bodies bobbing like corks. You ain't goin' to the Marine Corps."

There was no clear winner, so Mike pledged a sacred oath to his father, to preserve the honor between them. The oath was conducted under the approving eyes of their self-appointed referee, General Solomon.

"If you let go of me, Father, Sir, I promise you, I promise you, Sir, I will never let go of you."

Mike hoped for his own version of an honorable discharge from his father.

Solomon watched father and son part, on a promise of eternal faithfulness.

As Marine General Bull Baker concluded the story, he detected a gloss to Durant's eyes, uncharacteristic for a thick-skinned intelligence operative. All warriors, the ones who saw action, who saw the horrors of war up close, understand why General McRain did what he did. Baker knew that there was a soft spot, even in an unscrupulous bastard like Durant. General Baker shared a lot in common with Colonel Durant. He, too, had been marching to orders from C.I.A. for many years. Durant, Baker, and even Mike, at one time, had bowed to the same master.

"You know the rest of the story, Colonel Durant. Mike took his commission in the United States Marine Corps. He served three years under me in my best Force Recon unit. I never had a better officer. If I ever have a son, I hope for a clone of Mike McRain."

"Does McRain have any weaknesses, other than where I read he initially had trouble during sniper training, hitting moving targets at over five hundred yards?" Durant said.

"No. None."

Durant looked at the General as though he was exaggerating. General Baker picked up on the vibes that Durant did not believe that he was being fully forthcoming.

"Mr. Durant, or, I should say, Colonel, Delta Force was offered to Mike-O McRain, and he flat-ass turned it down."

"I saw that in his file. But why?"

"He got accepted to Harvard Law School."

Durant was perplexed, "Why would someone with all the athleticism and military tactical genius that McRain has want to go to Harvard Law School?"

"Because he could. Because he is that smart. Because he is that exceptional a person. He's the kind you see once in a lifetime, Colonel."

Durant seemed surprised that this General, who had made a career out of locating the weaknesses in different world leaders and military adversaries, could not find a chink in Mike McRain's psychological armor, other than an overprotective father.

"Don't listen to that bullshit about this man on CNN," General Baker said, in a flat, no-nonsense tone. "He is not psycho. He has the bullet and knife holes in his body to show you that he is as tough as they come. If he is your adversary, Colonel Durant, I wouldn't want to be in your shoes. This conversation is over."

Durant picked up his file and exited, on the General's handshake and salute.

After Durant left, General Baker sat down and opened his top-right desk drawer to reveal a pearl-handled Colt 45-caliber revolver. It lay next to a photo of himself with Mike at Mike's graduation from Harvard Law School. If Durant had stayed in Baker's office, he would have heard Baker speak to the photo as he would have spoken to his own blood.

"Whatever they're onto you for, son, keep your head down and your safety off."

Baker paused and sighed before he whispered his warrior's oath.

"*Semper Fi.*"

CHAPTER 66

# CHAPTER 67

*"A man will protect the honor*
*of his words; especially the liar."*
–Anonymous

I desperately needed sleep. But I feared sleep, actual sleep, into REM. I knew the dark fate awaiting me on the slip side of consciousness: Captain Carion and his crew of questionable souls. I poured myself some leatherneck-thick coffee and chewed on it to stave off sleep. It helped me plow through the age-old case law in preparation for oral argument—the defining act of an advocate. I discovered that Perjury on Admiralty was originally conceived as an underhanded legal means for the King of England to get rid of enemies without killing them. It served the dual purpose of eliminating an enemy and discrediting whatever his political views were, by labeling him a liar, much better than killing a political opponent and creating a martyr. Perjury on Admiralty left the opponent alive, a living lesson and warning to those who would try to change the world without permission of those who rule the world.

Two hundred years later, history was repeating itself in Jake Casteel's case. My caffeine fix lasted only so long. I found myself sliding into the clutches of The Nearly Damned.

*Captain Carion had me locked in the kneeling stocks. Head and hands clamped tight. He punched me across the face, his fist sporting a jagged black ring. I felt blood run down my cheek to the crease in my chin. I could see my blood begin a small pool on the deck. "You thought you'd be able to get a little shut-eye without having to meet me," Carion said, as he laughed. "I warned you before. You know better than to bring a woman on board my vessel."*

*Carion's madness infected my heart and soul. I was angry that he was denying my love for Ann. A sort of claustrophobia came over me, accompanied by a great urge to know my exact position in Purgatory.*

"Damn you and your sorry-ass [further deleted Marine-speak] crew right to Hell. I demand to know where I am in God's kingdom."

To my surprise, I was not hit. The Captain swaggered away from me tossing a comment over his shoulder. "Only prayers prohibit me from damning you."

Mr. Troubles grabbed the opportunity and ran front and center. He unfolded a weathered nautical chart drawn on sheepskin that crinkled as he held it on the wooden deck in front of where I knelt in the stocks.

"I know I am in Purgatory. But I am still alive. How can this be?"

Mr. Troubles face drew most serious. "You're not just in Purgatory, Michael O'Brien McRain, we're navigating through The Saints' Triangle for you, my Lad, for your dear soul." He daringly reached out to me and lifted my bloody chin and I saw a reflection of myself in his eyes. I was stunned by what he next said. "Your body is amongst the living, Michael, but your soul is about to die."

My face dropped through his bony fingers. I was crushed. I had always been prepared to die in war, with the belief that all I had done was absolved through a forgiveness of sins. I was faced with a reality that seemed beyond my control. But I am a United States Marine. I took action to command the destiny of my soul. My eyes focused on the chart lying on the deck.

I could see that the map was of an intricate detail. It was written in Greek and Latin and had worn well over the millennia for its appearance gave me every indication it had been drawn in the centuries near-following Christ. Mr. Troubles pointed his ash colored finger at a mysterious nautical location that looked like a lopsided pyramid with no latitude or longitude references. The pyramid on Troubles' chart surrounding the most perilous stretch of the Purgatory Seas had a name: The Sea of Communio Sanctorum.

The three points and sides of the Communio Sanctorum triangle were apparently plotted by a celestial sextant and, as Troubles explained, were drawn in martyrs' blood darkened by the centuries. Mr. Troubles interpreted the vectors and coordinates for me aloud as he pointed to each navigation point for the waters of the Sea of Communio Sanctorum, which he instructed, in Purgatory, is more commonly referred to as The Saints' Triangle.

There was a noticeable degree of civility and caring in Mr. Troubles' voice that was absent from all others onboard. "The uppermost point is Heaven, a place of love and light and the resting place for the saints, the souls of Heaven, who pray for the unfortunate souls banished to Purgatory; the second is Purgatory Cay, where there blows a perpetual, massive spiritual-storm raining doubt on the hopeful souls of the dead that number as raindrops, all clamoring

CHAPTER 67

for redemption, a hurricane of sorts that intermittently whisks up and carries deserving souls to Heaven's heights for sweet salvation; and the last point closing *The Saints' Triangle* is named *Terra De Spiritu Sancto*, inhabited by man and beast. It is better known as *The Land of Faithful Saints*, where the souls of the living must spar with beasts and pray for souls in Purgatory, in hopes that the Purgatory bound souls will be granted entrance to Heaven."

I nodded my understanding.

On the secret chart, Mr. Troubles pointed to a giant whirlpool much greater in size than Purgatory Cay. It was surrounded by horrid monsters that one could be sure were spawned in Hell.

"And what's that, that whirlpool aside the Cay?"

"That be the Gates of Hell for those whose souls who do not fly to Heaven."

"To Hell?"

Mr. Troubles made sure eye contact and offered an unmistakable, most sobering, nod. It was a clear message of damnation, if I do not succeed. I swallowed the stark information with a gasping gulp.

I said, "Is *The Saints' Triangle* the counterpart to *The Devil's Triangle?*"

"Me boy, the Devil has his own triangle, of that you can be sure. But 'tis only a baby's bath to *The Saints' Triangle*. You see, *The Saints' Triangle* hangs just above these waters that are the sins of man, for their depths hold the very creatures of Hell. *The Shoals of the Mortal Sinners* about the Cay have sunk many a well-meaning ship, with nary a soul to survive to Heaven."

Mr. Troubles' face brightened a hue and his mouth curled a wise smile in its corner as he lifted his hand skyward like a man who knows he is speaking the plain truth. "Only the Admiral himself and his Armada of Angels can lead a safe voyage through the Shoals of the Mortal Sinners onto Purgatory Cay."

Troubles pointed at the *Sea of Communio Sanctorum* triangle on the ancient chart while he cupped his skinny hand over his mouth to whisper to me the rest of the truth. A drop of my bright, red blood left my chin and splattered next to his finger on the chart. Mr. Troubles was unfazed.

"It's the Communion of Saints we're sailing in here, lad. It is berth to the everlasting supernatural forces under the direct command of the Admiral."

I exclaimed my frustrations much too loudly, with a distinct air of disbelief, for Mr. Troubles' fantastic story about a charted portal between Hell and Earth and Heaven above. "The Devil's Triangle? The Saints' Triangle? The Communion of Saints?"

Mr. Troubles hurried to me a more simple explanation for our whereabouts. "We are where Heaven ends."

Troubles then looked up at the dark force that loomed behind me. He yanked back the map and rolled away from Mr. Fetid's cat-o-nine-tails that rocked the deck planks where Troubles had just squatted.

"And where Hell begins," shouted Mr. Fetid. He quickly slapped his torture across my skin with a back-handed swing.

With fists on hips Captain Carion strutted back in front of me. He lit into me with righteous indignation. "The Saints' Triangle is The Communion of Saints, the existence of which you have professed in your faith ten thousand times — every time you said the Apostles' Creed, you bleeding idiot! But of course you don't remember what the Communion of Saints really is. You were a little heathen bastard throwing spit balls in the back of Sister Mary Patricia's catechism class, at Saint Simon parish, when she offered you the holy instructions. You didn't give a damn back then and you still don't!" Captain Carion punched the air in his exasperation.

It was partially true, I was guilty of the spitballs. But, as I looked up and beyond Carion, who was then caught up in his own blustering, I saw Mr. Troubles with his arms crossed and looking very pained in worry. The Captain stepped forward to continue his sadistic, Socratic method of teaching me what I needed to know to win Casteel's case and to obtain my own redemption.

"We would not give a damn about you if not for the dead and living souls who keep praying for you, although I do not understand why." He threw another accusing glare toward Mr. Troubles who, surprisingly, did not cower.

Carion was just getting started to slice my soul with his sharp tongue. "I don't care how much you pray, McRain, I think you're still a heathen bastard. You haven't succeeded for the Admiral, you haven't repaired the souls you're sworn to repair, damn it, you don't deserve redemption! Your actions are your character, McRain, that they are and ever will be. You are a deserter and you are still circling yourself like a damned dog chasing its tail!"

He jerked his fist and thumb like a baseball umpire calls out a runner. "As far as I'm concerned it's over the gunwale to Hell with you. But not yet. The Admiral sees in you what I do not." Captain Carion made a permissive motion with his giant hand inviting Mr. Fetid to approach me. "You may scourge the heathen, Mr. Fetid. Mr. Beelzebub likes his meat tender."

CHAPTER 67

Mr. Fetid wailed away at my back and arms with intense purpose and then interjected, smug and derisive, "That little tart you're fancying. She's nothing but trouble." Fetid and Carion quickly looked at Mr. Troubles, who shrugged, indicating innocence about my forbidden romance with Ann.

The Captain pressed forward with his intentions. "Well, Harvard geek, here's another lesson." He strutted around on deck, out of eyesight since I could not turn my head much, being in the stocks. "I taught you that law is war. You're a Marine. Where do you think you get the best intelligence information?" He waited for my response, which did not come. "Oh, cat got your tongue. You obtain your best intelligence from interrogating the enemy."

I was well schooled in Marine intelligence and counter-intelligence methods. I knew Carion was teaching me nothing new. The Captain brought his face close to mine. His breath stunk almost as bad as Mr. Fetid's. It assailed my nostrils and made my stomach flip.

"In the law, they call interrogation cross-examination. Now here's the cross." Carion ripped a hard punch across my nose. "And here's the examination." Carion forcefully grabbed my crotch, putting me into a blinding, white pain. "It's all very simple, McRain, once you get the hang of it." I whined as he twisted me. "Just get the witness by the balls, squeeze, and never let go, until you get what you want out of his mouth." I couldn't say a thing, for the excruciating pain. "What's wrong, Laddie? You know a man never really learns anything until he's spittin' angry."

"Let me out of these stocks, and I will kill you. You sonofabitch."

He released my manhood and said, "Here's one more tip, Harvard genius: a man will always protect the honor of his words. Remember that, you're going to need it."

Mr. Fetid leaned from behind the stocks and chimed in, "Especially the liars."

Mr. Troubles wiped my face with a fresh-water sponge and whispered, "And most especially the Judges." He ducked, barely missing the horrendous punch Carion struck across my face as he continued the lesson.

"Practice makes perfect, McRain. Now, let's take it again." Carion punched me and crushed my manhood—until I woke up, with a sore jaw and a fiery pain in my loins.

Lessons learned. Marine Corps style.

# CHAPTER 68

# THE MASQUERADE BALL

The whole Falic building was lit up, like a candle flaming at the top, a runny wax of limousines and people streaming around the base. Anyone who was anyone in the St. Martinsville legal community was at the Falic masquerade. Ajax was dressed in a "Star Wars" Chewbacca costume. It was so stretched over his enormous frame that it looked more like a King Kong outfit. Kraft, the law firm's conductor, was the only person not wearing a masquerade costume. He wore his workday, 1880s-era, black, railroad-train conductor's uniform, all the way down to the long, silver chain that secured a large, silver watch that he periodically pulled from the watch pocket in his vest. He would then pop open the watch face and bellow the time the next holographic train was to arrive. The crowd loved it.

Ann, Dalton, and I arrived as Cinderella and two priests. Ann suspected that Dalton had not picked up the costumes she had ordered, but had switched hers for a Las Vegas, dance girl's. The blouse revealed considerable cleavage, which I attempted to disregard. I failed, miserably. Ann was a striking, physical specimen. She had it going on. And there I was, dressed as a man of the cloth. The way I was enamored of Ann, I was soon to be defrocked.

Conductor Kraft announced the arrival of the next holographic train entertainer. "All aboard for the Cannonball Express and Charlie Daniels."

We entered in time to see the hologram fire up, recreating a steam-era locomotive. The detail was amazing, all the way down to the hostler, chucking shovelfuls of coal into the locomotive's blazing fire pit. A transparent Charlie Daniels was playing his fiddle in front of the Cannonball Express. Dalton and I were amazed at the realism, even down to the billow of black smoke that seemed to come out of the life-sized, holographic image. Ann was unimpressed and edgy, for what reason, neither Dalton nor I could figure out. Ann hooked her arm through Dalton's and mine, and we waded into the crowd of the rich and powerful. Dalton was in a good mood. He and I sported plain, black masks over our noses and around our eyes. While the mask worn by malcontent Ann was more in the spirit of a Mardi Gras: gay and all-consuming.

"Just a couple of good, Catholic boys, out to save some souls," Dalton said, as we approached the hors d'oeuvres and punchbowl.

The fiddle music was hopping. Ann seized her chance while Dalton was distracted with filling his punch cup.

"Father Mike, you wanna dance?"

CHAPTER 68

# CHAPTER 69

# THE DEVIL

Dalton's priest's costume had no effect on his actions. He was ogling a world-class set of ta-ta's. They were pushed up by a Victoria's Secret bra, wrapped around a hard body disguised as Elvira. I told him to stop staring, and he turned around to see me lead Ann onto the dance floor, full of ghouls and demons, comprised mostly of lawyers and politicians.

Ann and I found a good hole in the crowded dance floor in the huge lobby of Falic, Moore & DeVillay. The fiddle music reached its crescendo and stopped, much too soon for our liking. We held onto each other while I looked up into the seven-story-high atrium, with balconies on each floor overlooking the stadium-sized lobby.

"Where on earth do they get all their money?" I said as I wondered at the tremendous costs of all the glitz and glamour and extravagant architecture. On the other side of the lobby, the conductor was barking out the estimated arrival of the next holographic train.

"They get it like most lawyers. They just steal more than anybody else," Ann said, as a slow, dance song started. "Unchained Melody," sung by the holographic Righteous Brothers, on a backdrop of a slow-chugging, black locomotive, Number 99. Ann and I were excited. Nothing was said by either of us when I slid my arm around Ann's slim waist and held her tight. We extended our free arms in unison and moved to a beautiful, slow, waltz-style dance. Ann was warm and gorgeous.

She felt right in my lonely arms. She laid her head on my chest. Out of the crowd came a wanton hand, tapping Ann on the shoulder long enough that she released me. It was DeeDee, dressed in a skin-tight, Satan outfit. I could not tell who she was, but she looked very sexy. The she-devil slipped in to finish the dance.

"I don't usually go for men of the cloth, but you mind if I cut in?"

"Well, yeah. . . ," Ann said, because she knew who was behind the devil's mask.

I assured Ann, "Annie, I'll just be a minute."

Ann fumed and stomped back to Dalton and the punchbowl. "Sure, just leave me with the punchbowl and the other lonely souls," was how Dalton greeted Ann as she returned.

"Pour me a stiff one, Father."

Be careful when you ask Father Boyle for a stiff one, young lady," said Dalton, but his attempt at humor was lost on a thought-filled mind. Ann's brain raced in rage. She swore to herself.

*"Anybody, absolutely anybody, except for DeeDee DeVillay. That little bitch ran me off once before, and it's not going to happen this time. She is not going to win."*

When Dalton turned around, Ann's mask could not hide from him the anger her body language betrayed. Ann saw a waiter walking by with shot glasses of vodka, and she relieved him of the whole tray. She poured three of the shots into her punch glass and downed it like she was drinking a glass of water.

"Hit me." She extended her punch glass again to Dalton.

I was oblivious to the chug-fest going on between Father Boyle, the bartender, and Cinderella, back at the punchbowl. It seemed as though DeeDee was trying her best to press as much of her slinky body against me as possible. There was no doubt she was a temptress, and a shameless one at that.

"How do you like our little party, Father McRain?" I had now figured out who owned the set of double Ds pressed into me.

"So I saved you at the elevator, and now I have to save your soul?" I tried to keep my hands on the honest places. And there weren't many, with a body like DeeDee's. Her devil's tail bounced up in the air, S-shaped, with a heart-shaped point at its tip. How appropriate, I thought. I visualized her as a scorpion of love. Fated to kill off all her lovers.

"I never got the chance to thank you for your heroism. I might have been dead without you."

CHAPTER 69

I milked the situation and tried to shame her a bit, to see how she dealt with the concept of respect for those who risk their life for others.

"My number's in the book."

"I know, but with all that was going on with Uncle Jake."

"That's right! My client is your Uncle Jake. It's a mountain of work, representing him, and our deadline is next week. I don't think the Supreme Court will grant us an extension of time." It was just like me to be talking shop as I danced with a beautiful, flirtatious woman, her bosoms resting right beneath my chin, due to her four-inch stilettos. But my heart belonged to a scorned Cinderella.

DeeDee pressed her womanhood even closer. "All my resources are at your disposal."

"Thanks for your offer." I looked down briefly. All I could see was DeeDee's shameless display of her scantily covered bosoms. I immediately averted my attention. But her *Di Trina* ring caught my eye.

I nodded towards the ring. "Pretty ring. Family heirloom?"

DeeDee's devilish mask could not hide her surprise. "This?" She flaunted the ring for just a moment. "This old thing? Just a hand-me-down."

I milked it.

"Kind of beautiful—in a fraternal sort of way."

# CHAPTER 70

# CINDERELLA SCORNED

There was an awkward pause as the holographic Righteous Brothers wrapped up the number. I was eager to get the Casteel brief done and out of my life. I could not think of much else, even when I was dancing with a floozy who wanted me to take her body for a ride.

"About that offer. Truth is, I do need help. How about we start with some Westlaw legal research and a few typists. My deadline to file the petition for writ of certiorari in the Supreme Court is next week."

The slow music and the hologram ended. Ann was fuming as she swayed and watched the red devil dancing with Father McRain. Her man. Ann hit her trigger-point when she saw DeeDee seal the deal, hugging me and taking a nice handful of my butt.

DeeDee was as alluring as possible, "Sure, no problem. But I was hoping to make a lot more available to you . . . like tonight." DeeDee kept her hands on my derrière. I smiled at the nonverbal invitation.

"That's quite cordial of you, Miss DeeDee, but I have a date tonight." I remembered "Two Thumb's" tale, and the part about the black-and-white ring with the gold railroad spike in it. I wasn't born yesterday. I figured we could get close to DeeDee and her firm by using them for logistics to get the brief out on time. And then, maybe we might pull off a winner. A victory in the United States Supreme Court was the equivalent of a moon shot. Instant celebrity in America's legal circles, translated to a big clientele with fat wallets. I intended to use her like she intended to use me. Just without the flesh.

Ann did not know what I thought, or knew, or felt, behind my blue eyes. She saw the worst and tried to be big, understanding, maybe even open and mature.

Nada.

She flew past the bar and snared a pitcher full of beer on her vector towards DeeDee. She marched, double time, as if she was on the attack.

DeeDee pressed in and got a little too personal. "You mean, that little chambermaid you were whiling away your time with?" She did not know Ann's identity.

DeeDee hung on my neck and kissed me, her back to Ann. Ann moved towards us, even faster. Fueled by 80-proof Vodka and the innate energy generated by a woman scorned. She was the equivalent of a heat-seeking missile, locked on DeeDee.

"That little, red-tailed hussy. She thinks she's gonna steal my man."

Dalton was merely an observer of the fireworks to come. "Uh oh. Cat fight."

DeeDee was brazen, continuing to push for aerobics time between the sheets with me.

"I do feel devilish. Maybe some time soon. You are quite handsome."

The Absolute Vodka reached maximum volatility as Ann held the beer pitcher high, to pass over a pair of gargoyles doing the twist. One of them was Judge Lackey's clerk Annaleah, and she needed no mask. Ann went into a St. Pauli Girl, German beer server routine.

"Bier, mein fraulein?"

Ann pretended to stumble and poured the whole pitcher of beer down DeeDee's back. DeeDee shrieked and retreated before Ann could club her with the pitcher. For the short few moments when Ann was off balance, DeeDee grabbed and lifted Ann's mask and pulled back, astonished.

"It's you. You little . . . I thought I got rid of you. And you're here with whom? Mike?"

DeeDee left her mask on and turned and gave me a combined look of surprise and hatred. I immediately became a referee between DeeDee and Ann. DeeDee held a handful of Ann's hair and planted the *Di Trina* ring on Ann's chin. Dalton swooped in and pulled Ann back, as I controlled DeeDee in a very uncompromising position, right behind her, with my arms around her waist. DeeDee was bent over, trying to swing at Ann, while Dalton assumed the same position behind Ann. It probably looked like a

CHAPTER 70

provocative, M.T.V., clerical, sex-with-clothes-on music video for masochists. It was a bad scene that only served to make Ann even angrier.

The spectacle drew so much attention that they shut down the train hologram.

I was very apologetic to DeeDee, as Dalton continued to hold back Ann.

DeeDee glared at Ann and said, "That whore." But regained her composure and rephrased what she said to make whore sound like, "That horrible trash on the floor must have made you trip, dear. No harm done." DeeDee shifted emotions like racecar drivers shift gears. She cooed softly to me, but in plain view of Ann. "Nothing a hot shower won't fix."

Ann went ballistic again and darn near beat the Hell out of Dalton as he tried to restrain her.

I found retreat once again the intelligent option.

"I guess we better get going. I hope this doesn't change your offer?"

Poor Ann looked like a drunken sot.

"Your offer?"

Ann reacted as though I was referring to some type of offer of sex.

I headed it off at the pass.

"Right. DeeDee is Jake Casteel's niece. She has offered two typists to do all the typing for the brief. She gave me a kiss for saving her life on the elevator at the courthouse."

Ann was visibly ashamed.

"You're the one he saved?" She put her hands on her hips.

"But I should have known that it was you because you are the only woman I know who would not stay around long enough to see if Mike made it out of an elevator with a serial killer."

Ann wagged her finger in DeeDee's face. "What was it? A train derailment? A leg-off? Is that why you picked up and ran while Mike was trapped in the elevator with the man who tried to kill you?"

DeeDee knew Ann spoke the truth. It had been a derailment and a Hog Head's broken back that caused DeeDee to leave Mike at the courthouse. Ann's words rang true to those in the know. Most everyone at the party knew that Falic, Moore & DeVillay held the coveted right to chase personal-injury cases across the continent. They also knew that the firm broke a lot of laws in exercising it. But they didn't care. Falic, Moore & DeVillay was connected to the Senate Judiciary Committee, and they were wealthy. Most of all, the attendees were on the firm's "A" list. That seemed to make all the lying and thieving okay. Like the groupies who followed Enron. A house of cards, built upon a foundation of deceit.

DeeDee gave a quick, red-taloned squeeze to my bicep as she left.

"I'll leave the light on."

CHAPTER 70

# CHAPTER 71

# BOY CHASES GIRL

Ann flew out the front door of the law firm like a Cinderella who heard the clock strike twelve. She asked the valet to bring her truck around, while I was still inside, scurrying around, trying to find her in the crowd. I finally gave up and went outside to look for her. Dalton, at my side, said, "Was the boss thing getting a little personal here, my friend?" He bumped me in the ribs with his elbow.

"Because if it is, I don't know, but I guess you should . . . go for it! There she is, by the valet pulling up in her truck." I ran down to where the valet was getting out, relinquishing the truck to Ann. Ann was revving the engine and popping the clutch when I climbed up on the cattle guard over the truck's grill and up onto the hood. Ann stopped the truck.

I jumped down and opened the door while Dalton looked on. "Now, tell me what that was all about?"

Ann tried to push me back and close the door. But I wasn't budging.

"I'm not talking about it."

"Talk to me."

I switched off the truck's ignition, pulled out the keys, and held them in my hand. Ann turned to me and started thumping me on the chest.

Outside Ann's earshot, Dalton said, "Chest thumping. This is true love."

Ann needed to confess, "You want to know what it is?"

"Yea, I wanna know. Why'd you just go psycho in there?" I asked.

"I don't trust her because I know her."

"What do you mean, you know her?"

Ann looked at me full in the face and, in a bluster, said, "I used to work for her. I used to work for this whole, rotten outfit. I used to help them steal. I was a paralegal for the rotten bastards. I thought I could put it behind me.

I did things here that I thought I'd never do. I did them for all the wrong reasons. Now leave me alone."

I was shocked.

She grabbed the keys from my hand and restarted her truck. Ann placed her foot, wearing a sparkling, silver, Cinderella-costume shoe, on my chest. She shoved me away, as she shut the door, leaving me with a sparkling slipper in my hand. Ann dropped it into granny gear and popped the clutch. She lurched the truck in an attempt to get me off the running board. Cinderella wanted to run away.

"Don't talk to me," Ann said.

I was hanging onto the side-view mirror while I rode down the street, her silver slipper in my hand. I was oblivious to the traffic. I'd hitched a lot of rides out of bullet-riddled landing zones on the outside of a helicopter. I pressed her for logic—at a time when all she had was emotion.

"What do you know? What do you know about her that I don't?"

Ann hit a higher gear.

"She ain't no devil. She's a witch," Ann said, over the roar of her engine. She yanked the wheel to the right, causing me to fall off the truck. I rolled, ending up standing, on my feet. I watched Ann weave in and out of traffic, drawing honks from other cars.

I brushed myself off, straightened my cardboard, priest's collar, and said, "There's one Helluva woman."

Dalton was waiting for me half a block from where we'd taken off. He took the liberty of asking the valet to bring around my Mustang. I tipped the valet, and we got in. When I thought about DeeDee, I thought about the last advice Tony "Two Thumbs" gave us before we'd left our meeting at "The Couch." *"Keep your friends close and your enemies closer."* I intended to use DeeDee's firm's resources to get the Supreme Court brief done. And keep a close eye on the enemy.

A half-hour later, a country sky filled with stars found Ann driving down the gravel road to her modest farmhouse. She pulled up in the yard and stumbled up the steps. She flung open the screen door and stepped inside, to the warm glow of a table lamp, shining next to a worn, old couch.

CHAPTER 71

Her sixty-five-year-old mother, Chloe, sat on the couch with Kylee's head in her lap, deep in sleep.

Chloe looked up. She was surprised that Ann was already home. The night was still young. "You're home early. Kylee just went to sleep."

Ann kicked off her only shoe and ran on tiptoes to Chloe. She knelt in front of her and laid her head on her mother's lap, next to Kylee's head. Chloe sensed something was wrong.

"What happened? Why are you crying?"

Ann sniffed and hugged Chloe and Kylee together.

"Cinderella ruined the ball, and there ain't no glass slipper."

Ann sobbed, as Chloe consoled her with a gentle, motherly pat on the head. Ann told her the whole, messy story.

"Sounds like your Prince Charming will be back," Chloe said, while she rubbed her daughter's back.

"No, he won't. The way I embarrassed him, I think he'll hate me forever."

Chloe thought she'd seen a story like this once before, in a fairy-tale book. And she offered its pleasant ending.

"Oh, he'll be back. You'll see. Right after he tricks the witch and slays the dragon."

# CHAPTER 72

# A TRICK IN THE TRAP

The day after the Masquerade Ball, Felix Falic sat at his desk. The top seemed as big as an aircraft carrier's landing deck. He watched his long-legged secretary, Martinne. She'd started out as a paralegal and became much more than that after Ann had left. Martinne strutted into his office, carrying legal papers. She swung her hips to try to entice Felix. She knew he was a hopeless lecher, and she played to her audience. Martinne was Felix's new, first choice for romps at his lakeside getaway. The tall brunette was still in the phase where she was mesmerized by Falic's money, and she was trying to impress Falic with her body. She had not yet realized she was only a piece of flesh for Falic to use to pleasure himself. Martinne bent over, to give him a sneak peek of her cleavage, as she laid the papers on Felix's desk blotter.

"Mr. Falic, here's the legal research you requested I give to Mr. McRain when he comes in this afternoon."

Felix did not let Martinne get too comfortable with their cozy relationship. He insisted she address him formally while they were at work. But when they were alone, in the skin, she poured so many scandalous labels over him, it would burn a drunken sailor's ears. Felix knew she was a fine ride, all the way from bumper to bumper. But he treated her like dirt. A control thing, common among sexual sickos.

"Never set things on my blotter without asking. Don't be a dumb-shit. Just set it right there. I want to go through it personally, so I can make sure it was done right. After all, you don't have a law license like I do. Right?" But he ended it with a smile. The bastard. Martinne laid the two-inch-thick pile of court cases and Sheperd's citation, search lists on the corner of Falic's desk. She walked out, with her head held high to keep the tears back. Not to mess her mascara. Yet.

Falic rifled through the documents and located what he was looking for. "United States v. Gordon." "Ah, here it is. And just as I was told, *certiorari* granted." His eyebrows rose as he thought to himself, *"If McRain gets a copy of this case law, Casteel will surely win."* The facts of Jake Casteel's case were much more harsh and unfair than those of Gordon had been. And Felix was convinced that the Supreme Court surely would rule for Casteel. That is, if Felix Falic was honest and gave the case law to Mike to argue for the benefit of Jake Casteel.

Felix Falic removed the "U.S. v. Gordon" case from the stack of research for Casteel and he dropped it into the paper shredder behind his desk. He grinned as the critical case became confetti. Felix knew Jake's life depended on that case, the "Gordon" case. But he did not give a damn. It was gone.

Mike was relying heavily on the charity of DeeDee's firm to provide accurate, last-minute legal research. It was standard, legal-research protocol to double-check to determine if the Supreme Court were addressing any issues similar to those in Casteel's case. Mike had not yet found out about "U.S. v. Gordon" because, in 1995, on-line legal research was in its infancy. All of the hard-copy citation sources Mike had access to, in the law libraries, were not as up to date as the new-fangled, electronic research instantly available over a telephone line.

Over some crazy new thing called the worldwide web. The Internet.

That is why Mike asked DeeDee to provide a last-minute Sheperd's citation check, three days before deadline, in order to find out if there had been any recent cases he'd missed that might help Casteel win. Lo and behold. It turned out the Supremes were looking at an *identical* issue in the "U.S. v. Gordon" case. Felix knew he could not let Mike know that the Supreme Court had granted *certiorari* to hear "U.S. v. Gordon." Otherwise, Mike could cite "Gordon" in his brief, to make an extremely strong argument for Casteel. Maybe even convince the Court to grant Casteel certiorari, in conjunction with "Gordon."

If that happened, all the millions of dollars in expense and the hard work C.I.A. and D.O.D. had logged for the Hoffa Protocol might go down the drain. Felix did not want to think about how Durant would deal with such incompetence. DeeDee was a made lawyer in *Di Trina*, on the promise she would do *everything* necessary to make sure the Hoffa Protocol sent her uncle Jake Casteel to jail. Then they could keep Uncle Jake's Designation for themselves. She was proving that she came by her deceitful ways rather honestly, considering she had been raised by Falic.

Treachery was a talent Felix seemed to come by quite easily. Felix Falic had cut a deal with the government, the railroad union, and the railroad, to give Mike and Jake Casteel a false sense of security. He let Mike believe that Falic's wealthy law firm would foot the bill for the expensive, on-line legal research. For the time-consuming typing and the expensive $5,000 cost to have the Writ of Certiorari printed and bound, pursuant to United States Supreme Court Rules.

The deal that was struck for the benefit of *Di Trina* was that Falic, Moore & DeVillay would be allowed to continue to use Jake Casteel's "free" Designation in return for making sure that Jake Casteel went down. And stayed down. Convicted for good. If Casteel's conviction stood, he could never retake the International Presidency of the Rail Union and threaten a strike. He could never ask for his Designation back from DeeDee. Felix wasn't stupid. He signed agreements with the government and the Hog Heads Union. He left very little to chance.

Falic hailed Martinne back into the office. He instructed her to make copies of the incomplete case law and citation list for McRain. Falic was a dirty scoundrel. His withholding of critical research documents was going to derail Jake Casteel's defense. It was plain sabotage.

Falic told DeeDee the plan about withholding the "U.S. v. Gordon" case. She thought it was perfect. She explained an additional benefit to Falic's sleight of hand. Mike would look like an idiot for not citing "Gordon" because Felix's records would show that Felix had given Mike the "Gordon" case. Casteel would go down, and it would look like it was all Mike's fault. DeeDee and her stepfather Felix worked well together. They thought it was a perfect plan. The only thing they were missing was a witch's cauldron, to brew their pot of trouble for Mike.

But the conspirators had overlooked something critical to their plan. The jungle instincts and adaptability of a gung-ho Marine, who'd set a few traps of his own.

THE REDEEMER: IT IS WRITTEN

# CHAPTER 73

# CANDLELIGHT

The waiter poured a fine, Italian, red wine into my glass. I swirled it around and checked its color. I then sniffed the glass, sampling its bouquet. Finally, I tasted it. It possessed a wonderful dryness, embracing an oaky flavor and a smooth body. Perfect with beef. In a way, the fine wine reminded me of the beauty sitting beside me in the front dining room of "The Couch."

Ann.

But even though Ann had a smooth, hard body, like fine oak, she sure wasn't dry. Her intellect is what attracted me to her. She had a quick mind and a great sense of humor. Her great looks were an extra treat. She was intuitive and ran on gut instinct. I liked that a lot. Gut instinct keeps you alive. But I was like most men. I knew almost nothing about choosing wine and even less about women. I faked it well.

The waiter could have poured me the dregs of the barrel, and I would not have known the difference. All I knew was red wine traditionally went with beef, and Ann had said she was a meat-and-potatoes kind of girl. That was another good point for her in the tally I was keeping in my head. She was down to earth and didn't put on airs. I enjoyed her unpretentiousness.

We had our first falling-out at the Masquerade Ball, and I was playing makeup, for dancing with the wrong person when *our song* was playing. I didn't even know we had a *song*. But I went with it since she seemed to know much more about the many traditions of the heart. I learned from Ann's gentle instruction that the first slow song we danced to would be *our song*. Luckily, it was a classic. Forevermore, the Righteous Brothers' "*Unchained Melody*" would be special in our lives.

Ann wore a stunning, strapless, red dress that flattered her, and it did not make her look like the poster girl for a lingerie shop. The best don't have to flaunt it. I didn't know that Ann had borrowed the dress from her anorexic, second cousin, Noreen, and had starved all week, for fear she wouldn't fit into it. She looked marvelous in the warm candlelight. I told her I was a lucky man to be dining with her, and I meant it. She turned every head when we walked in.

The problem that kept eating at me was that Ann was my secretary. We shouldn't have been winking at each other, much less having an affair behind Dalton's back. But there we were, clinking our wine glasses together, toasting "*us.*" I relaxed in the moment and enjoyed Ann and the five-course meal. Ann seemed to pick up on my nervousness.

"Is there something wrong?"

I lied, "No, nothing, just thinking."

Right when I thought I could change the subject, I felt a strong hand grip my shoulder. Followed by, "And to what do I owe your attendance this evening, my friend?"

It was Marco. He moved around the table and took Ann's hand and kissed it. He said, "You are much too lovely to be dining with this man. Surely, he has no appreciation of your beauty. Otherwise, he would have taken you to 'Il Vesuvius,' where they have a wine cellar as good as any in Rome."

Ann blushed and waited to be introduced while she batted the long lashes of her big, brown eyes, like a butterfly flutters its wings.

Marco was the smoothest man I knew. I introduced Ann to my friend, Dr. Marco Falcone. She was taken by his aura of Mediterranean machismo. So much so, that she started to flush. She claimed it was the wine.

Then Marco unwittingly spoiled the whole atmosphere with the simple, logical question most friends ask when they see their friend with someone new.

"So, where did you two meet?"

It spoiled the evening for me.

I kissed Ann good night when I dropped her off at her truck, parked back at the office. I hoped she knew I cared for her and that she might see I wasn't just trying to get a roll in the hay out of her. I was disappointed the evening didn't end more passionately. But I was more disappointed with myself for not having the guts to make a statement to Ann and to the world that I loved her.

I was disgusted with myself and my life. I went into the office and read more about perjury. I plowed through a three-inch pile of old cases about liars, until the sun pushed a bloody sunrise over the horizon.

# CHAPTER 74

*"Steal a loaf of bread and go to prison.*
*Steal a railroad and become*
*a United States Senator."*
—Mother Jones

Ann stacked on my desk three, big boxes of the Falic, Moore & DeVillay client-loan documents she had copied before she left their firm. She kept them in her Daddy's barn, in a chest. They were her insurance policy if Falic ever decided he would do something violent. They were very damning. Lies, lies, and more lies about millions of dollars trading hands under the fictitious label of "litigation expenses." And they were passed off to their uneducated clients as a hundred different, fraudulent varieties. I assumed the I.R.S. knew nothing about this. If they condoned it, we would be looking at an extremely big conspiracy. One that would shake the Constitution.

There was some severe money laundering going on at the Designated law firms. I knew the *Di Trina* lawyers should be prosecuted. The government regularly sent experienced physicians to prison for submitting fraudulent Medicare and Medicaid claims. It would be only fair to do the same to lawyers who were racketeering and submitting fraudulent closing statements to their clients.

I knew the physicians did not have the political equivalent of *Di Trina* to throw all the right levers and push all the proper buttons in the Department of Justice. The political clout to make sure that nobody discovered the rampant fraud being passed off on the American people. Billions of dollars of R.I.O. bribes and racketeering every year.

It was the fraud Jake Casteel had courageously sought to eradicate from America when he tried to put *Di Trina* out of business. Anybody with a working knowledge of law and accounting could see the corruption if they looked at the client closing statements and the loan documents Ann had copied. By my analysis, the system had to have some big-time backers for it to have continued for decades so far outside the law. Sizing it up with an eye towards the way things really work, I concluded that Senator Moore and his cronies looked like the linchpins that connected the whole, damn trainload of manure.

I needed an honest arm of the government that I could tell about this widespread theft. If I told the F.B.I., there was a good chance they would come after me instead of going after the crooked lawyers. The Senate Judiciary Committee had a hammer-lock on the Department of Justice and its F.B.I. It seemed that the majority of the upper-level personnel at D.O.J. and F.B.I. owed their jobs to back-door-dealing Senators. And those Senators never hesitated to lean on their bureaucrats whenever they needed a favor. I got a flash.

The I.R.S. The Department of the Treasury. R.I.O. was controlled by the Judiciary Committee, but that committee had no control over Treasury. If the I.R.S. went after these lying, cheating, and stealing lawyers, Senator Moore would not have it his way, on his turf. And we might even surprise them. The Golden Rule of Combat: Maintain The Element of Surprise.

I thought of my older brother, Raford. He used to give me some severe, Dutch rubs. One of the caustic ways brothers show affection to each other. He was the brother closest to me in age. I idolized him. He became a Green Beret, traipsing the Earth for the U.S. Army for twenty-five years, until he left, to use his fighting skills as a Secret Service agent protecting the President. But jogging alongside the President's limo became a thing of the past. His knees eventually gave out. Rafe took a transfer to the Treasury Department, to the I.R.S., as a special investigator.

During my time in the military, I saw how things really worked against the honest men. I once knew a man who blew the whistle on three admirals who were helping an arms ring purchase Stinger missiles. The admirals worked the system to make it look like the whistleblower was the bad guy, even though he had never participated in the scheme. In the end, the whistleblower caught it in the neck—legally and literally. A dishonorable discharge and a garroting shortly thereafter.

I knew the whistleblower personally. He was an honorable man. But I knew how the circles of power work in the world. And they sure as Hell don't work for the little man. The honest man.

I was being careful, looking for legal booby-traps and evidentiary trip-wires that could get me, or my loved ones, killed. Rafe would be my only hope of seeing to it that the Designated lawyers stopped sucking billions and billions from America, like a bunch of parasites.

I drove down the street to a pay phone at a gas station and placed a call.

A strong voice on the other end announced, "Special Agent Raford McRain, may I help you?"

# CHAPTER 75

# DEADLINE

We had forty-eight hours left on the Casteel-brief deadline as Ann walked into the office and set her purse down on her desk in our small, front lobby. I walked out of my office. I looked like a train wreck.

"You get those last dictation tapes delivered to DeeDee's typists? The brief is due in two days."

"The typists just called and said they are having trouble printing out the brief. In fact, it sounded like they were having trouble finding the brief in their computer system."

My face looked horror stricken. An open-mouthed, terrorized look. I waved my hands in broad circles of protest. In the Marine Corps, we would take action, firing bullets, throwing knives, kicking butt. In the law, you're at the mercy of the secretaries. And they know it. But Dalton and I knew a secret.

"Take it easy, you're jumpy as a cat on a hot, tin roof."

"Thought you said you didn't trust DeeDee?"

"I don't trust DeeDee, but I do trust her typists."

"Maybe I ought to have a look-see, myself," I said. I picked up my coat and pulled it on as I walked to the door.

"Better go home and take a shower first, or they'll think you're a skunk. I haven't seen you leave here in five days."

Dalton walked out of his office, towards Ann's desk. He dropped off papers and walked back, holding his nose. I stood, with my hands on my hips, trying to feign that I was insulted, when actually I didn't give a damn. I'd once stayed behind enemy lines without bathing for over a month when I was in the Corps. Five days was nothing. I had grown accustomed to how I smelled as I worked on the Casteel brief. But to my co-workers, I smelled like garbage.

"What's the difference between a dead skunk and a dead lawyer on the road?" Dalton asked.

I obliged, "I'll bite."

"There are skid marks in front of the skunk."

Ann laughed; I waved my arms in feigned disgust as I left. Dalton winked and I nodded back. I didn't bother with the luxury of a shower. I splashed on some cologne and knocked down my beard with an electric razor on my way to DeeDee's law firm. I drove leisurely on my twenty-mile trek to Falic, Moore & DeVillay's Tabernacle of Torts in downtown St. Martinsville.

I walked into the lobby as their holographic machine displayed Old No. 148. A giant, coal locomotive, churning a six-foot-high drive wheel, with Johnny Cash singing *Two Feet High and Rising.* I marched past the man in black and over to Ajax. I demanded an immediate meeting with DeeDee and Falic. Ajax got the notion that, just because he was twice my size, I would turn tail and run when he got into my face and told me to leave.

Exactly one minute and twenty-one seconds later, he was crying like a baby, from a very painful, brachial nerve, stretching maneuver we taught to recruits in the Marine Corps' Linear Involuntary Neurological override Engagement (L.I.N.E.) course at Quantico. I took it easy on the dummy. I let him tap out, after he allowed me on the elevator. He did not want to see me again. Ever. I did the charitable thing and donated my handkerchief to him for the bloody nose I'd caused to set the tone for the rest of my M.O.M. lesson on how to treat a guest.

Word of my jar head ways made it to the top. They were afraid of me. Falic and DeeDee sat at one end of a conference table that was long enough to require two different time zones. I sat at the other end of the table, while they told me they'd "lost" the entire Supreme Court brief, and it could not be accessed in any way, shape, or form. In essence, they told me I was dead. That my Supreme Court brief for Jake Casteel had mysteriously disappeared from their computer network. And it had been totally completed—all the way down to grammar and citation checks.

CHAPTER 75

A mountain of work had magically vanished. It looked irreplaceable at that late date. The deadline to get on the plane with the brief was less than forty-six hours away.

I looked damned angry. I waved my arms like a wild man, in front of a picture window with a view of tugboats on the Mississippi riverfront. I paced back and forth and even jumped up and down a few times. I demanded answers to my questions. I wanted them thinking I was sunk.

What Ann and DeeDee and Falic did not know was that I had the whole thing covered. I did not tell Ann right away so I could preserve my fun at the expense of lying, cheating and stealing lawyers. None of them knew that I had downloaded a full copy of the brief every night by hacking into their law firm's computers. I just wanted to mess with these idiots who thought I would be stupid enough to trust them with a Supreme Court brief. I wanted to see them squirm so I could bring chaos to my enemy's camp. And I wanted to watch Ann laugh when I told her the truth about the prank I played on DeeDee and Falic.

I was coy.

"I know a little about computers. I received my degree in computer science from the Air Force Academy. So just tell me one more time how your whole system crashed, but the only document lost was my fifty-page brief and none of your firm's documents? How is that possible?"

Falic was a master at deception. Falic knew how to twist the truth and mix it with lies, to create a dark, elastic substance we lawyers call evidence.

"Mr. McRain, we didn't lose your brief. Our computer vendor tells us we just cannot access it because they cannot locate it. They advised us that these things happen quite regularly. It's somewhat unfortunate. I offer my deepest apologies."

Falic offered all the sympathy of a vampire who'd just drained a victim of all his blood. I noticed that Falic and DeeDee were wearing the same type of black ring on their pinky fingers. I turned my back to them and looked out the window to gather my thoughts.

"Zat so? Well, I guess I don't have any way of getting that brief reconstructed in time." I paused, like a man, deeply hurt, pauses to gather himself. To shake the pain. I milked the drama.

"Especially since the Chief Justice denied me an extension of time. Looks pretty bad, doesn't it?"

I saw the reflection of DeeDee nudging Falic, with her foot, under the table. And then, the two of them smirking, cute, little, thin smiles at each other, behind my back. DeeDee was a good actress, with ice in her veins.

"I can't apologize enough, Mike. Especially since it means my Uncle Jake will lose and stay in prison and lose his law license . . . and the worst." She was vying for an Academy Award. "The worst part is the federal labor laws. He can never be a union leader again. It's horrible." She blew her nose to end her dramatic scene.

I let them have their fun. With a woeful face, I turned around and faced DeeDee and Felix. I listened to DeeDee string out her act a bit too long.

"You know I'd do anything to help my Uncle Jake. He'll never forgive me."

Falic got into it, putting his arm around DeeDee to console her, "Don't cry, DeeDee."

I said, "It wasn't your fault. These things happen. I know you'll take care of your Uncle Jake if he loses his law license. That is, since the union will let you keep the Designation for yourself. Forever. For free."

Falic and DeeDee looked like they had just seen a ghost. They sat up in their seats. I walked towards the door, looking dejected. But I stopped, as DeeDee whispered to Falic, "How'd he know about the union deal?" I acted like I had not heard her comment, even though I plainly had.

"I know I cuss a lot, but I bet you didn't know that I'm a deeply religious man." I was sharing my inner self. And I elaborated.

"I think God gives us a sense of humor to live through these times." I turned to face Falic and DeeDee, who were nodding.

CHAPTER 75

I went on, "Reminds me of the story when Satan challenged Jesus to a typing contest." Falic gave DeeDee a look. He rolled his eyes, like I was nuts.

"They both started out, typing like crazy, burning up the keyboards. Then the electric blacks out." DeeDee rolled her bored eyes at Falic, "And God declared Jesus the winner."

I started to walk out of the conference room. Falic stopped me with an inquiry in his nerdy, nasal voice.

"Is there a point to your cute, little parable, Mr. McRain?"

I stopped and grinned, real wide and wise.

"Oh, the moral of the story?"

I pulled a floppy disc out of my jacket pocket. I held it up in Falic's face.

"Jesus saves."

My punch line left Falic and DeeDee astonished. They were disappointed and tried to feign that they were happy that the brief was not lost.

I walked out and looked at the fancy brass case protecting their precious Designation and its accompanying Supreme Court opinion. I stormed out of the firm's lobby, past 'fraidy-cat Ajax, past conductor Joe, out onto the sidewalk. I yelled, loud enough for everyone in a one-block area to hear, "Ooo-Rah."

DeeDee and Falic sat in the conference room, wondering if they'd been hit by a night train. DeeDee offered her own version of consolation.

"Pretty bad when a jar head Marine outfoxes ya'," Falic said.

"It isn't over yet," DeeDee said, "Remember McRain still doesn't know about 'U.S. v Gordon.'"

Out in my car, I felt confident. We'd carved out a beachhead. The only beach a Marine needs to fight is the sand under his feet. We still had the Supreme Court brief. We still had hope and a platform from which to fight for justice. We were still in the fight to prove Jake Casteel's innocence.

# CHAPTER 76

# BLAME THE LAWYERS

Halfway across the continent, in Washington, D.C., Colonel Durant sat in an office the size of a generous mop closet. The small quarters had Spartan furnishings: a plain desk, one filing cabinet, two client chairs, and the chair he was in which he sat. The only things that sat on Durant's desk were a telephone, two knives and to his deep dismay, a thick legal brief. Durant's forehead had a deep canyon running from his hairline to the top of his nose. And it grew deeper as he looked at a copy of the polished brief we had filed for Jake Casteel with the United States Supreme Court, a day ahead of schedule. He wanted answers about how the simple mission, to keep us from getting the Casteel brief done, failed. Being a Green Beret, failure was never an option or acceptable to Durant.

DeeDee's voice came out of the speakerphone. "We did everything you told us to do, Colonel. We destroyed the brief, and we even fed him bad citations and case law."

Durant did not have time for this mealy-mouthed excuse bullshit. He fantasized how he would kill Falic and DeeDee when this operation was done. Not because the Op called for it. But because they were dumb and they were not making his life easier. Add that they were lawyers, and he had three good reasons to off them. He pondered how he would do it. Perhaps throw DeeDee off the seventh-story balcony overlooking the atrium. And leave a forged suicide note, mourning the death of her stepfather, Falic, who she could not believe had stuck a shotgun in his mouth. Felix would have repainted the wall behind his desk crimson, with gray matter for texture. After it dried, it would be more of a grainy, dusty rose color.

Durant seemed to detach from his conversation with DeeDee and Falic, as his daydream expanded. He saw that DeeDee was probably like his third ex-wife, the interior decorator. DeeDee would be more upset that the color of Falic's blood and brains clashed with the Riviera-blue motif of Falic's office than she that Falic had killed himself. He liked it that she was a cold bitch. But she was a *stupid,* cold bitch, in his mind.

Durant associated his opinion of DeeDee with his memory of throttling his color-conscious ex. It was the time he'd held her head under water in the bathtub, while the children banged on the bathroom door for their mother.

He was getting more pissed off by the minute at the two stooge lawyers on the other end of the line. He was also pissed off because if it hadn't been for those damned children, he would not be paying spousal maintenance and child support. They'd screwed up his one good opportunity to make her death look like an accident.

Now Corrine, the decorator, was living with some guy while she raised their daughter and the two children he'd had from his previous marriages. Whose mothers had mysteriously died. Corinne was not marrying her live-in just so she would not lose the spousal maintenance Durant had to pay her every month.

He flipped one of his knives into the air, caught it by the blade, and immediately threw it into the back of one of the wooden, client chairs, sitting across from the desk.

DeeDee was still jabbering and Falic was chiming in with his two-cents' worth every now and then. Saying nothing at all, just damned excuses. By then, Durant was sure he was going to kill DeeDee after the Op was done. It was no longer a maybe. She was not even that good of a lay. He tried to lie to himself because she had been amazing on several occasions. He did not let that interfere with his bona-fide zest for violence against females. He enjoyed it too much to let rational thought prevent him savoring his secret rage.

Women had been deserting Durant his whole life. His foster mother hid her vodka bottle in the toilet tank. They never believed little Dirk. They always took the side of a string of foster stepfathers, when one of them decided to use him as a punching-bag. Until, one day, the last day he'd seen Mama, he used a tire iron to defend himself from his stepfather's army-drill-sergeant discipline. Hell, that's the reason Durant went into the service. He beat his father half to death. He'd dropped the tire-iron and quickly left his first, great work of art lying in a pool of blood. It got his step-father a Section Eight. Early retirement from the Army.

Enlisting in the Army at the beginning of the Vietnam war set Dirk in front of an I.Q. test. He found out he had been blessed with more smarts than he had ever been told he had. His brains bounced him into West Point's Prep School. He came up to speed in his math and science and went on to attend and graduate West Point. He was then shipped to Vietnam to hone his killing abilities.

Durant had been responding on his end of the phone call by giving a grunt, or an "Uh huh," or an "I see." He chafed at the two buffoons and their ridiculous tale of woe. Falic was just finishing the part of the story where Mike duped them. Falic explained that McRain had allowed them to believe he accepted their story that all was lost, that the Supreme Court brief had been erased, and that Mike was shit out of luck. But Mike had turned the tables on them. They didn't know Mike had been hacking into their computer system and downloading and saving a fresh copy of the Supreme Court brief every night.

"You do know that he is a member of M.E.N.S.A., don't you?"

Silence. DeeDee and Falic said nothing.

"You two aren't some of those idiots who think everyone in the military is stupid, are you?"

Silence.

Durant felt this was an opportunity for him to twist the knife and make them feel stupid because he, like Mike, was also a member of M.E.N.S.A., the high-I.Q. society.

"You two are members of M.E.N.S.A., aren't you?"

Silence.

Durant had twisted the knife long enough. He tried to act cavalier, to make the idiots on the other end of the phone lower their guard.

"Oh, whatever. So McRain skunked us."

Durant tried to make it sound like all was not lost. But he was livid at their failure. He knew he had to get off the line, or he was going to blow a gasket. He laughed, to break the tension.

"So super Boy Scout thinks he's going to get fairness out of the Supreme Court?"

Durant terminated the telephone conversation. He swore an oath to the empty room. "This Green Beret is going to kill that dumb-ass Marine." Colonel Durant threw the other knife into the second client chair, knocking it over and splitting its wooden back. "*Semper Fi* my ass."

CHAPTER 76

# CHAPTER 77

# THE LAW-GODS SPEAK

I sat at my desk in a mental fog. It was my practice to throw knives while I advised a client. Throwing knives helps me express myself. The inner, compassionate Mike McRain. The Supreme Court had only been in session a week and I was nervous about the Casteel brief. I tried to take my mind off of it by counseling a divorce client with my special set of knives in various lengths.

"We'll cut off their defenses with a motion to strike." I would throw a knife into the silhouette target on the wall.

"Then we'll attack with an amended counterclaim for damages." I'd throw another knife into the target.

"Then we'll go to trial." This would call for putting a big knife into the target.

A middle-aged divorcee, *wannabe*, a Ms. Jacobson, was afraid at first. Then she was amazed, "You got somethin' quicker?"

"Yes, Ma'am, but now you are talkin' settlement." I pulled out a tiny knife, the size of her thumb. I threw it into the crotch of the silhouette. It came to rest in a downward, flaccid position. Ms. Jacobson's eyes were as big as saucers. She was speechless. The silence was broken by Ann's voice, over the intercom, hailing me.

"We received an envelope from the United States Supreme Court."

I perked up. "The Supreme Court?"

I leapt to my feet and almost picked up Ms. Jacobson, escorting her out of my office, past Ann's desk, past the door to Dalton's office. We almost ran into Dalton, flying out of his office to get a look-see himself. At the front door, I gave Jacobson a nice send-off.

"You give all that some thought, and give me a call."

I shut the door and bee-lined it, back to Ann's desk, where Dalton was grabbing for the envelope, that Ann would not release to him. Dalton made what he thought was a funny complaint to Ann, as she held the envelope behind her back and out of his reach.

"Come on, you are dating one of your bosses, so you gotta be nice to your other boss, or I'll have to fire you both."

Ann's face went white for a moment. Dalton sensed he had trodden some forbidden ground and tried to mend the situation, "Or you'll have to date me, too." It was a nice try, but it made things worse. Ann and I each looked at the other, astonished. I pretended I was so surprised, I was holding my breath, behind Dalton's back. Dalton turned, and I acted like nothing had happened.

"Let's open her up." I handed Ann a letter opener.

Ann cut open the large envelope and took out a multi-page document that I snatched from her hand, "What the Hell. I gotta see it." I read quickly and dropped the document to the floor. I stumbled into my office, retreating as if I had been shot. I whispered to myself a blaspheme of my Lord and a cursing of saints.

I was angry, pissed off and about to go ballistic for the unfairness of the Supreme Court and the unfairness I believed I had been dealt by my Creator.

A full rosary had been offered by me every night for my client and I had called on the wisdom of every saint I could remember, and I was damn angry at God that Jake Casteel had lost. I was sure God had forsaken my client and me. Three knives went from my desk top to my hand and flew into the heart of the silhouette target on my office wall; between pictures of the famous professional football middle-linebacker, Dick Butkus, and the holy heavyweight, the Pope. I figured maybe those gentlemen could figure out how to kick ass and stay holy at the same time because the latest news from the Supreme Court said I was not doing a very good job of it for my client Jake Casteel, who around the office was being referred to simply as, J.C.

CHAPTER 77

In Ann's work area, Dalton picked up the opinion, titled: "Writ Denied," and read it aloud, loud enough for me to hear him through my office door. He was pretty darned angry too.

"We hereby rule that Casteel must lose. Although we struck down the use of Perjury on Admiralty today in the 'U.S. v. Gordon' case, it was the same day we ruled against Mr. Casteel. Therefore, under the doctrine of 'Teague v. Lane,' Casteel shall not receive the benefit of our new rule of law because that new rule was not created *before* our decision against Casteel." Dalton thought out loud about the Court's tortured reasoning. "Before is not the same day? Why, Hell, they are splitting some hairs there. Chief Justice Nelson, who wrote the opinion is being intellectually dishonest, and the other four justices are his lackeys. They decided the two cases the same day, the same damned day, and they say that Casteel can't enjoy the reversal of conviction rule in "Gordon" because "Gordon" was decided the same day as Jake's case. That's screwed up. It's rulings like this that give lawyers a bad name."

"What's all that mean?" Ann asked.

I stomped back into the room, "It means Casteel gets a real screwin'." I went back into my office, slamming the door behind me. Childish. But with real emotion. Dalton explained, "The Court made a new rule of law that favors Casteel's position, but he doesn't get the benefit of the new rule because the new rule would have had to exist before they decided on Casteel's case."

"Since they made the new rule on the same day they ruled on Casteel's case, they won't let Casteel win? That's not fair," said Ann.

"Annie, there is an old sayin' in this business: 'the law is an ass.'"

I came out of my office, angry. I punched the wall so hard, one of the pictures fell.

"Ain't that the truth," I said, with fire in my eyes.

Ann tried to make sense out of the most powerful court in the world playing word games with people's lives. "In baseball, they say a tie goes to the runner. So how do they know which case was ruled on first? Isn't there, like, an instant replay?"

Dalton and I looked at each other, in epiphany.

"Annie, you're a genius," Dalton said.

"We are gonna' type a subpoena to the Clerk of the Supreme Court," I said.

I leaned over Ann's shoulder, as she sat at the keyboard, waiting for me to start dictating the subpoena. "This is a subpoena duces tecum upon deposition, to be served on the Clerk of the United States Supreme Court, so we can take the Clerk's deposition to find out which order was signed and sealed first. If the Gordon case was sealed before Casteel's, Casteel is a free man. So type this . . ." I talked, and Ann typed.

This was going to be a first. Nobody had ever taken the deposition of the United States Supreme Court Clerk for anything like this. It was sure to ruffle a lot of feathers in the nation's highest court.

CHAPTER 77

# CHAPTER 78

# THE BISHOP

Service to charity can be a real benefit, from time to time. I was counsel for Catholic Charities. We had a board meeting coming up soon. My Mustang softly rumbled up the circular driveway of the Bishop's Chancery. I called ahead, and Bishop Stanley answered the door.

The government was running scared. The Solicitor General filed a motion to quash the subpoena we had served on the Clerk of the Supreme Court. They did not want us to take the deposition of the person responsible for sealing all the Supreme Court's orders, Deputy Clerk Anita Morrison. It was a typical, stall tactic. We only had three days to enter our plea to set aside the Court's ruling against Casteel. The clock was ticking, and I had to get the government and the judge to fight fair. I had a plan.

"Bishop Stanley, thank you for meeting me."

"Please, please, come in; you said it was important."

Surveillance Van #4 pulled up just across the street from the Bishop's residence. The men inside it watched me walk in the front door. Tech #1 shrugged to Tech #2 as though he was uncertain what this was about. Tech #2 hit the windowpane of the Bishop's front window with a laser, listening device, that measures the vibrations off the window and picks up sound like a big eardrum. It didn't work, though, because the Bishop and I went to the cellar.

"When my Catholic Charities Board attorney tells me it's an emergency, I better listen. But meeting in the cellar? You must have a lot to confess. How may I help?"

"It's about our upcoming meeting, Bishop. I couldn't use the phones. I have a problem—a lot like Pontius Pilate and Judas."

The Bishop raised his eyebrows, "I see."

"I've come to make a special request of you and the other board members about our quarterly meeting. I was wondering if we could move the meeting from the Pastoral Center to my office."

Bishop Stanley nodded while I explained.

Colonel Dirk Durant was in his hotel room when he received a late-night phone call from the graveyard-shift surveillance coordinator at Fort Meade, N.S.A.'s headquarters.

"What are you doing, calling me about McRain going to see a priest? No, I don't care if he meets with the Pope. For God's sake, he's a Catholic—and a lawyer. He's got a lot to confess. Don't bother me with this trivial shit any more. I'll read your typed briefing in the morning."

CHAPTER 78

# CHAPTER 79

# THE PENGUINS

They wore black and white. They carried black and white rosaries. Dalton said it was an invasion of penguins. There was Bishop Stanley and another priest, his administrative assistant, Father Killoren. Six nuns from the Order of the Sisters of The Most Precious Blood, adorned in habits, sat around the conference table in my law office: Sisters Mary Pat, Kimberly Anne, Andrea Rose, Carla Jean, Christina Catherine, and Mary Michaela. A telephone with speakerphone capability sat in the middle of the table.

"That adjourns our quarterly meeting. We will serve you lunch here in the conference room. Excuse me, please, I must take a teleconference call. We are arguing some motions with a federal judge."

I left Bishop Stanley and the rest of the Board of Directors of Catholic Charities to eat their lunch in peace. I went to my office, where we were to take the call from Judge Lackey. He was to hear our argument via telephone. Then he was to rule on the government's motion to quash the subpoena we'd served on the Clerk of the Supreme Court. We needed her sworn deposition to find out which case had been ruled on first: "Gordon" or "Casteel."

We only had three days before the deadline on Jake's right to ask the Supreme Court to reconsider its decision not to overturn his conviction. The government knew the clock was ticking. It had tried to stall, to run out the time, by filing its motion to quash our subpoena. We had to do something fast, so we'd requested an emergency hearing, over the phone with District Judge Lackey. We needed a fair hearing.

Lawyers overcomplicate even the simplest of matters. We were plenty angry that taxpayers' dollars were being used to contest such a straightforward issue. Jake Casteel's success or defeat depended simply on finding out if the "Gordon" case had been decided before Jake's. If "Gordon" had been decided before "Casteel," Jake would be a free man. If not, he'd lost. We'd lost. Simple.

~~~~~~~~~~~~~~~~~~~~~~~~~~~~~~~~~~~~~~~~~~~~~~~~~~

Out in the surveillance van, Tech #1 said to Tech #2, "This McRain guy must be pretty holy, with all these nuns and priests he hangs around with."

"Holy? Mike McRain? Holy? He's a lawyer. He checked his soul at the front door of Harvard Law School."

CHAPTER 79

# CHAPTER 80

# DAVID AND GOLIATH

Bridget was in her bedroom, chanting prayers, a rosary wrapped around her right hand. She prepared to do battle with the government and crooked Judge Lackey. She held a small statue of a black-robed figure in her left hand; a "Star Wars" Darth Vader figurine. She leaned forward in her big, overstuffed armchair and placed the black-robed figure at the top of her altar, in the middle of all kinds of candles and figurines of saints. With her right hand, she took some ash. She sprinkled a slight pinch onto the figurine representing the judge and onto a short candle burning next to it. Bridget blew out the candle, blowing the ash off the judge at the same time.

Bridget rocked hard in her chair. She picked up energy from the Irish ballads playing with uncharacteristic low volume on her stereo. She gathered even more spiritual force as she quoted the entire "Book of Judges," by heart, as fast as any human had ever recited it. "Now, after the death of Joshua, it came to pass, that the children of Israel asked the Lord, who shall go up against the Canaanites first, to fight. . ." As the beads peeled through her fingers, Bridget's left shoulder twitched more and more. It was Mohamed Ali's sledgehammer left jab she was warming up. The fight scene, onboard a train, from an old movie, "The Emperor of the North," between a murderous, railroad conductor and a hobo who dared to challenge him flickered through her antique television set. Gunny and Ace, ringside spectators, curled up in the corner. Bridget was in her zone.

"What we forget, in the darkest night, the Son gives us eternal light."

And then she quoted the whole story of David and Goliath out loud. Bridget was preparing for a donnybrook with Judge Lackey. He didn't stand a chance.

# CHAPTER 81

# BLACKMAIL

Immediately after leaving Bishop Stanley and the rest of the board in the conference room, I returned to my office. Dalton and Jake Casteel's father, Ben, were waiting. Ben Casteel knew his son had been railroaded. He wanted to hear Judge Lackey's ruling.

Dalton spoke to Mr. Casteel, "We are going to take good care of your son, Jake. This is going to be a teleconference between the white-collar crime unit in Washington, D.C., Judge Lackey in his chambers in Cincinnati, and us."

~~~~~~~~~~~~~~~~~~~~~~~~~~~~~~~~~~~~~~~~~~~~~~~~~~~

Tech #1 in the surveillance van said, "Oh, I'm hurt. He left us out."
Tech #2 laughed.

~~~~~~~~~~~~~~~~~~~~~~~~~~~~~~~~~~~~~~~~~~~~~~~~~~~

Jake's father asked, "What kind of hearing is this going to be?"

"It's a motion to quash, brought by the government. They don't want us to get the Clerk's sworn statement as to which case was decided first. So we have to put some lumps on their heads, to bring them around to our way of thinking," Dalton said.

"Isn't it bad if Mr. McRain gets the Judge angry?"

Dalton tried to cut the ice. He told a judge joke. "Hey, did you hear the one about the dumb judge that . . ." He didn't want to tell Casteel's father that pissing off a federal judge is like climbing a flag pole in a lightning storm. You are asking to be fried.

I left the conference room and walked into the foyer, where Ann was seated at her desk. Ann said, "I've got Judge Lackey's court reporter and the Department of Justice's attorney, H.T. Army, on hold. It will be three minutes until the Judge comes on."

I grinned at her while I started loosening up, rolling my shoulders and my neck like a boxer, taking short steps as I jogged in place. I thought a hearing by teleconference was best. It allowed me to remain loose, but stay razor sharp in my argument. I slowly jogged into my office, like a boxer jogs inside a ring.

Ann dropped her head into her hands in embarrassment and worry. Outside of Mr. Casteel's earshot she said, "Oh, my God, we are so screwed."

Jake's father watched in amazement and alarm. Fear was in his face as I jogged in my office. Dalton was looking at me, laughing and smiling at Casteel's father. But when Casteel's father gave Dalton a stern look, Dalton sobered. Nothing out of order. I threw right and left punches into the air. I acted like I was blocking and ducking punches, bobbing and weaving, shadow boxing. I jogged over to Casteel's father, where he sat in a client chair. I clasped both of Mr. Casteel's hands, as if I was approaching an opponent in the ring to shake hands.

"Your son isn't here, so I will give you the boxing salute in his stead. We are going over the top, Sir. Ooo-Rah. *Semper Fi.* Sit back and watch the fireworks."

Dalton was amused. But every time he looked at Mr. Casteel, he became solemn. Jake's father asked, "Do you know what you are doing?"

"Sir, we are going to win this today because we have the mojo from the Big Guy." Casteel's father looked at me with concern and disbelief.

There were six knives lying on my desk blotter. I jogged around to the side of my desk. "First, we have to start with a prayer. Good warriors pray before they go into battle." I prepared to pick up the knives, one at a time. I took up the first knife with my right hand. "In the name of the Father." I threw the first knife, and it stuck in the middle of the target figure's forehead. "And the Son." I threw left-handed, and the knife stuck in the navel of the target. That pitch had required that I throw slightly to the right of and above Casteel's father, who was in total fear.

"And the Holy . . . " I threw right-handed into the left shoulder of the target, "Spirit." I threw left-handed into the right shoulder of the target, "Amen." I threw another knife into the heart of the target.

Casteel's father watched my expert knife throwing. His expression changed from fear to amazement. Then, to intrigue, indicating he had some confidence in me. He was bewildered by the knife throwing. "And the sixth knife?" Ben Casteel asked. As I took it, nestling it down into my right boot.

"God, may we never forget your two greatest commandments. Number one: never leave your wing man. And, Number two: never give up your boot knife." I shoved the knife inside my boot.

I reached into my drawer and took out some camo paint. I painted stripes of war camouflage onto my face. I gestured to Mr. Casteel and then to Dalton, offering it to them. They waved me off, in bug-eyed amazement.

I spoke to Ann, who was waiting for Judge Lackey to get on the line, "Tell us when we are over the LZ."

I tied a camo bandanna over my head. I rolled up my sleeves, displaying the U.S.M.C. tattoo on my left, anterior bicep. A *Semper Fi* and a heart were tattooed on my right forearm. "The safety is off, gentlemen. We are jumping into a hot LZ."

"You're on stage, Jungle Boy," said Ann. I pressed a button on the speakerphone, and Judge Lackey's voice boomed forth. Judge Lackey was standing at his desk in his chambers, with his fists on his hips. He began the call, "We are in a teleconference regarding the motion to quash filed by the government."

Annaleah, Judge Lackey's clerk, was sitting in Judge Lackey's chambers scowling and filing her nails while she waited for the oral argument to begin. Her wart had been itching, as Annaleah had anticipated this show down all week. Her gum could be seen quite clearly as she chomped onto it with a mouth so open she looked like a shark devouring prey. She thought highly of herself, but Annaleah was not classy material. And she hated Dalton and me; we had spines. She was like many in the D.O.J.; she believed Jake Casteel was guilty until proven innocent. Annaleah tolerated the proceedings, wishing that they would all just proceed to the gallows to watch a hanging.

THE REDEEMER: IT IS WRITTEN

There were a lot of people listening in on the teleconference: Ann; Jake's Father; Dalton; the surveillance techs; Chief Justice Nelson; Big Dutch; Durant; and the Bishop, the priest, and six nuns in my conference room. One of the nuns held her hand to her mouth.

Sister Christina whispered to Sister Michaela, "Oh, my, should we be listening to this?" The Bishop assured her, with hand gestures, that everything was okay.

Judge Lackey spoke, "First, a few housekeeping matters before we address the motion. It is my clear order is that the only recording of these proceedings shall be by my court reporter. No electronic-recording devices are allowed. Is that understood?"

"Yes, Sir," I responded, as I threw a few left jabs.

"McRain, you have filed something with the Court that, in my twenty-five years as a federal judge, I have never been so embarrassed or angered. I believe that you should have your license to practice law stripped from you because your motion was filed in bad faith, and there was no proof."

"Sir, what pleading are you talking about?" I said.

"This motion to prohibit any more secret meetings between me and government agents. That never happened. It never would happen. I am an honorable judge. I have been embarrassed before the judicial system. I want your license for filing this because you have no basis whatsoever for the facts that are alleged in this motion."

He would have kept blathering, had I not interrupted him in a booming voice, "Your Honor!"

"How dare you interrupt me?"

"Your Honor, I have proof."

"That's impossible." The court reporter became worried, as she transcribed the hearing. Annaleah's eyebrows stayed arched but she stopped chewing her cud.

I raised two sets of documents into the air. "Your Honor, I am looking at hand-typed copies of the official proceedings of the Court, that have been certified. On five different occasions, you personally referenced that you met with government agents, in secret, behind the backs of Mr. Casteel's attorneys—*ex- parte.*"

"That . . . that . . . that is impossible. That. . . that document should not exist. Besides, I don't think my court reporter is taking down all of this that you are saying. And since you are not allowed to record this hearing, I think you are without a remedy, Mr. McRain."

"Your Honor, I figured you might say that. When I reviewed the Court file, the computer version had all these secret meetings erased. And, I should interject, Your Honor, that I don't have just one certified copy. I have six certified copies of the record of your secret meetings. The extra copies are distributed in . . . well, we'll say, they are in safe hands.

Back at home, Bridget sat at her altar, fanning herself with a certified copy of the records.

In my conference room, the nuns and priests were looking at two sets of the documents.

"You still do not have a typed record to appeal my ruling, you idiot. I am denying your motion to take the deposition of the Supreme Court Clerk. My court reporter stopped typing a long time ago. You have nothing to appeal."

One of the nuns, Sister Kimberly Ann, took a wooden ruler from her sleeve, as though she wanted to rap Judge Lackey's head for lying the way he did. All indicated by gestures.

Bishop Stanley whispered, "Someone needs to go to confession."

In my office, I said, "Your Honor, I am counsel for the Board of Directors for Catholic Charities. We concluded our quarterly meeting in my conference room, just prior to my taking this teleconference call. It appears now that Bishop Stanley, Father Killoren, and six nuns heard every word of this teleconference, on a speaker phone that I just happened to have turned on."

Judge Lackey said, "I'm tearing up the Order making these proceedings secret."

I interjected, "Bishop and you-all, could you say 'hi' to the Judge?"

"Hello, Judge," they said, in unison.

"That won't be necessary, Mr. McRain. I'm writing an Order right now, ordering you to take the sworn statement of the Supreme Court Clerk within the next two days."

In a rage, Justice Nelson, who was also listening via undisclosed conference call, used his semi-paralytic arm to fling his cane across the room, where it clanged off the wall and cracked the glass case of pressed flowers from the top of Noreen's coffin.

Back in St. Martinsville, tempers were also going up like a red flare. In a snit, Annaleah stormed out of the Judge Lackey's chambers. Sore loser. She could not believe that Judge Lackey was dunced by me. She hated losers.

In the conference room of McRain and Boyle, the Bishop, the priest, and the nuns celebrated.

In my personal office, too, there was celebration. Casteel's father shook my hand.

"You are one crazy S.O.B." He cupped his hand behind my head and gave it a shake. "And the best damned lawyer I've ever seen, or heard of, in my whole life." He looked me right in the eye. "Nobody gets a federal judge to back down in fear. Nobody, except you. You're unbelievable."

He left our office, whooping and hollering.

CHAPTER 81

# CHAPTER 82

*"The first thing we do, let's kill all the lawyers."*
*—Dick The Butcher,*
*in William Shakespeare's* <u>Henry The Sixth</u>

Colonel Durant had a great idea. He loved it so much that he did not tell Lieutenant-General Crowe or the C.I.A.

Durant determined it wasn't Casteel who was the reason the government was losing ground in the "U.S. v. Casteel" case. It was Casteel's *lawyer* who was making all the waves. The Hoffa Protocol required the C.I.A. to make sure the target, the union leader, was poorly represented. Judge Lackey was supposed to have selected an idiot lawyer to represent Casteel in the Supreme Court, to make sure he would not stand a chance of winning.

But fate makes no mistakes.

As fate would have it, even though Judge Lackey's pouty clerk, Anti-saint Annaleah of Botox, had tried to warn against it, a witless Judge Lackey purposefully selected a Harvard Law School graduate to represent Jake Casteel. And it made matters worse that, unbeknownst to them at the time of the appointment, Jake's new lawyer was a polished, ex-Marine Corps assassin, possessing all the smarts, guts, and controlled deviousness that come with the job title.

Durant thought it was interesting that Michael's and his psych profiles had general similarities. Both were willing to kill on orders from C.I.A., both were highly intelligent, both were classic over-achievers; but the one main difference between the two, and which caused a well-rooted network of neural passages ending at what Durant believed was an inferior concept of justice, in Michael, was that Michael humbled himself to a damning God, a God who kept a tally of how one treats others, in order to continually, and earnestly, examine his actions and if need be, seek forgiveness from God.

Michael's highest authority was GOD, not C.I.A., not money, not economics. Durant worshiped the world and all its material allure and he never admitted a weakness like Michael did in prayers to his weak God. But Colonel Durant could see another difference in their profiles. And the Colonel considered it his own strength, not a weakness. He was rather bent when it came to sex. His work had required him to consider it a weapon to exploit the weaknesses in enemies. And the attraction of sex no longer had any pretext of love to Durant. It was about control.

Dirk Durant toyed with Annaleah, one of the dark daughters of the D.O.J., a self-avowed sadist, one who enjoys seeing people in pain and miscarriages of justice, and is especially gratified, if allowed to help in the perversion of Lady Justice. Durant took special zeal in doing Annaleah. And in Durant's socio-path mind, she was a slutty surrogate for the blind lady holding the scales of truth, of justice. He even had Annaleah wear a red bandana blindfold while Durant exclaimed, "Mercy," to her to again and again, for the Psy-War expert needed to become as sick as his plans to conjure them up and so he knew Annaleah Eaves in a most biblical sense since they had enjoyed each other's flesh, repeatedly and in a rather erotic, stamina-driven and gymnastic manner, belying their age, from a penthouse overlooking Judge Lackey's courthouse and the Mississippi River, all of which was paid for by U.S. taxpayers out of the D.O.J., U.S. Marshall's Witness Protection Temporary Housing Budget; when slick Colonel Durant slid right into the role-playing that Annaleah requested for their tawdry interlude: he was her cowboy stud and she was his naughty cowgirl, chaps and hats and bilateral, sheriff's stars to boot, "Mercy! Gitty-up there! Oh mercy, Miss Cheyenne. Oh my, mercy!" He liked the perky stars a whole lot; Lady Justice would wear those he fanaticized. And then he could make her bark like a trained seal.

The prosecution of Jake Casteel had become a farce. But Colonel Durant enjoyed the perfect gratuitous tri-symmetry to it, the multi-decade *Di Trina* scheme. It was just plain old animal sex through the forbidden intercourse of corruption that groped and penetrated and violated amongst and between the government's own version of a holy trinity: the Legislature, the Judiciary and the Executive forces. Durant thought of it as a taking sex. An inhuman, heated, three-way fornication between the Executive Branch and the Judicial Branch and the Legislative Branch, with Lady Justice in the middle. And the U.S. Senators, led by Senator Moore, were shameless, cocky-assed pimps collecting more and more money from railroad barons and Designated lawyers alike, as they stood bedside like johns waiting in line, and as sick voyeurs watching all the sordid actions, in what the framers of the Constitution used much ink to avoid.

Colonel Durant put it into further perspective. If a crazy scheme like *Di Trina* had taken place in the church, it would have produced an insanely bizarre result; of priests and nuns and parishioners being allowed to freely copulate behind a veil of secrecy, in order to violate each other so as to produce money for those who made contributions on Sunday, which in turn, would allow the contributors to give a fraction of the money back to the church, so as to make the system run forever. And the Pope (as a metaphorical Presidential figure) would be required to turn his head and condone all of it by his silence and inaction. The fact that *Di Trina* had existed and thrived for over fifty years was a testament to how efficiently it had bought bipartisan support in the legislature and had infiltrated the bureaucrats in the Executive branch and used only greedy judges.

Colonel Dirk Eduardo Durant stretched a confident, evil grin across his face.

*Di Trina's* money and railroad money and blood money from the government made it all too easy for him to circumvent the Constitution. Money on money on money made the once pure lady eagerly jump on top of her corruptors. It even grabbed Durant, the marching soldier, and started him scheming a way to make his own fortune. The money kindled the dormant greed in Durant's soul, like a terrible, killing fire jumps to life after the snap of a match. Such fires become infernos and destroy much more than just the first victim. The government had perfected the technique; an entire labor movement can be stopped as killing a king or queen halts an army.

Snap.

Destroy labor leader Eugene Debs.

Lady Justice moaned.

Snap.

Destroy labor leader Jimmy Hoffa.

Lady Justice moaned.

Snap.

Destroy labor leader Jake Casteel.

Lady Justice was arching her back and moaning again.

She was not chaste. In the hands of greedy senators and Durant and over-zealous prosecutors, seeking to climb the ladder at D.O.J. by not questioning legalities but only plodding ahead as obedient soldiers, she was nothing more than a well-painted harlot. In retrospect, Colonel Durant sized it up. He had Lady Justice, figuratively, bouncing on top of him screaming an evil pleasure of injustice.

In Dirk's mind, it was not him, or the C.I.A., who was doing anything wrong, it was the once righteous Lady Justice, the D.O.J., who was allowing herself to be corrupted. He thought like most control freaks; forget the Constitution, might is right, it was the lady's fault that she was more resembling a gutter snipe than a beacon of truth and justice. He got off on her two-faced persona, her duality.

Plain and simple, the American people were getting fleeced. But it felt so good it did not stop. The railroad union officers kept filling their cups, like drunken sailors on a three-day leave that never ended. And the scheme continued from generation to generation like a sick parlay of deceit. And the profiteers, the Designated lawyers, like typical self-centered bastards, never even looked back at the panting train-wreck of injustice, curled in a fetal position, that they left writhing on the government's bed. They simply did not care.

Back in Washington, DC, Durant looked out his window, off into space, above the Potomac, and day dreamed; so far, they had been quite the debauched duo. Durant held his forehead and rubbed his temples and remembered what a potty mouth Annaleah had on her, what a wild thing; high-octane sport sex. And so easy to bend and take; he was not sure who bent whom the most. For their corruptions of each other had reached a singular, critical mass and took on a separate life of its own. Lurid. He felt comforted in being vile, in taking a married woman, a woman with a duty of fidelity. Triumphant. No strings attached. He smiled. She could teach hookers some street talk.

But the battle-hardened, professional warrior shook off his lustful memories and concentrated on beating up on himself; he knew his superiors would eventually be beating up on him. And he'd better have some damn good answers to why he was screwing up Jake Casteel's "shoo-in" conviction. Durant thought, as he looked out the window towards the Washington Monument, *"I should not have let Judge Lackey select McRain for me. I should have selected a loser lawyer and made Lackey appoint him."*

Fate selected Mike. God's will. But Durant did not believe in God's will. Bull crap. He believed only in himself and in his own version of the highest power, C.I.A. It allowed him to do whatever he damn well wanted to do: to take, to rape, to break, to murder both parent and child in order to get *the bad guy*, to steal, to enjoy without measure, and suffer no scars on his soul. For in his mind, he had no soul. No conscience. His ego was boundless. Perpetual want, want, want; take, take, take. Bestial, with a guttural voice of deception and evil. Just a God damned animal with no remorse or even a thought about any apologies or excuses. Might is right. He was a rakish, snorting non-human; the kind you read about in the Bible. One of Satan's minions if you may.

Maybe so.

Durant knew the mission would be a lot easier if Mike McRain was no longer Casteel's lawyer. Durant was frustrated because he was prohibited, by the Hoffa Protocol, from killing the union leader, Jake Casteel. He was used simply to killing his problems and he was angry that the alternative of murder was not available to him. Or, was it? The Colonel arrived at a solution. He believed he had overcomplicated things. He reasoned that the answer to controlling Casteel's conviction was simple, and right to the point.

Kill the lawyers. Kill McRain.

But Durant could not give Casteel an excuse for a continuance to hire a new lawyer. That would prolong the litigation. The clock was ticking for both Durant and Casteel. Durant had to do something quick, something that devastated Casteel's attorney. His mind was racing with the sinister realization that he was now like a giant, enabled by C.I.A.'s manmade power, black-operations magic; it allowed him to freely roam the Earth and step over the Constitution's high, impenetrable walls separating America's three branches of government.

He started to feel pumped and bulletproof like an over-confident fool feels after some long pulls on a whiskey bottle. He refined his plan and he decided to do what he was trained to do—psychological warfare. He would crawl inside the head of Casteel's lawyer with something wicked. He controlled the power of the material world as a demi-god. Colonel Durant felt a quickening surge through him sweet and sure. Completing it would satisfy his desires for letting red, innocent blood and fulfilling the rolling climax of *his* Lady Justice.

Assassinate the ones Mike cares about. Start close to home.

Snap.

Kill Bridget.

CHAPTER 82

# CHAPTER 83

# EVERYTHING IS GREY

In prison, Jake slept in a hard bunk that made the rocks and vines he had slept on, behind enemy lines in Vietnam, seem as soft as marshmallows. The bunks were cots lined up in a big room, twenty men to a room. Due to infectious diseases rampant in the minimum-security prison, the temperature was kept a cool, sixty-five degrees, to inhibit bacterial growth. The only privacy Casteel could enjoy was the escape he found between his ears. Life in prison was taking its toll on him. He was being sucked into the dismal, depression common to incarceration.

Casteel woke abruptly from a memorable dream. Rolling over, he saw one of his fellow inmates standing over him. It was a goofy fellow everyone called "Trashman Stan" because he went through the trashcans, no matter what was in them. It was believed that is where "Trashman" picked up the half-dozen, infectious diseases he carried. "Trashman" was standing over Jake, right next to his bunk, holding his manhood and fondling, yanking himself. Jake yelled at "Trashman" and walloped him in the gut with the back of his fist.

"Get away from me, you son of a bitch, or I'll yank your cock right off your body." "Trashman" whimpered and pulled up his pants as he stumbled back to his own cot. A guard opened the door to the room and warned Casteel.

"Keep it down, Casteel. And leave Stan alone. Ya pervert."

Casteel tried to employ the depression-neutralizing techniques he'd learned from men who spent years in North Vietnamese prisons. Memorizing multiplication tables, long passages from the Bible, and Shakespearean works. Jake recited them to himself, aloud, in a soft murmur, so he could hear the strong voice of one of the few men in this prison that had not yet gone insane, surrendering all hope to the cold chains of institutional depression. Those techniques, designed to ward off mental disease, worked much better when a prisoner held hope for life after prison—life on the outside.

Sadly, Jake's family–his wife and children—had all but deserted him. They believed the government's allegations that Jake was a liar. They were incensed that he would sacrifice their family's honor by being deceitful. Jake had been an Eagle Scout, as a young man, and a Boy Scout Troop leader. Jake harped on honesty and integrity as necessary ingredients to a fulfilling life. Then the government had trumped up the Perjury on Admiralty charges against him, and his family punished Jake for his apparent hypocrisy.

If only they knew the truth. It was the government that was lying– because Jake had been too good at representing railroad-union men.

Jake's mind wandered, thinking about how miserable his life would be, after he got out, if he did not have the love of his children. Much less, that of his wife. Unbearable and depressing to think about. But he could not stop thinking about it because there was little else to do in prison. Jake knew it was the government and *Di Trina* that had destroyed his family. And Jake promised himself that, if he got out, he would make them pay. Each and every one of the dirty, rotten bastards. *Who did they think they were, messing with his family? With their honor?*

Jake Casteel's elderly parents, Ben and Margie, drove a six-hour, round trip to visit him every week. No one else from his family came to see him. His hope for life on the outside was dim. Everything had turned gray.

CHAPTER 83

# CHAPTER 84

# THE CADENCE – THE ROSARY

Michael McRain and Dalton made the trip to see Jake in prison weekly, too. They communicated with Jake about sensitive matters by writing on tablets of paper, rather than speaking. They knew the government was listening. It was hard on everyone, especially Jake.

Driving home from a visit with Jake, Michael McRain would say a full rosary, concentrating on the Joyful Mysteries. When Michael McRain looked into Jake's eyes, he could see Jake slipping away, into a deep pool of depression. It was as if Michael McRain were watching a man slip under water, to drown. Michael McRain wanted to give Jake hope. The only way Michael McRain knew to do that was to work like Hell on Jake's case and pray to God to make Casteel joyful. In Michael McRain's mind, work would make it all work. Pushing beads and pushing papers, until the mission was accomplished, and no slowing down unless success is won.

Michael McRain's catechisms. His Catholic catechism. His Marine Corps catechism. They combined to make Michael McRain hard as a rock—and with the sight of an eagle, keeping a singular focus on Casteel's case. It was that focus that kept his faith strong and kept him going, like a marathoner. Quite regularly, Michael McRain listened to Marine Corps marching cadences because they reminded him of the catechism his instructors in the Marine Corps would yell at him.

*You don't ever leave a man from your squad behind—ever! How bad do you want it, McRain? What are they going to put on your tombstone, McRain? "Winner," or "Quitter?" Suck it up, McRain! Are you a maggot or a man? The difference between a Winner and a Loser is work. A pint of sweat will save a gallon of blood.*

And on, and on, and on.

It was the catechism of a warrior. Faith in your abilities. Faith in your training. No different from faith in your religious training. Faith in your fellow Marine. Faith in God. Faith in hope. *Semper Fidelis.* Always faithful. It was a catechism based on faith.

*Semper Fi.*

Michael McRain also had the continual fear that he would meet Captain Carion if he slept. So he stayed awake, working on Casteel's case like a one-man Marine Corps.

One evening, when Michael McRain had returned home from visiting Jake in prison, Bridget Mary McRain picked up on Jake's depression through Michael McRain's voice, sounding down and tired. For the first time in their adult lives, Bridget Mary McRain and Michael McRain held hands and prayed together, at the kitchen table. They concentrated their prayers on Jake's soul and on his release—as a prisoner of war, the war fought between the railroad barons and *Di Trina* on one side, and truth and the union men on the other. Michael McRain was so warmed by this prayer session that he even ate Bridget Mary McRain's cooking. Cleaned his plate. It seemed to Michael McRain that Bridget Mary McRain's cooking was getting better.

Quite a bit better.

CHAPTER 84

# CHAPTER 85

# JAKE'S DREAM

Jake Casteel knew how hard Michael McRain was working because he, too, was a lawyer. Jake could not believe the mountains of paper generated by Michael McRain in legal research and brief writing. It was both astounding and encouraging to Jake. But Casteel still had to deal with the harsh realities of institutional depression.

He remembered the dream he'd had before "Trashman" woke him. In it, he was in the rural countryside, at his grandparents' farm, sitting in the kitchen, drinking coffee. His grandmother was standing at the kitchen window, crying and wiping her tears. Casteel spoke to her.

"Nanna, why you cryin'?"

His grandmother never answered. In his dream world, Jake looked over at his Grandpa, sitting at the end of the table, in his blue overalls and a soft, flannel shirt. Grandpa Joe just looked down, into his white, ceramic coffee mug. Never looked up. Jake tried again to talk to his Grandmother because she was so sad. Little Jacob Casteel spoke to his Grandma Casteel, in the dream.

"Don't cry, Nanna. I'm all right."

Grandma never turned away from the window. She kept weeping, looking out the kitchen window. Then that dumb bastard, "Trashman," came knocking, and that was the end of his visit with his father's parents.

Jake wondered why he'd had that dream. His grandmother had been dead for twenty years, and Grandpa Joe had preceded her by five.

Jacob Holibrook Casteel spoke into the cold, prison air, words he knew would be heard by his Grandma.

"Don't cry, Nanna. I'm all right."

He slipped back into sleep, to the sound of a distant, train horn, blowing long and mournful, the way a coyote holds a howl.

~~~~~~~~~~~~~~~~~~~~~~~~~~~~~~~~~~~~~~~~~~~~~~~~~~~~~~~~~~

Two hours to the west, Colonel Durant contemplated how best to carve up Bridget's body, to maximize the psychological trauma to Mike.

He was an artist, you know. An artist who worked in the medium of mental pain. And his favorite color on the palette was red.

Blood red.

CHAPTER 85

# CHAPTER 86

# A LOVER'S QUARREL

I was charged up about our plan to take the Supreme Court Clerk's deposition, to find out which case became law first, "Gordon" or "Casteel." We were hoping that "Gordon" became law before "Casteel" so that Jake could take advantage of the new rule in "Gordon"; the "Gordon" rule did what should have been done two hundred years ago — it outlawed prosecutions under the ridiculous Perjury on Admiralty ruse.

Issuing such a subpoena was bold and it was made easier by Ann's caring manner. I knew we belonged together. But I could not let myself move into a relationship before I was done representing Jake Casteel.

By the time I'd finished dictating the subpoena, a full moon was high off the horizon. Ann finished typing. "There. The subpoena is finished." "All right. Now, off to Washington." I scooped up the subpoena documents, put them into a file, and made ready to leave.

Ann placed her hand on my shoulder to get a kiss. I shrugged her off, "Something wrong, Mike? You got jitters?"

"Naw, I don't have any jitters . . . You know, . . . about you and me. . ." "About us?"

Ann yanked me by the shoulder, so we looked each other square in the face. "You know, what we've been doing for the past month? I thought we'd kept it secret."

"Who told Dalton?" Ann denied telling anyone, and so did I. I was being a bit standoffish. I was more comfortable with a hot, hand grenade than a matter of the heart. Ann stepped in to narrow the awkward airspace between us.

I said, "You know I got feelings for you, but I. . . I . . . I . . ."

"But you don't think what we have been doing is right? Is that what you are trying to say?"

I blurted it out. "It wasn't in a marriage. It isn't right."

Ann dropped her hands from my hips to her own. "It wasn't right?"

I turned, to talk to the air with my hands, while I paced away. The subpoena pages fluttered in my hand. Almost as if they wanted to avoid what was coming, to take off and fly to the Supreme Court by themselves.

"It wasn't honorable. You got feelings for me. I got feelings for you."

"But what, Mike? What's wrong with . . ."

I wheeled around and faced Ann. I still talked with my hands, in a pleading sort of way. "A boss sleeping with his secretary? Isn't right, Annie; it isn't honorable."

Ann was taken aback with my viewpoint. This was news. That I saw any affair, any relationship, our relationship, this way. We had shared our bodies there in the office, in twenty different places. On my desk, on her desk, on the client couch in the foyer, in my chair, between chairs, against the filing cabinet, at the back window of the office—looking out at the stars. But most of all, on my U.S.M.C. area rug, under my desk and chair. It had been a fine and fancy affair, to date. And I was now coming up with this notion of honor. I admit that it sounded a bit suspicious.

Ann squinted and spoke softly to me, "It isn't honorable?" She turned away from me and chewed her thumbnail. Nervous. There was a lot on the line. Her heart was breaking. And she was too proud to show it because she loved me. She purposefully had not used the "L" word—yet. I moved into my office and leaned onto my desk, with my back to Ann. She faced away from me, too. She was gathering her thoughts, standing in my office doorway, clutching the neck of her blouse.

"Annie, I have strong feelings for you, but you know what they say about secretary and boss romances."

Ann exploded into action, turning towards me. I looked over my shoulder and saw her approaching, fast. She ripped open her blouse. Ann exposed her breasts to me. I turned around, quickly. Ann assailed my assertion of dishonor. "You don't think these are honorable?"

She cupped her hands under each breast, "These aren't honorable? Us making love all night on this floor, right on this honorable, Marine Corps rug, under your shining, fancy, honorable, Marine Corps sword?" Ann pointed towards my sword, hanging on the wall behind my desk. She was just getting started, "After you told me how men beat you as a little boy. And you stayed in the hospital for months. You weren't spilling your soul to someone you love? I gave you my body. And you think we weren't being honorable? That wasn't love?" Ann yanked her blouse shut. With hurried fingers, she began to button her blouse.

I was in a tough spot. I had to risk losing Ann, in order to save my client, Jake Casteel.

How could I tell her that Captain Carion, a sea-faring spirit in Purgatory, had forbidden me from associating with Ann until our mission to free Jake Casteel was successful? I feared she would have thought I was crazy and that she would have quickly ended our relationship. No, if I was to have any chance with Ann, I would have to take my licks from Ann's tongue like the floggings I received in my dreams. I tried to stall, to buy time, by throwing out the old saw about bosses and love. It seemed I chose wrong. I probably would have done better by telling Ann the bizarre truth about my soul being held captive in Purgatory as a ransom to win the case for Jake Casteel.

I stammered, like my first day at the Air Force Academy, when I was screamed at and turned seven ways to Sunday, by upperclassmen determined to make me focus.

"I. . . I . . . I didn't mean it that way. . ."

"Then what did you mean?"

Ann Parsons stabbed my chest, dead center, with her finger. She jutted out her chin, to make her points more clear. Then she wagged her long, index finger in the air and shook her head, taunting like the sisters do, to their men, when they are angry.

"Mr. Oh-So-Honorable, Decorated, Marine Corps Officer?"

"I . . ."

Ann finished it for me. "I'll do the talking, honorable maggot. Is that all you understand?"

Her fists were on her hips. "Honorable, Marine-Corps speak? You worthless pile of honorable horseshit." I was braced, at attention. "Well, I'm gonna introduce a new language to you. I'm gonna say it first . . . without the honorable bullshit."

Annette Parsons thumbed my chest, with a short, rabbit punch to emphasize each of the three words, "I . . . love . . . you," Ann said.

But I could not reciprocate.

I was tongue-tied.

I would rather have a knife fight with a Navy SEAL in a telephone booth than tell Ann how I really felt. There is no man more naked than one who reveals his true feelings for a woman he loves. I loved her. But I could not tell her that. It would be a sign of weakness. And I would be violating my orders from Captain Carion. Or so I thought, by the fractured reasoning of my emotion-inhibited male brain.

There was no response possible for the great communicator. "I . . . I . . . I . . ."

"What's wrong, cat got your tongue? Big, strong, tough Marine hit-man can't use the 'L' word?"

"I wasn't a hit-man. We neutralized. . ." My defensiveness about an irrelevant issue was not taken well by Annette Samantha Parsons.

She held her finger to my lips, shushing me, like a schoolteacher does to a child. "Ha! Daddy told me what you honorable Force Recon boys do and who you do it for. But you listen here."

She turned her back to me and stood, poised to walk out the door of my office. Out of my life. I was grateful she thought twice; she turned around quickly and pointed at me. Tears flowed down her cheeks. "If you can't understand love, and if you don't wanna love me back, that's just fine with me 'cuz . . ."

Ann seemed to lose her train of thought. I heard her mumble to herself, *"Oh, what does that one greeting card say?"* Ann's back was to me. She sounded a little squirrelly, as she wrinkled her forehead, patted her long fingers on her forearm and talked to herself. I knew I was in trouble. I knew better than to say anything, if I didn't want to lose the woman I loved. I had to take my licks because I was too big a jar head, an emotional coward, to say — "I love you."

CHAPTER 86

I came to one clear realization. She was even more beautiful when she was angry.

A re-composed Ann turned and delivered her best punch yet—loud, and straight to the point, laying it all out.

"I'd rather have loved you and lost than never to have loved you at all."

She saw my dazed face. I played it smart. Like a coward. I kept my tongue in my head.

Ann took my silence as indifference. She marched out of my office in a red-faced huff. The woman of my dreams turned the corner past her desk and legged it to the exit door, with me still standing there, not knowing what hit me. Ann put her hand on the doorknob. She hesitated long enough to say, "You can stick that honorable, Marine Corps sword up your honorable . . ." Ann yanked open the door. And screamed.

# CHAPTER 87

# A MOUTHFUL

I heard Ann's bloodcurdling scream. I ran, around the corner, out of my office, to find Ann lying on the floor, in the doorway, a bloody hog's head swinging above her, hanging from a tether. I rushed to help her up. We stood together, back from the hog's head for a moment, watching it swing and rotate.

I held Ann in my arms and said, "What in the holy Hell is that?" The grisly head spun slowly at the end of the rope, revealing its mouth stuffed with a piece of paper. Ann was shaken, reluctant to approach the bloody mess. The perpetrator had screwed a large I-bolt into the hog's head and hung it from the doorjamb of our office's front door. It was a message sent to rattle us.

"It's a hog's head, Annie."

"I know that. We butchered hogs lots'a times on the farm. I know what a hog's head is. But what is it doing here?"

"I don't know. But there's a paper in its mouth. Lemmee read it."

We stepped towards the hog's head, and, quickly, Ann reached out and stopped me. I looked back at her.

"Careful. It might not be an honorable hog."

She was being a smart-acre in a tense situation—I liked her more every minute.

I gave Ann a loving smirk. I was trusting her more and more. I felt I could love her, share my life with her and her young daughter, because she had a sense of humor. And now I knew she could crack jokes, even when things are at their darkest. That is a necessary trait in the Marine Corps. Force Recon men had to develop the ability to use a dark sense of humor, a *"C'est la vie"* attitude, now and then. It was necessary—if you did not seeing dead people, cut-up, mangled people, some who might have been your friends—or it would drive you insane. Such is life, so don't let it get you down.

I retrieved the piece of paper from the hog's mouth and read it out loud. "Pigs get fat. Hogs get slaughtered."

Ann turned to me. "I heard Daddy say that lots'a times when somebody was getting greedy. But what's it mean to us? How come they are telling that to us, Mike? And who did this?" Ann had plenty of good questions, and I had plenty of nothing for answers.

I turned my back to Ann as I looked at the message. I was thinking. I said, "It's the lawyers' mafia. *Di Trina*. They got the stranglehold on the Hog Head Rail Union."

Images of prohibition-era gangsters, with Tommy guns and the Corleone family flashed through Ann's mind. "Mafia? You mean the guys in the black Cadillacs and sunglasses?"

I gave no response. Ann moved over to me and put her face and hands on my back, then clutching my arms for reassurance. "Isn't Jake Casteel's union called the Hog Heads?"

"That's right." I snapped my fingers. "They are telling us to back off the Casteel case. Like we should count our blessings."

Ann looked at the hog's head, and a glint of something caught her eye from the back of the beast's mouth.

"And quit while we are alive."

Ann walked over to the porcine head and poked around in its mouth with an ink pen, trying to dig the object out from the back of the hog's mouth.

"They bugged this office. They don't want us going to Washington," I said.

"Looks like we got another message." To my surprise, Ann slowly pulled a rosary out of the hog's mouth. I grabbed it and looked at a small tag hanging on it. Ann read it out loud, "Made with loving hands at St. Cecelia's Workshop for the Blind."

We looked at each other, in a lightning-strike realization.

"Bridget!"

CHAPTER 87

We ran out of the office, leaving the hog's head swinging in the open doorway.

We sprinted to my car and peeled out of the parking lot. We did not bother to stop for a single red light on the five-mile route to Bridget, at home. About three miles from home, we flew through ran a red light, and a police car started to chase us, red cherries shining from its rack.

"Don't bother calling the police."

# CHAPTER 88

# THE ASSASSIN STRIKES

Bridget was home, sleeping, with Ace at her bedside. The glow from a late October moon shone through her lace curtains spraying tiny moonbeams of faded white light across Bridget's calico bedspread. Gunny pulled guard duty at his doghouse in the yard. He heard a slight rustling in the bushes adjacent to the house. He got a sniff of something he didn't like—evil. Gunny did his job. He bared his fangs and barked and tugged at the end of his heavy chain.

Colonel Durant cursed the mutt under his breath as he looked for the best way to enter the home. He decided it was through the kitchen door. He would have to pry it open. The problem was that it required him to step out into the open, right in front of Gunny, who had now pulled his chain its full length, twenty yards short of the back door. Durant knew the only person home was Bridget because he had just left the hog's head as a gift for Ann and me.

Durant referred to Ann as McRain's little "fornication station" when he spoke with the techies working the case. But that's the way Durant had referred to women throughout his whole Army career. He kept that opinion mainly to himself. But his actions spoke louder than words because that was the way he treated women. His devilish, good looks, his swagger, and a chest full of medals made many a secretary in his male-dominated world want a piece of his action. He was a natural lady-killer.

And he was very good at it—killing ladies.

Tonight, in a rare call, he was going to kill Bridget. He was forbidden by the Hoffa Protocol from killing Jake Casteel, but he'd realized the best way to get to Casteel was through Casteel's lawyer. Me. The best way to get to me was through my family. Durant knew Bridget was the weak link in my psychological armor.

Durant laughed out loud, in his car on the way to "neutralize" Bridget, at the thought that he could make a great living, intimidating lawyers for the lawyers' courtroom opponents. He figured it would be kind of like taking everything he'd learned in the Psychological Warfare Unit with the Green Berets and employing it in the lucrative, litigation industry. He'd make "a killing," he laughed to himself. He was one sick puppy. But very professional.

He came around the corner of the house, in full view of Gunny. My British bulldog exploded in a barrage of barking and growling, tugging and tearing at his chain. Bridget heard the commotion outside and sat up in bed. Ace walked over to the closed bedroom door and looked at it.

Colonel Durant jimmied open the kitchen door and pulled out a knife for his specialty, a silent job. Ace heard Durant coming up the steps.

Durant had grown fond of using knives in close quarters. Beyond being quiet, they were more convenient when conducting business, up close and personal. And they didn't leave you wearing the blood and brains of your targets, like when you shot them and got sprayed with blowback. Dirk believed there was an additional factor he enjoyed about cutlery; it allowed him to express himself, his artistic side. He wished that, some day, he could enter his work in the pumpkin-carving contest held every October. But, alas, he knew they would get picky about his subject matter. So each year, he practiced his craft in professional obscurity.

The fifth step made a loud, squeaking sound when he stepped on it. The sound confirmed where the intruder was. That prompted Bridget to begin the code she and I had worked out, exchanging alternating lines of lyrics to an old, Irish ditty. Said loudly in conjunction with particular squeaking steps for the staircase of Twenty-Three Oaks.

"Up the long ladder."

No response.

"To Hell with King Billy."

Silence.

Durant did not know what she was talking about. He previously had heard Bridget and me exchange the lyrics, on surveillance tapes. He didn't realize that was Bridget's way of making sure who was in her home.

CHAPTER 88

But that night, she was alone. That is all Durant cared about.

"Up the long ladder," Bridget yelled, this time with a twinge of fear in her voice.

Durant froze on the stairs, his knife in his hand. Then his weight rolled forward, onto the top step, making it emit its own unique squeak, a sound that Bridget had known for years. She knew, when she heard that squeak, there was somebody standing at the top of the stairs, right outside her door. Even though she was afraid, she was ready. She picked up her shillelagh and stood by the door, braced in a stance, like a warrior holding a spear. Ace started to bark aggressively. He sensed the evil on the other side of the door.

Out in the yard, Gunny barked, very loud. The miniature bulldozer pulled at his chain so hard, he started to weaken the screws anchoring it to the doghouse.

Two miles away, Ann and I took a corner on two wheels, with the police squad car in hot pursuit.

Gunny yanked the chain off the doghouse and ran in the kitchen door. But the long chain caught on the doorjamb, stopping him at the bottom of the steps. He acted rabid, showing his fangs as he barked, up, towards Durant.

Durant held his knife high, as he put his hand on Bridget's doorknob. Ace bared his fangs even more. Bridget repeated, over and over, loud and clear, "Up the long ladder, up the long ladder, up the long ladder."

Right when Durant chose to burst through the door, Bridget thrust her shillelagh into a space about the height of most of her brothers' heads. She chose wisely.

Her shillelagh struck Durant's face, knocking him backwards into the stair railing. It darn near knocked him out. Bridget landed another blow, as Ace tore into Durant's leg. Durant ducked Bridget's third, violent lunge. He wounded Ace with his knife. Ever the caretaker, Bridget's maternal instinct focused on Ace, if only for a moment. But Bridget was dealing with a highly trained assassin. Durant recovered, and he grabbed Bridget. He put his knife to her throat. "Say your prayers good night . . ."

Ace was bleeding badly, but he found the strength to deliver one more bite—to Durant's crotch. It made Durant let go of Bridget, allowing her to scramble on the floor and find her shillelagh. She stood up and swung it, hard, at Durant. She missed. And the force of it caused her to fall down the stairs, head over heels, in a looping, full-body-length summersault. She ended up at the bottom of the stairs, unconscious. But she was safely near Gunny, who guarded her mightily. Durant stabbed Ace three more times. On the third stroke, Ace let out a death moan and fell to the floor in a furry pile.

Durant looked down the stairs and saw Gunny, acting like a Marine, a Devil Dog, trying to get off his chain so he could attack Durant. Gunny was standing over of one of Bridget's legs, as she lay unconscious. The hair stood up on his back and he was braced for Durant's attack at the bottom step. Durant was undaunted by Gunny's ferocious show. He slowly walked down the steps, with his knife, to kill Bridget. He spoke to the unconscious Bridget, in anxious anticipation of cutting up human flesh.

"Feisty little retard, aren't ya? Gonna cut ya into Mulligan stew."

Durant stopped a few feet short of Gunny's frothing fangs. He calmly put his hand on his belt buckle. "But first, I'm gonna do what "The Slasher" would have done to you. See if you're *a real* redhead. I betcha you haven't had a real man before."

As quick as any boxer, Durant swung and sliced Gunny's leg. Gunny came back; he was not backing down. He doubled his ferocity, as he stood, braced and bleeding, at the end of his chain, between Durant and Bridget, at the base of the steps. Durant thought about leaping over the banister. Only a ten-foot drop to the far side of Bridget, and he could come at her from the back side, that Gunny could not reach. He thought for a second about how cool it would be to violate, kill, and slice up Bridget, right under the General's portrait. A real horror, an insult to the whole McRain family, living and dead. Durant would obtain the revenge "The Slasher" promised Mike, for capturing him, and not letting him escape, and for trying to teach him civility. Violating and chopping up the virgin, Bridget, was all very cool and alluring to the sick man, Colonel Durant.

Psy-War.

CHAPTER 88

# CHAPTER 89

# GOING DOWN

Ann and I were streaking to get home, to see if Bridget was in danger. One of St. Martinsville's finest was hitting my car with his spotlight and using his public-address speaker to demand that I pull over. I planned to explain to the policeman when we got home.

*What the Hell.*

The sirens of the police car chasing us pierced the house, over the din made by Gunny. Durant retreated, up the steps, to look for the best place to escape.

I stopped my Mustang in a power slide in the side yard, so I could go directly through the kitchen doorway. I motioned the policeman in. Ann and I ran up the porch stairs, through the kitchen door.

We found Bridget unconscious at the base of the stairs. She appeared to have a broken arm. The policeman called in an ambulance, as I stormed up the stairs. I found Ace's body at the top, with knife wounds. Dead.

"A pro," I thought. I moved, with cautious confidence, like I was back in the jungle, hoping I would find the bastard, so I could do to him what he deserved. My room was the last one I checked, and the window was open. Before I went to the window, I checked behind the door and found a message that sent a chill down my spine. The attacker had left his own bloody knife as a souvenir for me, and he had taken one of my favorite throwing knives from my dresser. I interpreted that as an assassin's nonverbal message that we were cut from the same cloth—we were both knife men. A loose brotherhood that shared killing instruments. He was wrong.

On top of the other dishonor, Durant had invaded my personal space, my room, my last bastion of privacy, in an attempt to rattled me between the ears. He'd tried to run a psychological-war operation, to get me thinking about the high price I would pay for continuing as Jake Casteel's lawyer. I read between the lines.

The message carved into the fine, wooden door was brief. But it told a complete story: "NEXT TIME."

It made me freeze, thinking about Bridget's life. It would be impossible for me to protect Bridget every hour of every day for the rest of her life. It pissed me off that I had brought this type of danger to Bridget, to my family, to the homestead.

I had been down this road once before. Back then, I chose wrong. I'd learned from my mistake and set my priorities, simple and linear. Family came before client. I could not risk Bridget's life to serve my client, Jake Casteel. I'd protected Bridget as a boy, and I would not let her down. Not ever. I was her self-appointed guardian angel, ready to praise God and kick anybody's ass who messed with her.

The message, between the hanging hog's head at my office and the carving in my door, was clear. Like a boxer who takes a fall, Durant wanted me to lay down my arms, drop my defense, and just give up. I was spitting angry.

I knew it. I felt it, down to my bones. I said, out loud, in earnest disgust, as I plucked Durant's knife out of my carved-up bedroom door, "This bastard is gonna die."

CHAPTER 89

# CHAPTER 90

# AN IRISH FUNERAL

It was a soft day, as the Irish would call it. Misty rain fell from a gentle, overcast sky. I patted the dirt into an oval-shaped hump. I hammered in the cross-shaped stake and hung the rosary on it that Bridget had given me to adorn Ace's grave. Ace was a good dog. A hero for saving Bridget's life. At that moment, I didn't give a damn about the Catholic Church's dogma that animals have no souls and do not deserve Christian burials. As far as I was concerned, Ace made a knowing, sentient sacrifice of his life, protecting Bridget. On those terms and according to my code, the code of a warrior, Ace had a soul. It was only fitting; Ace deserved a place of honor for burial on the homestead grounds. Out past the lower stand of hickory trees. There wasn't going to be any non-Christian burial on the grounds. Ace received a proper, Christian funeral, officiated by me.

I looked towards the house, across the long lawn where I played Indian ball, and football, and army, all day long, with my brothers, while Bridgy would swing or prance around in a blind whirl, playing games in her head. All the while, she would have a rosary, generating prayers in a galaxy-sized space in her mind that we knew, even at that young age, we could never visit. But they were nice memories of family and belonging. The unmeasured love of our parents. Always. Sweet memories of love and laughter.

I broke from my meanderings in the past and wished that Bridget could have found it in herself to come out to the grave. But she was still so distraught, so emotional, so absolutely destroyed over the whole incident, that she could not stand to bury her own dog.

I thought of Bridget, and I began to cry. Not a torrent, not at first. I thought of how Bridgy would never know the exhilaration of a romantic relationship and how she seemed trapped inside a beautiful world of perpetual prayer. Her life wasn't much different from the life of a Marine, out in the field. But worse. Lonelier. Perhaps she used the saints to keep her company, like the camaraderie between Marines united in a common purpose. A mission.

I wondered if she said her prayers to give her life a tradition, like we Marines chant, to keep time while we march and to build esprit de corps. Always marching onward, towards a righteous goal. I likened Bridget's rosaries; and her prayers; and her saints; and her God, Jesus Christ, to a Marine's cadences; and our Corps history; and our heroes; and our God, General Chesty Puller. *Was the God Bridget prayed to the same God that Jewish Marines, and Baptist Marines, and Muslim Marines, and Catholic Marines pray to, in a foxhole?* I did not know because I prayed right next to all of them, and all of us survived. I knew what worked for me. I am a Catholic man; I pray to Jesus, and Mary, and select saints, to focus on different things in my life. I am comfortable in that. I believe it is the truth. Jesus is my Lord, not C.I.A. Even though some people refer to C.I.A. as "Christians In Action," it no longer ran my life.

I cried. I never cried at Father's funeral. I was due.

I cried for Jake Casteel and the crooked prosecution. How it ruined his relationship with his family, his children and his wife, who endured the shame of Jake being branded a felon. It angered me so much, I was ashamed to be an American and a lawyer, for that kind of injustice to go on in our country, and nobody seemed to care. As long as the trains keep rolling, Jane and John Doe keep getting a paycheck and buying their six-packs to drink in front of their televisions, while *Di Trina* picks their pockets, slow and sure. I got very angry again, thinking about how they killed Bridget's dog. You don't kill someone's dog purposefully, especially a blind woman's dog, and not pay for it.

I'm not a very good Catholic—I could not forgive the cold, calculating bastards. I swore revenge. We would get even. Some way, somehow. I would make sure Lady Justice was redeemed.

And as a special note, if I am attacked, I want a well-sharpened Hibben, throwing knife. Not a handkerchief to cry on or to wave in surrender.

CHAPTER 90

# CHAPTER 91

# THE WING MAN

*"So be it,"* I thought, as I said some final words over Ace's grave. They were the kind of words I would have said over a man's grave. I treated Ace as an equal. As a true hero. Sacrifice should be respected.

As I leaned on the long-handled spade, I settled my thoughts for the while about Ace, and about Bridget, and about my late Father, and about my life, my yearning to build a family of my own, with Ann and Kylee. I crossed myself slowly. I made a simple decision, to protect my family and friends, first and foremost. But little did I know how difficult it would be, to stick to my new plan. I turned and walked back to the house, gathering internal resolve for the bombshell I was about to drop.

On the porch, I moved my chess piece to prolong the inevitable checkmate with which Bridget would snare me. She had me painted into a corner, covered by both her castles and a knight. Not good. I had to do something with my bishops. I walked off the porch, through the kitchen door. I did not know then that, in ten minutes, I would be in the most painful fight of my life.

Dalton and Bridget sat at the kitchen table, waiting for the breakfast Ann was cooking at the stove. Kylee stood close at Ann's side, watching her mother turn eggs. It was such a treat to have little Kylee in the house. It had been so long since the McRain home had had children in it. I thought it was about time that changed.

It had been a long night at the hospital for Bridget. And there was grim business before us. "United States v. Casteel."

Bridget's arm was in a cast, resting in a sling. That did not stop her from working her beads with both hands sitting at the kitchen table. I did not know if her head was twitching from her prayers or from the pain of her broken arm. Bridget was never one to complain much about pain or discomfort. She was always a trooper. A sign she was raised in a military family. Tough. Proud. Giving. Loving. That was Bridgey.

Dalton saw me walk in with a grim face. "Sad day, got to bury your dog," he shook his head.

Little Kylee ran over to me and offered her condolences, "Sorry your dog died, Mr. McRain, Sir. Mommy said Ace is in dog heaven."

Kylee was stealing my heart. I gently touched her face and rubbed her shoulder in gratitude, "You don't have to call me Mr. McRain, or Sir, Kylee. Yeah, Ace is up in heaven, where heroes belong." I moseyed across the kitchen and looked over Ann's shoulder at the yummy, breakfast fixings she was cooking. She worked the whole stove top, all four burners, and the oven down below, like a short-order cook.

Ann read my mind. "I'm cooking this way because Mom and Dad had six daughters, and I was the oldest, so I don't know how to cook for less than eight."

It smelled great, and I nodded to her logic. I tickled her side. She laughed and turned to the table to lay some southern-style breakfast on us: grits drowned in butter; eggs, every which way, cooked in butter; bacon; sausage; saw-mill gravy; buttermilk biscuits; and pancakes. But best of all—Ann's and Kylee's faces at my table. I took a seat at the head and poured Dalton and myself some coffee.

"Looks like we got 'til tomorrow to file that Motion to Reconsider with the Supreme Court," Dalton said.

I was abrupt, and loud, and almost mean, the way I said it, "We ain't filing it."

Ann stopped her fork in mid-air; Dalton's jaw went slack; and Bridge, although she remained stone-faced, stopped her mechanical, bead pushing. Kylee didn't understand what was happening and kept eating, until she saw her Mom's face. She stopped and scooted over, closer to Ann. I knew that I had taken this nice, placid pond of healing serenity—after last night's attack and dropped a big, black boulder in the middle of it, creating big waves, like a tsunami carrying heartbreak, confusion, and fear.

I was unfazed. I buttered my biscuit. "Pass the butter there, wud'ja?"

Dalton's eyebrows were raised. He couldn't believe his ears. "No more making legal history by taking the testimony of the Clerk of the United States Supreme Court?"

CHAPTER 91

"Yep. No more history. The price is too high. There are the innocent we gotta think about. I'm not gonna risk their lives, not for Jake Casteel, not for the Pentagon, and not for a lawyers' mafia. I'm not even gonna do it for good ol' Lady Justice. She's getting high on all that personal-injury money being thrown around. With judges and crooked lawyers putting her legs in the air. To Hell with it." I remembered there was a child present, so I cleaned up my angry language. But not by much.

"Yeah, good old Lady Justice. She looks a lot like a cocaine, you-know-what, lady right now, taking all comers just to get her next score. And the R.I.O. lawyers are her pimps and junkies."

Ann covered Kylee's ears. It had to be said, since it was the naked truth, and we were all affected by the government's atrocious gavel.

Bridget interrupted my tirade. "Never leave your wing man."

"Huh? Wud'ja say? My wing man?"

Bridget was rocking in her kitchen chair, getting all hepped up, working herself into a dynamo. I stopped buttering my toast, to listen to Bridget. I had seen this look on her face before. The time she stood up to all five of her older brothers and me, making us quiver in fear, as we braced against the shed. We were thinking we were gonna get whacked by her brand-new shillelagh again, the shillelagh Bridget had received on her thirteenth birthday.

I looked down at her hands. My eyes grew big when I saw she was working the same rosary she had that day, twenty years before. It was a magnificent, Franciscan rosary, strung with large, wooden beads, carved by yearning, African hands under the spiritual tutelage of a missionary Franciscan monk, Father Thomas Friedmann. It had an ivory Christ on the Cross, strung with water-buffalo leather. The five Miracle Stations were ivory, too. That rosary was breathtaking. Father Friedmann gave it to Bridget for her constant prayer devotions on behalf of his tiny mission in the Congo.

Over the years, I wondered if a witch doctor might have carved a few beads of that rosary himself, the way Bridget got results when she prayed with it. Don't ever bet against Bridgey if she's working her African Franciscan. She's a lead-pipe cinch on whatever she's praying for. I'll put it another way for you fighting men out there. If Johnny Rambo saw Bridget walk into his room with her shillelagh and her Franciscan, with beads as big as your thumb, he'd better high-tail it. Like most super-warriors of a different fighting style—prayer— Bridget did not brandish her results. She stayed centered, and within herself. She just kept working her beads, like karate masters continue practicing their Khatas; humble in their endeavor of a practiced art.

Bridget spoke, strong and direct, like she usually did when she had her Dutch up.

"Your wing man, Mr. Casteel, Mr. Jake. Don't be using me as an excuse to leave your wing man. He's counting on you. We gotta fight. We are McRains. Ace was my wing man, and I'm still here! Praise Jesus, Lord Almighty. Our Father . . ."

I shot Dalton a humoring look, back towards Bridget, as she droned on in prayer. Ann silently shoveled eggs onto her plate, and Kylee quietly poured herself some milk.

"Bridgey, you heard Daddy say it a thousand times. A wing man is somebody who relies on you and counts on you to be there, come Hell or high water."

My strong-willed sister tried to interject, "And . . ."

"And I'm not gonna risk your neck, for Jake Casteel, by going to Washington to take the riskiest deposition ever attempted in two hundred years of American jurisprudence. I almost lost you once already . . ." I was interrupted.

"This is about Daddy, isn't it?" I froze in place. A tennis-ball-sized bite of eggs, bacon, and hash browns was paused an inch from my mouth.

I was told it looked like blood welled up and flushed my face. I blinked, into open space and then at the choke-a-horse-sized bite on my fork.

"Daddy?" Dalton said.

I held up my hand to stop further questions from Dalton, who, it seemed, sat at that breakfast table more than some of my brothers. Ann moved away, giving me a questioning look. I wiped my mouth with my napkin and pushed away from the table, but remained seated.

"Bridgey, don't go there."

The fight was about to begin.

CHAPTER 91

# CHAPTER 92

# A MATTER OF HONOR

My older sister was dredging up some pretty smelly things from the past. Things I had been avoiding since Father died. It was the most difficult fight of my life. Bridget lit into me with some scalding facts, facts that I had not fully realized. I thought they were things not known to anyone else, only existing down in my subconscious, where they could remain hidden, so I could function even while they festered in my soul, like Mr. Fetid.

"Ever since you took on Casteel, I knew it wuddn't 'bout big onions, or a lawyers' mafia and railroads and government. It's about Daddy." Bridget had a way of speaking more clearly and lucidly when she was angriest. It was one of those counter-intuitive, autistic, Asperger Syndrome things.

"No, Bridgey, not here. Not with everyone here . . . I whip myself every day. And it's unions, not onions."

Dalton ran to Bridget's defense. "Some union guys smell like onions."

Ann smacked Dalton on the back of his head. She shushed him and told him to mind his own business. Even though Dalton was considered family, this was blood, and she steered him clear of it.

Bridget grabbed the arms of her chair and leaned forward, towards me. It was as though she could see right into my soul. "It's 'bout how you pray every night for God to fix your pain. Your pain from leavin' Daddy dying, an' you took off to do your lawyerin'. Daddy was cryin' for ya to hold his hand. You left, and he died, lonely for ya."

My chest swelled, I bulled my neck, and lowered my voice to a commanding tone. "Marines don't leave their posts."

Bridget stabbed an indicting, rosary-draped finger at me. "Daddy was cryin' for ya."

The others got up from the table. They hung back, away from the heated exchange between brother and sister. They were back by the kitchen sink, with Kylee behind Dalton and Ann, poking her face out, from between the two of them. Afraid.

Dalton whispered to Ann, "A father's deathbed, the most sacred post for a son."

I got up and began to pace behind Bridget, with my hands behind my back, as if I was cross-examining the opposition's star witness. I knew my jury of three would feel sympathy for Bridgey, which left me with a most difficult litigation maneuver. I knew I had to do what they refer to in the law as "Kill the Queen." It is based on the degree of sympathy the jury feels for the witness. If you attack "the Queen," you must destroy her credibility, or the jury will punish you because you attacked a likeable witness. I had to go for the jugular.

"I had to leave Father because I had to file papers in court. I had a deadline."

Bridget's head twitched involuntarily. But it did not seem to diminish her energy.

"Left your wing man."

I lost it. *How dare she assail my honor?* I bellowed in Bridget's ear—not to abuse her, but out of my extreme frustration, bottled up, without release, ever since our father died a year ago. I must have sounded and looked like a U.S.M.C. drill sergeant, screaming at a new recruit.

"I had a professional duty!"

I hammered my fist on the table so hard, it made everything on it jump three inches. A glass of milk bounced and spilled, pooling its contents into the platter of pancakes.

Ann, Dalton, and Kylee drew back, even further. Bridget seemed unfazed by my return fire, like the courageous, door gunners in Marine Corps helicopters. She continued to rock in her chair, and, with her tongue, she fired a withering assault on the honor so precious to my father and me. She had near-distance-effective-fire, so she discharged it in short bursts.

"You left Daddy dyin' and cryin'."

I bellowed it hard, "No!"

"Deserter!"

CHAPTER 92

With her shillelagh, Bridget swept the dishes off the table. They smashed on the floor, in a horrible clatter, the mess strewn across the kitchen, all the way over to Gunny's little bed by the stove. Gunny slurped up some eggs and lay back down to watch our firefight of words. At times, our words got so salty, you might think they were streaking, white, tracer rounds, shot by our tongues, back and forth, between us.

Bridget had no mercy, repeatedly stabbing me with her razor-sharp blade of truth.

"Daddy was strangling inside. He wanted to hold a warrior's hand. Daddy died right after you left him, Michael."

Bridget found the wound in my soul. She was almost unholy, the way she was pouring saltwater into it.

"No, Bridgey, no."

Bridget threw her shillelagh on the floor. She crossed herself and moved to rocking in her chair. I touched her shoulder. She brushed me off and retreated into her prayer, like a wounded, wild creature crawls into a hole. All the spectators were wide-eyed. Ann's lower lip was quivering.

Bridget referred to the ancient, Celtic practice of wailing: a traditional, half keening, half singing, ritual for the spirit of the dead, as it leaves the body. A throaty, high-pitched warbling that sounds like a banshee to the non-Celts.

"I was wailing him, best I could." She took a teary pause, "You broke his heart leavin' 'cuz you was his wing man."

"I didn't know he was gonna die so soon, or I wouldn'a left."

"Daddy said wingmen are meteors. I'm a wing man, too, Michael."

"A meteor? A wing man is a *metaphor*. A metaphor for someone you can always count on, to back you up."

"Ace was my wing man and you're my wing man, Michael, 'cuz you won't leave me. I can't get you out of the house 'cause you think you'd be leaving your wing man. So's if you treat me that way here, how come you can't treat me that way for Jake Casteel cuz it's Mr. Jake who you're supposed to be protecting? Mr. Jake is counting on you to cover his wing cuz youse is his wing man. You can't bail out on Mr. Jake now, not 'cuz of me."

THE REDEEMER: IT IS WRITTEN

She knocked her shillelagh on the table. "Damn it!"

Bridget's hidden intellect wasn't just peeking out, it was breaking down the door to my house of fractured logic. She continued to stomp on my reasoning.

"Daddy was lying in bed, ate up with a cancer, and you holdin' his hand, tellin' him to breathe and prayin' on him. You said you'd go serve some papers to court. You walked out, but ya had to walk back in 'cuz ya said Daddy's eyes were cryin' at ya, an' then ya left for good. And Daddy died grabbin' for your hand."

"Christ, Bridgey. No."

"And Daddy was stranglin' inside and needin' air, and I couldn' help him. I'ze praying, and Daddy died right after ya left 'im, Michael. Ya broke his heart, leavin 'cuz you wuz his wing man."

Tears streaked down Bridget's face, as she rocked and twitched in fervent prayer. I saw both Ann and Dalton crying. Little Kylee was standing in front of them, her tiny fists on hips and her lips pursed into a pout. She shook a finger of shame at me.

"You're bad. You're mean to your sister."

She turned and hugged her mother's thigh.

"Mommy, he's being mean to Miss Bridget."

I couldn't believe it. I was catching it from all sides. The old tactic of retreat was not an option. I decided that I had retreated, dodged the inescapable truth, long enough. I recognized I must get on with my life and listen to Bridget, as painful as the truth had become. I felt like Confederate, Civil War General Lee at Appomattox. But I wasn't surrendering to the Union, I was surrendering to an unbeatable army of saints, under the command of General Bridget Mary McRain.

I was certainly no General Lee. I was less than gracious in my surrender.

"Oh, shut up. Okay, you're expendable. And Jake Casteel is my wing man and I'm not gonna leave him to keep you safe. God help us all."

I made an attempt to go over and hug Kylee. But Kylee swung underneath the bridge of pity between Dalton and Ann, to put Mama between her and

CHAPTER 92

me. I smiled and chuckled a bit in the face of the emotional brush. I picked up a butcher knife and walked to the kitchen table. I stabbed it into the tabletop and motioned to Dalton.

"Come on, partner, we're takin' Washington."

As we marched towards the door, Dalton wiped his eyes of tears.

"Boy, I haven't seen you this fired up since half-time in the State Championship Game, when we were down three touchdowns."

"Oh, yeah? Didn't we win that game?" I said.

"Still got my letterman's sweater with 'State Champs' on it, hanging in my closet."

"Knowing you, you probably still wear it to pick up chicks."

"You saw me at the mall?" I stopped our jesting repartee at the door. It helped me cleanse myself of the emotional goo I felt covered with, from head to toe. I turned around and walked back to the woman I loved.

I kissed Ann firmly on the lips. Ann hung on my neck, looked me in the eyes, and smiled.

"Do your duty," Ann said, softly.

My mother used to do that for my father when the Pentagon's drums of war called him away. But we both turned around when we heard Bridget share some different wisdom.

"Remember, you can't catch a fish if he doesn't open his mouth."

"Now she's giving us fishing tips?" Dalton said.

Dalton and I headed out the door. Bridget snickered, gleeful and sly.

"Kissed her strong. Gonna be a war. Saint Michael, the warrior angel, please ask Jesus to protect Michael O'Brien McRain 'cuz here he comes."

Ann watched us pack up and drive off.

"Amen, sweetie. That's a man on a mission."

# CHAPTER 93

# FALCON AND SPARROW

Dalton and I took our three, pre-packed suitcases, briefcases crammed with ten copies of the "Motion for Reconsideration" and subpoenas in the back of my Mustang. We left in a hurry.

My right foot hit the floorboard, as the 'Stang roared out of the driveway, its top down. Dalton was not yet in command of the five-point, racing-harness seatbelt. At the end of the driveway, we blasted past a parked van we had all come to know as "the bad guys."

The local cop, a sergeant who'd played football with Dalton and me, checked it out weeks before. He told us who was really in the van, advertising "Plumber Bob" on its sides.

"They got more electronic gear in there than a nuclear sub. Yeah, somebody wants your asses, boys. Better watch out."

Dalton stood up in the car seat and flipped the bird, with both hands, at the surveillance van as we flew past, "You messed with his sister, and you killed his dog, and now he's gonna kick your ass."

My hard shift up to third gear threw Dalton over the roll bar and into the back seat. He scrambled back into his front, passenger seat and struggled with the five-point harness. He decided to break the tension with more humor.

"Whoa, hey, why didn't the shark eat the lawyer?" He paused, and delivered the punch line, "Professional courtesy." He tried another one, "Why don't lawyers go to the beach?" He answered it himself, "Cats keep covering them up."

I had focus, like a missile locks on a target. "Why can't you ever be serious?"

"Okay. Okay. Gentlemen, we'll be firing conviction-piercing subpoenas. So fix billable-hours bayonets and charge at my command." I gave Dalton a sideways look, to shut up.

"So what's the plan, Cap'n?"

I was winding out the powerful 351-Cleveland engine to punish the car's differential in fourth gear. "Hey, diddle, diddle," I threw it into fourth gear and popped the power clutch. It snapped back our heads, "straight up the middle."

Six hours later and one time-zone east found us landing at Washington's Dulles Airport, under the careful scrutiny of one of Durant's surveillance-team members. He spoke into his wrist transmitter.

"Falcon and Sparrow have landed."

# CHAPTER 94

# A KISS REMEMBERED

Bridget was still at the kitchen table with Ann. She was being pestered by Gunny for the meal that had been left behind.

"Did he kiss you hard on the lips? And squeeze the breath out of you?" Bridget asked.

"Yes, he did both."

Bridget drew a big smile across her normally stoic face.

"That's how Daddy loved Momma when he would leave for war. Amen. Saint Michael the Archangel throwing Satan out of heaven. All in the name of the Lord. Praise God."

Ann relented, giving in to Gunny's big brown eyes, that begged better than any whining or pawing ever could. She set a plate of eggs, toast, and bacon on the floor for him to eat. As she bent down, Ann saw the long, wooden, Franciscan rosary that Bridget had dropped, along with her shillelagh, during her heated debate with her little brother. The blessed beads had slid along the floor, to squarely under the middle of the table. Kylee scurried under the table, picked it up, and put it in Bridget's hand.

Bridget held onto Kylee's hand to deliver a message. The little girl was scared, with her hand trapped in the grip of this lady she just had seen act crazy and wild, shouting and carrying on against Mike. But there she stood, still, and listened.

"You good for Mike. Mike like you. You take care of him for me. Okay?" The little girl nodded, the index finger of her free hand hooked into her mouth, in anticipation and wonderment. Bridget released her hand.

"Mike good man."

Ann watched Kylee lean in and press herself into a warm hug with Bridget.

"He's the best," said Ann.

# CHAPTER 95

# THE SLIP

It was a solemn act offered to our Sacred Mother. I crossed myself, then rested, back in my seat on the jet. As I did most nights, I offered my soul to God, to do as God willed. Whatever came of the Casteel case, the lawyers' mafia, *Di Trina*, I knew it was all out of my control.

I learned long ago from my black ops days that, no matter how much control you exert by your acts—assassinating a dictator or causing unrest in a population, perhaps by blowing up, thereby disabling, a nuclear reactor being built by the wrong people, at the wrong place, at the wrong time—it still came down to God's will because there would always be flash-fires, caused by the greedy or the oppressed, that needed to be put out around the world. But worse, the same chaos went on inside every human's soul. I believed that daily prayer was the only way to keep the demons that raged inside me in check. Closely monitored, so they won't get out of line and lead me into life as a fool, a drunkard, or a philanderer.

I was a walking, talking, hypocrite. A man all about honor. But I was no angel. I enjoyed my share of the five-dollar whores in the Philippines and third-world countries. Three-day, drunken binges with the other members of my Marine recon team. Partially to blow off steam. But mainly to try to forget the faces of those we had killed, not knowing if they were innocent or guilty. Relying only on the word of our superiors—the suits, the guys from C.I.A., who really didn't look at you as though you were a human being. To them, we were just robots they sent by remote control to take out a target. If the robot got broken, if a man were killed, who cared? As far as they were concerned, it didn't matter. We were as expendable as bullets and cheaper than a smart bomb. Do the math. When they lost a man, they just plucked another one from the long line of wannabes, who bought into living a life they supposed was full of "sex and danger."

Dalton and I took a red-eye flight into D.C. I took the time to make two phone calls before I left St. Martinsville. The first, I used my cell phone to book a reservation in a hotel close to the Supreme Court. The next phone call, I made from the payphone inside the men's room at the St. Martinsville airport. With a pocket full of quarters I kept jamming into the payphone, I placed a call to a message recorder in Virginia, not far outside of Washington, D.C.

"Chieftain, this is Corporal Kick Ass." I went on, to leave a brief request to meet at a predetermined place. I added, "I brought you a little reading material." I was carrying a special package of documents for this special contact. "0300 hours, sharp. I need a favor."

I was a bit wily in the ways of counterespionage, making the first call for a reservation to ensure that Uncle Sam had the room bugged, seven ways to Sunday. Plus, they would probably have two or three surveillance units staking it out. That way, they would know every speck of dust in the room, and, if any of it moved, it would be documented and catalogued. We, of course, were not going to stay in that room.

When we landed in Washington, D.C., we took a taxi to a large, shopping mall in Arlington, Virginia. We walked through the mall, casually stopping to examine goods at various kiosks, which allowed us to look around. We saw we did have a distant tail in the mall. But we watched our backs as we carried our luggage into a "Victoria's Secret" store.

I told Dalton, "The tail won't think anything is out of the ordinary because they will think, he is buying himself his usual bra."

Dalton shot back, "Yeah, but, at least, I don't have to pad my bra like you do." It was great. We were cracking jokes while we ditched the C.I.A.

We went out the back door of a sporting goods store, to the loading docks, where we threw our bags in the back of a delivery truck and jumped into the cab. We simply drove off with a big truck that was not ours. Stole it, borrowed it, call it what you want. Ten miles down the road, we ditched the truck. We hailed a cab and took it, two miles, to a gas station, where we got out. We carried our luggage across the street to a hotel, not the one where I made the reservation.

CHAPTER 95

Dalton stayed in the lobby, acting like he was waiting for someone. I went into the bathroom off the lobby, with my largest suitcase, the only bag we'd checked. When we left St. Martinsville, I checked one large suitcase that contained disposable clothes and a small shaving kit. I knew we were being tailed by Big Brother and that they would put an electronic homing device on our luggage if we gave them the chance.

I opened the suitcase. Sure as shooting, there was the little homing device, about the size of a book of matches, in the lining of the suitcase. I took the time to remove the homing device C.I.A.'s friendly, baggage handlers had put inside. I was surprised they fell for their own trick, one they had trained me to do. I walked outside and put the homing device behind the seat of an idling, panel truck, with Utah license plates.

We laughed out loud at the image of two cars of government agents, tailing that truck all the way to Kansas before they figured out what was going on. We hopped into another cab and ended up booking two connecting rooms at a $45-a-night motel another five miles away. Clean and cheap. The hotel was perfect—off the beaten track. The beds were so broken down, they felt like hammocks.

Dalton thought the whole process was fascinating. He was excited by it.

"It's always an adventure traveling with you, Mike."

We laughed, hard and long, about our teenage years. We recalled the time we sneaked out with the General's Air-Force-issue sedan. We'd had the audacity to pull up in front of a liquor store and use the story that we were driving a government-issued car, on undercover surveillance, so we had no I.D. to buy liquor. The guy looked out and saw the blue, G.I. vehicle and figured that was good enough I.D. for him. He sold us a whole case of red ones, Budweiser. But we had no cooler, so we threw the beer and the ice into an open washtub and placed the tub into the trunk of the car. Then we drove to a late-night party at one of the colleges. Father, the General, never found out. Or, if he did, he never let on about it. We burned the candle at both ends, and we reveled in it.

I sneaked out of the room almost immediately after we arrived. We were sure we had not been tailed that far. When we wanted to be found, we would turn our cell phones back on, to let the government get a triangulated fix on our position. Until then, it was cat and mouse, and we didn't want the cat to know where we were. Dalton stayed at his room while I waited for my rendezvous with my secret contact—Raford. Special investigator for the I.R.S.

I had a lot of reading material for him, about the illegal loans *Di Trina* made to their clients. The loans were a key to their crooked system of theft from the American people.

I sensed the surveillance at the airport and its intended malice and I knew Durant wanted us dead.

CHAPTER 95

# CHAPTER 96

# A HIGHER POWER

It was 0130 hours, and I was in my hotel room. I finished praying before I slid into bed—fully dressed and my boots on. The night before the biggest day of my legal career. In my prayers, I called upon the wisdom of the Holy Mother for guidance. Not in the case "United States v. Casteel." Not in handling the assassins and the unfair, fixed legal proceedings I was fighting. But in my love for Ann and Kylee. Deep in thought, I pinched some beads in prayer and caressed others. When it came time to finish my Rosary, I let the Crucifix simply rest in my palm, applying no pressure against it, no grip on it. The rest of the rosary, I intertwined between my fingers and knuckles, ready to love or to fight.

My buddies in the Marine Corps made fun of me when we watched football on T.V. because I was always rooting for the underdog. I think my allegiance to the disadvantaged came from growing up with Bridget and from praying to Jesus, who was the ultimate underdog. Jesus' life story is about a man sacrificing himself for the well being of the wretched and overcoming the impossible, death. Nevertheless, I wanted to move on with my life, to get married, and to be a father to Kylee and whatever other souls of children God might grace us with.

I offered my fears and insecurities about my love life to my higher power, God, my Savior, Jesus Christ, to decide my fate with Ann and Kylee. I knew no more certain way to decide correctly. Listening to my gut instinct was how I looked into my soul. It is a conduit that brings me signs and messages from God. I learned to hold and follow the little, gut instinct voice inside me. The little voice served me well in all areas of my life, including in black ops, defusing explosive booby-traps not nearly as complicated as tying the knots and untangling the many, dangerous strings of love. I laughed inwardly and shook my head, in wonder and concern about the dream I'd had on the flight to Washington. It scared the Hell out of me, startling me awake. And it scared the Hell out of the flight attendants, who thought I was having some type of seizure. The dream was not about death or attack; it was about love. If there was anything that scared me, it was falling in love.

I dreamed I got married to Ann.

That scared me into a cold sweat. Love meant revealing a tender side, a vulnerability, a weakness. That grated against everything I stood for, as a Force Recon officer, as a trial advocate, or, for that matter, simply as a male because weakness is not tolerated in those circles. Because, to me, falling in love was all about giving in and letting yourself be sucked into the whole attitude, "Strong enough to be a man, but man enough to be tender." Was it malarkey? I didn't know. And I was not afraid to find out.

To me, acknowledging weakness was the same as surrendering my male ideals of being invulnerable. It was not a problem. And I was worried that I might be rejected by Ann because of Bridget. As though Bridget was a ball and chain. But God gave me an answer in that dream, that warmed me from the inside. I felt confident that we could all exist as a loving family. Bridget would be part of our nuclear family because she needed people to help her with most everything. *Didn't she?*

That was, of course, if Kylee and Bridget got along. Which brought up a whole ocean of fears, clouded with dangerous icebergs of emotion, capable of sinking any ship of love I tried to float. It was in God's hands.

In the still of the night, when the only sound was Dalton's snoring, the voice inside me told me to get back on my knees and offer another rosary, for guidance and wisdom, defending Casteel against Big Brother, big oil, and big rail—and against a bunch of greedy-ass lawyers. I finished the rosary, feeling stronger and more confident.

I had heard my Father explain his dog-fighting victories to many who pestered him to tell tales of his World War II, fighter-pilot days. At cocktail parties and picnics, fighter pilots are some of the few people asked to recount war stories in detail. It's probably because fighter pilots' stories are not that gory. I mean, nobody asks me how I broke into a room, where there were four heavily-armed terrorists holding a prisoner, or how I then killed three terrorists with a knife, snapping the fourth terrorist's neck before cutting the prisoner free, slinging him over my shoulder in a fireman's carry, and delivering him safely to the landing zone. Most people don't want the bloody details.

But fighter pilots, special forces teams, and lawyers have something in common. They must focus clearly and fly directly into trouble. To be successful, they cannot just believe they can do what looks impossible to others, they have to *know* they can do it. I knew I could beat Nelson.

It was time to rock and roll.

I set the alarm on my watch for a thirty-minute nap, and I shut my eyes. I finally got to sleep, with all the confidence in the world that the Rafe rendezvous at 0300 hours would pay off, in spades.

# CHAPTER 97

# A SILVER TONGUED DEVIL

I slept deeply.

My dreams carried me to the Seas of Purgatory, back on board "The Constitution," where I found the crew had fastened ropes to my ankles and hands and was now slowly hoisting me off the deck, belly up, spread eagled to the sky. Mr. Troubles stood to my right, Mr. Fetid to my left— thankfully, downwind—and, as I looked over my shoulder, I saw Captain Carion moving towards my head.

"What are you idiots doing to me now? You've beaten me everywhere a human can be beaten. I'm in it, now. Just show me where they are, so I can kick their asses," I said. "Send me in, Coach!" Carion's shadow fell over me, briefly. He stood to my right.

"Do you know who Daniel Webster was?" Carion asked.

"Of course, I do; he's the orator that defeated Mr. Beelzebub in a debate two hundred years ago."

"Aye, the Devil and Daniel Webster."

"Spare me the history lesson, Captain. I'm all ready to go, so get these ropes off me."

"You are not yet ready, Mr. McRain."

"I've done thousands of hours of legal research. I've written a fifty-page, legal brief to the United States Supreme Court. I just cut a federal judge to shreds, making him think he could go to prison for serious judicial misconduct. At the very least, he will be impeached by Congress. I'm on a roll, Captain; send me in."

Mr. Fetid laughed. He spoke only the spoiled and festered truth. I could see his breath come out of his mouth, in a gaseous, green wisp. It drifted away, knocking out a crewman who stood too close. Mr. Troubles was inspecting the binding on my hands and ankles. He looked beneath me, as if he were investigating some sort of a magic trick that caused me to levitate above the deck. It was obvious that the ropes were holding me up. Besides, we were in Purgatory, for God's sake!

"Do you know what ship you are on?" said Carion.

"All I see from here are puffy clouds and masts . . ." Carion interrupted my flippancy.

*"You are on 'The U.S.S. Constitution.'"*

*"' Old Ironsides.' I could not be more proud."*

*Mr. Troubles bent over me and said, "The very one."*

*Mr. Fetid cuffed Mr. Troubles for talking, in the presence of the Captain and out of turn. "Mr. McRain, I am in possession of intelligence that says you are going to be cross-examining a judge tomorrow. A male judge."*

*I laughed, "Well, your intelligence is wrong because I'm going to take the sworn testimony of a female, Supreme Court clerk. This is all a silly dream."*

*"No, where you are going, you will need extra ability. You must be able to speak so smoothly, you could sell snowballs to Eskimos. But it has to come from your soul. Given the state of your spiritual nature, I'm quite concerned. I do not want my operation to fail because, if you fail, I won't get out of Purgatory. And I do, so much, want to get out of Purgatory. Three hundred years is much too long. Wouldn't you agree, Mr. McRain?" Carion kicked me in the gut, knocking the air out of me. He stroked his chin, contemplating his celestial plan.*

*"Mr. Troubles, I need you to fetch me some souls from the hold. Let's see: of course, we'll need a judge. And, to endear the judge to favoritism, we'll need the tongue of a politician."*

*He shook his head, then he nodded, seeming not to know what else he might need. Then he snapped his enormous fingers and said, "We need something for that Catholic, guilt trip Mr. McRain is carrying around. We need to get rid of his conscience. Why, oh, yes, of course, someone shameless. A close cousin to lawyers everywhere—a prostitute."*

*" A judge, a politician, and a lady of the evening, coming right up, my Lord."*

*Mr. Troubles scurried off, to different hatches on the deck, of different sizes and shapes. He opened a medium-sized hatch labeled: "Judges," and Mr. Beelzebub handed up a medium-sized snake, full of venom and self-righteousness. Mr. Troubles dragged himself past hatches labeled "Robbers," "Muggers," and "Credit Default Swap Dealers." Troubles then ran to a very small hatch, with tiny letters that said: "Prostitutes."*

*While Mr. Troubles was fetching the snakes, Carion bent down and whispered into my ear, "That's a sweet, little tart you have, that Miss Ann. I'd be giving her the blade, if I were you."*

*"Yeah, well, Captain, I'm not gonna talk about my womenfolk that way. Cut me down, so I can kick your . . ."Carion screamed in my ear, "But she doesn't belong on my vessel! You are a Marine. You know better. Women on ship are bad luck! Wait until the mission is over, you dolt!"*

CHAPTER 97

Then Carion smiled a queer smile, of glory and gore. "That is, if you complete the mission. I've looked into your soul, Mr. McRain, and it's much too dark to gain ya admission to the Promised Land. So when the Crown gives you a double-tap to the head, you'll be swabbing my deck for the next three hundred years. Or, maybe, just straight to Hell with ya. Forever." The Captain roared, a hearty laugh that shook the ship's timbers. "Ain't no return from Hell, Laddie. Of that, you can be sure."

Captain Carion's laughter stopped when he looked over and caught Mr. Troubles taking the politician/snake out of the "Prostitute" hatch. "Get them out of the hatch with their name on it, Troubles, you lazy galoot ."

"Oh, but, Captain, Sir, Mr. Beelzebub handed them all to me. They all come out of the same hold, the same pile. Just different doors. What's the difference?" Troubles caught on fast, for he had been on board only a year, not like most of souls, whose voyages to purity lasted centuries.

The hold of the ship, its lower part, was the realm of Mr. Beelzebub, Satan, Old Jake, Lucifer, Mr. Nicky, Mephistopheles, the Devil himself. He went by many names. He was up to his knees in snakes, the souls on the lowest rung of Purgatory. The Nearly Damned. They sat in the bowels of "The Constitution." Below the water line, only an instant from the eternal, Hellish waters that never release a soul once it is fully consumed.

Just as Mr. Troubles said, there were no separate compartments for the snakes—the souls—but there were separate hatches. Beelzebub did not know the difference between the soul of a prostitute and that of a politician. But passing a soul through a hatch bearing a particular label resulted in the label sticking to that soul—for eternity. Such was the working of the system governing souls in the infinite, gray space between Heaven and Hell.

Mr. Beelzebub stuck his horned head out of a hatch labeled: "Dirty Cops" and snorted in disgust at Mr. Troubles' oversimplification of the complicated system he had been running for thousands of years. Beelzebub insisted on doing things his way. Simple. In Purgatory, that meant always erring on the side of damning the poor bastard's soul.

Captain Carion set Mr. Troubles straight. "I've told you, time and time again, you lazy Irishman, it's all in the presentation. Now, gather 'em right." Mr. Troubles shouted at Mr. Beelzebub, down a tiny hatch, labeled: "Prostitutes."

"Okay, ol' Beelzebub, I need a prostitute. One with swinging hips and singing lips, kind of classy, and still puts out, if you know what I mean." Beelzebub's red-scaled hand extended a tiny snake, a coral snake, to Mr. Troubles. Troubles double-timed the snake to Carion, with the other two snakes looped around his neck.

*Troubles cooed to the small snake, the one with the soul of a prostitute. "Oh, you are a fine one. I do believe I enjoyed your pleasures in Hong Kong. A splendid night it was, indeed. Oh, yes, a fine lady you are . . ."*

*"Troubles!" Carion scolded, at the top of his lungs, "After we are done here, perhaps you can pay the kind lady again, but we have business upon us, sailor."*

*Mr. Fetid whacked Troubles in the head for his inept ways.*

*"This man needs a tongue of gentle respect. Give me the politician first," said Captain Carion.*

*Troubles said, "Oh, sir, I got you a fine one—a governor!" Mr. Troubles handed a huge snake to Captain Carion. Mr. Fetid laughed as Captain Carion took it from Mr. Troubles, holding the head of the snake, with its forked tongue flicking out, again and again, to touch my mouth.*

*"Okay, here's a forked tongue. A judge is sure to understand that one, he will," Carion said. Mr. Troubles and Mr. Fetid looked on the spectacle, and Troubles served his purpose, as jester.*

*"Captain, Sir, don't you think it should be the tail first, since Mr. McRain here will have to argue both ends of the case?"*

*Captain Carion was unfazed and continued his task, shoving a large snake down my throat. Mr. Fetid still stood downwind. "Ah, so that's where they get the expression, 'talking out o' both sides of your mouth.'"*

*The ceremony continued a short while, until Carion had imbued me with the tongue of a politician, the scruples of a judge, and the wiles of a prostitute.*

*Upon finishing, he simply said, "He's ready."*

*Whereupon, I was rowed ashore and thrown from the skiff, onto the beach.*

I awoke on the floor beside my bed. I had to pinch myself to make sure I wasn't dreaming still. I was looking at a pair of well-polished combat boots, belonging to whom, I did not know.

CHAPTER 97

# CHAPTER 98

# BIG BROTHER

I snapped to and used a single-leg, shoulder-to-knee block to bring down the intruder. I quickly leveraged the knife out of the man's hand. The tables had turned. In the ten-second tussle, I was only half a second from sticking the knife into the man's kidney, a death wound, when I heard, "You stupid-ass, Marine, it's me, Raford."

I had rolled from my dream, aboard "The Constitution," to the floor, to awaken in battle mode. And the lesson I had just received from Captain Carion distracted me and dulled my usually keen warrior senses to the point that I had not heard Rafe invade our rooms.

I dropped the knife, and Raford said, "What are you doing, you crazy S.O.B.?"

"What do you mean? You were the one that sneaked into my room. I could have killed you."

"Killed me? I've got your law partner in the other room gagged and hogtied. I could'a slit your throat ten times, but you spazzed out in some kind of bad dream and ended up on the floor. You made a whole lot of racket. I'm just here to protect your ass."

"Protect my ass?"

" Hey, I'm early because I gotta get you outta here. This neighborhood has more federal agents than the Hoover Building. My guess is they want to kill you before you get to court today."

I started to Dalton's room to untie him, but Raford stopped me. "Before you untie him, I need to tell you that I read that first batch of loan documents Ann provided, and the Treasury Department is taking big action on all of it. The whole, freakin' mess."

Rafe looked me in the eye. "There'll be a lot of rats jumping off *Di Trina's* ship when we sink it."

"You're depressing me," I said.

"I thought it would make you happy; we prosecute *Di Trina*."

"I was hoping there wouldn't be any survivors getting off the ship."

To his great relief, I removed the sock from Dalton's mouth. "What is this? A McRain thing? I mean, tying people up in the middle of the night?" Raford knew Dalton quite well, as he had been my best friend since childhood. Dalton had been at our home hundreds of times when we were kids.

"You pencil-necked geek. I should'a slit you from one end to the other instead of just tying you up," Raford said, with all the affection of a Green Beret. "Come on, you two numbknuckles. We gotta get out of here within the next sixty seconds, or your asses are gonna be in a sling, on the wrong end of a nine-millimeter." Three minutes later, Durant's henchmen pulled up at the motel with a skid of tires. Raford had sneaked us out the back door of the hotel—luggage, and briefcases, and all. We went over a stockade fence and through some woods to his pick-up truck.

Durant kicked down the door of the hotel room, and, after a quick search, discovered we had evaporated. Colonel Durant was beyond angry. "What do you mean: you lost them? My God, they were in this hotel room. We have to find him and make sure he does not make it to the Supreme Court. You all are a bunch of morons. How do you lose men getting off an airplane?"

Dalton had always liked Raford and treated him like his own brother. Dalton was an only child and needed male camaraderie, growing up. I had been more than happy to share with him the Dutch rubs and other big-brother hazing Raford wreaked on me over the years. Imagine growing up, the younger brother of a Green Beret. Nobody messed with me. But that's because Raford wanted Dalton and me as his own personal, punching bags.

Now Raford was helping me bring *Di Trina* to justice through the I.R.S. A convenient aspect of Raford's job was that it gave him access to the Government's databases: databases of case files, databases of investigations, but, most important to me, databases created with a new technology—digital surveillance. I had been told, by a U.S. Attorney, that all the federal courts were equipped with digital-surveillance equipment that covered every inch of every federal courthouse in the country, including the United States Supreme Court.

I had a plan.

CHAPTER 98

# CHAPTER 99

# FISTICUFFS

Raford, Dalton, and I spent the rest of the night in a greasy-spoon diner in Maryland. We sat in a booth in the back. Out of sight from drive-by eyes that might be looking for us. Dalton and I told Raford about the *Di Trina* angle on this case—now a hold, full of smelly fish. He couldn't believe it, at first. But then, he acknowledged the Pentagon had some strange ways of making sure the trucks and trains continued to run in times of war.

Raford didn't give a damn if the Department of Defense saw him drive me to the Supreme Court Building, "Screw them, bro', I'm already drawing my Army pension. And, besides, I'll kill the sunz-a-bitches if they think about taking away my retirement. I'd have to hire some slick-ass lawyer from St. Martinsville, get me one of those twenty-million-dollar settlements for what-cha-call-it. Oh yeah, R.I.O."

Raford came to a stop, right in front of the Supreme Court building. Right in front of Colonel Dirk Durant, who was standing in front of the courthouse, coordinating surveillance units.

The smile left Raford's face. The Green Beret Cadre was a small world. "I know that son of a sea cook. I went through War College with him. Colonel Dirk Durant. You watch your backs." Dalton and I got our luggage out of the back of the pick-up truck. We walked right past Durant, not knowing that he was the one who had orchestrated the fix on Casteel's conviction.

Durant couldn't believe that Dalton and I made it through the dragnet he'd set up to prevent us from making it to court. Durant did not want the deposition of Assistant Supreme Court Clerk, Anita Morrison, to occur. He was embarrassed that he'd been caught, out in the middle of the terrazzo in front of the courthouse steps. It is never a good thing when a target gets a good look at your face, no matter whether he knows he's a target.

I picked up some bad vibes when I passed Durant, as Dalton and I marched up the steps, into the side entrance of the court.

After we got inside and through the security check, Dalton and I were assigned a personal escort to the anteroom where the deposition had been scheduled. Our escort was a huge bear of a man. Dalton whispered jokes about him, as we followed, ten feet behind.

"He is a government experiment gone awry. Half caveman, half buffalo." Dalton was not far off the mark. The U.S. Marshal's Deputy was massive. His hair was so black and so thick, it looked like it belonged to a buffalo. He sported no mustache. But he had a single eyebrow, an inch thick, that ran across his face uninterrupted, like someone had taped a black ruler to his face.

We watched him from behind as he walked. As he moved, I noticed his slouch, probably because, if he rolled his shoulders back, into a good posture, he would have ripped out the tent-sized, blue, Marshal's blazer he wore. "Buffalo Man," I quipped, quietly, making Dalton snicker. Dalton was at least partially right when he guessed about "Buffalo Man's" prior vocation. Later on, we found out "Buffalo Man" once played tackle for the Washington Redskins.

"Here is your room," Buffalo Man said, as he gently pushed open the heavy, wooden door, to reveal the court's stenographer, the Assistant Supreme Court Clerk, Ms. Morrison, and Assistant Solicitor-General, H.T. Armey.

Armey's face looked like the cat that just swallowed the canary. He was hiding something. I didn't know that Armey had been speaking with the Assistant Clerk for an hour before we arrived. Our opponents failed to come to a meeting of the minds about that vague and illusive notion, called the truth.

At Armey's meeting with Morrison, he said something like this: "Look, Ms. Morrison, you've been here, at the Supreme Court, for thirty years. How can you say you remember file-stamping the 'U.S. v. Gordon' opinion before the denial order for 'U.S. v. Casteel?'"

Ms. Morrison was fifty-two-years old, widowed, and black; and she had a law degree from George Washington University. She both carried and expressed herself with class, and she had an affable nature that made 'most everyone respect and like her. She'd lost her husband, a soldier in Vietnam, not long after she started working at the Supreme Court, as a secretary. She never remarried. Anita Morrison had only one regret in her life, as she looked back over a distinguished career of public service—she'd never had children. She made it clear to Armey that she didn't have room in her code of ethics for lying.

"Like I told you the six times before, Mr. Armey, I have always, for the past thirty years, file-stamped the opinions before the denials. So I don't have to remember the case name. All I have to know is that, for thirty years, I have never file-stamped a denial before an opinion. For me to characterize it any other way would not be the truth, sir."

Mr. Armey knew that I would be arriving soon, but now that he had tried so many times, he gave up, in hope that something would prevent me from learning the truth. Armey, after all, had his nose quite far up the butt of the D.O.J.'s liaison from C.I.A. The one who'd promised him serious consideration to become the next Solicitor General, if Armey could pull off this charade.

Mr. Armey threw in the towel, for the time being. "If that's the testimony you are going to give, so be it."

And then "Buffalo Man" brought in Dalton and me. I spoke first, "Mr. Armey, I see you found *my witness*. Having a pleasant chat?"

"We had one, at that, on just a few ministerial matters."

"Ministerial. I guess you mean which opinion was file- stamped first?" I went straight for the kill-shot. "I expect to be able to speak with my witness," I said to Armey, in a demanding voice.

Deputy-Clerk Morrison smiled at me, in a politely professional way. I extended my hand to her, to ease her out of her chair, so we could chat outside the anteroom.

She introduced herself. "Yes; Deputy-Clerk Morrison. Pleased to meet you, Mr. McRain." I introduced Dalton and myself and suggested we step outside, for a customary, pre-deposition interview of a witness. But, as I put my hand on Ms. Morrison's elbow to assist her out the doorway, Armey sprang from his chair and slugged me in the left jaw.

It was the damndest thing you ever saw, and it caught me totally by surprise. Dalton, too. He was all the way on the other side of the conference table, setting down his briefcase in preparation for the deposition. "Unhand her. Stop mauling her, you sonofabitch." Armey was making things up as he went, kind of improvising an excuse to start a fight.

After that, everything seemed to happen in slow motion. Armey hit me in the very spot where I'd first been struck by the bullies, that day in 1969, at the park, when I was beaten within an inch of my life. I was half knocked out, on my feet, looking out into the hallway, past "Buffalo Man," seated in a wooden chair, who was looking at a *"National Geographic."* Then something clicked, down inside my psyche, and I went into a flurry of hand-to-hand-combat action. I used my adrenalin as a super-charger for my fight.

It came to me, in an epiphany that hit me like a night train, like Armey's sucker-punch. I realized that Armey had to stop the deposition some way, somehow, to stop the truth from being told. Great Lord of Mercy. Armey never realized what he did. Being struck in the same place my childhood assailants hit me caused me to flash through, in a few seconds, what had taken me years to forget—the beating, the torture. As a victim of violence, I responded like a gut-shot bear. I grabbed Armey by the throat and threw him back, onto the conference table.

I mounted Armey, with a knee on either side of his chest. I slapped him, openhanded, back and forth, forehand and backhand, so hard that I lost feeling in my hand. But I continued to slap him because punching would have been too good for him. I wanted to humiliate Armey, and by slapping him, I would dispense with him as a man dispenses a weakling. I wanted to embarrass Armey and expose the government's whole case as a scheme to convict Casteel, an innocent man. To get in the face of the rich and powerful. People who believe they can twist the truth and run the world, at the expense of the little man.

I was accustomed to keeping my head straight in harsh and unforgiving conditions. But that training and experience were not applied as I continued to slap Armey, cursing a blue streak. The "Buffalo Man" barreled into the room and grabbed my hand in mid-swing. He applied a submissive hold, bending my fingers backwards, to get me to stop slapping Armey.

CHAPTER 99

All the while, "Buffalo Man" shouted for my submission. I protested, through the pain, "You trump up these charges against my client; you monitor me; you attack my sister; you kill our dog; you threaten my secretary; and now you punch me, you son-of-a-bitch."

At that point, "Buffalo Man" had my fingers bent all the way to the back of my hand, expecting either that they would break off or I would drop to my knees in pain. I drew on a spirit of calm as I held up the index finger of my free hand and said to "Buffalo Man," "I'll be with you in a minute, kind sir." His eyes blazed in alarm.

"Buffalo Man" was trying to exert a maximum amount of pain on me by contorting my fingers. I turned my free index finger to Armey, pointing it at him in a clear threat. All I did was point, and Armey knew that he was dealing with an opponent, the likes of whom, he had never seen before.

He tried to slide out the door, but not before Dalton grabbed Armey by the collar, "You're not getting away, geek."

It was a Mexican standoff, Dalton to Armey and "Buffalo Man" to me, with Ms. Morrison in the middle. She stomped her foot and made a fist of her own, hammering it on the conference table, "Order. I need order."

"Buffalo Man" protested, "He's under arrest."

I came back, "I could bring my palm up to your nose, shoving it into your brain, to kill you and perhaps bring a little color to this action."

Ms. Morrison demanded "Buffalo Man" release me, and she demanded the same of Dalton. "Good, now we can all act like professionals." Armey had been insulted—as a man and as a lawyer. He would be the brunt of jokes in every watering hole in Washington. He'd be known as the guy who got "bitch slapped" at a deposition after *he* picked the fight. He never would live it down.

Armey took one last shot at me. I dodged the punch and counterpunched so hard, I laid Armey out, on his back. Deputy-Clerk Morrison looked after Armey, as "Buffalo Man" pulled my hands behind my back and applied cuffs. "Sorry for the colorful language, Ma'am," I said.

We all exited the room, and I heard the court reporter say, "I think I got all of that."

# CHAPTER 100

# THE FULL NELSON

Dalton, Armey, Ms. Morrison, and I were led to the plush chambers of Chief Justice Nelson. Seated in Justice Nelson's chambers was the only black Justice on the Supreme Court, Justice Jackson. Chief Justice Nelson had just finished meeting with Justice Jackson about an opinion they were writing together. Jackson got up, inadvertently leaving his tape recorder on the Chief Justice's desk, by Noreen's picture. The recorder had been used, as a tool by the two Justices, to direct the law clerks how to write the opinion by Nelson and Jackson. Justice Jackson said, as he stood to leave, "Looks like you got a bit of refereeing to do here."

When we passed by Jackson, he said to me, "From what I saw, you're definitely a Marine."

I did not know what he was talking about. I could not understand how he saw anything, since he had not been present in the room where the fight occurred. Nelson gave Jackson a cold look, which only made Jackson smile. He shrugged his shoulders and left. He forgot his small tape recorder, still running.

"Let me show you something, gentlemen," Nelson motioned to our group. He pushed a button under his desk, and a wall across from his desk slid aside, to reveal a number of television screens, displaying different locations within the Supreme Court building. He pushed another button, displaying a replay of the fight that had just occurred. He hobbled over to the screen and pointed at it.

"This, gentlemen, and I use that term loosely, is unacceptable behavior in my courthouse."

We all hung our heads, except for Ms. Morrison, who stood defiant. "Due to technical difficulties, I don't have anything on this surveillance except you, Mr. McRain, jumping on Mr. Armey, beating him senseless, and defying a federal deputy marshal.

I tried to defend myself, "Mr. Chief Justice, he punched me first."

Nelson was unsympathetic, "Or, as they now call the evidence, a digital file, Mr. McRain."

"Buffalo Man" piped up, "It's true; Armey punched McRain first." All it took was a look from Nelson for "Buffalo Man" to shut up. Nelson redirected his attention to me.

"You're the same Mike McRain they call 'Psycho Mike-O' on CNN, isn't that right? For helping your sister to beat a reporter? You're the same Michael O'Brien McRain who is listed in the registry of lawyers certified to practice in front of this court, isn't that right?"

I answered in the affirmative. Guilty on all counts of the one-sided indictment Nelson was spinning.

"You're the same Michael O'Brien McRain who is under investigation for torturing a prisoner in an elevator at a courthouse? Isn't that right? Give me a reason why I should not disbar you this very second."

"Sir, these are only allegations, and they are not true. I am innocent until proven guilty?"

"Well, here in my courthouse, I don't need a jury. I can make a decision right now." He pushed another button and replayed the 'Psycho Mike-O' segment on CNN, where I was using a painful Aikido hold on the serial rapist in the elevator, "Slasher."

"Just allegations, huh, Mr. McRain?" Nelson shuffled back behind his desk.

I spoke up, "The law is not a bar of steel, but a willow branch, strong and flexible. It is meant to provide remedies, not excuses." I showed off my photographic memory, "United States v. Detweiler."

Nelson was surprised, "In my dissent, no less."

"Footnote Twelve."

Justice Nelson looked at me as though he should be concerned that he had underestimated me. He did it all with his eyes, his facial expression, his

CHAPTER 100

body language. He looked me up and down, reassigning me to the category of top-drawer threats.

"I will settle this issue this afternoon. You will take my sworn statement to settle this matter of which was filed first, 'Gordon' or 'Casteel.' Three p.m., today, in the main courtroom. You are dismissed."

"Sir, how can you say which one was filed first?"

"I was there."

Dalton and I raised our eyebrows in doubt. We all left, except for Deputy-Clerk Morrison.

# CHAPTER 101

# SCANDAL - SCANDAL

Nelson's door was closed. He spoke to Deputy-Clerk Morrison with authority and familiarity. "What were you thinking, to offer testimony that you file-stamped the 'Gordon' opinion before the 'Casteel' denial?"

"It was the truth."

"Is this still something festering between us? I thought we had this settled a long time ago, with quite a sizeable sum, plus I paid for your night-school law classes."

Chief Justice Nelson and Deputy-Clerk Morrison had a shared, dark past. Newly widowed by the Vietnam War, she had sought solace from Justice Nelson, as a father figure. Nelson took advantage of the situation. He even voted for "Roe v. Wade," to get rid of his little growing problem in Ms. Morrison's womb. Anita Morrison believed Nelson's baby had been Heaven-sent, to carry her through the profound heartbreak of losing her husband, her high school sweetheart, who had died months earlier in a Vietnamese ambush.

Back then, a pregnant Anita Morrison, thinking she had fainted, actually had been rendered unconscious, then whisked away, to Walter Reed Army Hospital, for a quick abortion by a government doctor, who stated she must abort the baby to save her life. He falsely represented to her that she had a life-threatening medical condition, when one did not exist. The abortion was botched and rendered her sterile. Because of the abortion procedure, she'd spent a month in the psychiatric ward, involuntarily. Nelson swept it all under the rug with money, and he got her into a local law school—on a fully paid sabbatical—to take her mind off her loss. Morrison went through law school at the expense of Uncle Sam.

Anita Morrison thought to herself, "*Well, Mr. High and Mighty, I've waited a long time for this opportunity to give you pain. What goes around, comes around.*"

"Am I excused, sir, or should I say, Sid, or, perhaps, 'SIN;' that is what your initials spell, you know?" Nelson knew, all too well: Sidney Ignatius Nelson, VI. Five before him had been stuck with those initials.

They glared at each other. Morrison walked to the door.

Nelson took a verbal stab at her under his breath, "Dumb bitch."

Morrison heard it. She clenched her nails into the doorjamb. She'd known pain at his hands, and she wanted to return the favor. He was the reason she had an empty house, no child and no grandchildren. She would make Nelson pay.

She hurried downstairs and caught me before I left the building.

CHAPTER 101

# CHAPTER 102

*"I find oral argument and athletic competition*
*to be a lot alike. Any time I tried to do either*
*one of them, without emotion,*
*I got skunked."*
—The Truth Warrior

Chief Justice Nelson sat in the middle of the bench of the main courtroom, the bench on which nine Justices usually sat. A court reporter was seated down one level and to the near right, pecking away in prelude to the historic deposition about to occur. Chief Justice Nelson was the chief administrative officer of the United States Supreme Court. He had authority over all administrative matters, including the filing and sealing of court orders, and that included "Gordon" and "Casteel."

The government's attorney, Assistant Solicitor-General Armey, was seated at counsel table on the right, looking like a raccoon, with two black eyes from my hammering his face. Dalton and I sat at counsel table on the left. Three large, Deputy U.S. Marshals, with "Buffalo Man" in the middle, stood guard in front of Justice Nelson's bench.

~~~~~~~~~~~~~~~~~~~~~~~~~~~~~~~~~~~~~~~~~~~~~~~

Back in Nelson's chambers, Colonel Durant sat, with his feet on Justice Nelson's desk, watching on the Court's closed- circuit, surveillance system. He cheered his cause, "Get this over with, pronto."

~~~~~~~~~~~~~~~~~~~~~~~~~~~~~~~~~~~~~~~~~~~~~~~

Back in the courtroom, Assistant Solicitor Armey stood to address Justice Nelson. "Your Honor, before this proceeding begins, I make a motion to quash Mr. McRain's subpoena."

"Overruled. Judge Lackey already ruled on its sufficiency. And, besides, this bumpkin is from the sticks." He rubbed his temple to stir his memory. "Where is it? Oh, yes, St. Martinsville. Thinks he can outwit me."

I stood to address Justice Nelson. The court reporter, young and flustered, kept her head low and her fingers fast. I walked to the podium and addressed the room. "May it please the Court, Mr. Armey, Your Honor. The legal and factual question before us, Your Honor, is, 'Do you run this court, or don't you?'"

~~~~~~~~~~~~~~~~~~~~~~~~~~~~~~~~~~~~~~~~~~~~~~~

In Judge Nelson's chambers, Colonel Durant was nervous, as he watched on the closed-circuit T.V. monitor.

"End it now, Nelson. Don't even let him step into the ring with you." Durant knew that Nelson was like a cat, wanting to play with his meal before he ate it. Durant jumped up and down in protest in Nelson's chambers.

Durant looked at Nelson's desk and saw that the white rosary, that previously had adorned Noreen Nelson's photograph, was missing.

~~~~~~~~~~~~~~~~~~~~~~~~~~~~~~~~~~~~~~~~~~~~~~~

"I am the Chief Justice, Mr. McRain. Of course, I run this Court. That, you can be sure of. And I run a tight ship, too." He paused, like he was reloading a shotgun. "I know everything about my courthouse."

~~~~~~~~~~~~~~~~~~~~~~~~~~~~~~~~~~~~~~~~~~~~~~~

Durant was coming unglued. He stood up, walked over to the monitor, and pointed at it, "You idiot, just walk away, and we win."

~~~~~~~~~~~~~~~~~~~~~~~~~~~~~~~~~~~~~~~~~~~~~~~

Durant watched Assistant Deputy-Solicitor Armey pose a question to Nelson.

"Your Honor, could you please state, for the record, which Order was sealed first, 'Gordon' or 'Casteel.'"

CHAPTER 101

This was the sixty-thousand-dollar question. The answer to which determined if Jake Casteel went in history books as a free man or a convicted felon. And if he ended up a convicted felon, he would no longer be able to run the railroad union. The Hoffa Protocol would be fulfilled. They would have stopped a nationwide strike. They would have stopped an economic debacle. And they would have disgraced Lady Justice.

Nelson testified, "Yes, I specifically recall that, at precisely one p.m., immediately after lunch, the 'Casteel' order was sealed. Then, at two p.m., the 'Gordon' order was sealed. I remember this because I was in the Clerk's office, helping with the slow procedure of twisting the fly for the pressing of the seal."

Dalton and I looked at each other, like we thought Nelson was lying. And he was. "That's all the questions I have," said Deputy Solicitor Armey. He looked at me, much too smug, if the proceedings were on the up and up. "Your witness." Chief justice Nelson stood and, using his cane as slowly as molasses pouring, started to move off the bench.

I was surprised, and I objected, "Your Honor, I must cross-examine you."

Nelson played dumb, "Cross-examine me?" He laughed, "You got your testimony; I'm done with you—forever." He pointed his cane to the court reporter. "Miss, you are excused. This hearing is finished."

I held up my hand to stop her, "Miss, if I'm talkin', you're typin'." Dalton and I exchanged shrugs and pointed at the court reporter, who had stood to leave, but sat back down. Nelson was angry and showed his temper.

"How dare you contradict my order, Mr. McRain. I am the lord of this house." He pointed his cane at me, as if he were in a duel, holding a long-barreled pistol. You Cretins exist at my mercy. He laughed and pointed his cane upwards. "Who is going to overrule me?"

Dalton tugged at my sleeve. I turned to listen. "Something's fishy. Looks like Casteel was right about the fix being in."

"I know. Fishy. Very fishy." I thought about the word "fishy." Something about that struck me as familiar. I snapped my fingers. "From the mouths of babes; Bridget's advice: a fish'll get caught if he opens his mouth."

Dalton didn't understand, "Wrong time for 'Field and Stream' stories."

"No, don't you understand? We gotta get the fish to open his mouth, get Nelson talkin," I said, as I turned back towards the podium. By that time, Nelson was off the bench and was being assisted down the steps by his orderly. I shouted, "Objection. Under the full and fair litigation guarantees of the Due Process Clause of the Constitution." I shrugged at Dalton.

"Overruled. You're wasting your careers." Justice Nelson stopped He drew his cane across his throat, in a slicing motion, a sign of death. I turned back to Dalton, who was hovering above my chair. Throughout Dalton Dennis Boyle's life, he had met adversity and high-pressure situations head on, with a smart-aleck joke and an in-your-face follow through. Even in the darkest situations, he was undaunted if he could find humor.

"If we're fishin,' we need some bait," I said. And then I knew what would come next. I could see my law partner was petrified and he wanted to crack some jokes to break the deadly serious air that Nelson had cast by promising we would lose our law licenses if we pushed too far.

"Well, he thinks he's God, so tell him the one where the archaeologist says that Moses couldn't have been a lawyer because the Ten Commandments are short and make sense."

I shook my head no. At least my buddy was entering the fight with me.

"Okay, then ask him if he heard the one about the lawyer's favorite song—'A Boy Named Sue.'"

I was imperative, and said, "Shut up with the corny jokes." Then I had an idea, "Wait a minute."

Nelson was now at the bottom of the steps and was about to exit behind the curtain.

"We don't have a minute," Dalton said.

"What's the one thing judges like to hear, most of all?"

"Their own words," Dalton said.

I snapped my fingers and returned to the podium, where I shouted, loud and clear, "The right to cross-examine shall never be violated. 'Abernathy v Public Service.'"

CHAPTER 101

Nelson popped his hand to his ear, hesitating at the curtain. Rone had seen Nelson's face growing blood red, as though he would soon fail. The orderly extended a bottle of heart medicine to Nelson to take, but the Justice inadvertently struck it out Rone's hand. The judge was visibly shaken, but riled. Even though he was getting close to a century old, he was ready for a fight. He was doing this for family. To have Designations held by his two sons would ensure that his grandchildren would live in luxury the rest of their lives.

~~~~~~~~~~~~~~~~~~~~~~~~~~~~~~~~~~~~~~~~~~~~~~~~~~~~~~

Back in Nelson's office, Durant was jumping up and down in protest. He banged his fist on the desk that fostered legendary opinions.

"Keep walking, you old fool. Don't stop. Follow the protocol!"

~~~~~~~~~~~~~~~~~~~~~~~~~~~~~~~~~~~~~~~~~~~~~~~~~~~~~~

Dalton gave me a thumbs-up as Chief Justice Nelson chortled, "My opinion, 375 U.S., at page 1207."

Dalton was my cheerleader, speaking to me in a stage whisper, "Set the hook."

I served another volley of *stare decises*, "Cross-examination is the test by fire required of all witnesses." Nelson had started back up the bench steps, but stopped as he responded, "'Senko v. LaCrosse Dredging,' 1957, one of my more plenary decisions."

I said, "Volume 352, U.S., at page 371."

Nelson couldn't stand to be outdone, "At headnote 10."

I looked over at Dalton, who was pantomiming his excitement that I had snared the judge. First, with his finger hooked inside his mouth, he acted like a flopping fish; then he acted like he was pulling against a fishing rod, reeling in a catch. Nelson was out of wind by the top of the stairs. His orderly shook his head in disapproval.

"Cross-examination is the bedrock of litigation. Without it, no case can withstand the withering gale of a Supreme Court review," I said, loud and confident.

Nelson raised his cane again, "'Terminiello v. Louisiana.'"

I had the audacity to interrupt the Judge by citing the case. "At 132, Lawyers Edition, page 444."

"You dare to cite Lawyers Edition in my Court? I'll disbar you just for that." Nelson referred to the longstanding rule for proper reference to past cases, The Harvard Blue Book of Uniform Citation.

I was undaunted, "At footnote 13."

It wasn't an oral argument. It wasn't anything civilized. It was an alley fight, fought with lungs and tongues, between men who meant each other harm. Nelson glared at me and resumed his original seat. His face was flushed with red, and a mountain-range of bulging veins had surfaced on his bald head. I motioned to Dalton to get something. Dalton passed behind me, offering me further support. "Keep him on the line; I'll get the gaff." Dalton walked straight to the door and motioned to someone standing just outside.

Chief Justice Nelson was now in a full, blustering gale. "Mr. McRain, you have tossed down the gauntlet—daring to match wits with me—and I have picked it up. As we speak, I am drafting the Order disbarring you from this and every court in America. Forever."

# CHAPTER 103

# "THE CONSTITUTION" VS. "THE NELSON"

I released my iron grip on the courtroom podium, and I walked to the middle of the dais, directly in front of Chief Justice Nelson, holding my arms out from my sides, my palms up. To anger Nelson even more, I thought I might tilt my head back, parading around the courtroom and howling to the ceiling while I flailed my arms and ran my fingers through my hair, like professional wrestler, 'Nature Boy,' Rick Flair. I wanted to get Nelson angry enough to make a dumb move on which I could capitalize.

My second thoughts were even more audacious.

Instead of putting on a show like a professional wrestler, I stood as if stunned, speechless while I watched Nelson draw up the death warrant for my legal career. Nelson's geriatric hand moved, slow and laborious, over the document he wrote with a 1950's-era fountain pen. He tapped the pen's gold-colored tip on the blotter a few times, to bring more ink to its point. While I waited for the old bully to finish off my life's ambitions, in the blink of an eye, I felt as if I had been struck by one of Bridget's prayers. My mind slipped into synaptic shadows, and I could see into my soul. There, I found strength and a vision of the future. I saw it all play out, in scant moments of time, as though I were a combatant aboard "The Constitution." Our souls were at stake—damn it.

*In the universe of my soul, the Seas of Purgatory churned black and violent with war. Innocent Bridget's prayers for the damned materialized, becoming militant in my famished breast. The mighty Captain James Cormac Carion commanded "The Constitution." At times, it seemed that his will, alone, carried our fight against Chief Justice Sidney Ignatius Nelson, the oppressor of good men everywhere. The immortal combat was on. It unfolded in my soul, as* it progressed in the Supreme Court. One was rooted in the other, and they became a swirling, spiritual mixture of the world and the divine. I was in the flow.

"The Nelson" was a man o' war, a massive, four-masted warship, sailing under the colors of corrupt law—the black flag of oppression. Never, in the history of men's souls, did a more powerful ship sail the Purgatory Seas than "The Nelson." She sported one hundred and three cannons of Hell's fury. And, making matters appear more bleak for "The Constitution," "The Nelson" was battle-hardened by war in the world, sailing undefeated in the ancient quest to corrupt the birthright of good men: freedom.

"The Nelson"'s voyages dated back over two hundred years, to its involvement in the English Crown's despicable act of operating it's Court of Star Chamber, where Perjury on Admiralty was first hatched, to deny fair trials to enemies of the Crown. Casteel's case was one of the last vestiges of such oppression, in America. That is, until The Terror Attack, yet to come, some years later, where the practice of Star Chamber was revisited under a similar claim of righteousness by the C.I.A.

"The Constitution," on the other hand, presented no easy dunking. Launched on October 21, 1797, she was a three-masted, forty-four-gun, heavy frigate, built for speed and brute strength. She entered the fray, under Carion's tough command, as a brash, untested claimant to the ideals of freedom and liberty and justice for all.

Although she carried more cannons, "The Nelson" was slower than her adversary, "The Constitution," which flew like an angel-winged prayer across the water. "The Nelson" plowed the seas with deep-drafting deliberateness. To Carion, such sluggishness was a sign that Nelson and his crew were much too confident.

Mr. Troubles ran up a blood-red banner, for freedom, and a blue one, for justice, upon his captain's brash order, "Now be showing our colors to the world, Mr. Troubles. And make it fast; I want her to know who will be taking her booty." Carion laughed, "The souls of Nelson and his merry crew, that is. Now be off with ya, ya lazy, Irish lout."

The two great ships stood, off from each other, yet close, in angry anticipation of their inevitable clash. Each ship's captain navigated his vessel to steal a tactical advantage. They were like two champion boxers, within each other's reach: circling, bobbing, and weaving, as the sea swelled and pitched. It was the eternal struggle, a timeless battle that would be repeated, again and again, throughout the ages. On its outcome was wagered not only Jake Casteel's innocence, but also the souls of "The Constitution" and "The Nelson."

CHAPTER 103

*Winner, take all—salvation. The losers were bound for Hell. Purgatory or damned for all eternity.*

*"The Constitution's" crew froze in fear when they heard Mr. Beelzebub's devilish, howling laughter rise from below. They knew he would take a bevy of souls to Hell that day. From which ship, they knew, he did not care.*

*"The Nelson" fired the first volley. A withering broadside from the most powerful cannons in the world. It rocked "The Constitution," down to its strongest buttress—an impartial judiciary. Carion was red-faced, blustering and swearing to allow Nelson no quarter to escape. "Fire, you buggery bastards, fire! For God and Glory, it be. We'll chase the blue-blooded bastards to the end of the seas."*

*In my heart and soul, Captain Carion, screamed encouragement to my tongue, that it might act as a warrior of truth. To finish my fight with Chief Justice Nelson. Now.*

*"And we'll be taking no prisoners, laddies, no prisoners at all."*

*Again and again, "The Constitution's" righteous, thirty-two pounder cannonades of courage fired: courage to pray openly; courage to speak the truth in the face of threats and ridicule; courage to stay the course, when representing a man who was much more a liability than an asset; and, of course, the courage of faith. All opened up on "The Nelson," ripping huge holes in her hull and destroying two of her three port gun-decks. Nevertheless, for what seemed an eternity, "The Constitution" took as much as she gave, although her hull did not give way, as did "The Nelson's." The battle between innocence and evil was harrowing.*

*Carion raised his cutlass, a Marine Officer's sword, into the air. "Give them the cannonballs of truth."*

*The unsung heroes, "The Constitution's" powder monkeys, carried the day. The souls of brave men who, filled with courage and stamina from Bridget's prayers and devotions, ran below deck, sprinting past the clutches of Mr. Beelzebub, to bring to the gun-deck the black powder of prayers and the cannonballs of truth. For truth first is forged in Hell's furnace of fear, and is told only by Heaven-made cannons of courage.*

*"The Constitution" weathered a blistering barrage of grape- shot, fired from "The Nelson's" bow chaser in a surprise, out-of-position, strike. It blasted holes in "The Constitution's" sails and ripped into some of its rigging, but the iron balls had no impact on the crew, the spirits of "The Constitution." The grape-shot passed right through them. Nelson realized, too late, that the spirit of "The Constitution", e pluribus Unum, could not be killed, for it was manned by Bridget's and a legion of others' prayers. In God we trust.*

THE REDEEMER: IT IS WRITTEN

*Chief Justice Nelson's minions fought hard for their cause—greed. "The Nelson's" cannons blasted round after round of hellish, twenty-four pounders, which struck "The Constitution," square. But the cannonballs merely bounced off the ship's side and dropped into the black seas of Purgatory. Ironically, the aged commander of "The Nelson" never knew that Admiral Jaundice, personally, had provided wooden stock most special and secret for the impenetrable inner layer, or soul, of "The Constitution's" hull. It was Southern Live Oak, which grows only in the land of the free and the home of the brave.*

*Nelson realized his worst horror: "Old Ironsides" could not be breached. He could not corrupt "The Constitution."*

*The seas teamed with the demons of Hell, swarming in anticipation of a feast, upon souls soon to be damned forever. It was then that Nelson understood he would be dunked and drowned, with no hope of salvation. Only eternal suffering in the infinite, deep and bestial waters of Hell awaited the loser. He was the captain. He would go down with his ship of lies, lies that he used to convict Jake Casteel. The practice of Star Chamber would sink.*

*The Chief Justice saw he would not win. But, instead of surrendering to Carion with honor, and admitting his sins, he stayed true to character, electing the course of a scoundrel. He tried to make a quick escape. Nelson still planned to leave his sons the millions of dollars per year in income the Di Trina Designations were sure to bring. That kind of money would provide for his family for many years to come. Greed for dynastic wealth. The type of wealth a judge would never obtain—not legally.*

*Bridget and her rosaries worked a miracle. The power of her prayers had become eternal, imperishable, like oak and steel, to protect "The Constitution" and stop Nelson's devious plan. But supreme victory over Nelson required more than a great defense. It required a Hell-born offensive; it required the truth. Wicked men prevail when good men do nothing. Nelson ran from the truth. But Carion pressed and pursued the fight.*

*The ships exchanged three more, torrid fusillades of cannon fire, and the smoke cleared. Mr. Troubles saw "The Nelson's" main mast had been blown into splinters. It laid across her deck, dipping into the Hellish waters. He waved his tri-colored hat in the air and let go a whoop. "The Nelson" was dead in the water.*

*Mr. Fetid rubbed together his skin-on-skeleton hands. "We should take her, Cap'n; she's but a crippled goose."*

CHAPTER 103

*Immediately, Carion saw his chance to end a three-hundred-year-long voyage for redemption. "Fix your blades and cutlasses, and prepare to board. Sharpshooters to the riggings. Toss the nets, and board her now. Board her, and claim our salvation."*

*What happened next was a crushing blow to "The Nelson's" original mission—to convict an innocent man. On a special dispatch from Admiral Jaundice, the spirit of Saint Michael the Archangel, the warrior angel, interceded, filling my heart with his superhuman strength, the spirit of the truthful and righteous. I argued in the Supreme Court with the power of the very angel who had vanquished Satan himself.*

My fantasy dissolved into the soft bars of the Marine Corps Hymn, and—elevated—I felt the music vibrate in my heart. I saw it clearly. Victory would be ours! We must stay the course and press the fight, no matter if Nelson disbarred us.

Dalton saw my blank face and wondered what it was that had mesmerized me.

"Mike, you Okay?" he said, as he touched my shoulder. I sloughed him off kindly. Looking at Dalton, I nodded towards Nelson. "Shame on him who evil thinks."

I realized I must engage the enemy—Chief Justice Nelson.

As quickly as I had zoned out, I returned to the world, where I found myself in the United States Supreme Court, cross-examining Chief Justice Nelson. I felt "The Constitution's" colors course through my heart. We were at battle—for truth, for justice. As I became more fervent, I was masterful in my oral argument. I spat words from my tongue, which swung like a Marine's cutlass, slicing through Nelson's weak armor of deceit and down to his frail bones of corruption.

The coaching Captain Carion had forced on me, the drilling in the tongues of great orators, paid off now. Nelson was about to slip out the exit door.

The world stopped as I spoke.

That moment, I will remember forever. It was the moment Chief Justice Nelson blinked.

Chief Justice Nelson stopped writing. He was made drunk by his unlimited judicial power. He brought down his gavel like one of Zeus's thunderbolts, ruling like a god, with great anger, by self-serving fiat. "I've heard enough of your off-point nonsense, you dolt. Get on with your examination! Now! Now! So I can watch you fall on your rusty sword of backwards logic."

At last, I had engaged my opponent.

CHAPTER 103

# CHAPTER 104

*"We do not remember days,*
*we remember moments."*
—César Pavese

In a very odd way, my past, killing men with my hands and a blade, had been a spiritual experience for me. From it, I knew, positively, that there is an afterlife.

I will never forget the first time I killed a man with a knife. When you force a piece of metal into a man, you hear the air escape from him. You also feel his life force and his spirit slowly weeping out. It changes you. Forever. Nothing else comes close to it. In law, forcing the truth into a man's mouth and then ripping out his honor is called cross-examination. It changes you, too. Into a wicked, demeaning bastard. You get a charge from both, a sick and inescapable excitement for accomplishment, which you cannot loathe if you are to do your duty. Detached from the acts, you therefore embrace each, and the murders of both man and honor are sanctified as necessary evils.

Like my namesake, Saint Michael the Archangel, I was a warrior—a warrior of truth.

Chief Justice Sydney Ignatius Nelson was playing right into my legal strategy. He persisted in his ornery, overconfident demeanor. He was an adverse witness. He was my opponent. As he was my opponent, I had to make Nelson do something, admit something, testify to something that would help Jake Casteel.

I love to cross-examine overconfident opponents. They are the easiest to defeat. Especially in a courtroom, in a metaphorical swordfight for the truth. On the witness stand, an opposing witness' overconfidence almost always produces sloppy recollection. Like a bullfighter with his sword, I knew when and where to stab the blades of truth to make the bull,

Nelson, angry and overconfident and charge at me. Chief Justice Nelson was definitely like a bull, and he charged at me, too confident. But I was about to find out that my strategy works only when the witness is *accountable* to someone. When the threat of a perjury charge hangs overhead like the sword of Damocles. My evidence, my sword of truth, appeared to have no effect on Nelson. None at all. Sadly, even the United States Constitution itself could not make Chief Justice Nelson accountable, save for a possible Congressional impeachment. And that minute chance could not come in time for my client, Jake Casteel.

I wanted to vomit when I thought about how the government was wasting taxpayers' money, litigating such a silly, silly legal issue. For God's sake, the Supreme Court created the "Gordon" rule *on the same day* it ruled against Casteel. By sticking to the Hoffa Protocol, Nelson made the court do something embarrassing—creating inconsistent results in two different, but identical, cases, *on the same day.*

Worse, the high Court had a longstanding rule that an appellant could benefit by a new rule only if that new rule existed *before* their appeal was decided. The government's lawyer, Assistant Solicitor-General H.T. Armey was a smart aleck about the government's bankrupt reasoning and obvious lack of common sense. He barely kept a straight face when he told us Jake could not use the Gordon Rule. Armey taunted us that the "Gordon" rule allegedly had been created after the Supreme Court ruled against Casteel, by mere minutes.

It was stupid.

It was intellectually dishonest.

It was our tax dollars, hard at work.

At the podium, I was facing off against the most powerful judge in the world. I would put on only a token defense to Nelson's threat to take law licenses. I needed to save my ammo for the real fight. I knew I must hurry in my cross-examination because I would be granted very little time with my primary target, Chief Justice Nelson.

"If you can take my license that easily, I don't want it," I said.

"Proceed to your folly."

"Your Honor, please tell me where you were standing when you allegedly saw the 'Casteel' order sealed before the 'Gordon' order?"

"I was standing three feet from the seal, helping to throw its fly."

"And you stated that Casteel lost because the new rule in 'Gordon' did not exist before the 'Casteel' denial was sealed?"

"You can read. That's what it says," said Nelson, who now was tiring, like a boxer in the last round of a championship bout. "But, Mr. McRain, this line of questioning is redundant drivel. I already testified the 'Gordon' rule did not exist until after the 'Casteel' order was sealed and made final and official."

I motioned to Dalton, still stationed at the courtroom door, now was the moment to bring in the person who had been waiting outside the door. Deputy Clerk Morrison wheeled in a cart containing a television and video equipment.

"I realize that, Your Honor, so I subpoenaed the Court's surveillance database for the day in question."

"And where did you get access to that database, Mr. McRain?"

I could not tell the Chief Justice that it was Raford who had located the database—through a confidential source, a hush-hush friend at the Treasury Department. He, in turn, had isolated the day in question, obtained the exact database coordinates and corresponding digital file, and given those to me. I specified the name and location of the digital file in the subpoena I'd had served on Deputy Clerk Morrison. She was more than happy to oblige our case if it could impact the downfall of Nelson.

"I subpoenaed it, Your Honor."

Nelson's eyebrows rose, and Assistant Solicitor Armey jumped up and objected. But Nelson batted aside the objection, with an analogy that revealed that he was a Civil War buff. "We're beyond objections, Mr. Solicitor; now it's down to blood and bayonets. Mr. McRain is reenacting Picket's suicide charge at Gettysburg, in a vain attempt to recapture his lost honor, like cowardly General Garnett." In shock, Armey slowly sat back down. His instincts told him he was about to bear witness to an unfolding legal massacre.

As long as Nelson was drawing energy for our legal battle from the Battle of Gettysburg, I would think of myself as Chamberlain, leader of Maine's Second at Little Round Top. When they ran out of ammunition, they fixed bayonets to charge into history, victorious. But if Nelson would have it that I take a role in Pickett's suicide charge, I was willing to sacrifice my legal career as General Garnett had sacrificed his life, leading a charge into certain death to restore his lost honor. Posthumously. I, like the Confederate general, had a matter of honor to resolve - a charge of cowardice. I had to clear my name with the dead.

If Nelson wanted to kill my legal career by disbarring me, so be it. Damn it; I was going to go down, slicing and swinging and shooting.

I was getting that little spark that Special Force operatives get when they first drop into a hot landing zone. Time and reality start to bend, like a length of rope. Fifty seconds is like an eternity. Everything seems to move in slow motion. This distorted combat universe is fully contained and can be turned to an operative's benefit only by his training, and by God. I knew that now was attack time. Time to draw blades of argument, time to charge Nelson and his unscrupulous position.

Nelson addressed me, "Go ahead; bring in your artillery. It's useless. I'm untouchable. Look," Nelson motioned towards the dormant court reporter. She sat, a mere spectator, recording nothing. "You have no record. No review is possible. You're desperate." Nelson paused for emphasis, "That's the sign of a dying man. This is your endgame, Mr. McRain."

I pointed to the picture on the television screen. "Your Honor, this shows the area in the clerk's office where the Court's orders are sealed. This picture is of the area at 1 p.m. the day 'Gordon' and 'Casteel' were sealed. But you are nowhere to be seen. Isn't that rather odd, since you said you were there at that time?"

Armey objected vigorously, but was batted down again by Nelson.

"Denied, summarily."

"Let's cut to the quick." I motioned to Deputy Morrison, "Give me a blow-up of the sealing of the 'Gordon' order."

CHAPTER 103

Nelson's eyes were riveted on Morrison. Her eyes stabbed back at his. Theirs was an obvious mutual hatred, fueled by circumstances that burned in their hearts. It was as palpable as if clouds smoldered above their heads. You could see pure loathing in their eyes. They were deeply in need of prayer—and Rolaids.

The screen showed the case style, "United States v. Gordon," being sealed, with a time stamp in the lower right-hand corner of the screen reading "1:07 p.m." I said, "Now, please split the screen, and show the sealing of the 'Casteel' order."

Armey tried, in vain, to object. "This violates the Best Evidence Rule."

"Overruled. I'm going to give a dying man his last request," said Nelson.

The television now displayed, on the left half of the screen, the "Gordon" order– sealed at 1:07 p.m.—and, on the right half, that the "Casteel" order was sealed at 2:19 p.m. This was conclusive proof that "Casteel" should receive the benefit of the rule made in Gordon. That rule pre-existed when "Casteel" was sealed. He was as good as freed. Except that a lot of judicial deception and dishonor stood in his way.

"Now, sir, here they are, side by side. I respectfully request you take judicial notice that the government's own digital records prove the rule in 'Gordon' was created before you ruled on 'Casteel.' Jake Casteel should be acquitted."

"That doesn't prove anything. You still don't understand. I am the god of law. Proof means nothing in my court. The only thing that counts is which result I want." I was angry, and it showed, as I yelled, "Enlarge it." I directed my request to Nelson. "Look at the proof, sir."

"The proof means nothing."

I gave sharp, perfunctory orders to Clerk Morrison. "Make it larger." "Make it larger." "Make it larger." "Make it larger." With each demand, the screen enlarged the names and times, clearly reflecting that Nelson was lying and that Casteel should win.

Nelson blinked—a slow, long, deliberate blink—and his eyes started to roll back in his head, like a boxer who has just been punched, hard, and yet does not know that he's been knocked out. Chief Justice Nelson looked directly at Clerk Morrison, who granted him no emotion, only an unforgiving stare. His moment of guilt was upon him: for taking Anita Morrison's baby and for convicting an innocent man. A death march, like a somber symphony of silence, played for what seemed like an eternity—without time, with neither past nor future. In that damning instant, he was trapped and his black soul was stripped naked by truth. But Nelson fought God's calling and continued the fight, for fear of the dark stakes that he glimpsed momentarily in the other dimension beyond our world. He knew he held only a sliver of mortality.

I dared to point at my powerful witness, with a damning finger, as I indicted Nelson, on the most serious charges, "Rape Lady Justice no more."

"Lady Justice does my bidding," Nelson said.

"Then Justice is dead."

Nelson held up the order disbarring Dalton and me. He shrugged off Rone, who was trying to calm him. "This is your disbarment. A death warrant on your profession. After the clerk . . ." He turned white, "seals it . . . it's official." The Judge's eyes bulged. "This ends the . . ." Justice Nelson's head hit the dais with a loud and resounding thud that reverberated throughout the world.

# CHAPTER 105

# PLAN B

Back in Chief Justice Nelson's chambers, the wheels of justice stopped. At least, the C.I.A.'s version of the wheels of justice. Colonel Durant threw Chief Justice Nelson's desk nameplate, like a major league pitcher, launching it straight into the T.V. screen, smashing it He could not believe that Nelson had gone toe-to-toe with Mike McRain.

Durant spoke aloud to the justice's empty chambers, in plain disgust, "That's why judges don't run the C.I.A. Bunch of egotistical sunza bitches!"

Durant realized a sure result of Nelson's collapse that day, and his resulting, imminent death, was that Jake Casteel would win. Soon, there would be an interim, unofficial, Chief Justice of the Supreme Court. Most probably, Justice Jackson. And the result of that would be honest—Casteel's acquittal. Justice Jackson still had a Boy Scout's attitude about the law, believing it was there for blind justice, not just as a tool for the rich and powerful.

Durant knew better. He knew how things *really* worked. He had taken the time to read the full dossier on Walter Sheridan, the famous C.I.A. operative. Sheridan, who was not a lawyer, spearheaded all the different prosecutions of Jimmy Hoffa. The Hoffa Protocol had been formulated *before* Hoffa was killed. Back then, it was called the Debs Protocol.

C.I.A. gave Bobby Kennedy the green light to create the infamous "'Get Hoffa' Squad," on the justification that Hoffa was a thief, which was never proven. But the C.I.A. simply wanted to convict Hoffa, so he could not hold union office. Killing Hoffa was sure to bring retaliatory, unofficial strikes from the Teamsters' truckers. The economy would take a hit, maybe even suffer a recession, when gas stations ran out of gasoline because the trucks were not delivering.

History.

Colonel Durant knew the real genesis for the Hoffa Protocol was the U.S. government's dealings with Eugene Debs and later in handling the

1946 rail strike. This predated the C.I.A., which was created in 1947, the secret, long-term, legislative fix President Truman requested in his rail-strike speech. C.I.A. began monitoring the international transportation unions back in 1947, and it never stopped.

Durant knew he'd failed, where Sheridan had succeeded.

Durant was a goner.

Colonel Durant knew he must think of what to do, now that he had squandered all the years of hard work C.I.A. had spent manipulating the world economy by preventing U.S. rail strikes and transportation stoppages.

Durant's mission had been a simple pop fly, a can o' corn. And Durant had dropped the ball.

The Colonel was angry. He had been forewarned by General Baker. The odds had been with Durant. The chance of winning a normal, federal, criminal case on appeal to the Supreme Court was over half a million to one, *without* the C.I.A. rigging the appeal.

McRain had won, against all odds. Durant thought, *"The lucky, God-damned Mick. Does he have a four-leaf clover tattooed on his ass?"* It made things worse when Durant admitted to himself that McRain wasn't just lucky. McRain was that good. Baker had been right. Colonel Durant made the stupidest mistake a trained warrior can make—he'd allowed his team, including Chief Justice Nelson, to underestimate their opponent.

Colonel Durant saw that another sure result of McRain beating him was that Durant would be retired early—without a general's star. Maybe even be retired the way they retired black ops screw-ups, with a one-way helicopter ride to nowhere. Durant certainly knew too much; that was sure. He patted the C.D. in his pocket.

He was glad he had Plan B. Durant looked out the window of Nelson's office and thought that there was still a way for him to get what he wanted from this operation.

Durant left the Supreme Court. He placed a call from a pay phone. The voice at the other end was deep, and thick as oil, piping English into Durant's ear with an Arabic accent.

"I have been waiting for your call. We have a deal, yes?"

CHAPTER 105

# CHAPTER 106

# CELEBRATIONS

Bridget prayed, in a fervor, over a toy soldier lying prone atop a Constitutional law book placed before devotional candles and an incense urn. CNN played loudly on her television, as the picture flipped and scrolled, unseen by her. The quality of the picture on her television didn't matter. She was blind. A news flash came across her television. A perky and professional female reporter told the audience, "This is a news break. We just received a report that United States Supreme Court Chief Justice, Sidney Ignatius Nelson, collapsed today during a heated debate."

With her rosaried hand, Bridget stood the toy shoulder upright.

The news reporter continued, "We now take you to Washington, D.C., for a live update on Justice Nelson's condition."

Bridget thumped the red tip of her shillelagh on the hardwood floor, in a resounding applause, heard only by herself and Gunny. She now considered Gunny hers, since Mike left her to feed him every night while he worked on that darn brief.

Bridget got up, and changed the channel, and adjusted the large, rabbit-ear antenna to make the sound less scratchy. She found an old "Wrestling at the Chase" professional wrestling match rerun from the '70s. Bulldog Bob Brown was catching the receiving end of a hammer lock from Jesse "The Body" Ventura's twenty-two-inch pythons. She'd never told Michael she was a closet fan of wrestling.

"Go, Jesse! Go, Jesse! Our Father, who art in heaven . . . "

Bridget had a fightin' spirit.

# CHAPTER 107

# GIVE THANKS

At the minimum security prison in Marion, news of a reversal of a conviction is rare. But good news travels fast. Inmates surrounded Jake Casteel, congratulating him on his victory. One of the older inmates, Ulysses Barbar, who had grown to be Jake's friend in the joint, patted Jake on the shoulder and said, "That's one Hell of a lawyer you got there. Went and off'd the old man for you."

"I sent in the Marines, didn't I?" Jake said.

That night, thunderous laughter filled the minimum-security prison camp. The prisoners rejoiced for Jake, their fellow inmate. And after all the whooping and hollering stopped, Jake lay on his cot, looking at the ceiling. He could not sleep. He was very anxious to get out, as soon as possible.

Jake likened prison life to being deep under water, smashed under its crushing weight. The deeper you go, the more weight on you, until it crushes you like a paper cup is crushed by a squeeze of your hand. To Jake, it followed that, the longer you are in prison, the deeper you go under, the more weight on you, until you eventually surrender to the never-ending, strong gravity of incarceration. It's inescapable.

He remembered the day the guards made him go across the road to Marion's infamous, maximum-security prison to help serve lunch to the guests of Uncle Sam residing there. Jake served mashed potatoes and carrots to Mafia Chief, John Gotti, "The Teflon Don," at the cafeteria line. Jake looked Gotti in the eye. Gotti looked hollow, like all the other prisoners. Casteel knew Gotti had given up, succumbing to the crippling, psychological weight prison life presses on its inhabitants.

Jake stared at the memory, so sharp in his mind. He shed one lonely tear of happiness. He was leaving! He was going to emerge, from the crushing waters of lock-down to life on the outside. It made his mind spin with excitement. But it was excitement tempered by caution. Jake would not believe he was free until he was sitting in a bar with a cold one in his hand. His family had disowned him. Casteel doubted he would see his wife and kids come to pick him up from prison. He fell asleep, saying prayers of thanks to God, for the good health of his family and for giving him such a great lawyer.

A never-say-die Marine.

CHAPTER 107

# CHAPTER 108

*"Set aside justice, and what are kingdoms*
*but enterprises of robbery."*
—St Augustine

It was not more than a minute after Chief Justice Nelson's head hit the dais before the machinery of death, dying, and the afterlife went into motion. When the crew of "The Constitution" saw "The Nelson's" crew hoist a white flag, in surrender, they overran "The Nelson," toppling all its masts into the water.

Captain Carion shouted, "To the victor go the spoils."

Mr. Troubles swung over to the defeated ship by rope, landing near Carion and Mr. Fetid. "And what is it to be for Nelson?" Mr. Troubles asked Captain Carion. Carion raised his sword, "Now, that *be the province of the Admiral, to decide the fate of Mr. Nelson. But if it were me deciding, he would go to the hold. With the other slithering souls."*

*But such was not the immediate fate of Chief Justice Nelson. Both crews looked on as two mighty angels flew down from above and plucked Nelson up, off the deck, out of the grasp of "The Constitution's" crew. They flew with him, high above the two ships, to where he could see his beloved Noreen and his baby Joan, who he had never met. Nelson felt unbelievable peace and serenity in his soul.*

*The angels then released him.*

*But Nelson did not fly.*

*His black robe flowed about him, like limp, lifeless wings, as he fell, scratching, clawing to try to grasp some humanity, and screaming—all the way down, to land on the deck of "The Constitution," where Mr. Beelzebub immediately snatched him up and, over Nelson's howling protests for mercy, took him below deck, down to the hold of "The Nearly Damned." Nelson's putrid soul then slithered amongst all the other serpents of sinners, which also were granted one last chance for redemption.*

"The Admiral decided his fate," said Captain Carion.

The dark cloud of battle blew away. I found myself on the deck of "The Constitution."

In full dress uniform, Carion assumed a ceremonious stance in front of the rest of the crew. One and all, they were squared away, in their best uniforms, at full attention, for their day of reckoning.

"The Constitution" was anchored in a beautiful, crescent-shaped lagoon. Deep, glowing, iridescent-green waters lapped its oak hull. A soft trade wind blew astern, barely able to loft a new flag, the stars and stripes of 1814. With rancid Mr. Fetid in tow, Captain Carion inspected the cut of each sailor's jib—his posture and uniform—as he marched down the long row of crewmen from every eddy of the seven seas. At the end of the line, Captain Carion stopped for closer inspection of one man, not in any uniform of the period. On his uniform, he wore a globe, eagle, and anchor, a sword and scabbard at his side. He was an officer of the United States Marine Corps.

Me.

I was downwind from Mr. Fetid. But the stench had no effect on me. I thought I might be destined to become one of the crew. I thought, "Am I to die? Have I been banished to Purgatory for past sins? And if so, for which deed? Was it for the assassinations I had executed upon a supposedly lawful order from C.I.A.? Was it for violating a variety of the Ten Commandments? Could it be solely for my transgression at my Father's, the General's, deathbed?"

I feared the unknown and the prospect of an eternity in Purgatory. But I also feared that I would not finish my business on earth. I knew that Bridget, Ann, and Kylee needed me as protector, provider, or perpetual caretaker. These were roles I would gladly serve the rest of my life.

Captain Carion marched out to where Admiral Jaundice stood at the head of the crew. Jaundice was still without eyes. His long, white hair was drawn back into a single plait that fell midway to his back. No hat adorned his head. Captain Carion knelt before Admiral Jaundice, who said, "You shall receive your redemption, Captain, as will your crew. Your next port of call is Purgatory Cay."

Carion remained kneeling, but, immediately, the crew broke into revelry, throwing their hats up in the air and thumping one another on the back in congratulations for they all knew that Purgatory Cay was where they would fly up to Heaven.

CHAPTER 108

*Mr. Troubles was especially gleeful. He beamed like a cherub at this new prospect of a life of Eternal Glory.*

*"Ah, the Rapture, laddies. An end to service on these seas, saving the souls of some, but drowning the rest—on a promise only that some day, we, too, might be saved. And here it is: the Rapture." He waved his pitiful three-cornered hat, of green, white and orange—the colors of Ireland, his isle of inheritance—and tossed it into the air to celebrate.*

*Through it all, I did not break rank or slouch from a posture of attention. Captain Carion rising from his knees before Admiral Jaundice, ordered, "Mr. McRain, front and center." I took two steps straight ahead; made a sharp, left face; marched to the middle of the ranks; stopped; made a hard, right face; and halted two paces from Captain Carion. I flourished a salute, swift, but deliberate, as I'd done as Cadet Wing Commander at the Air Force Academy.*

*"Captain Michael O'Brien McRain, United States Marine Corps, at your service, Sir."*

*Carion did not allow me to shift to at ease, but kept me at attention, "McRain, you know I would rather have killed you."*

*"Yes, Sir."*

*"But you earned your stripes. You are free to go ashore, amongst mortals."*

*My face beamed in appreciation. "Thank you, Captain, thank you very much."*

*Admiral Jaundice handed to Captain Carion a white scroll, secured by a black, wax seal of the McRain Coat of Arms. A black shield, with three gold stars on it, displaying the McRain motto on its bottom edge: "We Shine In Darkness." The Captain transferred the scroll, from his right hand to his left, and then extended it to me, "Your marching orders, Captain."*

*I gathered the orders in my hand. I felt a transfer of honor, an honor between men, an honor between souls. I felt what I had prayed for——the will of God.*

*"Do not open those orders until you are ashore, Captain." Carion said.*

*Holding the orders in my left hand, I snapped to the sharpest salute I'd ever given. I was a ramrod of humanity, pointed towards the heavens.*

*"Sir."*

*"You still have not made the connection have you, McRain? The line that ties you to me." Captain Carion smiled wryly at my blank face. "Those are my initials, J.C.C., carved into the tree you have been wetting every morning."*

*"You built Twenty-Three Oaks?"*

*Captain Carion extended his strong hand in a mutual respect that traversed dimensions.*

*"It's a grand house, isn't it?"*

*"Yes it is, sir. You run a tight ship."*

*Carion shared some secrets about the estate that not even Bridget knew.*

*"Carry on Mr. McRain. Oh, and keep a safe eye on your kind sister. She's who you have to thank for her prayers and your redemption."*

*I saluted Carion once more. He turned his back and he gave orders to his crew. "Set the sails and lay a tack for Purgatory Cay, mates. We're going home to the promised land."*

*The crew of yearning souls cheered again and laid heave to the ropes and riggings in anxious expectation of their imminent salvation.*

*I was happy for them. But most happy for me. I too was going home.*

CHAPTER 108

# CHAPTER 109

# PIECES OF THE PUZZLE

I'D HIT THE BIG TIME. The lobby of my hotel corralled over fifty reporters. Some held cameras, but most used stenographers' pads. All were poised like tigers, ready to pounce on me with biting questions. They wanted to pick clean the body of my story. The story of Jake Casteel, who was becoming known as the "comeback kid." An acquittal on a criminal case in the United States Supreme Court carried worse odds than winning the lottery.

Dalton offered to fly back early that morning, to draw some of the journalists away from me. I knew the real reason. He had a party planned, with the St. Martinsville University cheerleaders. I didn't blame him for bailing out. When he left by taxi, I saw two cars of paparazzi follow him towards the airport. Life in the spotlight was new to us. Dalton loved his new celebrity status. It was a chick magnet.

I took up residence in the hotel room I had originally reserved, the one I knew would be surveilled and bugged. After Nelson "took ill," as I referred to it, Raford had swung by the Supreme Court, and we drove out to his apartment in Falls Church, Virginia.

Only one car of paparazzi had the chutzpah to follow us. At a stop sign, Rafe put his four-wheel-drive Ford F-150, complete with step-up, steel bumper, in reverse and politely rammed the carload of professional voyeurs, not once, not twice, but three times. Hard. And not one of the idiots inside had the sense to take a picture of him doing it. Rafe calmly pulled away from the now un-drivable mini. My big brother asked me, tongue-in-cheek, if I could recommend a good lawyer for the rear-ender he'd suffered, due to the callous and inattentive driving of a motorist who'd rear-ended him. I laughed and jokingly suggested Rafe turn it in to the police as a hit-and-run.

We made our way to Rafe's apartment, where we cooked supper. Inch-thick T-bones and potatoes. Forget the salad. Afterward, we sat on his balcony and slaked some red ones, chilly Budweisers.

We went inside, turned up the stereo, loud, to foil electronic bugs, and exchanged notes on the progress of the Treasury Department's investigation of *Di Trina*. Rafe was having trouble keeping the investigation going, but secret, because Senator Moore kept sending D.O.J. liaisons to Treasury to ask questions about a unique audit of one of the Designated law firms. But the liaisons made sure not to mention to Treasury that it was an audit of a Designated firm— to minimize attention on the firm. Senator Moore's little spies wanted to know why Treasury was picking on that law firm.

Rafe was point man for dealing with the D.O.J. stoolies. He told them it was part of a random audit of law firms and not to get concerned. And just to make sure the D.O.J. ran away fast, Rafe would get in their face and ask why the D.O.J. was so God-awful interested in that one particular law firm. He never let on that Treasury knew the firm was Designated and that, according to their preliminary review of basic documents, the firm would be looking at a 188-count indictment for money laundering, income tax evasion, illegal cash transactions, etc., etc. Treasury planned to cut a last-minute deal with the Department of Labor, to give all railroad-union men full immunity if they came forward and testified against *Di Trina*.

It was beyond huge. Gargantuan. The names of the senators involved were household words around the nation. And the *Di Trina* firms enjoyed a combined net worth of over five billion dollars. Nothing like it had ever been attempted in the history of the United States.

And it didn't help the investigation that three different senators on the Judiciary Committee were calling Rafe's superiors at Treasury to get the audit of their Designated law firm friends stopped. Lucky for Rafe, the Secretary of the Treasury, Henry "Hank" Stinnelson, was the retired C.E.O. of DTX Railroad, headquartered in Santa Fe, New Mexico. He knew what was going on with *Di Trina*, and the loans, and Americans paying for a handful of lawyers to get richer and richer. And why there weren't a lot of rail strikes. Why the trains kept rolling.

CHAPTER 109

*Di Trina*. And its personal injury, protection racket.

Nobody but Stinnelson, his wife, and his doctor knew he had only six months to live. Cancer. He didn't want to leave this planet looking like he was covering up the biggest heist in history. The R.I.O. statute had just celebrated its hundredth anniversary. And Stinnelson painted his interest in justice to Rafe with a metaphor. "*Di Trina* has been milking that cow for a hundred years. She's dry. R.I.O. is over. She's out to pasture."

Rafe told me they will hit all the *Di Trina* firms simultaneously. Coast to coast. To minimize flights of escape to South America and to minimize Senator Moore's influence. Once one *Di Trina* firm cut a "State's evidence" deal with Treasury, the whole *Di Trina* lawyers' mafia would be trying to cut plea deals, too. And who could blame them in that situation? They would do five to ten years in a federal clubhouse, detention unit, while their money doubled in size. They would come out of prison a lot more wealthy than when they went in. Meanwhile, the American consumers and taxpayers will get a break.

About the time we'd finished rubbing our full bellies in front of ESPN's coverage of "Psycho Mike-O" McRain's "killer cross-examination," Rafe's latest girlfriend showed up with a bottle of wine and a rose. Rowena didn't want to interrupt us and offered to leave. But I would not hear a word of it. I could see Rafe had forgotten he had a date with Rowena, and she was a fine-looking woman. He'd been running around helping me. The very least I could do was help him. I was a third-wheel, imposing on their little party-to-be. I took a taxi back to my hotel. I wished I was home, with Ann.

I wanted a piece of that life that Rafe enjoyed. Not the bachelorhood, because I'd enjoyed plenty of that when I was in the Marine Corps. I enjoyed women, and they enjoyed me.

But when I went to Harvard, to Boston, I got all serious, pouring myself into my studies. I was determined to be number one in my class. And in pursuit of that high, class rank, I studied fifteen hours a day and experienced an unintended celibacy that had continued until I met Ann. I came home from Boston for my dying father. After the funeral, I decided I should stay in St. Martinsville, to honor my promise to my father to look after and care for Bridget.

"*A promise made is a debt unpaid,*" I would tell myself whenever I thought about leaving Bridget to her own devices.

And now I was in my hotel, I had to walk into the lobby, into the throng of journalists intent on picking my story from my bones. With the courage of a paratrooper, I went out the door; down the hall; and waded into, through, and past the journalists. During that walk, by the looks of the photographs that later appeared in twelve different newspapers, I apparently had experienced twelve different moods. I stopped at the curbside to answer the questions of a tiny reporter with a squeaky, little voice.

"Is it true Chief Justice Nelson died while you were cross-examining him?"

"No comment."

"The Attorney General says he's not going to press charges against you, even though he believes you caused Chief Justice Nelson's death. How do you respond?"

"No comment."

"Are you going to kill the new Supreme Court Justice, Jackson?"

I answered a question with a question, "He's already been named? It's Jackson?"

"Yes, the President made the announcement of his nomination this morning."

"No comment."

I jumped in a cab and took off.

Justice Jackson called me into his office after the paramedics had left with Nelson. Right in the middle of when the F.B.I., the Interior Investigations Bureau, and the Secret Service investigators were all asking me questions about what happened. Jackson cut through all the bullshit and had me brought to his office immediately. He cut off all the silly questioning. It was a simple case. Old man had a heart attack and died. Jackson wouldn't allow the other arms of the government, the Executive Branch, to use his courthouse for some type of grandstanding. Especially the F.B.I. since, for all practical

CHAPTER 109

purposes, it was controlled by the Senate Judiciary Committee, and not by the Attorney General, as the framers of the Constitution had intended. By putting our heads together, so to speak, Jackson and I succeeded in seeing the big picture revealing the amazing extent to which *Di Trina* had waged its treacherous scheme to make billions at the expense of the ignorant.

Jackson had his own agenda. He told me about the recorder he'd mistakenly left in Chief Justice Nelson's office, that recorded the argument between Clerk Morrison and Chief Justice Nelson. After Jackson listened to the tape, he knew Nelson was crooked. Jackson put two and two together real quick, given the recent appointment of Nelson's sons as railroad union-Designated R.I.O. lawyers and the sham of the prosecution against Jake Casteel.

Jackson wanted to do a swap, a quid pro quo. If I told him what I knew about the Designated lawyers, he would keep all the heat off me. I jumped at it—because it would help my client—and me.

Jackson knew he could do nothing, at the time. Going to anyone in the Department of Justice would surely bring about his own death. He had not yet made the connection between the Senate Judiciary Committee, R.I.O., and *Di Trina*. But he sensed something was not quite right at D.O.J. Weird stuff was happening. Like all these liaisons sticking their noses into his clerk's handling of opinions. The "Casteel" decision made Justice Jackson look like his right hand did not know what his left hand was doing. It was as though an invisible hand was moving around, changing procedures and papers in Jackson's office. Jackson knew something was amiss, but he could not put his finger on what it was. He waited until the right time to make his move.

I told Justice Jackson what I knew about *Di Trina*. All of it. He was intrigued, but not surprised. He said he, too, could not understand how so few lawyers obtained so much of the business. At least, not until he heard about *Di Trina*, from me. He said, "Ah ha," nineteen times, as I briefed him in his office, while the media frenzy continued on the courthouse terrazzo outside. It all made perfect sense to Jackson after I informed him of the truth I had discovered.

432

He played the tape for me. Not because he owed me anything as a jurist, not because he liked me as a lawyer, not because I had just accidentally killed the most corrupt megalomaniac in the history of the Court, but because we were both Marines who happened upon corruption. He wanted me to understand why what was going to be done would be done. Jackson informed me that he planned to make dozens of copies of the tape. He was going to distribute them to the other justices; to the President; to the Senate and Congressional committees; to the C.I.A.; and, finally, to the police arm of the D.O.J., the F.B.I.—with the promise that he would make the extra copies he possessed available to the world's media if anything at all happened to him.

He shared more with me. Jackson suspected that Durant and Nelson had something to do with the death of a F.I.S.A. judge, who died shortly after denying surveillance warrants on Jake Casteel's lawyers' homes, offices, phones, and cars—the basis of the warrant application merely that their client, Jake Casteel, belonged to an international union. Chief Justice Jackson also promised he would use whatever powers he held to ensure that I suffered no personal or professional repercussion for defending Jake Casteel.

Jackson could then see the entire *Di Trina* business model in his head. And he characterized his vision of reality to me, that *Di Trina* had succeeded in digging its own version of a secret tunnel under the United States Constitution's high fortress walls dividing the Legislative, Judicial and the Executive Branches of the United States Government to allow infiltrating each branch with the corruption and crime necessary to run *Di Trina's* lawyer mafia; railroad strike; protection racket. Justice Jackson even went so far as to faux-spit on his office floor and squint his eyes and grit his teeth and scrunch his face and point his finger at me, when he exclaimed that he now understood the full depth and breadth of *Di Trina's* criminal network.

"Hell, they even infiltrated the Goddamned Pentagon! I'll be a S.O.B."

I nodded my head in a quiet understanding of the gut-piercing truth spoken by the learned Justice.

Justice Jackson shook his head and worried about how he would now ensure the safety of Lady Justice. He decided that he would protect her the only way he knew how. Vigilant, aggressive, with honor; like a Marine who just happens to be a Justice of the United States Supreme Court. His fair and blind-folded Lady, who holds the scales of justice, was a Lady he fought to defend, as a Marine in Korea; she deserved nothing less from him, now, as an officer of the courts of the United States of America. His duty to protect the Constitution was no more or less than a newly sworn-in lawyer. He hoped he could bring the story to the entire country, the whole world, to serve as another lesson of what happens to our societies, when good men do nothing, in the face of clearly corrupt and evil situations. Decades of corruption was much too long.

As a final token of appreciation for my cooperation, Jackson was going to pick up the phone and convince the Bar Association's Disciplinary Bureau to drop any proceedings against me for roughing up "The Slasher" on the elevator. He said, "The son of a bugger is lucky it was you and not me. I would have killed him. Put that nail file right into his jugular." We worked fine together. Marine to Marine.

The C.I.A.'s secret, of the Hoffa Protocol, was safe. For now.

~~~~~~~~~~~~~~~~~~~~~~~~~~~~~~~~~~~~~~~~~~~~~~~~~~~~~

I left Justice Jackson's chambers and I confidently walked the hallowed halls of the United States Supreme Court, unescorted, back to Dalton who took his once in a lifetime opportunity to show his face to television viewers around the world. He was answering questions from reporters on the marble steps of the courthouse. I saw him through a window, waving his arms to the throng of journalists. He was in his element, the spotlight.

It was at that unpredictable time, when I was looking out and watching Dalton, that a warm peace moved over my heart and a bright understanding lit my soul. I realized that God had not forsaken me, when the Supreme Court first denied us victory for Jake. God had merely postponed our victory. All of the rosaries I had offered to God had not gone unheard. I felt bad for doubting God, after we received the bad news from the Supreme Court. I looked at myself as having been a Doubting Thomas. In a silent and solemn prayer, I thanked God and Jesus and the many saints I had prayed to and had cursed when I thought our ultimate victory had been denied.

I pushed open the door of the great courthouse and waded through the media crowd to stand beside my best friend.

# CHAPTER 110

# FIRE BOMB

Eighty acres of wheat waved good morning out the front door of Ann's tiny farmhouse. A heavy frost blanketed the yard, and it shimmered in the bright, morning sun. Ann looked out her window at her truck.

"Oh, Hell, gonna have to scrape the window again this morning."

It was quite frosty, even for the last Saturday in October. But with Mike and Dalton gone to Washington, D.C., Ann held down the fort at the law office. Her time had not been idle, with calls from new clients swamping her phone. And the reporters all wanted their ten-second sound bites. They combined to create a big pile of telephone messages, so high and thick, Ann had to rubber-band them together, separately for each day. She put the piles on Mike's desk, filling the blotter in front of his chair. Dalton had given her instructions to only take messages from female reporters. Of course.

She felt like she should change her name to "Suzie Switchboard" because she wasn't doing much, if any, typing; she was just answering the phone and writing messages. But, still, the fort had to be manned, and she meant to get in early that day to, at least, get some coffee started before the phone started jangling.

Ann put on her parka and headed out to start her truck and let it warm up. She had to defrost the windshield to drive the thirty-five-mile trip to the office, from the black soil where she lived, across the mighty Mississippi River, and into St. Martinsville. The old farm work-truck was a bit drafty, to begin with, and she preferred not to ride in a refrigerator. Ann pushed in the truck's clutch and pulled the knob for the manual choke halfway out. The way Daddy had taught her. She pumped the gas pedal, three times, and put her hand on the well-worn key, to start the antique truck.

Ann did not notice, as she walked up to the truck, that the frost in the grass alongside her truck had been partially melted by a C.I.A. mechanic, the technical wet-boy, ordered by Durant to wire four sticks of dynamite to explode when she started the truck. The truck was heavy. Good, old, Detroit steel. Its thick-gauge, steel firewall would have protected Ann and Kylee fairly well if the mechanic only used his customary, two sticks of dynamite.

However, Durant handpicked his crew. His explosives mechanic was an old-timer, who swore by dynamite for pick-up jobs and fishing. He knew that, due to the heavy-duty construction of the truck, this was a four-stick job as he had explained it to Durant. "Probably send the truck, oh, ten, maybe twenty, feet up in the air and probably flip on her back, too." Durant grinned.

The reasons for setting a bomb and killing Ann and Kylee were no longer applicable. Their deaths were supposed to shake Mike up, so he would not be able to function in D.C. and, maybe, even withdraw as Casteel's counsel. But Mike had uncovered the corruption of the Supreme Court Chief Justice and won a hard-fought victory for his client, Jake Casteel, in the Supreme Court. The jig was up. How could Durant have predicted this outcome? Who had ever heard of a man being cross-examined to death?

Casteel would be out of prison imminently. And according to Durant's intel sources, Jake would be back, running the union and calling a national strike, quite soon, if the railroad did not agree to its first wage increase in five years. But Durant couldn't call back the bomb. It had been set. He couldn't really send in his mechanic to say, "Oh, I'm sorry; I put a bomb underneath your hood. Please don't start your truck."

But, most importantly, Durant didn't care. He liked fireworks.

CHAPTER 110

# CHAPTER III

# KILL THE INNOCENT

The incineration of an innocent mother and daughter simply held no importance for Colonel Dirk Durant. He'd been an instructor at the School of the Americas' training ground at Fort Benning, Georgia, where he taught the harsh methods of military terrorism. A target was a target, without flesh and bone, without feeling, without emotion, and—certainly–without importance to the world. No emotion attached to the target once the higher-ups Designated a person a target. Zero emotion, no second thoughts whatsoever. It wasn't the assassin's job to wonder why the target had to be neutralized. It was the assassin's job to do, or die.

It was a code Mike once had followed, when he'd neutralized targets for C.I.A. as a Force Recon operative. Now Mike practiced as a lawyer by an equally unyielding code —destroy the other side at all costs. Simply destroy the opposing party, earn the fee, and walk away. But Mike wouldn't receive a fee for representing Jake Casteel.

Colonel Durant had made the decision that Ann and Kylee would be targets. Durant had turned a professional hit into a personal vendetta. Mike McRain had been skunking him. Making him look like a fool, on an assignment that should have been a cake-walk. And even though Durant had a personal plan "B," he still had a score to settle. He took advantage of the government's fast and effective lethal resources while he was still at the helm, implementing the Hoffa Protocol.

Colonel Durant indulged his favorite feeling. Scintillating, it was like a spark, running through his body, down his spine, and into his toes. He'd felt it when he murdered his first wife, Dani. She was a tall beauty he'd met in Germany. She mistakenly thought her life, married to a U.S. Special Forces operative, would be exciting. Killing her was simple enough. He had tired of her nagging. Dani nagged about most everything. But she complained especially about their lack of money. The pay of a Green Beret was little more than that of a bank teller, she told him. And the bills were piling up. But certainly not from any extravagances. They owned one car, a seven-year-old, white Chevy Impala. Dani drove it on a simple circuit—to and from her job as a bank teller, to pick up their one-year-old daughter from day care, to get groceries, and then drive back home. Their living quarters were quaint, too: a simple, little, two-bedroom, one-thousand-square-foot cottage, filled with used furniture and an old, black-and-white T.V., set atop two milk crates. And Dirk was never home; he was always out, chasing bad guys to the four corners of the earth. So Dani committed an offense, unpardonable in the circles of Special Forces wives.

She got lonely.

To cure her loneliness, Dani went out with her friends after work one night. The next day, she spoke with Dirk by telephone. He was at Ramstein Air Base, on a short layover in Germany. He'd called to tell Dani he would not be home for a few more months. He was being deployed to Afghanistan, as an advisor to the Afghanis in their struggle against the Russian Bear. But he couldn't tell her that—sensitive information. Just the lovey-dovey, miss-ya-baby, pining type of message from a lonely warrior. But Dani, being German and not fully indoctrinated in the protocols of American military wives, made a big mistake.

She told Dirk she'd been out with friends the night before and came right home. Dirk, who was a lowly captain at the time, saw Dani's going out with the girls as a type of A.W.O.L. He didn't believe her when she denied messing around with another man, like some lonely wives do. Dani did not know Dirk was a control freak. In his mind, Dani was not human—merely an object for him to adore, to screw, and to display on a shelf, to use like a fancy tool, whenever he needed it. If his Dani tool ever got bent or broken, he would throw her away. He convinced himself that she was damaged goods, that she was having an affair. When Dirk returned stateside, he took care of business as he was trained. Swift. Quiet. Smart.

Dirk made it look like a simple carjacking, gone awry. They found Dani's body in thick brush, alongside a Georgia stream, with two, neat, twenty-two-caliber holes in the back of her head. His daughter, Ingrid, was found abandoned, left in her car seat in the Chevy Impala, at an area shopping mall, to make it look like the carjacker didn't want witnesses. And didn't have the heart to kill a baby. Dirk just walked away from his little daughter, crying in the back seat. She couldn't talk; nobody would find out.

Finding someone to take care of his daughter prompted Durant's quick marriage to Suzanne, a young and pretty, Arizona cocktail waitress, working on a degree in Criminal Justice. Consistent with her penchant for law and order, Suzanne fell for the ultimate superman, for the mystique of law enforcer of the world that Dirk exuded, playing up his Special Forces status. Dirk met Suzanne after he had shamelessly milked the story, "I am —a —poor, grieving widower, whose wife has been murdered" to pick up chicks and get mercy loving, coast to coast for more than a year. Dirk had been taken by Suzanne at first sight. He put Suzanne on a pedestal, in the exalted position of his Number One "wiener cleaner"—his wife. If Suzanne had known her degrading new title, she would not have borne Durant another daughter, Sally. Colonel Dirk Durant had a certain recurrent pattern of using women for his own pleasure and gain. Then he dispensed with them, ushering them out of his life—and out of existence—with no emotion, as if he were shooting bullets from his Sig Saur semi-automatic.

As the Hoffa Protocol was being applied to convict Jake Casteel, Durant was bothered quite a bit that Mike verged on getting serious with Ann and taking their relationship to a higher level. Dirk knew Mike's intimate intentions because Durant had had the techs wire the whole McRain house for sound. Durant listened every night to Mike's prayers, *ad nauseum*. Aloud, Mike would beseech God and Jesus and so many damned saints that Durant, agnostic by upbringing, couldn't keep track of them all. Mike also prayed to restore Jake Casteel's honor, as payback for the dishonor Mike felt at his father's deathbed.

His prayers always included visiting on his rosary those damned stations of the mysteries. And the stations changed daily because the Pope had proclaimed that Catholics should focus on different Biblical mysteries different days of the week. Durant thought, *"Is this religious dial-a-prayer?"*

But Mike kept pushing those beads, on his knees, leaning against his bed, praying, on and on. Even for self-serving requests, such as a life of his own, love, a good woman, Ann and Kylee, more children, and the happiness and security of his challenged sister, Bridget. If only the women in Mike's life knew how much Mike loved them. But Durant chuckled, knowing that Mike was a guy, and guys don't tell women how they feel, emotionally. Durant smiled. That was one of the few predictable facets of Mike McRain. He was a guy. He was no angel. He was not a perfect Catholic. Mike kept praying, never attaining perfection.

*"What a fool,"* thought the Colonel. At least, Colonel Durant's prayers, requests to his C.I.A. god, were perfected with successful completion of a black op. *"McRain, you pray to a false god. My god is real."*

Durant considered Mike's prayers, and his Catholicism, a sign of weakness.

He could not believe a Special Forces operative like McRain, a Harvard Law graduate to boot, believed still in a celestial, Judeo-Christian God. *Hadn't McRain painted his share of walls with gray matter? Didn't Psycho Mike-O McRain remember that C.I.A. was God? And that the Chairman of the Joint Chiefs sat at that God's right hand?*

Mike's prayers were almost disrespectful, shunning and sacrilegious to Durant's God of War.

Durant lost all respect for Mike, listening to Mike pray to a weak god. A god inferior to his—to the C.I.A. and all its little saints, who carried guns and bombs and used electronic gadgets. A god with the characteristic of a *real-life god*— infinite resources. "Besides," thought the crazy colonel, "the C.I.A. god got things done right. Not like Mike's inferior god, who didn't answer all the prayers of his operatives. All of Bridget and Mike's saints were dead!

Death. That was how Dirk ultimately measured a discredited loser. At least, Dirk's idols were still flesh and blood, working at his religion—Might makes right.

Dirk worshiped at the temple of force.

Durant planned to make Mike's life miserable by striking him out, on all of his prayers. Mike's first prayer had been answered: Jake Casteel had been exonerated. And that pissed off Durant, to no end. But in Colonel Durant's mind, the game was not over. Dirk checked the odds in his head. Dirk's god of the world whispered in his ear—smart money was on the C.I.A. His god would defeat Mike's god.

He wanted to make McRain hurt. Durant wanted to see Ann—in her wholesome, old, blue, farm truck, with her daughter by her side—blown up and incinerated. It would give Durant a charge like the one that snapped through his body when he'd put the gun to his first wife's head. He loved it. Mike adored little Kylee, and Durant knew it would crush Mike if Kylee were barbecued, like a piece of burnt chicken, because Mike wasn't there to protect her. Kylee was cute and innocent, even wearing the plaid skirt of a Catholic-school uniform. The perfect target for terrorists around the world. Durant reveled at the prospect of seeing that burned skirt in morgue photos. Its torn innocence would make him giddy.

Killing the innocent was Durant's perverse means of applying Psy-war tactics to the Hoffa Protocol. It was like a rape. An act of violence. To murder Ann and her stupid, little daughter by blowing them up. Durant was visiting violence upon them because Ann had helped Mike defeat him.

*"How dare she help the enemy! She is sentenced to death."*

# CHAPTER 112

# GRACE

Ann needed to drop-off Kylee at St. Francis Parish gymnasium for her basketball practice and get to the law office. Pronto. She was running late. The manual choke on the dashboard of Ol' Blue was pulled all the way out, and she pumped the gas some more, to start the truck. Ann twisted the key again, and . . . there was nothing. No noise, no engine turnover, no explosion. Nothing. Ann looked up. Her truck door was open, but the tiny dome light was not lit.

Ann was not a perfect Catholic, either. She cursed out loud.

"Shit. The battery's dead." She was frustrated.

Ann got out of the truck, and slammed the door, hard, and raised the hood. She did not see the four sticks of dynamite, stuck to the firewall, wired to Ol' Blue's electrical system. Ann got an idea, which would have been a great idea, had her truck not been wired to blow up and fly twenty feet in the air when it was started.

She figured she would pop the clutch and start the truck that way, so she first needed to get the truck rolling.

Her yard was mainly flat. And she could not push the truck, popping the clutch at the same time, without a hill to keep the truck rolling. She went inside and tried to telephone her father, to ask him if he could come out and give her a jump-start. But there was no answer at Mom and Daddy's phone. *"Oh well, it can't get worse,"* thought Ann.

But her day did seem to be going from bad to worse. She had curled only half of her hair, and she was still in her pajamas, without a coat on, and it was cold. But Ann wasn't just pretty and smart. She was country. Resourceful and tough. She went back outside to take care of it herself. Ann watched her breath steaming as she strained hard, pushing the truck,

444

backwards towards the road, out where there was a slight hill down which she could roll the truck.

She stopped.

She heard Kylee yell, out the front door, for her to come in, right away. Ann wondered what was the matter, so she set the brake and slammed shut the door to the truck, and she shivered because she was cold and frustrated. Cursing under her breath, she left the hood up, marched up the porch stairs, flung open the front door, and stomped inside, to see what was so damned important that she had to stop pushing her dead-ass truck.

Kylee was jumping up and down, like she was on a pogo stick, excited, and a little scared. "Mommy, mommy, you know that man you work with? Mike-O?"

"Yes. Honey, you were supposed to be getting ready for school. You don't have your clothes on yet. Are you done with your cereal?"

"He's on T.V."

"*What? Who?*", thought Ann. She was still ticked off about her battery being dead, and Kylee wasn't talking sense. "What do you mean? Here's your knee socks. Let's go. You have to steer while I push the truck, and the Mother Superior is going to give you a tardy demerit if you are late, and you have perfect attendance for basketball so far," Ann said.

"Why are we pushing the truck?"

"Because somebody left the dome light on, and the battery is dead."

Kylee was embarrassed and evasive.

"Oh."

Kylee quickly changed the subject, back to Mike-O, as she ran into the kitchen, where they kept their small, thirteen-inch, color T.V., with a rabbit-ear antenna that was bigger than the T.V. itself. Kylee was half squealing, half speaking, and still bobbing up and down, like a Mexican jumping bean. "Yeah, Mike-O, the psycho, or something like that. They say he killed somebody, Momma. Even had his pitch'r on T.V., pushing some reporter dude. They were all ganging up on him and yelling at him."

Ann scrambled and got partially dressed. She ran into the kitchen in her blue jeans and bra, her hair still not curled on one side. The T.V.-news

CHAPTER 112

reporter told the audience they would be cutting to their special correspondent outside the U.S. Supreme Court for a live telecast. The picture changed, to a reporter standing in front of the Supreme Court, microphone in hand, speaking in a charged tone of voice.

He reported that they were following up on an announcement that Chief Justice Sidney Ignatius Nelson had died, shortly after leaving the Supreme Court. He'd apparently suffered a massive coronary, simultaneous with a cerebral aneurysm—a double-whammy death knell. For the first time in the history of the U.S. Supreme Court, a Chief Justice had taken the witness stand and undergone cross-examination. The reporter continued that it had not been a friendly cross-exam. It was a blistering interrogation, conducted by none other than the infamous "Psycho Mike-O" McRain. The inflammatory newscast further reported that it was believed that McRain and his law partner were hiding inside the Supreme Court, to avoid any on-camera interviews. The unreported truth was they had answered rapid-fire questions from three different investigative agencies before they were allowed to leave.

The newscast switched over to a live picture of Nelson, on a gurney, being raced to an ambulance. As they were lifting Nelson's gurney into the ambulance, his right arm slipped out from under the sheet. Chief Justice Sidney Ignatius Nelson, VI, had a white rosary wrapped around his dying hand. The reporter picked up on that, immediately labeling Nelson a devout Catholic.

Ann's knees started to buckle, and she dropped the kitchen's wall phone, in the process of dialing Daddy's number on the party line they shared.

It seemed, by the way the reporter was presenting the facts, that Mike was a murderer. As reported to the world, old and frail Chief Justice Nelson had been cross-examined to death in a relentless barrage of questions by a lawyer who was already on the hot seat for torturing a prisoner in a courthouse in St. Martinsville.

Then there was a voice-over on a fifteen-second short of the S.W.A.T. team tape, showing Mike putting the Slasher in the Aikido hold, to teach him manners.

"Now, say, 'I'm Sorry,' Mr. Pells. I know you can do it."

Pells shrieked and pleaded for the pain to stop; however, M.O.M. continued his charm-school lesson, unheeding, not knowing it would be broadcast to the world. Mike was messing with the Slasher's mind, like a U.S.M.C. drill instructor makes a recruit shed his old ways, so they can be replaced with Marine Corps ways. The right ways. The ways of a gentleman. Mike's taped instruction to the Slasher was somewhat tongue in cheek. Mike was offering the Slasher a personal, hands-on, crash course, for which Marine recruits do not qualify.

"We can get through this together, and you can shed that whole 'Slasher' serial-murderer persona."

Then Mike screamed in the Slasher's ear, "Is that what you want, mister; is that what you want? Do you want to change? Do you want good manners? Because if you do, I can't hear you. And if I can't hear you, we are going to continue our little finger-focus exercise." All the while, Pells was screeching and moaning in pain.

The newscast shot back to the reporter, outside the Supreme Court. "The spokesman for the Supreme Court made no comment regarding how a sadistic man like McRain was ever allowed to appear before the most respected and powerful court in the world." There was no mention whatever of how Mike had saved DeeDee's life, or how he'd saved his own, trapped in an elevator with a serial murderer, twice his size. Mike already had told Ann and Dalton what really happened. And the truth was, Pells tried to choke and punch Mike the first three times Mike unhanded Pells, allowing him to stand up. The media did not show those parts of the video captured by S.W.A.T., the parts that exonerated Psycho-Mike-O, to show he was just a good guy. They chose not to present the full truth to maximize their media splash.

Mike was being persecuted by a press that wanted only to report the sensational. The Bar Association Disciplinary Bureau would see the whole tape and that Mike was defending himself, as much as he was dishing it out. McRain knew the bar would see he gave Slasher ample opportunity to act civil and not attack Mike, so they could get off the elevator like gentlemen.

CHAPTER 112

"Don't you want to surrender with style and honor?" Mike said to the Slasher after the Slasher punched Mike in the jaw the second time Mike let him stand. The only thing Mike was guilty of was trying to talk reason into a psychopath as he defended himself. No good deed goes unpunished. He could not even trust Slasher to the end, when they got off the elevator. That was why Mike decided to ride Slasher off, with a horsey-back leg-scissors, in order to keep control of the massive brute.

The whole newscast made it sound like Mike took advantage of Nelson, as if the Chief Justice were a harmless senior citizen, sitting on a park bench, and Mike ran up behind him, whacked him with a club, and took his wallet. It was a one-sided media ambush, and Ann did not buy into it. But she thought to herself, *"Oh, great, and I was going to introduce Mike to Daddy at this Sunday's Supper." She visualized the introduction. "Daddy, this is Psycho Mike-O McRain. He's crazy, Daddy. But I love him."* She wondered how Daddy, the Marine and Medal of Honor recipient, would take to his little girl hooking up with a psycho. Ann fidgeted wither hair. *Just great!*

The unflattering newscast made Ann bump her forehead with the palm of her hand, astonished. Kylee hugged her leg and acted a bit timid, seeing the shocked look on her mother's face. "See, I told you he killed somebody."

Ann defended her man, "He didn't kill anybody, honey. He didn't do it; I mean, I don't know. He's a good man. He wouldn't do that, Sweetie."

On T.V., the talking head finished the report, with a promise of more information as the day progressed. Ann was having a good, old-fashioned anxiety-driven thumbnail chew when her father walked in, holding four sticks of dynamite and a detonating harness. It was a C.I.A., standard-issue harness. "Is this a new accessory you had installed on Blue?" Her father placed the dynamite gently on the kitchen table.

Ann's eyes bugged out in her head. Her father, Sam, leaned to his right, away from his prosthetic left leg, and he spoke slowly, low and matter-of-fact.

"Well, I took hay to the west herd, and I did a little rabbit hunting along the scrub, and I was driving back and saw you had Ol' Blue's hood up, so I thought I would stop and have a look-see. Lucky for you, your battery was dead; otherwise, . . ." Her father spread the fingers of his hand, pantomiming an explosion.

Kylee blurted her confession, "Mommy, I was playing in your truck last night." Ann had found the overhead light switch on after she tried to start the truck. They all realized immediately why the truck battery was drained. The chilling fact was that the only reason Ann wasn't killed was that Kylee had turned the truck dome light on the night before and forgotten to turn it off. Sam seemed nonchalant about the dynamite. But he jammed his hands into both of his front pockets. He kept his money in his left pocket and his old rosary at the bottom of his right pocket, in a small, snap-top purse, for safekeeping. If he had shoved a hand only into his right pocket, Ann would have known he was worried about something. And Sam did not want to make a bad situation seem worse than it already was. He was a Medal of Honor recipient, for Iwo Jima—he did not sweat the small stuff.

His rosary was one of a kind with special significance all its own. Each of four of the five miracle stations were represented by a trinity of kernels of sweet corn, strung together with baling wire. Those kernels were part of a miraculous crop. In a bad storm, eleven years before, ninety-mile-per-hour, straight-line winds knocked down every cornfield in St. Francis Parish, destroying all, except Sam's. As they spoke, Sam was secretly pushing beads. He didn't want to upset Ann. Sam ran cool. But he, sure as Hell, wanted to know who was trying to kill his daughter. Samuel Parsons was in a protective, fatherly mode, although it did not show outwardly, not then and there.

Sam acted rather clinical. Explosives weren't anything out of the ordinary for a Marine. "I didn't think they were using dynamite any more. I thought they were going to plastic explosives. Oh, well, must have been an old-school guy, rigged it up. Did a nice job on the wiring harness."

Ann looked at Kylee's startled face, then at the television, with more dark news, and then at her father. She instantly felt nauseous and lightheaded. She fainted, into Sam's arms.

She'd dodged the bullet. Twice.

CHAPTER 112

# CHAPTER 113

# CIRCLE OF PROTECTION – CIRCLE OF LOVE

Forty miles to the west of Ann's home, Bridget shook a little more holy water on the two Raggedy Ann dolls, large and small, draped over her altar. Circle of protection prayers that she had customized from the Ninety-First Psalm were what she was working that day—over and over, going into a type of trance. Her right arm started twitching pretty badly, too. Bridget had to keep Ann and Kylee safe if her little plan was going to work.

Bridget was chanting in an uncharacteristic falsetto. But instead of using two rosaries and saying them simultaneously, she said one rosary and, with two hands, recited the prayers, so that one followed the other, respectively, like an inch-worm gathers itself together before it moves on. There was a price to pay that day.

No pain. No gain.

Bridget Mary McRain's fingers were blistered from pinching the rough beads of her rosary of Chilean granite fragments, strung with stainless steel, barbed wire, to resemble Christ's crown of thorns. She called it her "biker dude rosary." It also had a chrome Jesus on a three-ply, Andean, lama-leather cross, blessed by a bishop who had been visiting Our Lady of Guadalupe, the Mother of The Americas. A Bolivian nun in the Order of the Adorers of The Blood of Christ had previously used that exact rosary to pray a novena for landslide victims, who—afterwards—were spared casualties.

Serious, serious mojo.

How Bridget got her hands on that instrument of spirituality was a secret. And she wasn't talking. She paused for a few moments, sipped a little herbal tea, and petted Gunny. Tommy Macem and the Clancy Brothers were singing, from the belly, a heartbreaking tragedy of the Irish and of love. She felt the Irish—the Celtic in her— down to her bones. And she paused in her prayers to revel in the warm glow of ancient belonging. The glow of family, of friends, and of a saintly, maternal love, washing to her on the tides of time.

Bridget loved Ann and Kylee, and they loved her. Bridget could sense they had pure hearts. Ann was not like the other long-legged skirts Mike had brought into her house before: gold-diggers, who just wanted to snare a lawyer. She had no shame in running them off. Because Bridget had run off so many girls, Mike became gun-shy, and now he didn't bother even bringing Ann home to get a concussion.

Mike didn't know it, but they were all praying for each other. Their little prayer circle began one day, when Bridget called Mike's office and, unconsciously, started a "Hail Mary" while she was waiting for Mike to get on the line. Ann had put Bridget on speakerphone and heard her prayer. Ann chimed in, and the rest was history. From then on, they had themselves a little prayer group. Ann would call Bridget and say a rosary with her when the boys were out of the office. She would put Bridget on speakerphone and try to keep up. But usually, she sat back and gave the reins to Bridget, to be the prayer leader, seeing as how Bridget spoke and prayed so fast.

For a matter of the heart, Bridget secretly conspired with Kylee and Ann against Mike.

And so it began. First by happenstance, then by natural courses, it had developed into a plan to get Mike and Ann together. Bridget, Ann, and little Kylee worked as a triangle of prayer trained on Mike's heart. Mike didn't know a whisper of it. The poor man didn't stand a chance with those women, ganging up like snipers, shooting prayers at him like that, from three different directions. But it was all secret and holy. A conspiracy of love is what it was. Bridget even taught Ann and Kylee to say "Hail Mary's" in Gaelic, to give them a bit of a double whammy on poor, unsuspecting Michael.

The three of them—Bridget, Ann, and little Kylee—were a conniving trio. Saint Patrick was playing his golden harp to bachelor Mike's heart. Whatever else he was, the man was sure to become a groom.

CHAPTER 113

Bridget fired up the biker-dude rosary again, with a kick-start, for the long version of the "Apostles' Creed." She carefully let out the clutch on her tongue, and she quickly gained speed, rumbling off another couple of rosaries of devotion for Ann and Kylee's safety and a few more for her dumb brother, Michael.

Bridget was a-rockin'. And getting ready to roll.

# CHAPTER 114

# GREEN SNOW

Durant acted fast. Sixty million dollars will light a fire under your tail. He was excited. He was a pure capitalist, and he was in business for himself. But he wanted a partner, to make the job a little easier. He'd rid himself of one obstacle, Sergeant Butler, before he left D.C. They'd gotten together for one of their little rendezvous, the ones Butler used to keep tabs on him for C.I.A. Durant knew what she was doing, and he treated her accordingly. He eliminated her.

Characteristically, they didn't waste much time getting naked. He slid behind her. But he was careful; he knew all about the forensic use of DNA. The only evidence he left on her body was the place at the base of her brain where he'd stuck his stiletto. Then he threw her body in the trunk of a stolen car, and he sunk it in a remote Virginia pond. He'd meant to have a talk with her, about how he wanted the freedom to perform economic terrorism. But somehow, Durant didn't think Butler would let their relationship grow in that direction.

Then it was off to Colorado for a little meeting with Big Dutch. He felt some mountain scenery would be good for his focus—and his pocketbook.

In Colorado, Dutch had just finished a three-day, elk-hunting trip with the president of the railroad. The railroad helicopter landed at C.A.R.'s secluded mountain chalet, and the ground crew escorted Dutch aboard for the short flight to Peterson Field in Colorado Springs, where he would take a jet to St. Martinsville, for an emergency *Di Trina* meeting. They'd never planned for Casteel winning. That changed all scenarios. They needed to make some big decisions, with C.I.A. and Durant.

The helicopter was airborne for less than a minute when the co-pilot removed his helmet, with its dark visor, and came back to the passenger cabin. Dutch looked up and saw it was Durant. Durant was expressionless. There was no hint of a smile or grin on his face.

"Looks like our little plan sort of imploded."

"You should have called to let me know you were going to be meeting me. I would have been better prepared," said Big Dutch, regretting that he had not come aboard armed. He remembered their last meeting quite clearly. Dutch could forgive that Durant shot Davis and butchered Knuckles. But he could not forgive Durant shooting his dog or stabbing his hand onto his desk. Dutch had had to put down his pet, Kerbelos. And that angered Dutch to no end. Don't mess with a man's dog.

"You must be very well prepared because you are heading to St. Martinsville for our meeting about Jake Casteel and the whole *Di Trina*, Hoffa Protocol situation."

Big Dutch explained that he had no authority to discuss how the Pentagon, the Department of Labor, and the C.I.A. were going to handle the Jake Casteel situation. Colonel Durant gathered that Big Dutch had gone behind his back and struck a little agreement on the side with Lieutenant-General Crowe. Durant thought Big Dutch was a good politician, that he would have done well in the military, especially at the Pentagon. Which gave Durant that much more reason to make Big Dutch his own offer.

Now that Casteel had won in the Supreme Court and would retake leadership of the union, it looked like there would be a national strike, and the economy would be shut down. A rail strike would be the linchpin for the whole economy to begin to fail. The money lost on the stock market and the commodities markets. The credit default swap and derivative hedge funds that printed money as if they were U.S. Mints. The funny money. Lost, short-term profits would be in the hundreds of billions of dollars and would eventually accumulate into trillions. A worldwide financial blood bath. Only the countries and monarchies that controlled the most valuable resources, oil and gas, would be able to bribe, barter and battle their way into world leadership position. This had all been explained to Colonel Durant at the Afghanistan Embassy.

CHAPTER 114

And the colonel, who was paid ninety-three-thousand dollars per year by Uncle Sam, wanted a piece of the multi-trillion-dollar action. He wanted to be a player on the level of the software, and oil, and manufacturing magnates. He wanted to look down his nose at the railroad barons. Maybe even ask them to shine his shoes.

Durant needed professional help.

He did not care that a rail strike also would wreak a terrible impact on average citizens, in homes and businesses and hospitals, as the country would be quickly drained of its critical needs: fuel, energy, food, medicine, and hope. If the strike lasted longer than a few days, its ripple effect would dwarf the anarchic scenario President Truman predicted in his landmark speech of 1946. Starvation and pestilence would visit the world.

C.I.A. was going to do everything in its power to prevent that. Durant expected to be erased from the picture as a failure. He would never get his general's star. He would be labeled always as the fool who'd lost the operation of the Hoffa Protocol. It was supposed to have been a simple operation, that would have slammed Casteel with a conviction through the criminal justice system that, in turn, would have prevented Jake from running the C.U.RT.I.S. Hog Heads Union and calling a strike.

Nobody expected Mike McRain to screw it all up. Mike turned out to be an unexpected master at merging guerilla warfare and lawyering. Durant shook his head in stunned disbelief. But it was true. McRain was nothing short of a tactical legal genius. He rewrote the manual on how David could slay Goliath. Durant knew, plain and simple, if it had not been for McRain, the C.I.A. would have won. An innocent man would have been convicted. And the economy would not be thrown into a recession caused by a rail strike.

Durant made his sales pitch to Big Dutch, "I have a plan B."

Big Dutch didn't want to hear anything about any plan "B" the colonel was selling. Durant had failed, and he was expendable. Big Dutch knew Colonel Durant would be asked to retire quietly. Which Durant knew. So he pressed his case. He had nothing to lose. His head was on the chopping block. Literally.

"My plan will keep Casteel away from the union forever."

"Well, I have a plan 'M,' for money. I've been approached by some very powerful people, who would like to see the price of oil fluctuate," Durant said.

"What are you getting at?"

"You told me that I should let nothing and nobody get in my way of making a profit."

"Yeah, but what is this money and oil about?"

"We knock off Casteel and make it look like the railroad did it. The wildcat strikes will spike the price of oil. We get ten percent, sixty million dollars." Dirk's plan was a model for how to merge terrorism with capitalism. Durant kept his sales pitch upbeat and candid.

"Hey, if we are going to wreak worldwide economic terrorism, we might as well make a buck doing it."

Big Dutch's face screwed up with worry. Durant had figured out the formula for profit between transportation and the oil business, real fast: create an emergency, and jack up the price. Simple. It worked every time, on a public that was like a kid so stupid, he keeps putting his hand on a hot stove. A kid with a long, long, learning curve.

Big Dutch's face tautened, as though he had just been slapped.

"The Hoffa Protocol prohibits that, Colonel. I gave the President my word. Killing Casteel would probably cause a recession. With all the wildcat rail strikes and all . . ."

Dirk interrupted the crooked lawyer. "Recessions come and go. Profit opportunities like this only come once in a lifetime. I figure that we lost the Hoffa Protocol operation. But, you and me, we could turn a bad situation into a good one."

"So you want me to help you make a silk purse out of a sow's ear?"

A smug grin crept over Colonel Durant's face.

"Mr. Van Killman, let's once again recall the secret of your success. 'Don't let nothing or nobody get in the way of making a profit.' Now, we both know Casteel is going to call a strike. All I am saying is, why don't we profit from what is going to happen anyway?"

CHAPTER 114

"This is nonsense; it's crazy, and I don't want you to say one more word about it. The wildcat strikes that would result if Casteel dies will be unpredictable, much worse than a full, primary strike. If there is a primary strike of the whole country, the President will use the Army to get the trains running after three days, until the stupid-ass union men get their uneducated heads out of their butts and get back on the trains. Furthermore, the railroad president advised me he wants to make another year's profits before he gives the union any wage concession, so a primary strike is inevitable. Plus, we gave the President our word. And last, the one-time sixty million you will receive is chicken feed compared to the revenue I get from my R.I.O. practice and as the head of *Di Trina*. Why would I want to screw that up?"

Dirk nodded in an exaggerated way, seeming to be mocking Big Dutch, who'd now said everything except what Durant wanted to hear. Durant seemed to contemplate his next move, as Big Dutch pulled out his cell phone to make a call.

"The mountains are beautiful this time of year," Durant said, as he pointed out the window. Big Dutch turned to look, away from Durant's sucker punch. The punches landed hard behind Dutch's ear, slamming his head four times against the window. Dutch was dazed, but not knocked out. Colonel Durant quickly unbuckled Big Dutch's seatbelt and yelled, "Now," to the pilot, who pitched the helicopter to the left as Durant flung open the door and pushed Big Dutch out. As he watched the horror on Dutch's face as he fell away from the helicopter, Durant could not resist being a smart-ass.

"Don't let nothing or nobody stand in your way of making a profit. Asshole," Durant shouted from the helicopter, with a big, shit-eating grin. He and the pilot watched Adolph "Big Dutch" Van Killman claw at the air as he fell, thousands of feet, into the remote, rocky, mountain valley below. He impacted on a large boulder beside a mountain stream.

Durant patted the pilot's shoulder, "Your share just went up." The pilot set the helicopter down in a clearing fifty yards from Dutch's body, allowing Dirk to jump out, run over, and confirm the death of the super-lawyer and to remove any electronic gadgetry from Big Dutch's body. He did not want locating it to be assisted by the use of homing devices.

Durant thought that Big Dutch's landing had been a perfect splat. He smiled; it would allow the wolves and bears to dine on tenderized meat.

Durant ran back to the helicopter. He boarded, and they flew off on a short hop, to where the pilot dropped Durant at an S.U.V. parked a mile away. The pilot thought it odd and asked, "Aren't you concerned that we are landing so close to where Van Killman went down?"

"Hell, no. Our tracks will be covered when the bears get his body." Durant handed the pilot a steel briefcase. The pilot opened it, revealing its contents: row upon row of bundled currency, lined up neatly in multiple stacks. He rifled through a few of the bundles. They were all hundred-dollar bills.

Durant gave final reassurance to the pilot. "Capitalism is good."

The pilot shut the lid and offered Colonel Durant a salute. Durant shook his head, "NO."

"We don't have to do that any more. Our working days are over."

Durant watched the helicopter rise to a height of about two thousand feet before he took the remote control out of his pocket and pushed the detonator. The helicopter pilot's share of the money floated towards earth, like huge, green snowflakes over the Colorado Mountains. The money was Durant's way of telling the intelligence community who he was. He knew he would have to get a new face and a new identity, in a forgotten corner of the world. Durant got into his S.U.V. and drove away, through the snowfall of greenbacks.

"Snow forecast for today? Green."

CHAPTER 114

# CHAPTER 115

# THE WAITING SPIDER

I came home to a dark house, in the early morning hours on the eve of Halloween. My red-eye flight from Washington was delayed in Cleveland and Chicago. It put me into St. Martinsville late. My Mustang muscled up the driveway half past midnight.

There wasn't any need to have lights on in the house when Bridget was home alone. But Bridget usually left the porch light on at night to fend off robbers, burglars, and whatever else went bump in the night. She prayed to a string of saints that I couldn't keep track of, but I'm sure she had prayed to her 'home alone" favorites, Jesus and Saint Dismas, the patron saint of criminals. It was great to see home as I walked up the steps to the porch, a bag in each hand and roses for Ann under my arm. It was even better to see that Bridget left our chess game just the way it was before I went to D.C. My move. While I was away, I'd thought about my next move—in our chess game and in the game of life. Ever the gambler, I'd decided to sacrifice my castle to a pawn. It was a strategy to open the flank of Bridget's white king to a possible checkmate in, oh, three or four more moves. I doubted that Bridge would fall for it. She didn't miss much. I supposed she would parry and continue her offensive. Bridget style. If you are not attacking, you are praying.

I dropped my bags and took my move on the eight-foot by eight-foot chessboard. As I was picking up my castle, a female voice behind me made me freeze.

"All the right moves, isn't that what you make, Mike? All the right moves?"

I turned, in a snap, to see DeeDee on the unmoving, porch swing. In the shadows, she was posed like a lounger on a warm, summer's day. Her tight skirt taunted the cold, Midwestern Fall of St. Martinsville.

# CHAPTER 116

# DONNYBROOK

DeeDee blended with the evening. She always wore black. Locomotive black. It suited her well.

"What brings you here?" I said, putting my hands on my hips.

"Is that any way to welcome a guest?"

"I don't recall inviting you."

DeeDee had already learned that Big Dutch was missing. News in *Di Trina* moved swiftly, on the tongues of conspiracy. She knew something big was about to come down, and she wanted to ally herself with a white knight who would give a damn and protect her when the indictments started flying. She stood up from the swing and sashayed over on her spiked heals, real sexy-like. The best rainmaker in the hundred- year history of R.I.O. looked like a princess of darkness. I felt sorry for her. All those wicked, good looks and smarts wasted on whoring. She wore a waist-length chinchilla-fur coat, cut in a style you might see on a Paris model and a short, black skirt, with fish-net stockings and black-checked high heels. Very chic and of the world.

"I came to make you a proposition," said DeeDee, as she bellied up to me, real tight and sensual. I knew this meant only trouble.

Her big eyes were alluring and very hypnotic. She was the sharpest-looking woman I'd ever met. If it is true that the eyes are the window to the soul, then DeeDee was all about money. Her eyes looked golden, with flecks of diamond and silver.

Her motor was running. I could sense fear of rejection in her voice. I kept my hands off her hips.

"A proposition, huh? What 'ya talkin'?" DeeDee didn't hem and haw, "I wanna offer you a partnership. A partnership in my law firm."

The offer caught me by surprise. I looked DeeDee in the eye, and I almost kissed her—just because she was beautiful. My heart belonged to Ann.

"This isn't the normal way business alliances are formed. You know, belly button to belly button," I said.

DeeDee picked up on my reference to her sex-filled proposition. She rubbed her right leg into mine, "True. I like to keep business separate from pleasure."

She was gorgeous. But DeeDee and *Di Trina* were directly responsible for Jake Casteel's conviction. And she'd sabotaged my work on appeal for Casteel. If DeeDee had been a man, I would have beaten her like a dirty rug. A couple of times.

When I looked into DeeDee's eyes, I recalled the information I'd received in Washington from Supreme Court Justice Jackson. Jackson and I spilled our guts to each other. Jackson knew he needed my help to discover the background of the whole affair of the Hoffa Protocol. And he knew he would never get the full truth from the D.O.J. and F.B.I. investigators because half of them still owed Senator Moore their jobs. He was conducting his own unofficial investigation. Justice Jackson detested *Di Trina*.

"*Di Trina* is a boil on the ass of the rest of the American Bar. It gives honest lawyers a bad name," he said.

I gave DeeDee a flaccid response, "No, thanks."

DeeDee looked down at the chess board where we were standing.

"Isn't this the part of the game where you jump me?" She batted her eyes and pushed her flat pelvis, hard, into me.

DeeDee grabbed the roses from beneath my arm, where they had been tucked, reserved for Ann. Right then, the front door burst open, revealing the faces of both Bridget and Ann.

"Surprise!"

They both yelled, as Ann flipped on the porch lights. DeeDee and I looked like two raccoons caught in the headlights. At the surprise, DeeDee jumped onto me, putting me in a provocative-looking scissors hold with her legs. With her arms around my neck and holding a dozen roses, it looked damned bad. Bridget could not see what was happening, but she heard an unknown woman's voice and then Ann labeling the stranger in a very unflattering way.

"You whore. What are you doing here? And, Mike, what are you doing, jumping her bones?"

That was all Bridget needed to hear before she went into full attack. She ran towards me and DeeDee with her shillelagh outstretched, like a knight on his steed in a jousting match. In the short time before Bridget would have impaled us, I peeled DeeDee off and grabbed Bridget's shillelagh with a sidestep, like a matador dodging a bull. But Bridget was persistent, pulling her shillelagh back and swinging it at the area where she thought DeeDee was. Bridget's guess was rewarded. The shillelagh caught DeeDee squarely in the ribs. She emitted a pain-filled scream as she crashed through the porch railing and into the icy water of a decorative fishpond.

Bridget was about to jump off the porch into the fishpond, without even knowing where she would land. I grabbed her by the waist and held her up, off the ground, while Ann ran behind us, screaming from the porch at DeeDee.

"I see what you've been doing, you back-stabbing bitch."

Then Ann turned to me, with her finger in my face, "And I thought I could trust you, you two-timing . . ." I tried to say something in my defense while Ann struggled with her words. But she shouted me down and left me with the worst thing she could call me, given our past argument.

"Now I see why you can't say the 'L' word. You aren't *honorable*. You're a damned, two-timing lawyer."

Ann ran away, to her truck that she'd hidden around the back of the house.

Meanwhile, DeeDee struggled out of the fishpond and sneaked off towards her two-seater, Mercedes coupe, parked out on the street. As DeeDee slinked away, Bridget spewed a long string of colorful language at her, with "Harlot" and "Jezebel" interspersed about every third word. Finally, Bridget broke into a staccato of saints' names, beginning with Saint Ignatius Loyola, the soldier, turned saint, and ending with a plea to Saint Thomas Aquinas for help with me and my philandering ways.

The battery on Ann's truck was weak, and she couldn't start it. She came stomping back onto the porch, demanding I gave her my car keys, so she could go inside, get her sleeping daughter, and leave. I quickly obliged, but tried to explain that the roses were for her and that DeeDee had been there, uninvited. She was so angry, she would not let me carry Kylee out to the car or help her recline my passenger seat, so Kylee could sleep lying down. Ann popped the clutch like she was driving her Daddy's tractor. She threw gravel back at me as she spun my Mustang's tires, roaring off down the driveway. DeeDee started her car and took off, too. Not like I was going to stop DeeDee.

Bridget stormed into the house and locked all the doors. She dared me to try to come inside. I think she would have killed me in my sleep.

I laid the roses for Ann on the square on the chessboard for the queen. I shook my head. I couldn't call Ann on her cell phone because she didn't own one. Not everyone had a cell phone in 1995.

I slept in the loft of the carriage house, using some old horse blankets as both cover and pillow. I swore vengeance on DeeDee. I had no idea how I would get Ann back. I would have chased after her, but she'd taken my car and hers wouldn't start. I was stuck.

Now, Ann thought I was seeing DeeDee behind her back. It was impossible. I reflected on the irony that a dark lining came with my silver cloud. I had succeeded in battle. I'd exonerated Jake Casteel. But my ship had sunk. I'd lost Ann. She and I—as in "we"— was my ultimate objective, and it looked like she was no longer within my reach.

I did not sleep. This wasn't supposed to be happening to me. I was born in the Celtic Great Year, 1959. Bridget told me repeatedly over the years that I was not supposed to have a sign with a crossed star.

I slept up in the hayloft, above where my grandfather had stabled his horses. And I stewed all night long.

CHAPTER 116

# CHAPTER 117

# THE AWARD

The next day, Colonel Durant was sharpening his knife on railroad-ballast rock. He dropped the rock, sheathed the knife, and swung himself up, onto a rolling freight car.

An hour to the east, Ann typed at her desk at the law office as I walked in the door. The phone rang, and Ann answered it, with her back to me. I walked over and hovered by Ann's desk, anticipating good news.

"Yes, ma'am. I gave Mr. Casteel your message." She listened, "Jake said he'd report to the railyard right away." She listened again, "Goodbye."

We still needed to mend the fence about DeeDee on my porch. Although I'd spoken with Ann on the phone to explain the truth about what happened, Ann was still rankled. She was treating me pretty cool. This was the first time we had been face to face since the incident. I had called Ann a dozen times and offered my explanation. But she had been hurt by it all and it would take time to mend her heart.

She hung up the phone and started typing again, somewhat oblivious to my presence. "What's that about?"

"The railroad wants Jake to report right away for his re-certification train ride."

"Re-certification train ride?" I put my hands on my hips, showing disbelief. "Why would the railroad re-certify Jake if the arbitration panel hasn't yet given Jake his job back?"

"I don't know, but it's only from East Martinsville to Franklin City. It can't be that bad. Oh, I forgot! The arbitration board just sent this big envelope by overnight delivery. You think it's a decision about Jake getting railroaded and restoring his job?"

"Isn't that convenient."

I took Casteel's arbitration award home with me for safekeeping. I wanted to deliver it personally.

# CHAPTER 118

# A NEW LIFE

Jake thought it felt good to be out. Free of constant fear—of disease, of being jumped with a shiv, or of picking up hepatitis, which was rampant in prison. Prison life was an experience he would carry with him the rest of his life. It humbled him and moved him closer to God. While Jake was in prison, his wife had filed for divorce and his children had turned their backs on him. They believed the Government's case, that he'd lied and disgraced them. His only daughter had shared with him that she was taunted at school by some "cool" fellow students, who called her dirty names, like "whore," and smashed her ego by saying, "I heard your daddy went to prison for pimping you out." Kids are vicious and cruel. They will use 'most anything to step over other kids to try to correct their insecurity and as a way of creating their cliques.

Jake had not been allowed by the minimum-security prison even to attend his son's high school graduation. The boy was a member of the National Honor Society and the recipient of a scholarship to M.I.T., where he would study physics and mathematics. Jake missed it all.

Now he had a chance for a new life. He showed up at the rail yard at the direction of a telephone message he'd received from Ann at his lawyer's office. "Mike McRain walks on water," thought Casteel, as he walked the uneven rocks of the railroad track's ballast. Jake slowly made his way to the three-engine locomotive consist, where he would make his first ride to be re-certified as an engineer. The railroad had fired Jake while he was in prison as a felon. A clean criminal record was a prerequisite for employment. That applied to all railroad engineers. You pick up a felony, you lose your job. Simple.

But Jake's felony had been erased by the artful and dogged work of his persistent legal team, to whom Jake was eternally grateful. Across the nation,

Jake had men to lead. But that required Jake to be re-certified, so he could become, once again, an employee of C.A.R. He would then be qualified to resume his office as international president of C.U.R.T.I.S. The Hog Head Union.

Jake saw the face of someone that he'd called friend for twenty years on the rail. S.T. Mareau, who everyone knew as Snaggle Tooth, or Snags, for short. Jake walked between the tracks of rail cars and locomotives. Casteel held out his hand to greet Snags, who was inspecting a locomotive.

"Hey, Snaggs, you know what you're looking for?"

Snaggle Tooth stood up right away when he saw it was Jake. His face beamed, as he showed his perfect set of false teeth.

"Jake, Jake, they told me I was gonna get to re-certify you. Seems how you have been off the rail for a while." A loose reference to Jake's recent prison stay.

"You ol' son of a bitch. You would have been off the rail twenty years ago if I hadn't saved your job for you, five times over." Jake playfully patted Snaggle Tooth, as though he were searching him.

"You're not carrying that pint of Old Crow still, are you?"

They both laughed again, remembering how the railroad had tried to get Snaggle Tooth fired half a dozen times. But Jake did his lawyer's magic and found some loophole each time, to get Snaggle Tooth his job back.

Jake Casteel had been a thorn in the side of the railroad even before he'd gone to law school—after the railroad fired Jake for insubordination. Casteel had refused to move a train he believed was in a dangerous position and should not be moved. So the railroad fired Jake for insubordination, and Jake had appealed the firing. During the time he was off work, appealing his firing—and unknown to the railroad—Casteel applied to and attended law school in St. Martinsville.

He was bright and hard working, and he graduated six months early, just in time to learn that he'd won his appeal. He got his job back, and he did not bother telling the railroad that he had become a licensed attorney when Jake returned to the job because he knew they would have thought up some other reason to fire him. Jake was reinstated as an employee. When he sprang the good news, that he was a licensed attorney, it made the railroad's vice president in charge of litigation go ape.

The railroad had not had a licensed lawyer in its rank-and-file unions for over a hundred years. For a whole century, C.A.R. enjoyed an easy go, not having to deal with lawyers in its one-sided, investigative hearings, convened whenever a man got hurt. They would simply fire the man with the blessing of the *Di Trina* lawyers; for without a job, the *Di Trina* lawyers were able to ask juries for more money due the injured man. And of course, that meant more of a contingent fee for the *Di Trina* lawyer. Such a deal, for the fat lawyers.

Casteel turned the tables on the whole railroad industry. His name was known in every railroad boardroom across America and Canada. Some of those rail directors ended up as powerful secretaries in the cabinet of President of the United States.

Jake Casteel pissed off the wrong people.

Jake and Snaggle Tooth finished their pre-trip inspection of the locomotives and climbed the ladder to the lead locomotive's cab. Jake walked over to the locomotive's control panel and held the throttle, a phallic shape, like a long pistol grip. When you push it forward, the train pulls forward, and vice-a versa. Casteel thought he would get right into Hog Head mode and be a bit raunchy. Jake had some fun, stroking his hand up and down the throttle.

"Hey, Snags, this one needs a little lubrication." That drew another white-toothed smile from Snaggle Tooth, who shook his head and laughed.

"No. Those new ones are pre-lubed. All set for where it goes after an investigative hearing."

Casteel was anxious to get back to the trade he plied before his imprisonment.

"Let's fire this mother up."

# CHAPTER 119
# GOOBY-SHAMMER

The warm autumn sun hovered over the Mississippi River valley's horizon, in a blaze of crimson glory, as though it struggled to keep Halloween from arriving. The day's final, yellow rays of life pierced Twenty-Three Oaks, through the cross-hatched windows of the big, country kitchen. I had not cooked for Bridget in over a month, while I had been hammering away at the Casteel brief. That absence from the kitchen had turned out to be good. It had forced Bridget to learn to cook, without a flame-thrower and a fire extinguisher.

I was frying eggs at the stove, drinking my coffee and reading the newspaper. Some Bob Dylan song played in the background. His *"Blood on The Tracks"* album. I loved to eat breakfast food for supper, and Bridget liked it, too. I was a bachelor, and breakfast was easier than cooking a roast. I fished two pieces of browned Irish soda bread from the toaster. Bridget's cooking was certainly getting better. She'd done a great job with the soda bread. It was something she would not have dreamed of baking before she gained her new culinary skills. Soda bread tended to be on the dry side to begin with, so I buttered the toast, taking care not to crumble it.

My mind moved to Ann. I did not know how to keep my mind off of her. I loved her. She and I made up at the office. A kiss, a hug, an exchange of "I love yous," and a lot of talking. Strangely enough, I opened up to her about my feelings—with me sitting in my desk chair and Ann in a client chair. Isn't it odd that I needed that big desk between us to feel comfortable enough to reveal my feelings? As though they were a frog we would dissect on a lab table. But that's me; I'm a red-blooded American guy. An emotional coward.

The other reason I used the desk as an emotional buffer when I told her I loved her was to let her see I wasn't just saying "I love you" to get some of the good thing, but that I was serious about "us" and about building a relationship on trust and friendship. And not on the weak foundation of lust.

The whole thing went great. We kissed, and I told her, "I love you," plenty before I left the office. I was on Cloud Nine. Using the "L" word was pretty heavy for me, emotionally. But, after I did it, I felt as if a ton of bricks were taken off my back.

We wanted to go to supper together, to be more intimate, at some warm restaurant, with a bottle of wine. But the responsibilities we bore in caring for others dictated the calendars of our social and love lives. Ann had to pick up Kylee and take her to basketball practice. And I had promised Bridget I would cook supper for her. Such were our lives—lives of split households.

Ann and I swapped car keys. She said, "Nice ridin' your Mustang, cowboy."

I hitched my thumbs into my pockets, like a cow puncher on a Montana cattle ranch.

"You can ride on my spread any time, ma'am."

"Your bedspread?"

"No, I mean, yes; I mean, you know what I mean by my spread. My ranch."

"Oh, you have a ranch I don't know about?"

"No, it's just a figure of speech. But I'd like to have a ranch."

"I know. I was just messing with you. It's been a while, and I missed you a lot."

"That makes two of us."

We kissed. We hugged. We told each other, "I love you," again. It was warm. And very exciting.

Later on, as I was cooking supper, I was happy, humming the tune, *"Get Me to the Church on Time."* I did not know all the lyrics. So I faked the parts I didn't know. I belted out the lines, "I'm getting married in the morning. Ding dong, the bells are gonna chime." Then I would hum, faking it for a while, till I picked up the send-off, "So get me to the church on time." There was a little extra zing in my step. Life was grand. I was in love.

CHAPTER 119

I slid fried eggs onto a plate, along with the toast; picked up the plate and my coffee; and headed towards the table. I stopped in my tracks when I heard a long, blood-curdling howl come from Bridget's bedroom. I set the food down on the table and sprinted up the stairs. When I got to the top, I opened Bridget's door and flew in.

"Bridge?"

Bridget was holding a toy, a model of an old-fashioned steam locomotive in one hand, which also gripped her special Easter rosary. The purple and white one, that had a nice caricature of Jesus on the front medallion and little, silver beads at the mystery stations. In her other hand, she held onto Ace's empty harness. She was lonely for Ace. Gunny sat on the rug beneath her, not knowing what Bridget was up to. Gunny's wrinkled, bulldog face tightened with fright.

She was seated, but acting like she was trying to get up. I tried to help her, but discovered that she wanted to remain seated, with her left hand on Ace's grip. She flew off the handle like this, now and then. I learned, over the years, to let her go. But I had to make sure she was safe. Every time this happened to Bridget, it looked as though she was having an epileptic seizure. The doctors told her and the family that she did not have epilepsy. They opined that she got so darned excited, during some of her autistic revelations, it just seemed like she was having an epileptic seizure.

Bridget was shaking hard, like she was freezing to death. Every now and then, she opened her eyes with a flutter, giving me a rare peek at the blue of her eyes. Father claimed it was the same blue he'd seen in the sky at 70,000 feet, when he flew once in an SR-71 Blackbird.

"Bridge, Bridge, what is it?" I was trying to help her into the here and now. I disregarded the lessons I'd learned over the years about leaving her alone. I was concerned about her. She shook when she spoke.

"It's Jake. There is something wrong. He is on a train."

She put it in oral overdrive, speaking in Gaelic. When she spoke the Irish, there seemed no way to bring her back until she was darned ready. She was in her own time and place. Interspersing some English in reference to certain saints, she continued to speak mainly Gaelic. About the only word I could pick out was "killing." I knew that word well because I'd heard her say that, in reference to us, her brothers, hundreds of times.

"*Ag marú, ag marú, ag marú* Casteel." It sounded like Bridget was trying to say the word "Jake" and ended on a high note that made her sound like a banshee. I knew she was visiting another world.

"Criminea, Bridgy. You're as crazy as a bit raccoon." I took a step back. What I saw looked like someone possessed by demons, who needed an exorcism.

I was half disgusted. There was simply nothing I could do. I stood up from my station next to Bridget's chair by the altar, and I walked back down to the kitchen. In the hallway, I flailed my arms as though it all was beyond belief. I felt sorry for Bridget, and I wanted to forget about the whole spooky episode.

Besides, my coffee and eggs were getting cold.

I went back to the kitchen and sat down to eat my eggs. I accidentally knocked my fork to the floor. As I reached under the table, Bridget slammed her shillelagh down onto the table, clearing my plate and coffee mug right onto the floor. I was astonished as I watched Bridget back up and raise her stick, like a baseball bat, assuming a fighting stance. Then she lunged at me as though she were going to spear me with her loaded stick.

"You think I'm a faker? Well, how about 'law is war,' for starters?"

I threw my hands in the air, and I threw my napkin on the table in disgust. I stood up and walked towards my bedroom.

"I can't even eat a plate of eggs around here without getting my chops busted."

"Gooby Shammer," Bridget said to me, as I retreated.

This stopped me in my tracks. It was an old phrase, that Bridget and I used just between the two of us, the two youngest, the babies in the family, when Bridget was serious about something that her autism prevented her from saying in detail.

"Jake. Save him. Train. Danger . . ."

I knew, in my house, "Gooby Shammer" meant there was a five-alarm fire somewhere. I needed no more. I was already heading out the door, wearing only my tennis shoes—no socks, windbreaker pants, and a sleeveless U.S.M.C. shirt. I grabbed a jacket, the denim one with the fleece lining. It made me look like the Marlboro man, dressed to pick up some milk at the corner store. I jumped in my Mustang and fired her up.

Worst of all, I'd brought only one knife in my calf scabbard. No boot-knife —sinful.

If there was one thing that I had learned in my life, it was when Bridget said, "Gooby Shammer," she was right every time, never wrong. And that I damned well better act on it. I scratched the tires in all four gears as I shifted like a madman, making my way to the rail yard in East St. Martinsville. My speedometer hurtled forward at over a hundred miles per hour and hung there, as I flew down the highway with Frank Sinatra belting out "My Way" on the radio. I had been playing the radio more, instead of the Marine cadences, since I began seeing Ann.

I downshifted as I roared into C.A.R.'s East St. Martinsville rail yard. I pulled up to the trainmaster's building. I talked with the assistant trainmaster, who refused to give me any information about where their mile-long train was headed. I guess he thought it was a national secret. Or maybe he knew it's a set-up, and he didn't want to blow it.

Instead of thrashing it out of the man and dealing with the railroad dicks' goon squad, I decided I would take the roads that paralleled the tracks on the route to Franklin City. Jake and whoever was training him had a two-hour head start on me. But I figured they would be stopping to cut-out some rail cars, at factories and other places needing supplies, along the railway. And my pony was a Hell of a lot faster than their train. I just hoped I could make it to Jake before dark because that is when most "accidents" happen.

# CHAPTER 120

# SHE'S GONE

Bridget prayed at her altar from her big, overstuffed chair. She kept moving a tiny, toy train in a circle, chanting in a very low voice, almost a whisper as the train circled around and around. Then she stopped playing with the train, and she stopped chanting and praying over it. She picked up a small figure of a man, sprinkled holy water over it, and prayed–hard. Some of the usual Hail Marys and the like, but she customized it a bit, "What we forget in the pale moonlight, the Son gives us eternal light."

Bridget started twitching, and she let go of the rosary in her left hand. Then that hand spasmed, knotting up like a fist. With the fingers all knotted up. Her body froze, stiff. And not a muscle did she move.

Gunny whimpered and reached up to lick his master's hand. Bridget drifted away, and Gunny started to howl, but not like a coyote, with high-pitched yips and yipes. Now and then, the spotted white bulldog would lick her hand, then go back to baying, soft and smooth, like he was singing to her, letting her know where he was, so she could find her way back.

My little redheaded Bridgy was lost to the world.

# CHAPTER 121

# THE RECKONING

The night hours seemed to pass as quickly as the mile markers alongside the railroad tracks. Jake Casteel was in the poorly lit cab of the loud locomotive with Snaggle Tooth. A man Jake had known on the rail for over thirty years. Casteel had saved Snag's job for him when Snags had not deserved to be saved, more times than he could count. The recurrent theme of Jake's life continued to play out: "No good deed goes unpunished." Casteel was running the train, keeping his eyes on the tracks. This was Casteel's re-certification run, so he had to do everything right.

Finally, they got the green light to head straight through to C.A.R.'s brand-new, billion-dollar, Franklin City rail center, and they got rolling again.

It was on the starboard side of the second locomotive that Dirk Durant boarded, swinging himself up, climbing the stairs, and ducking into the cab at the last possible second. That is where Snaggle Tooth had told him to wait for Casteel.

The train Casteel was piloting chugged slowly out of the East St. Martinsville rail yard, headed towards Franklin City. It was a short hop and a piece of cake for Casteel. He'd made the run, to and fro, thousands of times in his days as a locomotive engineer. Before law school.

A light came on in the control panel, indicating a problem with the second locomotive in the three-locomotive consist.

"Hey, Snaggle Tooth. We got a problem with Unit Two."

Snags motioned to Jake that he would take over running the train while Jake went to check out the problem.

"Number Two's compressor. Go on back and check it out. I'm too old to be jumping cars at night."

"Sure; be glad to," Jake said.

Casteel made a windy exit from the cab of the locomotive. Jake made his way to the back of the locomotive. He hesitated, as he swayed, to time his jump between the undulating platforms of the lead and second locomotives. He jumped, slipping a bit, but he saved himself from falling between the locomotives by grabbing the iron handrail. He looked back and down, to the railroad ties whizzing by, under the train. He said, out loud, like he was defying a great beast, "Good ol' meat grinder."

I saw the train from the highway. I goosed the accelerator and zoomed ahead and got off the highway and ditched my car on the side of a country road adjacent to the train tracks. I ran up to the tracks believing that Jake was in grave danger. I laid low in the tall grass to conceal myself until the last moment and then I sprinted to the side of the thundering machine to a try to get on the train as close to the locomotives as possible. I was unlucky. I missed the grab iron on the third locomotive and I had to get on three cars behind the consist.

The next ten minutes were spent jumping from car to car and I lost my footing on the last jump. I held onto the top of the car and scrambled up knowing that I would be dead in pieces if I slipped to the tracks.

Jake pulled himself to the safety of the side rails of the second locomotive and made his way back to the cabin. He yanked open the cab door and stepped into the dark cabin of the second locomotive. Moving to the control panel to hit a light so that he could see better, Jake was jumped from behind. A shadowy figure tried to put a garrote around Jake's neck. Jake succeeded in slipping one leather-gloved hand under the wire. He fell to the floor, together with his assailant.

My jump up onto the third locomotive went fine. I checked the cab of that locomotive and found it empty. I too had to navigate a tricky jump between locomotives, on my way up to the second in the three locomotive consist.

Inside the cab of the second locomotive, the lights of billboards beside the track illuminated Jake's and Durant's faces with a strobe effect. Both men were straining—one for death, one for life. Casteel was about to lose consciousness. He's stopped the garrote with his buckskin-gloved hand. But it was cutting off his blood supply, though it had not severed his carotid

CHAPTER 121

artery. Grabbing his boot knife, he stabbed it into Durant's leg. Durant howled and released Casteel. But Casteel was too weak from the loss of oxygen to get up quickly. Durant recovered, pulled out a large, combat knife, and raised it.

At that moment, I flung open the cabin door opposite where Durant squatted. He was about to plunge the knife into Casteel's chest.

"Can I play, too?" I said.

"McRain." I moved to attack Durant with my only knife.

"No, Frankenstein, asshole."

Durant pressed his knife to Casteel's throat. "Drop the knife, or Casteel's dead."

I violated a rule; I did not have a back-up boot knife. But I dropped the knife anyway, "Won't killing him violate your Hoffa Protocol? Out of the corner of my eye, I glimpsed a huge, railroad-sized screwdriver, rolling back and forth on the control panel.

"You know about the Protocol?"

Some slack action made me sway, away from the control panel and over to the opposite wall of the cab. "Enough to know you aren't working for Uncle Sam any more."

"I can't clip Casteel with you here 'cause then, it wouldn't look like the railroad did it. If your blood's in the cab, I don't get paid."

"Your blood doesn't matter?" I asked.

"For sixty million, I'll spill a little of my blood." Durant pulled out a nine-millimeter Glock and pointed it at me.

"Whoa! Economic terrorism pays well."

"I'll give you a chance to jump, McRain, or I'll kill you, too."

"Jump? Then you grease my client, and we get a nationwide rail shutdown." I leaned towards the rolling screwdriver and continued, "That's what you are getting paid for, right? Creating mass hysteria in the world markets? Slowing down the economy, so the terrorists get what they want?" The train lurched again, and I fell towards the control panel, by the screwdriver, but it rolled away again. I steadied myself. "Drive up the price of gas to ten dollars a gallon, and, in a couple weeks, let it stabilize at twice today's price."

"Something like that."

"Well, well, you got a neat and tidy retirement plan. And big oil makes an extra five hundred billion over the next decade?" Bright lights from a cigarette billboard briefly hit the cab. I glanced at the screwdriver on the control panel. I knew he could not see my eyes because the light from the billboards was at my back.

"Any chance your money men are fanatic terrorists, bent on destroying America? Mister?" I was fishing for his name.

"You are a quick study, McRain. It's Colonel Durant, to you."

The train horn blared, up ahead. Snaggle Tooth took a pull off a flask of Old Crow and squinted at something on the tracks, something blurry. Some cows, up ahead on the tracks.

He hollered, to no avail, "Get off the tracks." The locomotive horn blasted, with Durant and me in a standoff.

"I bet you didn't think about your blood in here." Casteel struggled, but stopped when Durant pressed the knife harder against his throat.

"I'll mix it with his; anyway, it will be the Feds that will investigating this Einstein." He said it with the knowledge that the results of any investigation would be predetermined. Jake's throat started to trickle blood. "See, Harvard Boy, that's what makes us different. I don't need a fancy degree to make my millions."

The train horn blew three more times.

"Colonel. You're an officer. And a Westie at that. You know that, without a good education, . . ."

The train's brakes locked up, into emergency, throwing everyone forward. I grabbed the large screwdriver off the control panel, and, with a quick, underhand pitch, I threw the screwdriver into Durant's eye. All the way through. The long screwdriver stuck out the back of his head. I'd impaled Colonel Durant.

"You're screwed."

CHAPTER 121

Colonel Durant slumped back against the side of the cab where he had been when I first came aboard.

Jake was still not fully recuperated, but he was lucid, "That was some pretty fancy knife work, there, counselor." I helped Jake sit up.

"That's the way they taught us at Harvard."

"And how's that?"

"Always dot your eyes."

"And, for good measure, to make sure the job is done right ..."

From his seat on the floor, and even as weakened as he was, Casteel punched Durant's corpse across the jaw.

"And cross your 'Ts'."

"A little something for the afterlife, eh?"

Two Marines with law licenses. We bonded well together.

# CHAPTER 122

# JUDAS

Inside the cab of the second locomotive, Durant lay dead against the wall. Casteel was sitting up, but still suffering from loss of oxygen. I rushed to pull Jake away from the bloody corpse.

"That was a Hell of an economics lesson. You should have taken the money," said Jake."

"Naw. The pay was great, but the health benefits sucked," I said, as I got Casteel up. We moved out the cab door and towards the front locomotive.

Casteel opened the lead locomotive's cabin door, revealing a surprised Snaggle Tooth. He turned around, quick, to see a bloody Casteel. Snaggle Tooth stuttered.

"Wha, wha, what? Jake? Jake, what ya so bloody for? Thought you got yourself a nap back there. And who's he?"

"Cut the crap, Snags. Surprised to see me? Where's your grip? My lawyer wants to inspect it."

Casteel rummaged through the cab storage while I stepped into the cab. Jake found Snaggle Tooth's grip and unzipped it. Bundles of money fell out, onto the floor.

"Now, I can explain about that money. That's for my old lady's cancer surgery."

"You lyin' sack of shit. You left your old lady for the bottle ten years ago."

"A runner from Miss DeeDee's law firm brought it out to me. Like the big union men get. You know. The ones who send all the business."

Jake and I looked at each other. Blood money. Sent by a relative of Jake's. That was pretty cold behavior between relatives, considering Miss DeeDee was Jake's niece. Jake filed that fact away, in the "Revenge" section of the filing cabinet in his mind.

Casteel began his revenge with Snags, dragging him to the cab door. I opened it. Jake pulled back his fist and punched Snaggle Tooth.

Snaggle Tooth pleaded, holding his hands up to stop another punch.

"Wait a minute there, please, Mr. Jake."

Snaggle tooth popped his false teeth out and handed them to me. "Cost me a month's wages." I took the teeth and put them on the throttle. They chattered away, to the heavy vibration of the locomotive on the phallic-shaped locomotive throttle. They looked nasty, like they were giving the throttle oral sex.

Jake Casteel pointed at the throttle and got in Snag's face.

"Look, Snags. Even your teeth know who owns ya."

Jake nodded at the teeth, chattering on the throttle, as he held Snaggle Tooth's shirt, in a fistful of flannel.

He punched Snaggle Tooth in the face.

"You son of a bitch."

He punched Snags harder.

"You Goddamned son of a bitch."

He punched him again, swinging from way down, from his heels. He delivered a crushing roundhouse into a turncoat friend.

"You Goddamned, traitor, son-of-a-bitch."

Casteel punched Snaggle Tooth one last time and let go of Snag's shirt. The sudden release made Snaggle Tooth fall, through the open door and off the locomotive. He rolled in the weeds and ended up somersaulting into a tree of thorns. Winded, Jake staggered back a bit. He collected himself, wiping the blood from his knuckles.

I was a Marine first and a lawyer second. I offered Jake support, "U.C.M.J., Uniform Code of Marine Justice."

"Damn Judas, what he was." I put a consoling hand on Jake's shoulder.

"You okay? You oughta have a doc look at that line from the Sicilian necktie you were wearing."

Jake waved me off.

CHAPTER 122

He turned to see me still ogling the money. "You know, my electric bill is overdue," I said, as a joke. There was a hundred thousand dollars in the bag.

Jake looked at the money. He bent over and picked some up. He stood up and pulled on the throttle of the locomotive, and the train slowed.

"I need you to get off, Mike."

I argued that, whatever he was going do, I was with him. Marines had to stick together. No, they didn't teach me that at Harvard. I learned that with bullets whizzing by my head, carrying a two-hundred-pound Marine out of a bombed-out hell-hole in Beirut, Lebanon. The door gunner had caught it in the shoulder. That son of a sea cook grabbed hold of his weapon and covered my ass with a hail of bullets, allowing me and my package to escape. That is where I learned that we cover each other's backs in all we do.

"Don't tell me you are gonna break any laws 'cause then I'd have to turn you in. I can't violate the rules of ethics," I said, tongue in cheek. I wanted to hit the railroad right in the gob. And that train had the right punch for the job.

"Boy Scout days are over. I hereby relinquish my Eagle Scout rank. Now, get off the train. I'll see ya."

"What ya gonna do? How come I don't get to play?" I replied. "You're gonna trash the train, aren't ya?"

"I'm gonna tape down the throttle, and this baby will come off the grade, doing about a hundred miles per hour, all the way to the new rail center. What with all the volatile shit we are hauling in the tank cars behind us, this train will go up in a mushroom cloud."

"Then we're in it together," I said.

Immediately, Jake went out the door and jumped to the second locomotive.

"Where you goin'?"

"Every pirate ship needs a flyin' lady."

The mile-long train slowly inched up the grade, ten miles from the new rail center, while we ran up our own version of the Jolly Roger. The C.I.A.'s dead ramrod, Colonel Durant, on a spit.

We secured the body of Colonel Durant onto the front of the locomotive, leaning out the draw-bar on the front railing. Durant looked a lot like the flying lady on a sailing ship, only much more grisly. Durant's corpse was now equipped with a ten-foot draw-bar, going in one end and coming out the other. Like a pig on a barbecue spit. We were waging psychological warfare right back at the people who sent Durant to us.

I took a C.D. out of Durant's pocket and kept it. I thought it might make some interesting nighttime reading.

Sure. What we were doing was not perfectly legal. But what can I say? We were Marines, and they ticked us off. I wish I could say I was Jesus Christ, but I am not. I'm not a perfect Catholic. Guilty, as charged.

This is why I pray so much.

Jake laughed when he thought about what the Franklin City trainmaster, up in his control booth, would think when he saw the train through his binoculars, coming at the yard at one hundred miles per hour. Durant out in front of the lead locomotive. Their dead assassin coming back to them. There would be a hellacious collision and huge explosions. I wished I could stay and watch.

I knew it was Halloween, but I love fireworks any time of year.

CHAPTER 122

# CHAPTER 123

# THE BLOW

Jake and I were wrapping up—transforming Durant into our own version of the flying lady—and the colonel was starting to color up a bit.

"Hey, the Chicago Arbitration board decided about your job. I thought you should be the one to open it." I handed Casteel an envelope. "Go ahead and read it; I'll finish up."

Jake went aft while I applied tape to the dead body we were proudly displaying on the front of the locomotive. I stuffed thirty C-notes—hundred-dollar bills—of the blood money into the dead man's mouth. Then I finished the tape job and followed Jake aft. The train was slowly lugging to the top of the hill. I opened the cabin door and stepped in.

Snaggle Tooth's teeth were still chattering on the now duct-taped throttle. I saw a note: "*Semper Fi.*" Duct-taped to the window. The arbitration award was crumpled up into a ball on the floor, the envelope shredded.

I heard Casteel's voice call to me from outside, "McRain."

I threw open the port-side door and went flying onto the catwalk. I looked forward, then aft. Casteel was standing on the front of the second locomotive. I moved towards him. But he stopped me.

"What are you doin,' Jake? We gotta get our asses offa here."

"You see the screw job they gave me? My own union voted against me. The lawyers' mafia *won.*"

"Hell of a blow, Jake. Forget the mafia. Come on. Let's get out of here."

"I'm getting off here, Mike. Right here."

"Whadda ya mean?" Jake looked down, at the rail ties and train wheels.

"No. No way, Jake. *Di Trina* and the railroad think they won. Forget 'em."

"I get to shoot last."

"Bullshit."

"I will be a great martyr. A lot better martyr than a leader. *Semper Fi*, and all that shit."

Jake jumped to down between the first and the second locomotive. But I grabbed for his jacket collar and held on, though he tried to break free of my grip. I struggled mightily and held Jake against his will. But my grip was slipping.

The consist of locomotives crested the hill, and the train began moving faster. We had to get off soon, or the train would be going too fast and we would die when we jumped.

I came close to falling off the locomotive. I wrapped one leg around the iron railing of the deck. I'd held more than one Force Recon teammate like that, off an extraction helicopter. But those men had not been working against me.

Jake's feet pedaled in mid-air, inches above where the railroad ties whizzed by, under the train. "You gotta stay, Jake. Your men. Your men need you."

"My kids disowned me. My wife divorced me. The only thing that matters to me is the union." Jake punched the air in protest.

"And my men fragged me."

"*Semper Fi*, mister. You're coming home with me."

"Let me die, God damn it. This is the only way to hurt the bastards. Nobody invited you to my war."

Jake unbuttoned a button on his jacket, so he could slip out of it. But, against his will, I continued pulling Jake from behind, up towards the safety of the deck.

"My war is about over," I said. Jake could not undo the last button. It looked like I would be able to haul him to safety. I was laboring, very hard.

"The war will never be over, McRain. *Di Trina* will never die."

I hauled Jake up to the safety of the deck. I put him in a chin-drop and an arm bar, to hold him until he cooled off. I hooked him under the armpits

CHAPTER 123

and dragged him back a bit, away from the lip of the locomotive deck, like I was dragging an unwilling wrestler back onto the mat.

Jake said, "You don't understand, McRain, they were supposed to kill me tonight. God damn it. This was my fate. My Alamo."

I put Jake into a snake headlock that pinched his carotid artery. It's a bit tricky. But I knew what I was doing. Jake went limp as he tried to grab his boot knife. He was unconscious.

I said to my quiet client, my fellow Marine, "We'll still have our Iwo Jima."

I grabbed the money bag and lifted Jake into a fireman's carry. As the train crested the ridge, it was picking up speed. I slowly moved down the locomotive steps, holding Jake over my shoulder and gripping the bag full of money. I looked for a nice place to jump, tuck, and roll.

Geronimo!

I got up and watched the mile-long train thunder past, on its way to an explosive ending. I got to Jake. After his rough roll off the train, Jake was coming to, and I freshened him up. We started walking out of the rural woods.

U.C.M.J. Uniform Code of Marine Justice. Ooo-Rah.

I knew revenge was a vexation to the spirit and, by helping Casteel get even with the criminal bastards, I was not being a perfect Catholic. But this was not just revenge. The railroad had sent us their hit man, who we'd killed in self-defense. Jake Casteel and I were just sending him back to the railroad via express delivery. It was our little gesture of protest, like when, in the temple, Jesus overturned the tables of the moneychangers. He shamed them and hit them in their pocketbook. We were just two Catholic Marines, trying to apply our Catechism to the dangers God set before us.

I kept Snag's grip, filled with money, on my shoulder. I am a lawyer, after all.

I figured we could turn it over to Rafe, to see if he could trace it to one of the Designated firms. If not, Jake could put his kids through college with it.

I figured Dalton and I might have a fee coming. I didn't know how the Bar Association would allow me to list some of my legal work on our billing statement, so I thought wryly of submitting the following to Casteel as this day's bill:

McRain & Boyle
Attorneys at Law

Billable Hours: "U.S. v. Casteel"

Locate adverse parties via Gooby Shammer 2.4 hours

Whack bad guy for client, saving client's neck 0.3 hours

Deliver screw-job arbitration award to client 0.1 hours

Prep bad guy to ram into railroad's terminal 0.2 hours

Save client's neck, preventing suicide 0.2 hours

Secure blood money placed on client's head 0.2 hours

Walk angry client to safety 1.4 hours

Total 4.5 hours
Total Costs, Some gas money
Total Due.........No Charge

Total Profit......Priceless:
A true friend for life

I wondered how my parish priest, Father Dempsey, would take my confession the next Saturday. My bet was my penance would be ten "Hail Marys," ten "Our Fathers," and ten "Glory Be's." And a special meditation on letting things go. Live and let live.

CHAPTER 123

I promised myself, and God, I would try to change—if only the bad guys would cooperate and stop sending assassins to our doorstep. I, too, was once an assassin, claiming the blessing of the C.I.A. god of "might makes right." Now, I was living life on the other side of my previous employment; I was seeing violence as a victim of oppression. I began to understand some of the wisdom of the ancients, of God's word.

To stop sin, we must begin in our own souls. I can live with that. But can the enemy live that way too?

Just don't mess with my family and friends. If God was going to send me to Hell for using deadly force in protecting the innocent, then get me some S.P.F. 200, suntan lotion because I am going to fry.

*Semper Fi.* And carry on.

# CHAPTER 124

# RECESSION ELECTIONOMICS

The President was in the Oval Office watching television coverage of the huge catastrophe at the largest rail center in America. He spoke to his Chief of Staff.

"Mr. Trenton. What have you found out about the railroad mess?"

"Sir. They located Van Killman's body. It does not appear that it was blown out of the helicopter when it exploded. The cause for the explosion is still under investigation."

"Will the bad news never stop?" the President said.

"This isn't on CNN yet, Sir. But there is more bad news, Mr. President."

"How could the news get worse than the violent death of Big Dutch Van Killman? He was my biggest donor and my campaign manager."

"And a dear friend," Trenton added.

The President looked out the window in a mournful way. His arms were crossed, and his face wrinkled in thought.

"Lieutenant-General Crowe advises that the toxic train that slammed into the railroad's new, billion-dollar switching facilities caused much more damage than what first appeared. Preliminaries from the E.P.A. are that the site will take a few years to clean up. The toxic payload was in tank cars headed to the Army's chemical weapons manufacturing facility. The tank cars ruptured."

The President put his head and face into his hands. He could not believe the news. With the rail center destroyed, there surely would be slow-downs in rail traffic. This would result in an economic slowdown, which would cause a bona-fide recession. And that meant there was a good chance he would not get re-elected.

There would probably also be a couple of dozen short wildcat strikes because Jake Casteel had been screwed on his job appeal. C.I.A. was damned if it messed with Casteel and damned if it did not. This would seal it: he would be a one-term president.

He could already hear his political opponent rant and rave.

"It's the economy, stupid."

CHAPTER 124

# CHAPTER 125

# MICHAEL, ROW YOUR BOAT ASHORE, HALLELUJAH

My prayers, of course, were actually dreams with God. And vice versa.

I was full of the truth. I did an abrupt about-face, turning from Captain Carion, and marched away from the ceremony. Mr. Troubles escorted me down the ladder to a rowboat. He took a seat aft and told to me to row ashore.

I asked Mr. Troubles if he could hold my orders while I rowed. Troubles laughed hard in refusal. "You never want Troubles touching your marching orders, Laddie. Best you keep them to yourself. That is, if you don't want a black cloud following you the rest of your days," Troubles said, with a wise grin and a twinkle in his eye. It was advice from the ancient, to be heeded.

"It figures I would have Troubles taking me ashore."

Troubles laughed again, "Ah, you'll never get rid of Troubles, Laddie; you will never get rid of Mr. Troubles."

I wrapped a hand around the handle of each long oar and began to row. The water was placid and clear. Fish of all colors darted throughout its depths.

The skiff entered the white, foaming surf, and I got out in knee-deep water and dragged the boat to a stable berth. Troubles did not get out, for fear of touching the Hellish waters. "I've come much too far through Satan's black ink with nary a drop. It would be a spoil of my rapture."

I understood, and we shook hands as men—as mates communing with the spirit of one soul to another. "Good luck to you, Laddie," Troubles said.

I knew Mr. Troubles was going to have his rapture. I put my shoulder to the bow of the skiff and pushed it back out into the surf to help Troubles get back to "The Constitution." I turned to walk up the beach and towards the jungle. But I was haled by a voice so familiar, it sounded like my Father's voice, calling my name. I turned around to see that Mr. Troubles was now in the uniform of the man in the portrait above my own homestead's stairs. Indeed, it was my Father, General McRain, pulling on the oars and hollering back to me, "Remember, Mike-O, the ghosts of guilt. They haunt only their masters." I was in awe. I could not believe my eyes. I felt my heart spring from my chest upon seeing my Father again. I ran into the surf to swim out to Father's boat. I needed one more touch of my father, of his spirit. I wanted an eternal moment in his eternal love.

But the Hellish waters had turned to acid. They belonged to a dimension into which I was no longer allowed. The waters burned me, and I made a shameless retreat to the shore. From above the surf-line of sin, I could only watch the General, Father, the irascible Mr. Troubles, row the boat back to "The Constitution" and away. I heard my Father's voice drift gently across the water as "The Constitution" filled her sails.

"Be gone with you, Mike-O, be gone. Live and love," Father said. He punctuated his farewell with a broad wave of his hand. Father turned away, to his duties in the afterlife. He was off to Purgatory Cay with the rest to the deserving souls. It became apparent to me that Father stayed in Purgatory, he postponed his salvation, risking his soul to make sure mine made safe voyage back to the living.

It was a quick flick of his hand, at his full arm's length, and my dear Father was gone.

I paused on the sacred Father-Son moment. It was gut-wrenching, life-turning and immediately up-lifting. My soul was charged with the joyous power of my Creator.

I felt the crinkle of my marching orders, tucked inside my officer's coat. I fetched them out and broke the ancient family seal, the symbol of my family name. The break in the intricate, wax seal ran along a line that separated the bottom of the midnight-black shield, with its one gold star, from the top of the shield, with two stars. First, as I read my spiritual orders, the battle plan for my soul's redemption, my eyes grew cold and stern. Then a knowing smile, the smile that belonged to a determined man, crept across my face. I stuffed the orders in my coat and drew my saber. Churning up the powdery white sand, I marched into the jungle, back into the world. Like a Marine on a mission.

Ooo-Rah.

CHAPTER 125

# CHAPTER 126

# TAX REFUND

It came in a bumpy envelope and carried a bumpy message.  A tax refund, payable to "Bridget Mary McRain," spelled out in Braille and in ink for the total sum of $2.00.

Bridget Mary McRain clutched the check from the United States Treasury to her chest, as though it had ten zeros behind it.

Now Bridget Mary McRain believed she was *somebody*.  She had power and rights, and she could live however she pleased.  She didn't pray to Jesus in thanksgiving, not right away.  Instead, she rested on her accomplishment and chose to meditate.  Her thoughts turned to St. Theresa of Avila and how she might meditate like that saint to look inward, into her soul, instead of searching amongst the man-made, ego-driven distractions of the world, for answers to one of the biggest questions in Bridget's life.  Her powerfully fast, autistic brain slowed and she began to think deeply and smoothly and rock and twitch surely  and rhythmically and curl her long, red hair around her ring less finger.

Bridget Mary Bernadette McRain had a decision to make.

# CHAPTER 127

# WHO KILLED JIMMY HOFFA

I went to the kitchen and tried out my new laptop computer. I put in the C.D. that I took out of dead Colonel Durant's pocket the night before. The CD's formatting had been ironed out by the Afghanistan Embassy's I.T. staff. There was a lack of sufficient encryption, which indicated to me that Durant distrusted computers. The information displayed without a hitch. But I had to make sense of it.

Bridget and I sat at the kitchen table. Gunny lay in the corner, chewing on a bone. Bridget, with her arm in a sling, was reciting the rosary and praying to Saint Catherine of Siena, a politician within the church, and Saint Francis of Assisi.

After a couple dozen clicks, I brought up a text titled "Termination." I clicked on it. What it displayed changed Bridget and me forever.

I read out loud from the laptop screen:

"On July 30, 1975, primary operative for *Di Trina* met with James Riddle Hoffa at safe house regarding possible merger of Teamsters and rail unions. . ."

"Sweet Mother of God. That's who killed Jimmy Hoffa? Bridget, you have to hear this. This is incredible." I read on:

The report reflected that Jimmy Hoffa walked from his car and into the target home with Big Dutch Van Killman and the Rail Union president Sal Macon. The audiotapes produced from the surveillance bugs in the residence provided the text of the dialogue. I skipped ahead, towards the end of the dialogue.

"If you do it our way, Jimmy, the Teamsters and the C.U.R.T.I.S. unions will merge. I'll step aside as Curtis Union International president right before the merger, and you will take my place after the unions are merged. You will end up president over the Teamsters and the rail unions.

But your title won't have nothing to do with the Teamsters. The teamsters will be underneath you. Yous understand? Verstehen?"

"Verstehen. I got it. I got it," said Hoffa.

"You will be back in business 'cause you'll be president of all the land transportation unions," said Big Dutch.

Jimmy Hoffa said, "My parole prohibits me from dealin' in Teamster politics, but yous are sayin' I can get around that by becomin' president of the railroad union. The Hog Heads." Hoffa made hand gestures indicating he saw the big picture, "And then merge the rail union and the Teamsters?"

Macon and Big Dutch nodded. Hoffa understood the deal.

"We got the Senate Judiciary Committee gonna give us a friendly judge. Senator Moore got it all hooked up for us. He is the on the Senate Judiciary Committee, and he made the deal foolproof."

Big Dutch threw in his two cents' worth. "The judge that Senator Moore gives us will make a very cooperative interpretation of the pardon you received from President Nixon." Big Dutch motioned towards the rail union president, "And I'll take good care of Sal with a very nice retirement package." Macon hushed Hoffa and flashed his Masonic ring in Hoffa's face. "You gotta keep it on the square, Jimmy. Hush, hush." Sal was referring to the Masonic oath of secrecy that Mason's refer to as "Keeping it on the square.", or in other words, what happens in Masonic business dealings stays secret.

Hoffa couldn't sit still. He acted like a bronco with a burr under his saddle. "Hey, we are just negotiatin' here . . . Teamster style . . ."

Hoffa pointed at Big Dutch, "Wudda you get outta this, Big Dutch, ya rich personal-injury lawyer?" Dutch's face remained as cold as ice. "I've been in the joint and I've seen some smelly Mafia crap, but this takes the cake." Hoffa counted factors on his fingers for Big Dutch to consider.

"I mean, the F.B.I. is your muscle, Masons here run your union, and the Mafia runs the freakin' railroad. And it's all C.I.A.'s plan? Why should the F.B.I., the C.I.A. and the Masons give your Mafia more injury cases?"

Big Dutch and the rail president shrugged at each other. Hoffa reached across the table and grabbed Big Dutch's shirt, mangling it into a crumpled mess.

CHAPTER 127

"So yous get to cut and cripple my Teamsters, and ya greedy injury lawyers keep a monopoly on pain and suffering? Off my men?"

Big Dutch explained later he was very angry that Hoffa would even lay hands on him. Hoffa released Big Dutch and turned to Macon "And you, you limp-dicked, son of a bitch.

You'd sell your position of trust to these lousy *Di Trina* lawyers— Mafia, stoolies, whatever they are?" Hoffa pointed a finger in Big Dutch's face. But he looked at rail union president Macon. "Government stoolies, just so's you can sip margueritas on a beach the rest of your life?" Hoffa said, as a further indictment of *Di Trina* and Big Dutch. "You get outta my sight before I beat the holy horse piss out of you, ya cocksucker." Jimmy lurched out of his seat and punched Macon, who fell out of his chair. "I mean it. Scram."

The rail union president got up and got out of the kitchen—quick— leaving Big Dutch and Hoffa alone. For just a moment. Before the door closed behind Sal, two huge men came in, carrying ax handles and a roll of duck tape, and stood behind Hoffa.

Big Dutch sat across the table from Hoffa —seething at the way Hoffa refused the offer. "Go head, negotiate." Big Dutch said.

"Ya tol' me yous had it all worked out where I'd get back the Union. And now I come here and find out you want me to let your *Di Trina Mafia* run my Teamsters Union for the Goddamned C.I.A.? So ya won't ever have any strikes? What's the price we are all payin'— you gettin' personal-injury cases?" Hoffa slammed his palm on the table.

"And so we can all have a nice, little, circle jerk on my men with the Mafia, the Masons, and the Goddamned government? To make yous more tort fees?" Hoffa pointed at Big Dutch, who sat with his arms crossed offering no denial of the truth. Van Killman looked like he was about to explode. But Jimmy kept boring in on Dutch.

"Lemme tell you somethin', Mr. Big-Shot Lawyer. I know what you're up to, and I will never sleep." Hoffa leaned over the table and got in Big Dutch's face, "'Cuz I know you're going to sell my Teamsters' body parts to your frickin' juries."

Big Dutch motioned to the two huge men behind Hoffa. The mafia strong-men grabbed the union leader, and the bigger one put Jimmy in a double-hammer lock.

I paused there and explained to Bridget. "A double hammer is a powerful wrestling hold on the neck and shoulders that immobilizes a man."

Bridget showed she was a television wrestling aficionado, "Double hammer illegal. Only counter is bull your neck and pull down with your arms and stomp on other guy's feet. Maybe flip him off."

I was astounded. I knew wrestlers who could not explain it that well. It looked like there was a lot I did not know about my big sister, Bridget. I shook my head and read more of the report.

They duck-taped Jimmy Hoffa onto his chair. Hoffa struggled all the while.

"I'm sorry it came down to this, Jimmy. I thought we could do business. But you don't leave me an option."

"You thought I'd be some desperate sap who'd sell out my men?"

"They aren't your men any more, Jimmy. Your pardon says you're out of the Teamsters' Union. If it wasn't for me, you wouldn't even be able to dream about getting close to a Teamster office."

Hoffa stood up, with the chair taped to him. "Ya sum bitch. They'll always... they'll always be my men. I've had men's heads beaten in; men shot, burned; kids made orphans—to make a better life for the living. For my men. For my Teamsters."

Jimmy Hoffa tried to ram Big Dutch, even while taped in the chair. But the two torpedoes yanked Hoffa back down. They held his chair down while Big Dutch picked up one of the ax handles. Hoffa struggled hard against his restraints. The veins in his neck bulged.

"We'll just negotiate the Teamster way," said Big Dutch, in a stance like a baseball hitter, as he drew back the ax handle.

"I will fight you all the way to the grave and beyond," Hoffa said, spitting on the floor. "*Di Trina* Lawyers' Mafia, my ass. You think I'm afraid of you? Verstehen, Dutchie? Verste ..."

Big Dutch swung the ax handle and hit Hoffa on the side of his head. The impact made a sick, snapping sound as it cracked Hoffa's skull.

CHAPTER 127

Van Killman showed his psychopathic side. "Nobody takes food offa my plate. Nobody . . . Verstehen? Verstehen, Hoffa? Verstehen, Jimmy?" Big Dutch hit Jimmy's head, again and again. "Jimmy Goddamned Hoffa." Then Big Dutch started to play with Hoffa's head like it was a baseball.

"And here's how Stan Musial would do it," boasted Big Dutch Van Killman.

Big Dutch swung left-handed, hitting Hoffa on the other side of the head. Big Dutch was getting sick with it. Hoffa was unconscious, but Big Dutch took another swing that sent blood onto the wall. Dutch was a sick S.O.B. Big Dutch swung and swung, on and on, until C.I.A.-operative Turner came into the kitchen.

"What have you done? Oh, you dumb, dumb son of a bitch," Turner said to Big Dutch. The C.I.A.'s Mr. Turner was extremely familiar with Big Dutch and Hoffa. Turner had helped Walter Sheridan orchestrate a number of prosecutions of Hoffa for Attorney General, Bobby Kennedy.

Lieutenant-General Crowe, at that time Major Crowe and assigned to the Pentagon's Intelligence Bureau, came into the kitchen, stone-faced behind aviator sunglasses and in plain clothes. Crowe nodded to his men, who then shot Big Dutch's henchmen. They went to work bagging the dead and cleaning up the carnage.

"You have no idea what problems you just caused us for the next fifty years," Crowe said to Big Dutch.

I stopped reading and Bridget immediately gave her assessment, "Hoffa good man," her voice trailing off in sorrow.

I figured out what Colonel Durant tried to do, "So Jake was set up under the 'Hoffa Protocol' because a felony conviction would prevent him holding office."

Bridget rocked back and forth, working the beads, saying, "C.I.A., C.I.A., C.I.A."

"And, when it came to Jake Casteel, the C.I.A. made sure that the economy didn't stop because a transportation-union officer got whacked. Otherwise, there would have been wild-cat strikes that would have been worse than any primary strike."

Bridget was into it now, "Hoffa good man."

# CHAPTER 128

# LOST AND FOUND

Bridget and I were in the kitchen, listening to the television: "The toxic firestorm at America's largest rail yard was finally brought under control." CNN showed a picture of the raging fire and toxic cloud. "After a runaway train slammed into the railroad's new billion-dollar rail yard three days ago." Eating, I paused and used a napkin to wipe away some egg sticking on the corner of my mouth.

"Meanwhile, wildcat rail strikes against all carriers have shut down America."

Bridget tried to get a word in edgewise. "Mike. Listen to me."

I tuned Bridget out. I was in my own little world, and I turned up the TV's sound even more. "In a minute; now listen."

I listened to the television reporter say, "And you better get out the ax and chop some firewood. Blackouts are expected again in forty-two states, until coal trains can get to the power plants." Electric-company officials say existing nuclear-power plants simply do not have enough capacity to service the whole country." The story ended, and the screen went to a commercial for new gas-guzzling S.U.V.s.

Then the house lost electricity. The T.V. went black. Bridget knocked with her shillelagh on the table, like a judge raps a gavel. I looked indignantly at Bridget.

"You don't need me any more," Bridget said.

"Wudda ya mean? I'm the one's been takin' care of you."

"The house is mine. Michael, leave. I can't mother you no more."

I stood up and shook my finger at Bridget, as though she could see my finger. "You can't do this. You can't live on your own."

Bridget stood, and grabbed the sleeve of my sweater, and, with her tears spurting, she shouted me down. "I can't mother you no more. You get your own family. Get happy." Bridget's head bounced up and down, in short spasms, like one of those bobblehead dolls people put in the back windows of cars. She was delivering the bad news.

"I don't need you any more? You're confused, Bridgy. I'm the one who's been takin' care of you." I waved my arms in frustration. "I've been doing the shopping." I turned and staggered away from Bridget to the sink to look out the window because I realized that what I'd said to Bridget wasn't true. I corrected myself.

"No, I haven't shopped in months."

Gunny rubbed up against Bridget, and the old bulldog turned his head away from me.

"My ol' *'Semper Fi'* buddy."

"Go see Daddy. Go see Daddy," Bridget said, as she shooed me out the kitchen door.

I staggered out of the kitchen. Out the door, onto the porch. I stopped at the big chessboard to make a move. But Bridget had put my black king in checkmate. There was no move for me to take. Only surrender. Like a trained warrior, I cut my losses, buried my dead, and moved on. I let go of Bridget. Just like Dalton had told me to do. For my own good. For Bridget's good. I let go.

But let her go or not, Bridget kept praying, right and strong, for me, her little brother. She never stopped.

Bridgey was exuberant, sprightly in her claim to holy words, words of an ancient parable taught throughout the millennia, each time as though the parable was a new-found prize. With sensing fingertips, Bridget coursed over and clung to her relics, chanting and rechanting with glee, a sparkle beneath the eyelids of one who possessed a spiritual eyesight as sharp as an eagle's. She saw all–in her soul and in her heart. Holy words were trapped in the strong talons of her mind. She perched high on the rock of what has been written.

". . . and be glad: for this thy brother was dead and is alive again, and was lost and is found. Lord praise a'mighty."

CHAPTER 128

# CHAPTER 129

*"All that we do with our lives is laid,*
*as an offering, at the altar*
*of our gods and goddesses,*
*on Earth, our parents."*
—Michael McRain

On my way to the National Cemetery, I stopped at Jefferson Barracks V.A. Hospital to see the sick men society had forgotten. The orderly told me that the 'Admiral,' Bob, my favorite of the injured and ailing veterans, had died a short while back, when I was engrossed in the Casteel case. Damned Agent Orange had attacked the old, Navy, U.D.T. frogman's endocrine system. Liver failure had made him so debilitated and jaundiced, his whole body shut down. He died alone, except for the wishes and prayers of the other men in his hospital wing. An honorable death for an honorable man.

The orderly asked me why I was dressed in my Marine Corps dress blues.

"I have some unfinished business up the hill."

I tilted my head in the direction of the National Cemetery. He nodded with an understanding grunt. He knew all too much about speaking to the dead. The drive up to Father's gravesite took only three minutes. But I was tortured by what seemed an eternity of anticipation.

I felt armed properly to do battle with the past. I wore my Marine regulation white gloves. As offerings to my Father, I held Colonel Durant's "Hoffa Protocol" C.D.; a stack of Polaroid pictures of the stone; and a scroll, tied with a red bow, the Supreme Court's order exonerating Jake Casteel. I stood at attention before my father's tombstone. I heard a train power by, down at the base of the bluff on which the cemetery sat. It was headed downstream.

A shiver went down my spine. I looked over my shoulder, expecting to see some beast or monster because I now realized the evil spawned in our legal system by trains, and lawyers, and railroads, and greed. It would never stop. Not for anyone. I thought it ironic that the train's booming horn blasted right after I got those goose bumps. It was as if it was signaling to me, *"I'm here; I'm still alive; and I'm strong as ever."*

I accepted that my size was tiny in relation to the strength of the railroad. The strength of the world. I moved on to much more important things.

I dropped to one knee and laid my offerings before Father's tombstone. I bore through them all and stuck them firmly to the ground with a small American flag on a stick. Only the offering of triumph—proof of my manhood, my bravery, my skills as a truth warrior—allowed me to approach my dead father for his blessing from the grave.

The tombstone read:

FRANCIS T. MCRAIN
MAR 6, 1919 – SEPT 3, 1986
BRIG. GENERAL USAF
WWII, KOREA, BERLIN CRISIS,
CUBAN MISSILE CRISIS, VIETNAM

I braced at attention, maintaining a strong salute.

"Sir."

I severed my salute, did an about-face and marched off towards my Mustang.

Music stopped me cold. Bagpipes. I turned to see a kilted piper, playing "Taps" at a funeral high on the hill. Servicemen saluted and fired a twenty-one-gun salute. A single tear rolled down my face. I doffed my hat and ran back to my Father's tombstone. I hugged the stone as "Taps" continued from the distant Irish funeral. I wept freely.

"Father. I'm sorry . . . Oh, I've missed you so . . . I didn't leave my wing man."

I gripped the stone as I would hold my Father in a bear hug. I respectfully kissed the top of the tombstone, then slowly let go of the stone with my white-gloved hands. The hands of a Marine. The hands of an ever-faithful son. *Semper Fi* hands.

All the good and bad we do, as sons of men, is laid upon the altars of our Gods — our Fathers. Some say without those offerings, offerings of respect, duty and honor we are hollow, incomplete men existing only to serve and sense the world.

I recalled when I first feared losing my Father.

I steadied myself by the stone, for my head swirled with emotions. My mind harkened back to a time when the world was much colder—a time when the Russian bear roared at Uncle Sam and discovered that Americans are not easily bluffed. It was October 1, 1962, and the Cuban Missile Crisis was upon us. I was my Father's son, and Father was my god. He wore the hat of a warrior: a fighter pilot's helmet. When America called him to serve, he was the best. I knew he wasn't really God. But I treated him that way.

We had to say goodbye to Father. He was the commander of a fighter wing preparing to leave for a nuclear war. I was only four. I was trying to prove my courage to my Father. It was an offering to my god on Earth. When he let me come onto the tarmac at the Air Force base, to climb up and stand on the ladder to his fighter jet, I wanted him to see I would not be scared.

I clung to the jet's port-side ladder. My knees knocked, my teeth chattered, and I pussied out. I held hard onto the narrow, yellow rung, my brother Raford next to me. The voracious nose air intake of the F-84F fighter jet was only nine feet to my left. It screamed, an ear-shattering roar, for air or anything else on which to feed. I buried my face between the rungs of the ladder, only lifting it from a shivering stare into the fuselage long enough to yell a plea to my Father, to leave. "Daddy, the jet is going to swallow me!"

I wanted to bail out, like a coward. I was a coward.

I could not yet read. But I knew what quotation marks were, and painted on Father's helmet was his pilot name, his call, "Bubbles." It was a fun sounding name that masked Father's deadly skill in the most sophisticated warfare — aerial combat. My eyes returned to the ladder I hung onto and the jet fuselage that was only seven inches in front of my nose. The ladder and I shook as the jet idled, warming up.

Father's crew chief held the ladder and made sure neither Raford nor I fell. He chuckled when he heard that I wanted to jump off the ladder and go back to my Momma's side. I was scared to death, and I did not want to offer anything more to my warrior god. Raford was nonchalant, asking Father questions about the dials and levers in the cockpit. Father complied while he ticked down his clip-boarded, pre-flight checklist.

"I'm scared and I'm getting off the ladder!" My shameless offering was rejected in a summary manner. Father said, "Never leave your wing man!"

The jet's engine was whining so loud, I could barely hear Father. And it looked like the crew chief was blocking my exit— at Father's request.

"Never leave your wing man!" he repeated, even louder.

I stammered and almost cried. But I tried to show a stiff upper lip. Some backbone. I yelled, above the din of the screaming jet engine, "What's a wing man?"

Father did not seem to hear me. He was absorbed in his work. Father was still looking at his pre-flight checklist, going down it and checking things off as he concentrated on preparing for battle against the biggest air force in history. The Russians. I repeated my question.

"What is a wing man?"

Finally, he pulled his attention from making sure his fully armed fighter jet could fly, to school me on a fine lesson of honor.

Father spoke in a firm voice. "A wing man is the man counting on you. Your brother Raford is next to you on the ladder. You cannot bail out on him." He saw I was bewildered, and he extended the analogy. Life paralleled air warfare; it was a familiar reference in our military family. "You must stay because, if you leave him alone, the enemy might shoot him down.

Something bad might happen to him. You have to be faithful. You cannot leave your wing man. The Marines call it *Semper Fi*."

I was unhappy and angry that he wanted me to stay. But it became easier after my older brother Raford insulted me.

"Aw, Dad, he's just a pussy."

Father passed over Rafe's sniping and continued his lesson. I did not know it yet, but my Father, Frank "Bubbles" McRain, a full-bird Colonel at the time, had already been honored in the Fighter Pilot Hall of Fame at The United States Air Force Academy for being the top-scoring Mustang Ace in World War II. He had lived and suffered many harsh and deadly lessons of duty and honor. Father stayed upbeat and told Raford and me his favorite quote, from General Robert E. Lee. He lowered his voice to his most serious tone, and it boomed over the noisy jet engine on which he was sitting.

"Gentlemen, always remember what General Lee said, 'Duty then is the sublimest word in the English language. You should do your duty in all things. You can never do more, and you should never hope to do less.'"

I could tell, even at a young age, that Father found great strength and solace, a warrior's intellectual bond, in that quote from General Lee.

There were seven kids in my family: six boys and one girl. I felt like the black sheep because I was the only one who had Black-Irish hair like Father's. All the rest had different shades of Momma's red. Father quoted General Lee to us seven kids more times than I could remember, at the dinner table, in the car, or most anywhere. Father's favorite time to pass along General Lee's words was after a bedtime story or after he'd recited "*The Cremation of Sam McGee.*" Father told us that whole ballad was a story about duty and honor, even though it had a funny ending.

I did not know what half General Lee's words meant. Only that *duty* was important, and it had something to do with honor. That you always wanted a lot of honor, and the only way you got it was by doing a lot of duty stuff. But, as a four-year-old, that is all I could understand about General Lee—duty and honor.

It came time for Father to go fight the Russians, so he pulled me up the ladder with one arm, and he hugged me and kissed me good and told me he loved me. He did the same with Rafe. Then we got down, off the ladder. Momma said I ran like a scared bunny, all the way back to her. Raford just walked.

In his jet, Father taxied out onto the runway. When he took off, he hit his afterburners—as he had promised us kids—for esprit de corps. There was a loud, popping sound and a long, blue flame blasted from the rear end of his silver fighter jet. Momma and we kids were all lined up, in order of descending height, with me at the end, holding hands with my blind sister, Bridget. We jumped up and down, waving wildly to Father, as though he could see us. Bridget thrust her white cane high into the air, and the rosary around her neck bounced off her belly. We clamored so, until Father had traveled up beyond our worldly sight, up to heaven—we believed—where other winged warriors, like Saint Michael, like warrior angels, waited for him to rendezvous.

Father's lesson always to be faithful, never to leave your wing man, consoled and warmed me in his absence—even if my wing man was just my obnoxious brother on a ladder. It was not merely a security blanket when I thought how Father might be blown up by the Russians as I went to sleep, stared at the ceiling, or cried into my pillow. It was a concept that stuck with me, allowing my father to materialize to me. He was a friend I could always visit, repeating those last words he'd offered before he bravely flew off to harm's way, toward battle, into history.

The Cuban Missile crisis passed, and Father came home safe and sound. But the ageless lessons he'd passed to me, lessons of love as strong as oak, continued in varying shades: *"Never Leave Your Wing Man," "Always Be Faithful," "Semper Fidelis."*

My focus returned to the stone and the ceremony with the dead that I found necessary.

CHAPTER 129

# CHAPTER 130

# REDEMPTION

I still needed my redemption, in the mortal world. I could not hear any message of forgiveness from Father, while I was still confined in a self-made prison of guilt. Its unbendable bars had been shaped by the harsh hammer of duty.

I hugged the stone, strong and tight, as though it were a life preserver and I a castaway adrift at sea. I was overwhelmed by a message of eternal love, which I more felt than heard. It came to me directly. I understood the power of its forgiveness, pure and plain, as if my Father, in the flesh, had spoken it right into my ear.

*Yes, son, I was gone toward Heaven. But I watched you rush back to my bedroom, after you'd taken care of your client. Your inescapable duty. You feared that you'd chosen wrong. You wept hard and grieved over my dead body, that you'd let me down. Forsaken me, your father. You believed abandonment of me to be a mortal sin. That you failed, sinfully, as a son, in your duty to provide comfort during my last, painful breaths. That you deserted me, as a fellow warrior, in your duty to hold my hand and escort me into the presence of God's light, where all good and honorable warriors go to rest. To Valhalla. To Heaven. To glory with God.*

*A deserter you are not. You were doing your lawyerly duty for your client. Duty is duty, no matter how painful. I forgive you for leaving, Michael.*

I'd represented Jake Casteel, not just as a client, but as a wing man. I'd protected Jake, in his impossible case, to prove something to my father, to clear my name with Father, to remove my name from the eternal roll of Goddamned cowards. I never left my wing man, like I had left Father on his deathbed. It was worth the long wait for Father's forgiveness.

I realized that Bridget had prepared me a great feast.

Redemption.

Father granted me amnesty through a message that wrapped my soul in certainty and spiritual understanding; duty and love are continuous, complete and unbroken, like the Celtic rings. Never ending.

With wet eyes, I spoke to the stone, "Thank you, Father."

When I stood there, in reflection, looking back at my Father's tombstone, a sudden wind rattled through the trees along the top of the river bluff. A blizzard of autumn oak leaves fell on and about me looking like huge, gay-colored snowflakes, as though children had colored them with crayons. I do not know how long I meditated there, while the oaks' sun-timed shadows grew longer and longer to cover me with a comforting blanket of natural progression; a deeper understanding of family, past, present and future. They all cast shadows, if we have the faith to see them. I felt sad and lonely, until the soft, familiar sound of bugled Taps filled the cemetery, signaling an end to my mourning. My breast gently swelled and my heart and soul felt mended. I turned away from the stone and staggered to my car, emotionally spent. There was still work to be done to set my life straight.

I moved on.

CHAPTER 130

# CHAPTER 131

# THE JUSTICE OF THE WOOD

Casteel high-stepped as he marched at the head of his Hog Head Union men, through the gaping hole in the facade of the Falic, Moore & DeVillay Law Firm building, into which I had just driven Ann's truck, smashing through the glass front of the atrium lobby. Carrying baseball bats and ax handles, Casteel's men were all business. They demanded they see Felix Falic and Senator Moore. Jake didn't care to see his niece, DeeDee, since he was there on a mission of some violence.

Even one-armed Billy McAvoy was there, wielding an oak ax handle. He wanted to leave with his case file so he could get a different lawyer. An honest one.

Billy planned to sue the britches off the whole C.U.R.T.I.S. union and its Designated lawyers for its conspiracy against its own men—the working men. He had a corpse-cold stare as he chanted like he was storming the Bastille during the French Revolution. "The dirty bastards." Billy repeated it over and over, with a nervous tick, knocking the ax handle against his leg in anxious anticipation of meeting someone he could swing it at. He wanted to make contact, come hell or high water. He had a score to settle for the amputation. All of the psychiatric treatment he'd received after he lost his arm went right out the window. He ached to spill blood.

Ajax saw them come in, like invaders at war, barbarians set to sack Rome, and he locked the elevators to prevent them reaching the upper floors. Jake looked up and saw Falic peering over the fifth-floor balcony and Senator Moore peaking out from his seventh-floor perch. "I can see those sons of bitchs sittin' up there like treed raccoons." Jake pointed a black baseball bat at Ajax. "You tell him to come down here," and Jake lifted the black bat toward Falic.

Jake yelled up at the Senator, "I'll deal with you later, Mr. Moore. I don't call you 'Senator' because your politicking days are over. You son of a bitch. You aren't accountable to anyone. No wonder you voted against having an ethics commission to oversee the U.S. Senate, you damned thief. You and your family are too busy making money."

Senator Moore cringed at Jake's bright, hot truth. And, like a vampire who shuns sunlight, he quickly shied away from the balcony's edge.

"Mr. Falic wants to know what this is about," Ajax said, with a look of deep concern on his face, thinking, any second, he might get an ax handle upside his head.

Jake slammed the bat into his hand in anger, "Tell him I'm going to give him a good-bye card from Mr. Rawlings here, and I'm going to take back my Designation."

Ajax's face showed his surprise. He whispered Jake's message into the phone.

After a few moments' time, one of the elevator doors opened, and DeeDee came strutting out acting like we should bow to her as though she was Cleopatra. Jake's face softened, and he lowered his bat in the presence of family.

"Uncle Jake, Uncle Jake, Uncle Jake, what is this all about, sweetie?"

I wanted to vomit because I knew the truth about Miss DeeDee. I'd told it all to Jake.

That it was DeeDee who set up Jake and cooperated with Colonel Durant to assassinate Jake in return for making DeeDee the replacement for Big Dutch as the *Capo* of *Di Trina.* With Durant dead, DeeDee knew the bottom line. Jake spoke deep and direct, no bullshit.

"Party's over."

DeeDee acted as though she didn't know what he was talking about. She tried to buy more time to smooth Jake's feathers, to make him feel like he could trust her.

"Young lady, I used to bounce you on my knee when you were a child. And I've never hit a woman in my life." He paused, "So I brought a friend." The crowd parted, and Bridget stepped forward. She whacked DeeDee in the shins with her shillelagh. DeeDee went down hard.

As she looked up from the floor, Jake said to DeeDee, plainly and clearly, "You messed with my family and turned my children against me. You turned the world against me. And you were family. I have disowned you."

As Bridget pursued DeeDee blindly around the lobby, Ajax did not dare intervene, although inwardly he was laughing at the hilarious sight of a blind woman chasing DeeDee with a shillelagh. DeeDee hid by Ajax, who was behind his security desk, right when the holograph fired up. A new train was leaving. The train's conductor was hiding in the broom closet and didn't bother to emerge to call the train's arrival. The locomotive barely got underway before Johnny Cash started singing *"Folsom Prison Blues."*

"That's appropriate. *'Folsom Prison Blues.'* To prison. That's where you sent me," said Jake. "And you tried to kill me so you could take over Di Trina."

"But you can't prove it. Uncle Jake; I didn't do that." DeeDee denied everything. The vamp tried to remove her *Di Trina* ring without anyone noticing. But I yelled at her. "Leave the ring on, or I'll put it where the sun doesn't shine. Lady or no lady."

Jake grabbed her hand and looked at the *Di Trina* ring and he dropped her hand with disgust. "Where'd you get the pretty ring?"

DeeDee looked away and stayed silent, wiping tears from her face, smearing her mascara. Jake felt no compassion for his ruthless niece.

I had strong I-bolts screwed into the Designation showcase set into the marble wall. And big logging chains hooked from the bolts to the bumper of Ol' Blue. I left the motor running and got out of the truck. I walked over to DeeDee and asked to borrow her cell phone to make a call. She obliged. I stepped to the corner of the lobby, away from the conversation between uncle and niece. I returned a minute later and handed the phone to Jake.

"Take a look at those numbers, Jake." Jake made a quick scroll through the phone numbers on DeeDee's cell phone contact list, reflecting it contained

520

phone numbers for Colonel Durant. Numbers that DeeDee could have in her electronic phonebook only if she had been part of the scheme.

"They say dead men can't talk, but his numbers are sure screaming at me right now. Durant's numbers are in here. And so are Big Dutch's," Jake said, as he pointed the black bat at DeeDee.

"You're lucky I don't kill you: family or not, you're lucky. You turned my wife and children against me. You disgraced our family name. And all for money?" Then Jake motioned for his men to destroy the hologram machine and yank the Designation out of the wall. Ol' Blue tightened the slack of the thick logging chain and yanked forward. The Designation came crashing out, falling on the floor in a big cloud of dust.

Ax handles and broad backs made short work of the hologram machine. Jake said to me, "Mike, I am giving this Designation to you—for giving me back my life. You earned it." Jake assumed I would accept his kind offer, potentially of millions of dollars per year.

"Put that Designation in the back of his truck, men."

"Thank you, Jake."

We shook hands, making it a deal. The Designation and the potential to make millions of dollars per year was now mine. I turned to DeeDee. "In about twenty minutes, there are going to be more Treasury agents crawling around this firm than there are ants at a picnic. If I were you, I'd meet them at the curb, to be the first one to cut a deal because this ship is going to get torpedoed by the I.R.S."

DeeDee was stunned. All her fears had come true. "The I.R.S.?" she said, a dazed look on her face.

I jumped in the truck. I looked to my right at Bridget, sitting in the passenger seat, working her beads. All the excitement had her twitching. I looked to my left, back at DeeDee. I put it in gear and revved the engine. "Yeah, DeeDee, the big, bad, freaking I.R.S. You know anything about client loans or great big cash transactions?"

DeeDee's mouth fell open. "How did you know? I mean . . ." DeeDee's face said it all. She was flabbergasted. She understood.

"It was Cinderella, wasn't it? That's who told the I.R.S.?"

Ann served her revenge cold.

"Your firm left a trail a mile wide, DeeDee. And don't be crabbing. You should know better than any. If you are going to dance with the devil, don't cry if you get burned."

DeeDee was speechless. I twisted the knife.

"You better go get your papers in order because the I.R.S. is on its way to look into all your dealings. And I think the U.S. Attorney has a nice indictment in hand."

I knew it would be the worst thing possible for her to start shredding papers. It would be considered evidence of guilt since the firm's computer records would be seized immediately. If she was dumb enough to go inside and shred papers, she deserved a longer sentence for obstruction of justice. But that wasn't my problem or Bridget's. I would leave that to DeeDee's conscience. Her character would dictate her sentence.

I told DeeDee that if she were smart, she would cooperate with I.R.S. Special Agent Raford McRain when he showed up. She nodded that she understood.

Bridget and I drove Ann's truck, with the Designation in the back. We were headed towards other business, much more important than lassoing a bunch of lying lawyers.

DeeDee's whining was making me nauseous. I gunned the engine and drove back through the big hole I'd made on my arrival.

I'd promised Bridget I would take her to mass, across the Mississippi River at Saint Clare's. It was a cloister of the Sisters of the Poor Clares, tucked away in an isolated forest in the woods. I always felt a little cleaner when I came out of mass at a church that served nuns so serious about their business that they shut themselves off from the rest of the world, concentrating only on serving God through prayer.

Very cool. Not very sociable. But very cool.

# CHAPTER 132

# GOOD RIDDANCE

Jake and his men followed me through downtown St. Martinsville. I pulled onto a hundred-year-old bridge across the Mississippi River. It is a bridge not many use because it's narrow and rickety. I swung the truck across both lanes, and I backed it up to the guardrail. I got out. Jake and some Hog Heads stopped their vehicles and came trotting up, wondering what I was doing.

"You guys give me a hand? This thing's pretty darn heavy," I said.

They all looked at me like I was crazy.

"You aren't going to throw that in the river, are you, Mike? I gave that to you to make money."

"I know you did, Jake. And I appreciate the gesture. But I'd have to be looking over my shoulder every day. You think I want to live like Big Dutch? The poor man lived on a farm, protected by a six-foot-high electric fence, clear-cut perimeter of two hundred yards, in-ground motion detectors, and a motorized security gate surveilled by two cameras, twenty-four, seven. With guard dogs to boot. And I'd be having to bribe union men and politicians and pay illegal money to whores and case runners and God knows who else because the Designated firms all compete against each other. So even if I'm Designated, I would still have to compete with firms pulling illegal crap, and if I don't do what they do, my Designation won't be worth a damn. Prison ain't worth it, Jake. I'll make my money the honest way."

Jake knew I was right. All of it.

Before Jake could speak, I added some more. "This Designation is cursed, Jake. If it wasn't for this, you would not have had a problem, would you?"

Jake looked stunned by the clarity of my logic.

"You do with the Designation what you want, Mike. It's yours." Jake had a new-found respect for me. He didn't want any more of what the Designations brought—trouble.

We pitched the Designation and its heavy, brass case into the river. I shook Jake's hand again.

"Now, you want to practice law with Dalton and me?"

"No, but thank you. I've got to find a way back into the union. The railroad will run right over my men if I don't," Jake said. Jake was getting smarter. He knew I'd be Hell to practice law with. Running the Hog Heads Union would probably be a lot safer. We parted as friends, exchanging an ancient oath of friendship and loyalty.

"*Semper Fi.*"

I drove across the Mississippi with my dignity. While Bridget prayed to Saint Rose of Lima, the saint of the New World.

Ann met us at the church, and she and Kylee attended mass with Bridget and me. Kylee enjoyed the unique way mass is performed at the Poor Clares, with the cloister of nuns worshipping, hidden behind a high wall behind the altar. Only their voices, in prayer and in song, could we enjoy. A Franciscan monk, Father Chris, gave mass in Latin. It was a moving and beautiful experience. But my time with Ann and Kylee was much too short. After mass, we swapped vehicles and went our separate ways, to our separate homes and our separate lives. Isolated; stuck in our separate sorrows.

On the parking lot, our kiss and hug good-bye was brief and respectful. Kylee was watching. But I looked into Ann's brown eyes and said, "I love you. Thank you for coming into my life."

Ann smiled. With a joyful mist in her eyes, she gave me a last hug, "No, Michael, thank you."

It was a lonely ride home, even though my sister was praying, out loud, the whole way. And in Ann's truck, little Kylee, in a high-pitched and taunting voice, teased Ann with "Love you," all the way back to the farm. She punctuated her teasing with a fun, little laugh.

Ann smiled and stuck her tongue out at Kylee. And Kylee laughed at her Mother, in love.

CHAPTER 132

# CHAPTER 133

# A NEW LIFE

The next day, I emptied another can of gasoline into my Mustang's tank. A jeep loaded with teenage girls directed cat-calls at me. They even stopped, then started to back up, but they chickened out and peeled off instead. My hair was long. It touched my ears. I chuckled at the zany girls as I poured the last drops of gasoline from the can and tossed it, empty, into the back seat of my Mustang. The wildcat railroad strikes had hit America hard. People were not driving. Fuel was scarce. I looked up the road a ways, and I smiled as I read the road sign, "Entering Chakateptkee County."

I chuckled, thinking of Chakateptkee County's reputation. As legend has it, God mistakenly put Chakateptkee County above the Mason-Dixon Line, then filled it with Catholic good ol' boys. It was a county-wide contradiction in cultures. But there was no place I would rather live. *Who, me? Live without conflict?* I said, out loud to myself. "Where Bubba meets the Pope." Heck, we might even get beer in church. And with this new thing called the Internet, I could be hip and erudite in the middle of a cornfield.

I got into my Mustang and fired it up. Familiar Marine Corps cadences barked a measured beat. Listening to them was my warrior's equivalent to saying a rosary. It was a meditation of muscle and machismo and militarism. I put the car in gear and started to drive off. I stopped abruptly. I looked at my stereo and listened, deliberating, to the cadence's marching, marching, marching through the speakers.

I pushed a button on my car stereo and ejected the U.S.M.C. tape. I looked at it with a smile that held a curve of mischief. I tossed the Marine Corps tape over my shoulder, into the back seat, with the gas cans. Then I selected another tape, "The Rolling Stones," and slid it into the stereo. *"Start Me Up"* rocked and rolled loudly as I slapped the car back into first gear, hammered the accelerator, and popped the clutch. The tires spun, furious and wild, and smoke rose from where my tires met the road. My muscle car's rear-end squatted and fishtailed. I straightened it out, rocked it into second gear, and pointed the nose of the pony hood-ornament down the road with a jolt.

I took off—to a new life.

I was free. I'd settled things with my father. I did not have anything further to prove; not as a man, not as a lawyer, only as a want-to-be husband and father. I knew there was only one destiny for me. I was going straight for it. I red-lined the engine and hammered the stick into third gear with a resounding scratch of my Mustang's rear tires.

I drove a few country miles, then turned my Mustang down a one-lane country road. The Mustang's fat wheels churned up a cloud of dust that cycloned behind it as the car rumbled past cows pastured behind barbed wire.

With all the dust I was stirring up, Ann and Kylee could see my car coming a good half a mile away. Kylee had her head on Ann's lap, and she saw my arrival first.

"Momma, we got company." They were watching television, a Disney movie, spending some good mother, daughter, quality time.

I pulled up into the yard of Ann's farmhouse just as The Stones began thumping out *"Miss You."* Kylee was shy and hid around the corner while Ann walked out on the porch. I got out of my car, carrying a dozen roses and the hopes and dreams of a man ready for marriage.

If Ann would have me.

Ann Parsons acted nonchalant, waiting for me. She leaned against a porch post, reading a newspaper. She was looking pretty sweet in her blue jeans and a sweater. Then again, Ann could wear a burlap potato sack and make it look like a high-fashion dress. She was terminally hot.

"So what brings you out here?" Ann said to me, as I stood at the bottom of the steps, looking up at her like a loyal serf looks at his queen. She glanced to her right and saw Kylee hiding, around the corner, outside my eyesight. Kylee was jokingly giving her the loser sign, her hand forming an "L" at her forehead. It made her mother laugh.

CHAPTER 133

"I came to see you."

Ann Parsons played it cool. She turned back to the newspaper and acted like she was reading it. She held it up, in front of her face, to show the huge headlines, "LAWYER MAFIA EXPOSED." But she made no reference to the stories of greedy lawyers who had lied to America for fifty years. What was news about that? And, besides, she knew she would be testifying for the United States for a couple of years to come. Maybe even longer, if the State Department succeeded in extraditing the few *Di Trina* fat cats who flew the coop to South America. All that could wait. Ann and I had more important things to concentrate on.

Us.

"How come?"

"I love you, and I need you," I said.

Ann's pretty eyes flashed a sign of relief and joy; I did not even stutter on the "L" word.

My cowboy boots climbed the seven steps to the porch where Ann was. The fall day was warmed by an Indian summer. I could almost hear the birds chirp. But that would not happen for months.

I extended the roses, as they were a special offering. The ends of the long stemmed red roses were laced into the shimmering Cinderella slipper that Ann had smashed onto my chest as I fell off her truck outside the Masquerade Ball. I fished a jewelry box out of my back pocket, and I immediately got down on one knee. Ann dropped her newspaper. It filled with wind and flew up, above her home, and off North across the wheat field towards the heavens. Annette Samantha Katherine Parsons covered her mouth with one hand. She couldn't believe what was happening. Ann grabbed hold of the porch post, for fear she would faint. My second offering was well received.

"Oh, my God. It sparkles."

"I tried to pick out an *honorable* stone. But the jeweler said that costs extra."

"I guess we'll have to work on the honorable part."

"Guess so. Will you marry me?"

Before Ann answered, Kylee ran out to join the party. She jumped up and down, cheering. She grabbed Ann and me in a three-way, group hug. As a family. But Kylee stopped her celebrating and stepped back from us. She put her hands on her hips, and she drew herself erect and became assertive.

"O.K. You can marry my mom. But I have one condition," said Kylee.

"Anything," I said, trying to wrap up the deal as quickly as possible.

"That I get to use Grandpa's cattle prod on you?"

## THE END

# EPILOGUE

The Bishop officiated a quiet wedding ceremony on the farm.

They said grace together at the supper table that night, holding hands in a circle, as a family; Kylee and Ann and Michael McRain. Little Kylee said her bedtime prayers with her Mother and Michael. She crawled into bed and she laid her head onto her goose-down pillow. Kylee Reneè smiled and looked to Heaven and wished on a new star hanging outside her bedroom window.

That night Michael McRain slept in Ann's lace-canopy bed. Closure. Contentment. Commitment.

Due North, at the edge of Sam's eighty acres of waving winter wheat, a train rolled on, slow and sure, to all points known. The Hog Head blew the train's horn three times. And the coyotes yiped and howled and began their wild dance.

# The Author's Post-Script Note:

The below account reflects some of the important occurrences that led up to the writing of <u>The Redeemer: It Is Written</u>.

## <u>A LOVING SON – A FORGIVING FATHER</u>

Today, November 15, 2003, I opened my small cedar box, where I keep some life mementos collected over the years. I found the newspaper clipping for when I passed the bar exam, my old baseball umpire strike-ball-out counter and some other cool keepsakes. The neatest, most revealing items I visited were the Polaroid photos I had taken of Dad's gravestone. The date on two of the photos was June 20, 1993 and the date on the third was May 31, 2000. The fact that I took Polaroids of my father's gravestone and for years kept them pinned just above my bedroom light-switch, where I would be forced to see them a number of times every day, revealed that I visited Dad's grave in a holy and solemn, yearning for redemption sort of way, *before* I took on Mark Waldemer's case. I specifically remember taking the latter photo – to get closure.

Those before and after photos show a glimpse of my earnest search for a task of sufferance that would serve two purposes: as a rite of passage sufficiently difficult to allow "Bubbles" Moran's son to become a man, and much more important, to serve as a proper offering to God and to my father to redeem myself for deserting Dad.

I left my knelt position by Dad's deathbed and let go of his feeble, desperate, clenching hand at the only God damned time in Dad's life that he specifically asked for me to help him. He had beckoned me at 3:30 AM to help him, the life-long warrior, to sever his painful, earthly bonds and pass through the gates of Heaven – to Valhalla. A final place of sure salvation for men who killed in the name of war. At the time of his greatest need I left his bedside for ignorant, if not selfish and trivial reason as a mistaken superior duty to deliver some Returns of Service for three subpoenas I had served for a divorce hearing set that day. Stupid. Insensitive. It was a sinful failure to honor my father's dying request. Dad died fifteen minutes after I deserted him.

I violated Dad's primary rule of an air warrior – never leave your wingman. Desertion of my dear and faithful father, The Triple Ace, The Trial Lawyer, The Legend was by far my life's worst failure and believed by me to be a mortal sin; a ghastly, disfiguring, crimson scar raked across my face of honor. That transgression resulted in a secret, gouging wound to my psyche. It became emotionally crippling. Thus, Mark Waldemer's case became my best hope for redemption, healing and an honorable manhood. It was what my heart, my soul, my existence as a son and man needed to capture, to repair, to prove and move on.

At Jefferson Barracks National Cemetery atop a limestone bluff overlooking the slow, wide Mississippi River, the secluded, tearful ceremony was respectfully, tenderly conducted. In a sacred sacrifice, I laid on Dad's, the General's grave the 1997 Seventh Circuit Court of Appeals' winning Habeas Corpus ruling in Waldemer vs. United States, 98 F. 3d 306. I lovingly hugged my father's tombstone – tight, as between two wrestlers. Then, in a heartfelt speech at parade-rest, I made a plea for forgiveness, a prayer for redemption, a braced salute and a sharp about-face to march away. The ceremony and the court's ruling were the physical manifestations and a combined culmination of over five thousand *pro bono* hours fervently waged fighting for truth, for Mark Waldemer, a good and honest union man. That cemetery rite was the armistice of my spiritual crusade. It marked a peaceful end to my very own private little war.

God help my soul.

# Additional Material

This is for all you Zoomies at the United States Air Force Academy (USAFA), and other military types out there, who might want to read the original Chapter 130. It was abbreviated considerably through editing. This passage was written from observations of a general throughout much of his life, by hearing his stories and from being with him at his final days and hours; a "what if" look into the next dimension. You might enjoy its perspective.

# The Death of a General

Even with all the prayers I said, pleading to be redeemed, I had never felt forgiven, not until my dream in Purgatory. But I had been confined in a self-made prison of guilt. Its unbendable bars had been shaped by the harsh hammer of duty. I hugged the stone, strong and tight, as though it were a life preserver and I a castaway adrift at sea. I was overwhelmed by a message of eternal love, which I more felt than heard. It came to me clearly. I understood the power of its forgiveness, pure and plain, as if my father, in the flesh, had spoken it right into my ear.

The words were those I had fought for, with all my being. Yes, I knew it in my heart. I was guilty of what Captain Carion accused me: being a selfish bastard. I had fought for Jake Casteel so I could be redeemed, by showing my father I was not a coward, that I had not left my wingman, that I had brought honor to our family through victory. I hadn't represented Casteel and damn near bankrupted myself because I was a champion of the union cause or because I was a man of justice, bent on setting free one innocent man. It wasn't for either of these reasons. I'd represented Jake Casteel in his impossible case to prove something to my father, to clear my name with Father, to remove my name from the eternal roll of Goddamned cowards.

I did it for me. For my soul. For redemption.

Jake never knew the depth of my selfishness. He thought I did it for him and his union crusade.

I did it for me.

Captain Carion had been right. I was no good Samaritan. I'd offered my earthly time and energy, good works for others, as a penance to get square with Father. For the eternal record. For love.

And there it was. Finally. A timeless rite in the cemetery. I was on my knees, making an offering to my father of my victory on behalf of an innocent man. I accepted Father's message: of how he'd died alone, except for Bridget and her two-fisted, rapid-fire rosaries, and how he'd felt about me leaving him to die alone. Father spoke to me, through our spirits, and I claimed my redemption right there as I hugged his tombstone.

Redemption at last. Father spoke from the grave:

*"My other children loved me no less than Bridget and you. They visited for a few days, here and there, and called and sent flowers, that Bridget put in vases. But Bridget and you were there for me through the worst. You even carried me to the lavatory in the final months. You saw me all the way through to the last aggressive chemo. You were saintly; of that, you can be assured.*

*I left you, my children, the single, most prized possession in the world: faith. A profound and inescapable belief in a power greater than yourself: God. I told you children, "Catholics don't hold the patent on holiness," after one of you blurted at the dinner table that people of other faiths are lesser souls. The horrors and hardships I saw in my decades of war made me forget my ageless catechism. Over the years, seeing the worst in life through the death and misery of war, it became a warrior's catechism. A jaded, jaundiced view of God.*

*Mike, you need not worry about me. At the end, God took me kindly. Not in a wicked swirl of horrid darkness. But in a cocoon of bright love. The cancer, that spread from my stomach to my lungs, disabled my ability to breathe. It felt like a great snake, crushing my chest for seventy-seven hours straight without sleep and with constant, conscious effort to draw breath. It was the ultimate marathon. And there you were—the whole way—coaching me, holding my hand, loving me, praying for my recovery and for my soul. I taught you well. Cover your bets.*

THE AUTHOR'S POST-SCRIPT NOTE

*You held my hand as you kneeled on the floor by my bed. You repeated General Lee's words on duty, interspersed with "Hail Marys," seeking her wisdom because you didn't know which duty to choose. To stay with me or to meet the court's harsh deadline.*

*You chose the more difficult of the two duties. You knew the more difficult a duty is, the more likely it should be done first. You chose the more difficult: the duty to the living, to your client. Your choice was correct. But, of course, you didn't feel that way when you discovered I'd died shortly after you left. You were convinced you were a cowardly deserter.*

*Fear not. God cradled me.*

*My body failed me, and my earthly existence folded in on me, as though my creator laid a veil over me through which my spirit immediately passed. I saw my whole life in one unbroken moment.*

*I found myself when my family was young. I was surrounded by my wife and seven children, saying good-bye, staining my uniform with their tears as they saw me off to war. I was coddled in my sweet mother's arms. I was playing football, working in the Granite City Steel foundry, boxing on the same card as Joe Louis, kissing my wife on our wedding day. All the fear I'd felt in war and life melted and congealed, like candle wax, into an object that hung before me, like an apple from a branch. I observed it without terror. And then I found myself in the cockpit of my P-51. But even with all the people with me in the cockpit, it was as spacious as ten ballrooms. I was at an endless receiving line, greeting a montage of people who had gone before me. My wingman, Punchy, who I'd lost to a ruthless Kraut, who cut Punchy's parachute strings with his fighter's wing. My beloved wife, Annette, who, when she saw me off to war in Vietnam, surrounded by our six children and pregnant with our seventh, kissed me and whispered the bravest words I would ever hear: 'Befehl ist Befehl.' Duty is duty. My tireless and my ever loving mother, who raised seven children by herself after Father died. And then my father, John Michael McRain, who I never met; he died in the 1918 Spanish flu epidemic, three months before I was born. Each and every man I had killed in war—all of them: the good and the honorable; the bastards; the ones I'd killed in rage because they'd killed my comrades, my squadron mates; German pilots and air crews; the defenseless German soldiers I'd strafed, trapped in closed freight cars on troop trains. The innocent civilians I'd killed and maimed when my bullets and bombs went astray, one, Yvette, a little girl just six weeks old. And then all my squadron mates, bright and ready for a new day's hop as we gathered in the Ops Room. My wife and children and our entire lives together. And the face of God.*

*Heaven opened.*

THE REDEEMER: IT IS WRITTEN

*I was gone from the world.*

*I felt warm. I belonged in the light, my spirit merging into an infinite power I understood. I saw and heard Bridget, giving me a good, Irish wailing. She was lonely, hurt that you'd left her alone with me, to die under her care alone. She and you were my youngest and the closest—my Irish twins.*

*I watched you rush back to my bedroom, after you'd taken care of your client. Your inescapable duty. You feared that you'd chosen wrong. You wept hard and grieved over my dead body, that you'd let me down. Forsaken me, your father. You believed abandonment of your father to be a mortal sin. That you failed, sinfully, as a son, in your duty to provide comfort during my last, painful breaths. That you failed, as a fellow warrior, in your duty to hold my hand and escort me into the presence of God's light, where all good and honorable warriors go to rest. To Valhalla. To Heaven. To glory with God."*

*Then Father cut through all the malarkey of my guilt trip. He granted my soul amnesty. "You are forgiven, son. Go. Live and love."*

Father had spoken to me from the grave! Redemption felt sweet to my heart and sustained my soul.

The wisdom of an ancient general, repeated by Father to us countless times over the years, came into my mind like a beacon of truth. "Duty then is the sublimest word in the English language. You should do your duty in all things. You can never do more, and you should never hope to do less." And my mother's brave and wise words, whispered to my father as he left for war, "Befehl ist befehl." Duty is duty.

It was then that I understood the meaning of those words. They are continuous, complete and unbroken, like the Celtic rings. Never ending.

There is an inescapable, imperfect order on this earth. The world. Duty offers both redemption and damnation.

All the lessons I had learned of the world— the beating I had suffered when I protected Bridget; my years as a cadet at the Air Force Academy and as a warrior in the Marine Corps, when I had killed men with my own hands; my studies at Harvard Law School; my work as a lawyer, when I had stripped both men and women of their honor. Those lessons paled in comparison to this final truth my father taught me as I hugged his tombstone.

Men are emotional cowards. They bestow upon the objects of their ultimate aspirations officious names like "duty" and "honor." But women know the truth better; they call it "love" and "forgiveness."

Bridget had one up on me. She had it all figured out. There will always be war between duty to God and duty to the world in order to capture the flag of honor. But, in the end, love and forgiveness conquer all.

I had been forgiven.

I moved on.

"Thank you, Father, for forgiving me."

I staggered to my car, emotionally spent. There was still work to do to set my life straight.

# America's Lawyer Mafia: Railgate

The following documents and transition and commentary text are excerpts from a, non-fiction book, presently titled, <u>America's Lawyer Mafia: Railgate</u>, which is intended to be released in the future. Please note that we reserve the right to change the formatting and content of the following excerpts prior to printing/publishing; the below is offered in condensed form.

~~~~~~~~~~~~~~~~~~~~~~~~~~~~~~~~~~~~~~~~~~~~~~~~~~~~

<u>Excerpt: DOCUMENT I from America's Lawyer Mafia: Railgate</u>

The first document is a copy of the Court Order, by Federal Judge Sim Lake, wherein he briefly, but unequivocally, describes the lawyers who admitted, under oath, to ongoing, racketeering activities, in order to obtain railroad injury cases and union designated status. Unless you are a lawyer, you might find the rest of the eighteen page Order rather boring. That is, until the end of the Order, where the Court rules that the names, of the dozens of admitted organized crime lawyers, be kept from Bar Associations' disciplinary authorities across the United States. The most relevant text is <u>underscored</u> for your convenience. Note: the middle pages of the opinion have been omitted.

~~~~~~~~~~~~~~~~~~~~~~~~~~~~~~~~~~~~~~~~~~~~~~~~~~~~

Case 4:03-cr-00362 Document 306 Filed 09/13/2005 Page 1 of 18
IN THE UNITED STATES DISTRICT COURT
FOR THE SOUTHERN DISTRICT OF TEXAS
HOUSTON DIVISION

UNITED STATES OF AMERICA,

§

§

Plaintiff,

§

§

v.

§ CRIMINAL NUMBER H-03-362-SS

§

BYRON ALFRED BOYD, et al., §

§

Defendants.

§

## MEMORANDUM OPINION AND ORDER

On January 5, 2005, the United States of America (Government), acting through the United States Attorney for the Southern District of Texas (AUSA), filed, ex parte, a Sealed Motion for Disclosure Order Under Federal Rule of Criminal Procedure 6(e) (Docket Entry No. 256) seeking an order allowing disclosure of grand jury transcripts and interview reports to "relevant state bar disciplinary authorities" having jurisdiction over each of 38 attorneys who testified before a federal grand jury in Houston in connection with this case between October of 2002 and December of 2003. On January 19, 2005, the court entered a Disclosure Order (Docket Entry No. 258), and then on February 24, 2004, stayed that Order to allow counsel for the attorneys identified therein to file a memorandum in opposition. Before the court are the Memorandum in Opposition filed by counsel for 31 of the 38 attorneys named in the

Case 4:03-cr-00362 Document 306 Filed 09/13/2005 Page 2 of 18

Disclosure Order (Docket Entry No. 262), the Brief in Opposition filed by an attorney-intervenor (Docket Entry No. 282), the Government's responses thereto (Docket Entry Nos. 268 and 285), and replies to the Government's responses filed by counsel for the 31 attorneys and the intervenor (Docket Entry Nos. 302 and 304). For the reasons explained below the Disclosure Order will be vacated, and the Motion for Disclosure Order (Docket Entry No. 256) will be denied.

## I. Factual Background

<u>The four defendants charged in this case are former officers and members of the United Transportation Union (UTU) who have been convicted of conspiring with others to violate the Racketeer Influenced and Corrupt Organizations Act (RICO) through the commission of two or more predicate acts in violation of 18 U.S.C. § 1962(d).1 Between October of 2002 and December of 2003, 38 attorney-witnesses testified before Grand Jury 02-1. Many of these attorneys admitted to paying cash and other things of value to UTU officials to acquire and/or to maintain the status of designated legal counsel (DLC) for the UTU. Other attorneys made similar admissions to government agents.</u>

1See Plea Agreement of Ralph John Dennis (Docket Entry No. 38), Plea Agreement of Charles Little (Docket Entry No. 102),
Plea Agreement of John Rookard (Docket Entry No. 156), and Plea Agreement of Byron Boyd (Docket Entry No. 160).

-2-

Case 4:03-cr-00362 Document 306 Filed 09/13/2005 Page 3 of 18

## II. Motion for Disclosure Order

Citing Federal Rule of Criminal Procedure 6(e)(3)(E)(i), the Government moves that certain transcripts of testimony secured through a criminal grand jury investigation and reports of interviews leading to an indictment in the above-referenced case, be disclosed to relevant state bar disciplinary authorities having jurisdiction over attorney witnesses whose testimony may have revealed misconduct that calls into question their fitness for the practice of law.2

The attorneys argue that the Disclosure Order should be vacated and the Government's motion denied because the Government has failed to satisfy Rule 6(e)(3)(E)(i)'s requirements that disclosure of grand jury materials be "preliminary to or in connection with a judicial proceeding," and that the moving party make a strong showing of particularized need for the disclosures.3

A. Applicable Law
I. Grand Jury Secrecy

[PAGES THREE THROUGH SEVENTEEN WERE DELETED HEREIN. But, in the future, you may access the document in its entirety, at http://www.lawyermafia.com or other websites as may be designated by the author.]

III. Conclusions and Order
For the reasons explained above the court concludes that the Government has failed to show that the disclosures it seeks to make

25Id. at p. 10.

-17

Case 4:03-cr-00362 Document 306 Filed 09/13/2005 Page 18 of 18

are "preliminary to or in connection with a judicial proceeding," and has failed to make a strong showing of a particularized need for the disclosures. Absent these showings disclosure of grand jury materials is not authorized by Federal Rule of Criminal Procedure 6(e)(3)(E)(i). The Disclosure Order entered on January 19, 2005 (Docket Entry No. 258), is therefore VACATED, and the Government's Motion for Disclosure Order Under Federal Rule of Criminal Procedure 6(e) (Docket Entry No. 256) is DENIED.

SIGNED at Houston, Texas, on this 13th day of September, 2005.

SIM LAKE
UNITED STATES DISTRICT JUDGE

-18-

[Portions of order reformatted to fit electronic viewing page. The text remained the same.](EMPHASIS ADDED)

Excerpt: DOCUMENT 2 from  America's Lawyer Mafia: Railgate

This document was obtained via the internet, in the public domain, at  http://radio.weblogs.com/0118868/categories/straightTrack/2004/07/index.html.

It is an excerpt from the in-court transcript of the sentencing hearing of UTU International President, Byron Boyd.  There are portions of the text highlighted:

First, where Mr. Boyd testifies that the railroad injury case racketeering has been going on for generations.

Second, that the corruption reaches throughout the entire international union, from top to bottom.

And third, that the "son of a United States Senator" was amongst the lawyers testifying about the racketeering in the railroad injury case system.

The following portion shows how distrustful the rank and file are of their leadership at the international level — they are not receiving the whole truth. Misspellings, formatting etc. are displayed exactly as they appeared in web posted materials.

~~~~~

http://radio.weblogs.com/0118868/categories/straightTrack/2004/07/index.html
(accessed/downloaded 01 15 2008)

If so, consider joining UTU's Members Against Corruption Caucus (MAC) by visiting
www.reformit2004.org

getting informed, and signing up with the only organized group of UTU members working to uncover the real story of past and possible ongoing corruption.

Also, please consider signing the online petition to get the Boyd/Little/ Rookard/Dennis court records unsealed which can be found at www.PetitionOnline.com/syzygy/

UTU posts sentencing transcripts of Boyd/Little/Rookard/Dennis at www.utu.org/worksite/detail_news.cfm?ArticleID=15546

~~~~~

Below is the web-posted rendition of a portion of the Federal Court transcript referencing the United States Senator. The Defendant is Byron Boyd, International President of the railroads' United Transportation Union (UTU), at his criminal sentencing, after he plead guilty to participating in an on-going, organized-crime conspiracy with personal-injury attorneys and law firms whose identities have remained super-secret. Misspellings, formatting etc. are displayed as closely as possible to the way they appeared as web-posted at: http://radio. weblogs.com/0118868/categories/straightTrack/2004/07/index.html

~~~~~

From Boyd Sentencing

THE DEFENDANT: Thank you, Your Honor. The first thing I need to say, and I want to say publicly, is I accept full responsibility for my actions. The shame and responsibility falls squarely on my shoulders, no one else.

The other thing about the tragedy of this whole event that I think is not so obvious to the word is the personal and private tragedy that I've caused a number of people, my family and my close friends. We all know what the public outcome of it is.

Publicly I would like to apologize to my wife and my son and daughter, grandson and some very dear friends and members of the organization and other friends throughout the country who expressed their support. In trying to think of the words to use to ask for forgiveness or the apology, there's only two words that come to mind and those are to them I say thank you for the love, kindness and support and I'm truly sorry and ashamed for my actions. And I have been overwhelmed by that support and particularly overwhelmed by the folks that I've sat across the table from and argued against my whole career and I'm truly amazed. I'm not entitled to it, but I'm gratified by it.

The other concern that I have is and I wasn't a victim. I was a participant in a perverse corruption and

THE COURT: Let me ask you, what can be done to correct this scheme? The DLC program provides an inherent incentive for lawyers to be referred these very lucrative cases. How can this system be corrected to destroy or reduce that incentive?

THE DEFENDANT: My belief, Your Honor, is this, that I think maybe to define one thing first and then I'll answer your question, because I think the two go together. The system has gone on for generations. The system goes on as we stand here or I stand here today. The system will go on tomorrow.

What needs to be done, in my opinion, is to look at the very genesis of the system. It just isn't at the top level of the organization, but at the bottom level of the organization. I know from dealing with the politics and the inside of the organization that there's a huge amount of control that's generated by these DLCS, and you have to be able to counter that. And the way you have to counter that, I think, is with the ability for government to get in and have the knowledge and understanding and to follow the trails that need to be followed and where they go to get to the core base, the political base of these DLC's within the organization. And I would say this, I don t think this corruption is limited to UTU. I have a firm belief it goes way beyond that, into all rail labor. And the genesis of it is at the very lowest level. And trying to control the internal politics of the organization becomes extremely difficult when you have all these forces coming from below up. They're the ones that control the votes. They're the ones that control a lot of the policies of the organization.

THE COURT: So, you're saying the DLC's control the local union officials?

THE DEFENDANT: Absolutely, absolutely. <u>They're more pervasive there and more powerful there than they ever were at the international level, because they control the absolute base of the organization.</u> And you can believe their support is either generated because the individual members think they're wonderful lawyers or do a good job or for other reasons. And to some they're very good lawyers and do a very good job.

There are many other reasons that they get their support. And I think the government needs to look into that. And one of the things that I was going to say, and it also answers your question, is I've committed to the government and Mr. Gallagher to do whatever I can, now and in the future, to help clean up that corruption and try to get that control away.

THE COURT: Yeah, I think this — it's become apparent to me reading the information in this case that this situation is longstanding and systemic, and I'm not sure case-by-case criminal prosecutions are the most effective way to root out the inherent incentive that exists under this regime. Has the government thought about some legislative solution?

MR. GALLAGHER: The government has, in fact, Your Honor, and we're hopeful that we can address that issue, but Mr. Sussman and his folks would probably have a greater influence than the U. S. Attorney's office in trying to get audiences with those folks. In fact, one DLC, an honest DLC, <u>is the son of a U.S. Senator.</u> So, certainly there are ways to provide influence to change this system , but as Mr. Boyd mentioned, it goes back — it actually goes back to the turn of the Nineteenth Century when the FELA came into existence in 1906, which <u>created this limitless amount of money that could be awarded to damages. So, it's very lucrative for lawyers to get that FELA work and in competition, there are so many lawyers that want it, they are wiling to pad the pockets of union officers or help their campaigns in order to get or retain that designation.</u>

Saturday, July 24, 2004
<u>Help MAC Petition to Unseal Court Records</u>

United Transportation Union <u>MAC Caucus</u> members seek help from the Houston US Attorney in getting the court records of the Boyd/Little/Rookard/Dennis case unsealed. There is now an <u>online petition</u> that UTU members can sign to lend weight to this effort. Go to

<u>http://www.petitiononline.com/syzygy/petition.html</u>

and help us do some heavy lifting for the membership.

(EMPHASIS ADDED)

## Excerpt: DOCUMENT 3 from America's Lawyer Mafia: Railgate

This document is a portion of the transcript of proceedings before the United States Senate Committee on the Judiciary for Mr. Alberto Gonzoles' confirmation hearing, which began January 6, 2005. This is the day <u>after</u> the day when U.S. Attorney and Ex-Navy S.E.A.L. intelligence officer, Michael T. Shelby, filed in Judge Lake's court a motion to reveal the names of all the organized crime/racketeering-testifying lawyers to respective bar disciplinary authorities.

The following transcript and the foregoing sentencing transcript beg many questions regarding corruption that might have reached all the way to the United States Senate and the Oval Office. Here are some important questions to start with.

(<u>Remember: Not all work-injury, rail union designated lawyers are corrupt</u>.)

QUERY:

Who is this mysterious senator whose son was investigated in a shocking crack-down on organized crime's influence in the UTU railroads' union?

Is there a United States Senator who has a son that is, or was, a "designated legal counsel", a DLC, for any railroad unions?

How much money has the mysterious senator and the senator's family members made from railroad injury cases legal fees, kick-backs, referral fees?

How much money has the mysterious senator received in political contributions from railroads? From railroad unions? From defense lawyers? From personal injury lawyers representing injured railroad workers?

If that mysterious senator was on the Senate Judiciary Committee at the time of Alberto Gonzales' confirmation hearing, why did he not immediately disqualify himself from any participation in the Judiciary Committee's confirmation proceedings for Alberto Gonzales, as the Senate Rules require in situations involving a senator's family?

Was the mysterious senator threatened or coerced, through any means or manner, by the UTU's designated lawyers who had previously testified and admitted their participation in organized crime; that they would take the mysterious senator's son down with them if their names were released to the bar discipline authorities?

Was there a deal struck between the secret lawyers and the mysterious senator? And if so, was money or referral fees (for regular railroad injury claims and for the multi-billion dollar fund for railroad asbestos claims, which were specially exempted from an asbestos bill proposed by a powerful senator on the Judiciary Committee) to the mysterious senator, or to his son or his son's law firm, discussed as payment for the senator's profound influence in such a deal?

Where, exactly, did the billions of dollars of personal injury lawyers' fees for railroad work-injury and asbestos cases flow? Into whose pockets or political campaign fund(s)?

Has the mysterious senator built his political career by attacking or defending wealthy plaintiff personal injury lawyers?

Is it that simple; that the mysterious senator thought it was all so secret that he, and any co-conspirators, could just plain old get away with it?

What sort of deal might have been struck with the other members of the Senate Judiciary Committee to make it all stay quiet?

Was a quid pro quo deal struck with Mr. Gonzales to keep the mysterious senator's son's name out of the bad light cast by the existing federal investigation, through firing or forcing the resignation of the Texas U.S. Attorney handling the investigation involving the mysterious senator's son, in return for the mysterious senator making sure Alberto Gonzales was confirmed by the Senate Judiciary Committee?

Will the subject mysterious senator willingly admit the nature and extent of his family's involvement in the designated union lawyer organized crime investigation, "US v Boyd, et al", or will he force us Americans to discover this critical information the expensive way? ~ Does his political party have the courage to push past the embarrassment, due to the possible involvement of one of its own leaders, in order to reveal to the American voters a corrupt system run primarily by the opposing political party and its contributors?

Is the mysterious senator, or his family members, already hiding funds off-shore, or in non-profit organizations, in anticipation that the government's investigation into Alberto Gonzales will lead to the doorstep of the mysterious senator and reveal the enormous amount of money his family has received through the railroad injury claim industry?

Has the Alberto Gonzales criminal investigation Special Prosecutor, Nora Dannehy, investigated this high-level cover-up as another possible instance where a U.S. Attorney might have been fired, by Alberto Gonzales, for political purposes?

If not, is it because of the possible position of the mysterious senator's on the Senate Judiciary Committee, where he can influence the progress of the investigation... and the careers of the prosecutors on the case?

How much did President George W. Bush know about this secret deal given to wealthy personal injury lawyers who admitted to participating in organized crime activities in order to secure railroad work injury cases?

How much about all of this does the new President of the United States know? ~ Will he give the union workers full immunity, including for bribery/tax violations, to testify, in order to finally reveal the truth about how some rail injury lawyers are taking advantage of railroad workers?

Considering that President Obama is a licensed lawyer, a constitutional law professor and is the Chief of the Executive Branch of the federal government, how much access will he allow the American people to the warehouse full of documents gathered during the investigation regarding the nature and extent of how and why and through whom organized crime infiltrated the UTU railroad union?

Why did U.S. Senator Orrin Hatch suddenly withdraw his name as a candidate to replace Alberto Gonzales? ~ Did the UTU railroad union organized crime secret somehow get in his way of becoming the next Attorney General?

Does the Teamsters Union even know about the UTU organized crime conspiracy convictions and of some railroad union personal injury lawyers' direct participation in the scheme?

Will the Teamsters Union's subsidiary, affiliated railroad union, the Brotherhood of Locomotive Engineers (BLET) require the lawyers who admitted to participating in the organized crime conspiracy and predicate acts, with the UTU rail union, (and the other lawyers who gave similar statements to federal agents during the investigation) be prohibited from affiliation with the BLET rail union, or any of its membership, in order to avoid violating the long-standing federal court order requiring the Teamsters Union to immediately report any organized crime activities or persons associated with its union to the Teamsters Union's Internal Review Board (IRB)?

Are any of the lawyers, who participated in the "US v Boyd, et al" investigation into UTU organized crime activities, now members of the BLET's circle of designated legal counsel?

Has the Teamsters Union's IRB adopted a special exception for the lawyers of organized crime that allows known, admitted-under-sworn-oath, organized crime figures/lawyers or law firm participants to be associated with the Teamsters Union, as long as they are rail union designated lawyers or are working for such lawyers?

If so, has the mysterious senator, perhaps through his un-matched connections at the Department of Justice, participated in helping the IRB implement such an unwritten policy to allow his son to be a designated lawyer with the BLET?

~~~~~

Transparency in government – it is a constitutional right, not a privilege.

These and many other questions need to be answered for the good of our United States Constitution and for the good of American citizens who have been fleeced for billions of dollars, for generations of time, by a secret circle of personal injury lawyers. We all deserve the transparent truth, no matter which political party is in power, no matter the political fall-out.

To redeem the integrity of our nation's judicial system, we hope President Obama does the right thing and makes this information about our elected officials, the officers of our courts and the running of our government available to the concerned citizens and voters of the United States of America. ~ Most respectfully, Mr. President, please ask yourself, "What would President 'Honest Abe' Lincoln do?"

~~~~~

(Excerpt From January 6, 2005 Confirmation Hearing For Alberto Gonzales's Nomination to Attorney General of The United States of America.) (EMPHASIS ADDED)

SEN. SPECTER: "…The department will have a major role in implementing President Bush's proposals to revise our nation's immigration laws and to deal with the 10 million aliens who are in this country illegally. <u>The committee will also be interested to know of any new ideas or programs Judge Gonzales has for fighting organized and violent crime, cracking down on fraud</u>, especially on federal health programs and protecting U.S. intellectual property rights.

The committee will be interested in Judge Gonzales' views on the Patriot Act since the attorney general will obviously be a central figure in consideration of reauthorization of that act. That act provided considerable assistance to law enforcement by eliminating the so-called wall between the gathering of intelligence once obtained for intelligence purposes to be used in criminal law enforcement, but there are other questions which have been challenged by a wide array of people on all facets of the political spectrum with the issue of probable cause to obtain records, library records, and the so-called "sneak and peek" orders, and we will be interested in what Judge Gonzales has to say about that very important matter.

We will also be interested to know Judge Gonzales' views on the issue of detention and standards of detention.

The attorney general has exercised the authority to overrule conclusions by the immigration judge and a board of immigration appeals. And this is an issue that lingers after considerable questioning of Attorney General Ashcroft as to what standards ought to be used. And the attorney general, John Ashcroft, conceded before this committee that it's not sufficient to simply cite national security. And that will be a question which we will want to inquire into.

We will also be looking for commitments from Judge Gonzales to appear before this committee at least twice a year and to be responsive to our inquiries. And we will seek his commitment on the oversight authority of this committee, as recognized by the Supreme Court of the United States — our Constitutional obligation on oversight.

As we begin a new term, I pay tribute to my distinguished colleague Senator Hatch who has chaired this committee for most of the past 10 years and has been responsible for some of the most innovative and far-reaching legislation which has ever come from the Congress of the United States. And he has handled these duties in an atmosphere sometimes contentious, sometimes difficult, but always with good cheer and always with aplomb and always with balance. And I have admired especially his stamina.

SEN. HATCH: (Chuckles.)

SEN. SPECTER: We affectionately refer to him as "Iron pants" as he has chaired this committee with such great distinction. And it is an honor to receive the gavel from him.

If you will make that formal presentation, Senator Hatch.

SEN. HATCH: Well, I'm very honored to make that presentation to Arlen Specter, who's one of the best lawyers we've ever had serve in the United States Senate, among a whole raft of very fine lawyers. And so I'm very proud to have you as my new chairman, and I appreciate your kind remarks. And I appreciate serving with Senator Leahy and all of our colleagues on this committee for such a long period of time. But I'm anxious to serve under you, and I'll enjoy sitting beside you.

SEN. SPECTER: Thank you, Senator Hatch.
SEN. HATCH: Here's the gavel. (Applause.)

SEN. : There you go.

SEN. SPECTER: I commend Senator Leahy for his very distinguished service as the long-time ranking Democrat on the committee, and chaired the committee for most of the 107th Congress.

Senator Leahy and I have been colleagues going back to the late 1960s, when we were district attorneys together. Senator Leahy was the district attorney of Burlington, Vermont and I was district attorney of Philadelphia. And we have worked together for 24 years on the Judiciary Committee.

And in the past several weeks, we have talked extensively, we have sat down, we have gone over the agenda of the committee. We are obviously keenly aware of the difficulties of gridlock, and we're looking for a new beginning with more consultation in an effort to avoid some of the contentiousness of the past if it is at all possible and to avoid, if we can, even consideration of the so-called nuclear option. So it is with pleasure that I work with Senator Leahy, a friend for four decades.

And now I yield to you, Senator Leahy, for your opening statement..."

Excerpt: Electronic Documents For Your Reference

Please forgive the formatting. It is extremely difficult to neatly format these web addresses and other references to comply with certain formatting for electronic screen viewing. The below information will also be made available at lawyermafia.com or other internet site(s) designated.

1)   Retrieved/accessed 06 06 2008 at:
     http://blogs.chron.com/legaltrade/us_ag_gonzales/
     March 13, 2008 Chron.com
     (Houston Chronicle blog)
     Copyright Houston Chronicle
     "Gonzales visits, Shelby quits, Gonzales returns"

2)   Obituary of Michael T. Shelby, US Attorney who filed the Motion To Reveal the Names of Organized Crime Investigated Attorneys.
     Retrieved/accessed 06 06 2008 at:
     http://www.chron.com/CDA/archives/archive.mpl?id=2006_4155618
     Copyright Houston Chronicle

3)   Cleveland Plain Dealer News Article
     Web posting dated: Saturday, March 27, 2004
     http://radio.weblogs.com/0118868/categories/straightTrack/2004/03/index.html {retrieved/accessed 01 15 2008}
     "Lawyers, leaders capitalize on railroad workers' injuries"
     03/26/04; Alison Grant; Plain Dealer Reporter

4)   Houston Chronicle News Article
     By HARVEY RICE
     Copyright 2004 Houston Chronicle
     "Defendants describe corruption in railroad unions"

Article retrieved/accessed at: http://radio.weblogs.com/0118868/categories/straightTrack/2004/07/11.html
(Retrieved/accessed 01 15 2008) © Copyright 2005 The Usual Suspect.

5) Houston Press
http://www.straighttrack.org/2003/11/13.html
(Article retrieved/accessed 01 15 2008)
"Pens and Needles"
Federal turf fights and deals mark the legacy of a union bribery case
BY GEORGE FLYNN
george.flynn@houstonpress.com

<u>Excerpt: A CALL TO ACTION from America's Lawyer Mafia: Railgate</u>

Contact your senators and congressmen to get transparency and accountability in our government!

We hope the "mystery senator", who is the father of the subject attorney referenced in the "US v Boyd" sentencing transcript, will reveal herself/himself, in a forthright and respectable manner, without the necessity of appointing another Special Prosecutor. Furthermore, we hope that US Attorney and Special Prosecutor, Ms. Nora Dannehy, will use this information to help complete her pending criminal investigation of Alberto Gonzales regarding the United States Attorneys who were allegedly fired for political purposes.

It appears that, given the foregoing, such allegations against Mr. Gonzales might include a review of Southern District of Texas US Attorney, Michael T. Shelby's hurried resignation, which occurred only days after Mr. Gonzales paid Shelby a closed-door visit, in early May 2005. (Before Judge Lake changed his initial ruling and decided to keep secret the names of the RICO investigated and testifying lawyers.)

This scenario raises a number of questions about the lack of transparency of our government. Who was the mysterious, unnamed United States Senator? Who, by the admission of the government's lawyer, AUSA Gallagher, was the father of one of the lawyers involved in the RICO investigation. Was that senator a member of the Senate Judiciary Committee when it held hearings and a vote for confirming Alberto Gonzales as Attorney General, in 2005?

If yes, wouldn't that be a disturbing conflict of interest? (Especially since the Attorney General oversees all federal criminal investigations and prosecutions). Does it not make the influence peddling obvious when the mystery senator's son is under federal criminal investigation and about to have his name and grand jury testimony released to his state bar disciplinary authorities, by Southern District of Texas, US Attorney Michael Shelby? Influence pedaling? Criminal?

If such influence peddling is not criminal, does that not sanctify what Gov. Rod Blagojevich is presently charged with? Criminal influence peddling? Or is there a separate set of laws for railroad union lawyers that de-criminalizes what might ordinarily be treated as criminal conduct?

Do Americans care that they are repeatedly paying for the racketeering of a few? Was it a *quid pro quo* deal between Gonzales and the mystery senator?

Did Karl Rove, the "mystery senator" and Alberto Gonzales make a deal to let the mystery senator's son off the hook, along with dozens of other designated lawyers, in return for ensuring that Gonzales would be confirmed as US Attorney General?

We reserve the 1st Amendment and other constitutional rights to protect the identity of any confidential sources we have regarding these matters. (Especially since the government already possesses all this information.)

You can access the names and respective email contact information for your United States Congressmen and Senators at: congress.org; or house.gov; or senate.gov. Do not be afraid to ask questions and demand accountability.

Remember Harry Truman's rule for investigating fraud involving Congress: Follow The Money.

(End of Excerpt materials from America's Lawyer Mafia: Railgate).

## Notice of Charitable Intent

A portion of the proceeds of this book, <u>The Redeemer: It Is Written</u>, will be donated, in equal shares, to: The American Autistic Society, Catholic Charities, Generation Rescue (Autism Is Reversible), The Injured Marine *Semper Fi* Fund and The Innocence Project, all of which support those in need on a non-denomination basis. We suggest you too consider contributing to these fine charities. They are in the trenches doing God's work daily, by helping many people in need, from all walks of life and religions, even those who do not believe in God. These charities are the real-life embodiment of being Good Samaritans. Note: As of time of press, none of these charities formally, or informally, endorse <u>The Redeemer: It Is Written</u>.

## Freedom of Religion

American veterans served and fought with courage, and many died, to preserve for all United States citizens the constitutional right commonly referred to as Freedom of Religion. You may see how one such veteran fought, in open combat, to preserve Freedom of Religion and other United States constitutional rights by visiting the website, <u>www.lawyersmafia.com</u>. There, the late Brigadier General Glennon T. Moran, Sr.'s (when he was only a I<sup>st</sup> Lieutenant) P-47 and P-51 live-combat, gun camera film is available for viewing, courtesy of his loving daughter, Jeanne Moran. (The video download takes a minute or so, but it is worth the wait).

Think about it. What religion, if any, would we be allowed to be practiced, if Hitler had won WW II? Or, if Stalin had won the Cold War? How about under Chairman Mao? Or, if present day despots have the landscapes and peoples and temples of worship of the world painted in their intolerant, self-serving ways?

History's lessons have taught us, century after century, in layers upon layers of bright warning, the morbid stories, upon terrible stories, upon horrendous stories documenting horrible genocide and suffering, of those souls who are punished merely for worshiping in their own peaceful way.

These lessons teach us that Freedom of Religion is not free. And it never will be free.

Whether you are an atheist or you are devoutly religious, please, thank a veteran for his or her service spent helping to preserve our United States Constitution and all the rights we hold dear, including what might be our greatest right, Freedom of Religion.

(All of preceding written and formatted by Mark Moran Copyright © 2009 Wild Horse Literary Works, LP.)

## *It Is Written*

3647328

Made in the USA